WITH THE DEVIL'S
OWN DETERMINATION . . .

Young Gurney called up all his fortitude for a long and dangerous odyssey of revenge . . . Across seas and distant lands where a tall, blue-eyed Christian could expect no quarter.

Following his resolve square into the face of uncharted hazards, he would witness strange things, undergo cruel hardships, and know exotic women . . . especially the high-born Grecian beauty.

But with the stubborn luck of a born fighter, Gurney would turn risk into riches . . . holding a true course back to England and Arabella.

SEA DEVIL

ABOUT THE AUTHOR

Born in 1948 in Scilly Isles, SAM LLEWELLYN was educated at Eton and Oxford. In the course of his extensive traveling he took part in such diverse activities as running a Spanish nightclub, baiting shark-hooks professionally, living off the land in Norfolk, working at Sotheby's in London by day and with a rock group by night, and finally became an editor at Pan books. Now married, he lives in Canada and divides his time between Toronto and a desolate cabin on Georgian Bay where he pursues his hobbies of sailing, fishing and bird-watching on cross-country skis.

SEA DEVIL

BY SAM LLEWELLYN

BANTAM BOOKS
TORONTO · NEW YORK · LONDON · SYDNEY

This low-priced Bantam Book
has been completely reset in a type face
designed for easy reading, and was printed
from new plates. It contains the complete
text of the original hard-cover edition.
NOT ONE WORD HAS BEEN OMITTED.

SEA DEVIL
A Bantam Book

PRINTING HISTORY
First published in England 1977 by
Arlington Books (Publishers) Ltd., as "Gurney's Revenge"
Bantam edition / February 1979

ISBN 0-553-12442-0

Bantam Books are published by Bantam Books, Inc. Its trademark, consisting of the words "Bantam Books" and the por-
trayal of a bantam, is Registered in U.S. Patent and Trademark
Office and in other countries. Marca Registrada. Bantam
Books, Inc., 666 Fifth Avenue, New York, New York 10019.

PRINTED IN THE UNITED STATES OF AMERICA

Prologue

A bitter northeast wind was driving eddies of snow-flakes through the pillared courts of St. James's Palace as the travel-stained black carriage rounded the corner of Pall Mall and turned north toward Piccadilly. The coachman shrugged deeper into the collar of his greatcoat and muttered a curse at the whims of a newly fashionable master who could choose a February night as vile as this to go out on his gallivantings so soon after the long drive from Dorset. As he pulled up before the imposing stone portico of Vernon's Assembly Rooms, his thoughts turned to the convivial circle round the fire at the Mulberry Tree. He ran his tongue over his lips. Hot gin-and-water against the ague, and plenty of it, was what he needed. And soon.

The little groom jumped from his step at the rear of the carriage, ran to the near side, and opened the door, touching his forehead with blue-frozen fingers as the bulky figure in the interior struggled out of the thick fur wraps and heaved himself into the snow. The double doors at the top of the broad stone steps swung open in a blaze of lamplight and a tinkling hum of music and voices, then shut. The tiger blew on his nails, jagged viciously at the horses' mouths, and began to walk them back and forth, sticking his tongue out at the coachman, who was slipping down a side alley towards the inn.

Mathias Otway, owner of the coach, horses, and servants, stamped his dress pumps in the paneled hall-way and cast a complacent eye over his reflection in the gilt pier glass as the porter took his greatcoat. He never failed to be impressed by what he saw. A stout, sallow man of two-and-fifty years, puffy jowls confined by a high wing collar with a white cravat, thinning hair brushed, curled, and cropped à la Brutus, he could pass, he told himself, for a youngish forty. His close-fitting three-quarter-length coat of black broadcloth with silver buttons and his buff knee breeches and hose gave him an air of the no-nonsense countryman with a hint of the fashionable cleric. A combination, he assured himself, calculated to inspire confidence. A confidence which was no more than the due of a merchant as successful as himself. For Mathias Otway, despite his recent acceptance by the noble and influential members of the *ton,* made no secret of his mercantile past. Though there were, admittedly, men of ill will who whispered that his recent marriage to the impoverished widow of Lord Mountolivet, herself now unhappily deceased, had been contracted in pursuit of ends less spiritual than self-interested. And those same ill-wishers would from time to time intimate that in earlier years he had been over-closely concerned with such dubious activities as the stuffing of companies and the short selling of stocks not his to sell. Still, the stones of the debtors' cells in the Fleet told no tales. Besides, it was now obvious to the most censorious eye that the excesses of his youth were well behind him. With a final ingratiating smirk at his reflection, he turned and waddled into the assembly room, bowing to right and left as he drew his white gloves onto his pudgy hands.

The soirée was well advanced. The brilliantly lit room was almost filled with a throng of ladies and gentlemen; at the far end a small orchestra was sawing its way through a piece by the newly fashionable Italian composer Rossini. Otway remembered his dancing master playing it to him a short while ago. He smiled inwardly. He was beginning to feel quite at ease with these glittering lords and ladies, emptyheaded idiots for the most part, with their foolish prattle of the play, the concert, and the rout; yet it had taken a long and concentrated effort to learn the manners and codes that constituted the key to their select and immeasurably powerful circle. But then Otway had been fascinated by the machinery of power for as long as he could remember—since the day he had turned his back on his parents' few poor and windswept acres on Cranbourne Chase and set out, his father's small savings in his satchel, for the navy yards at Portsmouth. It had taken thirty-five years—years of bullying, wheedling, conniving, bribery, and unscrupulous manipulation; but now there remained but one small gambit between himself and the happy outcome of his schemings.

Otway took a sip from his glass and let his eye rove over the crowd. There was old Lady Montague-Stanley, one eye fixed adoringly on a dancing-masterish foreigner and the other keeping a close watch on her brandy-nosed husband lest he slip away to his opera girls. It seemed likely that the foreigner, whose flashing teeth were doing journeyman service, was more interested in the famous Stanley diamonds, which crusted most of the visible portions of his admirer's wrinkled anatomy, than in her conversation, limited as it was by her complete deafness and incipient senility. And in the corner farthest from the orchestra a circle of young bloods bayed around Fenella Markham, belle of last year's season, whose incorrigible flirtatiousness had become the despair, Otway had heard it whispered, of her noble but penurious father. My lord Markham, already broken by his enormous gambling debts, had pledged what remained of his estates to the moneylenders in an attempt to find a suitable match for his daughter; but the light-minded hussy found it more diverting to spread her favors widely among the romantically inclined throngs of young officers on half-pay like the pup Gurney, unemployed since the cessation of hostilities with France and America, who now haunted the salons of the capital.

George Gurney, unaware of Mathias Otway's unflattering cogitations on him and his ilk and locked in an extremely shallow conversation with the undoubtedly beautiful but even more certainly bird-witted Fenella Basset, stiffened as he saw the merchant's heavy figure framed in the doorway, the cold

eyes sweeping the crowd. "Mr. Gurney!" Miss Markham was looking at him strangely. "I declare for a
moment I thought you were in a taking! What a
fierce, cruel look you sometimes have!" She fluttered
—engagingly, her mother told her.

George forced a smile. "No doubt 'twas at the
thought of having to leave you so soon, Miss Markham. For there is Bruiser Carstairs, and I am sure you
have much to say to him." And with a smile that lit up
his pale blue eyes he turned and made his way swiftly
through the crowd.

A tall, well-made young man of some two-and-
twenty years, this Gurney. As he walked across the
room, he drew many eyes, admiring and disapprov-
ing. His admirers said, to themselves or whoever was
near at hand, that he was *such* a charming boy—so
brave, they heard—quite a fire-eater—poor fellow was
wounded off Cuba, you know, which accounts for
his limp—charming, frank, open face—eyes a bit mad,
of course, but you can't have everything. His detrac-
tors muttered similarly, though they tended to stress
other facets. Impertinent young devil—natural result
of being too lucky too young—gambles like a crazy
Chinee—bound to come a nasty tumble soon—shan't
be sorry—disturbing influence—off to the tables again,
no doubt. But Gurney paid no heed to the emotions
he aroused in the breasts of those around him, even if
he recognized them, which was doubtful. He was
deep in talk with Ivo Dauncey, whom he wished to
consult about the undoing of Mathias Otway. Dauncey, a tall, dark youth wearing the same sort of semi-
naval uniform—blue coat, brass buttons, white
breeches—as Gurney, waved a dismissive hand. "Sorry,
old boy, urgent business. Game o' whist and a good
'un, I hear. Shall I keep your name in reserve?" Gurney grinned. "Yes, please do. My creditors are becoming somewhat importunate. I'll speak with you later."

Dauncey waved again and disappeared towards
the orchestra. Gurney returned to the tables by the
door, where he was buttonholed by a fat admiral with

a theory about sea bathing. Groaning inwardly, he prepared himself to smile and agree. Admirals were few and far between, and for such as himself, with little "interest"—influence in high places—promotion, or in his case a posting from half-pay to active service, could rest on the whim of some cranky old windbag like this. He fixed a look of polite amazement to his face; but his mind was far away, and his foot tapped restlessly on the floor. The hunt was up, and Otway was the quarry.

Otway drained his glass and picked his way across the room to a table set apart behind a small ornamental railing, where a dark Frenchman with small, shrewd eyes and an unfashionable abundance of lace at his throat sat deep in conversation with a foppish, pale-haired exquisite whose beak of a nose failed to compensate for his lack of chin. Otway addressed himself to the latter, bowing.

"My lord Fotheringham! It is indeed a pleasure to renew your acquaintance! What brings you to Vernon's on such a desolate evening?"

The youth rose to his feet, bowing awkwardly. "Mr. Otway, is it not? It is indeed a *great* pleasure, don't ye know, to see you again. Monsieur le Comte de Fauvenargues and I were just discussing his new venture in the Peruvian mines, which he declares are the veritable Eldorado. But you do not know each other? Allow me to present you."

As Otway rose from his bow, he caught the Frenchman's eye. The foreigner nodded almost imperceptibly, and Otway allowed his right eyelid to droop the merest fraction.

The three men seated themselves, and Otway composed his features to a look of fascination as the callow Fotheringham stammered his enthusiasm for the schemes of the enterprising count. "I take it, then, that you're a man not averse to a little . . . speculation?" Otway smiled fatly. "Well, well, this is the stuff of the rock on which Albion stands. How fine it is, in this day and age, to meet a man with the adventurous spirit of a Drake, the imagination of a Pitt, the resolve of a very Nelson!" The Frenchman hid a smile behind his jeweled fingers; Otway threw him a warning glance. "I declare," he continued, "that it would be a vast pleasure to hazard a rubber or two with such a spirit. If Monsieur le Comte would be pleased to join us"—the Frenchman waved an acquiescent hand— "we need find but one more to make up our four." He beamed at Fotheringham, who returned a loose-lipped smirk. "Well, that's settled. And unless I am mistaken, that's young Ivo Dauncey. Duke of Carlisle's nephew, don't ye know. Charming young fellow, great friend." He waved a white hand.

The lieutenant raised a languid eyebrow, rather less friendly than Otway had implied; but he professed himself ready for a rubber and the four passed into the card room, where beeswax candles burned low over green baize tables. The room was hushed but for the grunted bids of the players, the riffle of cards in the dealers' fingers, and the chink of gold sovereigns. Otway took a long, deep breath. This was his element. The cool, quiet computation of odds and probabilities, the passionless logic of a man's future staked on the turn of a single card, had always set his blood racing. And to manipulate this system, to use not only the turn of the cards but the players themselves for his own devious ends—this was the greatest game of all.

He seated himself opposite Dauncey, noting the half-amused, half-suspicious flicker of the young man's eyelids. He was a strange, wild one—twenty-two years old, with seven years' experience of life at sea on one of Her Majesty's ships and two years ashore, one of London's most promising young rakehells. Rumor had it that he had won and lost three fortunes already; but his smooth features betrayed little but quizzical surprise at his card-partner's untypical warmth, and a slight edge of disdain. Otway chose not to notice the disdain; there were issues afoot in furtherance of which he was prepared to suffer a good deal more than the scorn of a whippersnapper like Dauncey. A servant brought a pack of cards. Otway cut and passed them to Fotheringham on his right. "My lord Fotheringham, perhaps you would be so good as to shuffle?"

It soon became apparent that Otway and his partner were by far the better players. Though the Frenchman was obviously a veteran at the game, Fotheringham revealed himself as an abysmal duffer from the moment his fumbling fingers touched the cards. Dauncey watched in some puzzlement as Fauvenargues commiserated with his partner for a lost hand that any five-year-old in skirts could have won, then shrugged mentally. If Monsieur le Comte wished to lose his gold in partnership with this babe unweaned, that was his affair. Meanwhile, he was quite happy—nay, delighted—to continue taking their money, particularly in view of the two large and aggressive gentlemen who had appeared at his digs that afternoon bearing bad tidings of his account with Isaac Rubin. He took a long sip at his glass of claret as Otway won the final trick of the hand and struggled to his feet.

"If you will excuse me, I must take my leave. But the night is still young, and we must not deprive milords de Fauvenargues and Fotheringham of their revenge. Dauncey, did I not see you earlier in the company of the brave Lieutenant Gurney? I know that he is one of Fortune's favorites, so perhaps you could prevail upon him?"

Dauncey vouchsafed him a formal bow, but his voice was loaded with irony. "Delighted, though I am naturally desolate to lose so brilliant a partner as yourself. If my lords permit?" Fotheringham, who was commencing to wilt under the incisive play of the merchant, nodded eagerly, and the Frenchman spread his hands in acquiescence. Dauncey rose and left the room with Otway, returning a few moments later leading a tall figure in a uniform similar to his own.

De Fauvenargues leaped to his feet. "But can it be? Is this the very Lieutenant Gurney of the *Vam-*

pire? The intrepid argonaut who single-handed put a
stop to the heinous maraudings of the usurper Bonaparte in the West India Station?"

The intrepid argonaut's unfashionably bronzed face
broke into a grin. "I wouldn't put it as strongly as that,
mylord. I merely did my duty as I saw fit."

"No, no, a thousand times no! *Parbleu*, but how can
I demonstrate the depth of my feelings towards one
so instrumental in the removing of the iron heel of
tyranny from my beloved France?" And the excitable
Gaul flung his arms around Lieutenant Gurney and
kissed him loudly on each cheek. Gurney went scarlet
as the room fell silent and two-score pairs of eyebrows
lifted as one. Really, he thought, these Frogs, Jaco-
bins or Bourbons, were impossible.

"I am deeply sensible of the honor you do to me,
and I look forward to an evening of interesting play.
Shall we set to?"

As the Frenchman dealt the first hand, he looked
narrowly at the new arrival. A well-set-up young buck,
this; his square jaw bespoke a firmness of resolve
entirely at odds with his youthful awkwardness, and
the lines at the corners of his blue eyes betrayed a
wealth of painful experience. But straightforwardness
would avail him little this night. For a moment, the
look on de Fauvenargues's face was that of a grazier
assessing a prime bullock he means to send to the
slaughterhouse; then a veil of urbanity dropped over
his countenance and he sent the first card spinning
in front of Gurney's hands, folded on the baize table-
cloth.

It seemed that Fotheringham's luck had not
changed. His neighing laugh became more forced as
trick after trick fell to Gurney and his partner. And de
Fauvenargues's black brows knit aggressively as finesse after finesse failed. The swarthy foreigner
seemed unable to concentrate; his play now seemed
almost as incoherent as that of his partner, who was
covertly glancing at his watch.

It was midnight when Lieutenant Gurney leaned

back and ran his long fingers through his close-cropped yellow hair. "Well, milords, I must commiserate with you on your atrocious luck. Shall we play another rubber and call it a night?"

De Fauvenargues scowled. "Yes, *parbleu*. And for these last hands, perhaps you gallant rulers of the high seas would agree to playing for a somewhat increased stake? Milord Fotheringham agrees?"

The pale fop gulped and nodded. *"D'accord.* According to my calculations," the Frenchman continued, "milord and I are some fourteen hundred guineas to the bad. May I suggest that we play, *désormais,* for a hundred guineas a point and a thousand on the rubber?"

Dauncey looked at Gurney. "Pretty steep that. You game, Gurney?"

Gurney nodded. A small voice at the back of his mind kept telling him that his choler was getting the better of his common sense; but he angrily silenced it and picked up the cards. God knew that he hated this humiliating grind, playing whist with nincompoops and sharks to supplement the pittance that the peace-time navy called a lieutenant's half-pay. But it was the only way for a gentleman and a thousand times preferable to the sort of shabby-genteel living death he had seen creep up on his former shipmates, marooned in their lodgings in Deptford or Portsmouth just as surely as on any Bahamian cay.

At least he was still fighting, and the winner's laurels were enticingly close. For if Gurney's plans matured aright, Mathias Otway's days as cock of the walk were numbered. The days when a blackbirder—a slave trader, not to dignify so vile a commerce with a pet name—could openly come the nabob in the salons and gaming rooms of London had passed with the coming of Fox and Wilberforce. Now, with the information Gurney had at his disposal, Otway would find his Whig friends avoiding his eye, becoming suddenly engaged in confidential conversation when he entered a room. The rotten borough to which he currently aspired would be quietly transferred to a more

discreet man—not because of any deep scruples in
the Whig conscience, but because of its solemn ad-
herence to the tenets of the Eleventh Commandment,
"Thou shalt not be found out." To turn a blind eye to
the orders of one's superiors and act on one's own
initiative might be a permissible naval tactic—Nelson
had proved as much—but in politics a more searching
regard for the proprieties was the rule. Otway would
founder without a trace, and the fair Arabella, his step-
daughter, no longer a lucrative match for some scat-
terbrained lordling, would be Gurney's for the asking.
As she already was, had her own preferences counted
for anything in the matter of her life's partner.

Gurney grinned as he contemplated the ruin of his
enemy's schemes. But as he dealt the cards, he caught
the count's eye, in which lurked a hint of—was it
avarice? cunning? His whole body was suddenly tense,
imbued with a curious numbness, the dull oppression
he used to feel before action, rocking heel to toe, toe
to heel on the pocket-handkerchief quarterdeck of
the *Vampire*. Last time, it had been the precursor of a
sweat-soaked hour on the surgeon's table with the
sawbones carving at his leg after a privateer's musket
ball . . .

Gurney took a pull at his claret glass and dealt.

The size of the stakes seemed, if anything, to have
discomfited de Fauvenargues and his partner. Fotheringham was drunk, beyond reason, unable to play his
cards otherwise than at random. De Fauvenargues's
cards were better and his playing improved, but not
enough. After two honors hands had gone to Gurney,
the Frenchman began to mutter under his breath.
Now it was Gurney's deal. The two lieutenants, if
they won this final hand, would carry away between
them as much gold as they would have got from a
fair-sized prize. It was too easy. Far too easy. Gurney
could understand the gaping Fotheringham, always
anxious to impress, pouring good money after bad;
but the Frenchman looked to be too experienced to
play for such stakes against two such notoriously cool
heads as Gurney and his comrade-in-arms. The short

hairs at the nape of Gurney's neck prickled warningly as the count leaned towards him, his thin lips twisted into a disagreeable smile.

"It seems to be your lucky night, *hein?* I fear that my poor skill has deserted me completely. Such cards! And my partner"—Fotheringham was swaying glassily—"will, if I am not mistaken, soon be indisposed. I have played in many places, from Pondicherry to the Americas, but I have seldom seen one so young or so lucky as yourself. Fortunes of war, I think? Your exploits on the high seas, I have heard, often hinge on subtle *ruses de guerre. Tant mieux.* But when these *ruses* are applied to the card table—"

Gurney's face drained of blood. "What exactly are you trying to say, monsieur?"

"Simply that there comes to me a slight suspicion that the cards you are dealing have more to them than meets the eye. Or at any rate, the eyes of milord Fotheringham, Lieutenant Dauncey, and myself."

Gurney leaped to his feet, the Frenchman's mocking grin dancing before his eyes. Fotheringham's mouth hung open, and Dauncey was leaning wearily back in his chair, minutely examining his fingernails.

"You realize this means blood, sir? My friends will be calling on you shortly. Meanwhile, I must ask you to consider this game at an end."

"Not so fast, my fine young friend." De Fauvenargues was squinting at the back of the queen of clubs. "Gentlemen. You see that the roundel in this pattern resembles the face of a clock? If you look closely, you will see a light pen stroke in the one o'clock position. It is not easy to see in this light; but Lieutenant Gurney is famous for his excellent eyesight."

Dauncey put out a languid hand and picked up the card. "He's right, you know. But I must say that I feel it's a little early in the day to level such serious accusations. The scandal will be frightful. So, *entre nous,* should we not turn out our pockets? I am sure that we will thus allay all suspicion. Admiral Jessop? If you could arbitrate until we have cleared up this deeply embarrassing misunderstanding?"

The portly red-faced officer nodded and rose.

A heavy silence spread from the gaming tables to the ballroom as the four men placed the contents of their pockets on the table. Gurney dug into his waistcoat, produced watch, seals, chain, card case, and purse, and thrust his hand into his coat. Dauncey grinned as a mummified blackbird's wing flecked with albino white joined the small pile on the table; then his jaw dropped as Gurney drew out his handkerchief and flung it down, scattering from its folds a pack of cards of the same pattern as those already on the table.

The admiral's eyes were cold as he turned to Gurney. "Hrrmph. In the circumstances, it seems that you have no cause to ask satisfaction of Monsieur le Comte. Perhaps you should withdraw to put your affairs in order." A rustle of whispered conversation swept through the gathering like a breeze. Gurney, white to the lips, swept up his possessions and limped from the room, the crowd parting before him like fairgoers before an itinerant leper.

From the Lady Arabella Mountolivet:

> Mendlebury House,
> Dorset
> February 14th
> in haste

My darling George,

What, oh what have you been at, my only love? There has been the violent brouhaha here since you left; I think that the odious Mathias has quite taken leave of his senses. But wait. Let me begin at the beginning.

Three days ago that gamekeeper Zebedee Watkins came up to the house—the *house*, my dear; the gall of the man!—looking for Mathias. A rational man—and you know how my charming stepfather prides himself on his rationality—would have sent him packing forthwith (he does stink so of ferret). But Mathias took him by the

elbow and steered him into his writing room.
I didn't exactly listen at the door, but I couldn't
help overhearing some of what they were saying.
Watkins was mumbling—you know, you could cut
his accent with a knife—something about "that
damn' young lieutenant tumbling to the blackbirding lay," and Mathias was squealing like a pig.
Then he flung out of the door and up into the
attic (our attic, George; you remember? Oh, how
I miss you). A few minutes later he came stump-
ing down again with a chest of papers, the same
chest you spent so much time with just before
you set off for London. Then he burned the
papers in the library grate and bellowed for his
carriage. George, I hope that this letter reaches
you before he does, for I collect that he means
you no good. I need not tell you of all people
that he is a hard man to cross—my poor mama's
fate bears testimony to his hypocrisy and malice.
Beware!

Meanwhile, with all my heart, dearest George,
I remain your adoring

Arabella

Gurney laughed mirthlessly and poured himself another half-tumbler of cognac. He felt bloody awful.
The air in his room was cold and damp, and from time
to time he coughed raspingly. His throat was sore,
his head ached, and his eyes were red and gritty in
their sockets.

Since he had arrived at his humble lodgings at the
Three Tuns in Whitechapel at four A.M., he had not
slept a wink. It was now nine o'clock in the morning,
and a dingy light was glimmering through the cob-
webby mullioned windows. The snow had turned
to a raw gray drizzle, beaten by the wind over the
marshes to the east, moaning listlessly in the rigging
of the ships lying moored in the West India Dock.

Gurney thought back to the first time he had seen
Arabella. He had been coming out of the card room at
Wattier's when he noticed the fine-featured blonde

girl sitting demurely, white-gloved hands folded
in her lap, in animated conversation with some blub-
bery exquisite at a table by the doorway. He had noticed that she was positioned so that she could see into
the gaming room, and that every exclamation of disgust, chink of gold, or riffle of cards from within that
exclusively masculine preserve set her delightfully
rounded bosom to heaving and her hands to clutching her fan. Gurney had stood entranced, staring as
she led her swain on through painted little gardens
of small talk with half her mind and drank in the gambling with the other. Then she felt his eyes on her,
and her cool, probing gaze locked with his. Once,
Gurney had watched a repetition of Professor Gal-
vani's experiments with electricity and a frog's legs.
The jolt that had twitched the amphibian's limbs then
was nothing to the shock that crashed through him
now, from the crown of his head to the soles of his
feet.

The next thing he knew they were being introduced
and she was making a pretense of maidenly confusion, but all the time the wide-set blue eyes, almost
level with his own, were telling him things which
would have sent Mrs. Mippins, her chaperon, into a
black swoon. That night they talked until la Mippins
clucked her way across the crowded assembly rooms
and dragged her charge away. After she had gone,
Gurney sat like one stunned. Arabella was not only
beautiful—though beautiful she surely was, with her
golden ringlets, violet eyes, and fine-boned, faintly
aquiline cast of feature—but, unlike the vapid spawn
of the petty nobility to whom a dashing but youthful
lieutenant was expected to pay court, she had a mind
and she was not afraid to use it. During that first two
hours with Arabella, Gurney had an inkling of a depth
of companionship for which the casual chatter of the
ball and the rout and the claustrophobic intimacy of
the midshipman's flat had in no way prepared him.

He groaned and buried his face in his hands. The
thoughts tramped endlessly through his mind, keeping

time with the pounding of his head. Lord, what a fool
he had been! To have landed himself in this hideous
imbroglio would have been almost bearable. But to
have drawn Arabella with him! He knew that he,
Gurney, had represented to her one single hope of
salvation in a universe made horrible by offers of marriage from overbred guffins with purses as light as the
contents of their heads. Now, with him in disgrace,
Otway could force one or another of these suitors on
her. Gurney ground his teeth. The unctuous Mathias
would use Arabella as he had used her mother, as a
pawn in the game he played to his own rules for his
own ends.

He picked up Arabella's letter for the hundredth
time. Too late, too late by one meager day. That swine
of a gamekeeper, with his confidential manner and his
fund of rustic lore. What a fool Gurney had been to
question him so closely about Otway's comings and
goings! Once he'd seen his line of inquiry, he'd strung
him along until he was sure of his man and then simply reported the conversation to his master. Good and
faithful servant indeed! He'd certainly cooked Gurney's goose for him.

It had been prettily done; the Frenchman must be
a past master at the noble art of cardsharping. First
his careful dealing of the cards to put himself and the
idiot Fotheringham onto their losing streak, then the
switching of the cards on the table for the marked
cards in his pocket; and finally, the planting of the
original pack in Gurney's pocket while he was going
through that Bourbon rigmarole as they were introduced. The whole thing stank of Otway. And it was
clever. Devilish clever. Impossible, now, to reveal Otway for what he was; the word of a man on whom lay
the disgrace of cardsharping (Old Jervey Hutchinson
had once told him, in Jamaica, "Three disgraces,
George. Adultery—not good, can get you killed.
Drunkenness—beastly. Cardsharping—worse than dis-
honor. No redress, no excuses.") would have no influence with the worthy merchants on 'change; and

still less with the toadying Whig lickspittles, "radicals" in name only, in Parliament. But there were other ways . . .

He coughed, wincing at the pain in his raw throat, and lit a cigar, wondering as he put taper to tobacco why he was doing it. The smoke stung like hell, and he pitched the weed into the cold ashes of his fire. He lifted the hand bell from the rough table which, with a narrow bed and a couple of upright chairs, comprised the room's only furniture, and shook it violently. A dispirited-looking young woman shuffled through the door, trailing a powerful smell of boiled cabbage, wiping suds from her forearms with somebody's shirt. Her small eyes flickered over the empty bottles in the grate, the unwrinkled counterpane on the bed, and George's hollow cheeks and red eyes. She sniffed twice, wetly.

Gurney winced. "Coffee and a biscuit, please, Maria. And would you send a boy after Romeo Copley, the actor." The slattern shot him such a look of hurt dignity as was obviously intended to make his eyebrows curl, spun on her heel as if to say that her mum kept a decent house and times was hard enough without a lot of theatricals cluttering up the taproom, and slammed the door behind her.

Half an hour later, two voices raised in violent altercation floated up the stairwell. Gurney grinned, stuck his head around the door, and yelled, "Romeo! Romeo! wherefore art thou, Romeo?"

The small man disentangling himself from the slattern's apron, in which he had become raveled during what looked like a determined assault on her honor, turned his face upward, an expression of deep romantic passion printed large on his narrow brow. "But, soft! what light through yonder window breaks?"

He was up the stairs in two bounds, a ragged little Cockney, his twinkling eyes barely separated by a lengthy crimson toper's nose, a broad grin on his face. Gurney ushered him to a chair, and with all due ceremony offered him coffee. An expression of deep disgust swept over the mobile features.

"I am surprised, werry surprised, that a gentleman normally so goodsensical as your lieutenantship should indulge in a beverage so harmful to the spleen and generally deleterious to the internal plumbin' as the juice of the bean."

Gurney grinned and poured him a half-tumbler of gin. Romeo stuck his long nose into it, took a pull, wiped his mouth fastidiously with the frayed sleeve of his overcoat, and made an expansive theatrical gesture signifying that he was all attention. Gurney told him of Arabella's letter and the events of the previous night. The actor, head rolled back on his scrawny shoulders, pursed his lips in a soundless whistle and leaned forward in his chair.

" 'Ere, try a drop of this." And he poured a generous measure of Gurney's gin into Gurney's coffee cup, topping up his own tumbler as if inspired by an afterthought. Then he fell into ruminative silence.

At length, he joined his hands fingertip to fingertip under his nose. "Werry pretty. Ho yus, a most attractive tale of skulduggery and mayhem. It occurs to me that were this to get into the wrong hands, a most scurrilous and damaging broadside could be made of it. Most unfortunate for the upright Mr. Otway, of course, but then a man of his bottom has nothing to fear from the ravings of the gutter press. Provided, that is, he can prove his case."

"Very good, Romeo. I knew I could count on you to go straight to the heart of the matter. The way I see it, Otway had so much money tied up in his slaving that when he cuts his connections—and by God he'll be bound to, with the world watching his every step—his affairs will be in a highly precarious state. Then we must watch which way he jumps and try to catch him off balance."

"We'll cover the town from Bow to Hampton Court. No peace for the wicked, oh dear me, no."

"Excellent. One more thing, though. I need you to take a letter to Dorset for me. Do you still ride as well as you used?"

Romeo's diminutive chest swelled like a turkey-cock's. "Hi should say so, not half. Tomorrow noon I'll be there, you can bank on it. Ho, hum, 'partin' is such sweet sorrow,' as the Bard said. Back in an hour. Don't worry about nothing, just get your letter writ." And clapping his disreputable hat on his even less reputable head, the great actor sped down the stairs and into the street.

Gurney found himself much cheered by his interview with the resourceful Mr. Copley. The symptoms produced by the emotions and overindulgences of the previous night had withdrawn into the background of his consciousness; but still he plunged his hands into his pockets and stared gloomily from the diamond-paned window of his room over the gray, glistening cobbles and slates without. How, in God's name, to tell Arabella that he intended to separate himself from her for a period in excess of a year? He knew her too well to think that she would let him go meekly. She was not one of your accommodating doormat sort of women, thank the Lord. Even Otway had from time to time been given cause to regret that he had caught the scornful side of her whiplash tongue, and Otway's hide was notoriously impervious to such lashings. Gurney's heart ached with longing at the prospect of seeing Arabella again; but he was also conscious of a lively trepidation at the thought of breaking the news to her about his plans. He turned on his heel away from the window, sat down at the table, and began to write.

1

The *Lady Ellen*'s white wake stretched far astern over the short gray waves of the Bay of Biscay. Gurney, the taste of his breakfast porridge still in his mouth, peered unseeingly at the horizon. For three weeks now the *Lady Ellen,* a portly brig of some three hundred tons burden, had been beating her way against a succession of hard southwesterly blows toward the Strait of Gibraltar. Gurney made a mental note never again, under any circumstances, to take passage in the *Lady Ellen.* As well as rolling like a dead cow in a hurricane, the old tub sagged off to leeward like a crab in any breeze stronger than a zephyr, despite the valiant efforts of her captain and a crew that would have done credit to any proud East Indiaman.

The skipper, coming astern, watched narrowly as the tall young man in strangely ill-fitting civilian clothes began to pace back and forth, back and forth, on the windward side of the quarterdeck—the spot traditionally sacred to the captain of a man-of-war. The young man checked himself, realizing what he was doing, and hurried below. The skipper shook his head slowly. He hadn't spent twenty years in His Majesty's Navy for nothing; he knew an officer when he saw one, and he'd have sworn that this young rip hadn't been off a king's ship more than a year.

As Gurney clattered down the companionway, he was conscious of a sense of profound embarrassment. It was a deplorable lapse of self-control in him to have slipped into his old habits; the kind of slip which, at the wrong moment, could be fatal. He turned into his small cabin, which contained no other furniture than a cot and a tiny table, and sat down. The smell of the sea coal with which the brig was loaded impregnated every plank, but Gurney remembered once having been told during his childhood that it was a healthful vapor. His lungs were still a little congested; his grippe had turned into a fever from which he was only barely fully recovered. He inhaled deeply, slightly ashamed of his temporary return to the nursery. Then his eyes went cold and he took a much-folded and thumbed piece of paper out of his coat pocket. He already knew it by heart—every minute scratch and stain; but as his regard traveled over it, he felt the same lurch of the heart he had experienced when it fell on the breakfast table at the Three Tuns.

"Their Lordships of the Admiralty," he read, "have asked me to convey to you their extreme displeasure at the events of the evening of February 28th. They have asked me to inform you that it would redound to the credit of His Majesty's Navy were you to resign your commission forthwith."

How like that pompous ass Jessop. Not only had he run eagerly back to Whitehall with news of the hot-head Gurney's disgrace, but he had doubtless asked particularly if he, who had been present at the disgracing aforesaid, could perform the act of execution by writing the letter. The whole sordid performance showed a propensity for nit-picking that rivaled anything that even Otway could have conceived.

But be that as it might, Gurney had sent in his letter of resignation, received a curt acknowledgment, and passed, as far as Whitehall and the rest of London polite society were concerned, beyond the pale. Though even as he had stepped onto the grimy deck of the *Lady Ellen* at Rotherhithe, the capital was beginning to hum with a juicy new item of scandal. It was rumored—nothing certain, mind—that a very prominent merchant, a sure bet for the next Parliament, had been larking with the slave trade, and that his embarrassment at the fabrication of these extraordinary facts was so strong that he planned to leave the country until the rumors had died down. Having first, naturally, sued all concerned in the rumor-mongering for their last penny and seen them clapped in the Fleet. The first part of this Gurney knew to be true; Arabella, in her response to the letter which he had sent to Dorset in Romeo's loving care, had told a sad tale of shuttered rooms, and furniture lurking under brown Holland covers. Otway, it seemed, had been caught on the hop; all the money tied up in his blackbirding had slipped through his fingers; and he was now deeply financially embarrassed.

All that Arabella knew of his plans was that he was heading for the Far East. She had once heard him speak familiarly of a countinghouse in Macao, so she assumed that that could be his destination. Meanwhile, she was to be dispatched to Bath as companion for a household of elderly aunts of bigoted religious views. She longed for George in her hour of trouble; could they not meet before she was immured in Bath?

Gurney had made a rendezvous with her at the Dovecote, an inn on the Wimborne Minster road south of Blandford. The landlord, Daoud Brulette, a French sea cook who had been released from the prison hulks when the war ended in 1815, kept a fine table and could be relied upon to be cheerfully discreet. The damp cold in the bowels of the *Lady Ellen* crept into his bones, but he was far away, in the courtyard of the Dovecote, the jets of steam from his horse's nostrils hanging in the frosty air as the hostler took the bridle. Arabella had run into the yard as soon as she heard the clatter of hooves on the cobblestones, dressed, despite the freezing air, in a high-waisted gown of muslin, her shoulders bare, the skin gleaming like ivory in the light of Brulette's lantern.

"Lord, my dear, you'll catch your death of cold."

"Oh, bother the cold, George, you're a sight to melt the Pole itself. Quickly, come in. Daoud's put up the most delicious dinner."

And she swept him, laughing, up the stairs and into a room where a fire of beech logs blazed and twin candelabra set rubies glowing in the hearts of the decanters on the sideboard. A bowl of white crysanthemums, from Arabella's beloved conservatory at Mendlebury, stood at the center of the table.

Gurney ate prodigiously, the food sending warmth coursing through limbs stiff and icy after the long ride west from London. But he did not notice what he ate. Arabella, sitting at his side, the firelight striking golden glints from her ringlets, her skin thick as cream in the candlelight, occupied his whole attention. As always, he was struck dumb by her beauty, and it was only gradually that her spell drifted over him and he found his voice again. She was telling him about her latest enthusiasm, an enthusiasm she knew he shared, for her correspondence with David Douglas at the Glasgow Botanical Gardens; then she seemed to remember that Mendlebury was up for sale, her conservatory with it, and a shadow passed over her face. She fell silent, staring at the chrysanthemums.

The tapboy drew the cloth.

Gurney took her hand. She turned to him. Her face was serious as he told her of the events of that evening at Vernon's.

"George, what will become of us now? Do we flee together? Can we go and soon? Mathias has departed, and I can give my aunts the slip. Let us go to France or Italy, set up house there, live free and pay no attention to the calumnies of Otway and his toadies."

Gurney shook his head. "No, my love, I have made a compact with myself. I shall not rest until I have ruined Otway and forced him to acknowledge his guilt. It will not be an easy road to travel, and I must travel it alone."

"Oh, a pox on your honor! Can we not live apart from the world, you and I? How can you go half way round the globe, leave me for the pursuit of a pompous nobody like my dratted stepfather? I have no wish to wait until I am old and gray for you to return from your wild-goose chase." A glistening teardrop hung suspended beneath her long lashes, and she turned her head away.

The skin of her neck was hot and feverish under Gurney's hand.

"My darling. How can I aspire to you, I, a man

dishonored? The world must know of your stepfather's villainy. Otway is a vile bug, and only I have the means to crush him. Reflect a moment. This man has dragged your mother down into the grave, tried to use you as his creature in his disgusting quest for power and gold, sold and bartered all you hold dear for his own petty and venal ends. And you would let him get away scot-free?"

Arabella sighed. "You are so stubborn. Why should it matter, what the world says? Why should we not fly to France, live in the country as man and wife, pure and simple, concern ourselves like Candide and Cunégonde with our garden and let the world go to hell in its own way?"

"Come, love. We would go stark crazy in a year. Have you seen the eyes of the Boulogne gallopers, that haunted wistfulness as they stand on the sea walls, gazing at the horizon day after day, at the white cliffs of Dover lying like a tombstone to their hopes at the gates of England? No, we belong here. I know it is a hard thing I ask, but it is the only way."

Though the tears were coursing down her cheeks, Arabella smiled. "Hell take you, George, you are a stubborn devil. How shall I bear the separation? I shall go mad in Bath, reading Walter Scott's latest drivel to my bird-witted aunts. Ah well, perhaps I shall become a proper bluestocking, a paragon of refinement and learning. When you return I shall doubtless be the mother of five squalling and bespectacled brats, all spouting Homer and digging for antiquities under the Pump Room, kowtowing to some blockheaded paterfamilias my aunts and Otway have fobbed off on me between them."

"I'll be damned if you will!" It was a possibility that had occurred to Gurney, and even though Arabella was quizzing him, her remarks struck deep. "I will make you a pledge. You see this ring? It was my father's and his father's before him. Wear it for me, Arabella, and tell me that you will be waiting when I return with Otway's head on a charger." He took her left hand and slipped the massive gold and onyx jewel onto the ring finger. "Wear this for me, Arabella, and never forget what it means."

She flung herself into his arms, her face wet against his lips, sobbing helplessly. "Damn you, damn you, George! Why must you leave me here? It's not fair! I shall, I tell you, I shall find another! But damn your arrogance, you know full well there's none other like you."

Her hair was smooth as silk under Gurney's hand, the lines of her body soft and firm under the sheer muslin of her dress. His lips found hers, and their mouths locked, twisting, as Arabella's sobs died and she wound herself round George's body, clutching at the back of his neck and raking his shoulders with clawed fingers. He felt fire begin to pound through his veins. Arabella was breathing hard now, eyelids lowered and red lips half open, head flung back. He kissed her again on the lips, then stepped away, holding her at arm's length. "No, Ara. I must away now, to Rotherhithe."

She clung to him. "No, George, don't go. You have already compromised me past hope of redemption; don't you think you should see it through?"

Gurney grinned and bussed her roughly. "Away with you, hussy. I ride tonight. Farewell, my darling! Pay mind to the ring!"

And he strode out of the door, slamming it hard behind him.

As the horses' hooves clattered in the courtyard without, Arabella sat bolt upright in her chair, eyes staring unseeing at the glow of the ashes dying in the grate. The hooves drummed into the distance, and she cast herself on the bed, turned her face to the wall, and began to sob bitterly.

By noon of the following day Gurney was on the London road from Salisbury, and early the next morning he had boarded the *Lady Ellen* at Rotherhithe, bruised and sore from hard riding.

He climbed to his feet and went on deck. The *Lady Ellen*'s roll was noticeably more pronounced than before, and the skipper was conversing in a muffled roar with the helmsman, both of them casting the occasional worried glance at the foretopmast, curved like a whip under the pressure of the freshening breeze. He looked at the wake. Despite her bulk underwater, the *Lady Ellen* must be making a mile to leeward for every ten she sailed.

A voice sounded in his ear. "That's not a very pretty sight, eh bor? She do sag down to leeward like a ghillie crab. But I hope you never do see har goo in ballast. 'Twould fair make your hair curl."

Gurney nodded abstractly, looking at the fore-top-mast. If that spar were to carry away, they'd never get to Gibraltar, let alone Naples, their official destination. He turned to the speaker, a stooped, sun-burned man of about sixty, a filthy old hat pulled well down over his ears and the lower half of his face obscured by a tobacco-stained white mustache. But it was his accent that had caught Gurney's ear. The rising inflection of the interrogatives, the curiously Germanic vowel-sounds, and the choice of words reminded him irresistibly of his childhood.

"Norfolk man?"

"Yew could say that, though I've been bledderin' round the coast fer so many a yare now that I'm more a citizen of anywhere you like than elsewhere. But I was born to the west of Sheringham there, an' my owd man were a fishing man from Moorhouse."

"Moorhouse! I myself spent the greater part of my youth there. You remember Jedediah Priest?"

"Blast I do. He were a good ol' boy, that one. I used ta reckon that what he didn't know about that coast wud fit into a right small barrel. He's long gone now, o' course."

And the seaman lost himself in a torrent of reminiscence, much of it softened by the kindly lens of time.

It had not been a pretty place, Moorhouse. Beautiful, yes, with a strange and cruel beauty of gray sea, yellow beach, and washed-out blue sky; sometimes, in summer, charmingly romantic, the sea lavender glowing purple under a fierce sun, the tidal creeks rushing urgently through their deep cuts in the marshes, and the dunlins drifting in flurries on the mud flats; but most often iron-hard, terrifying, wracks of cloud driving down the cutting east wind, mysterious currents shifting without rhyme or reason; shoals, tiderips, squalls. And Jedediah had taught George to read the shifting patterns of sea and marsh like a book; had shown him the migrations of geese which presaged foul weather from the northeast; had taught him to unravel the currents that could build up mud banks and sandbars where no banks or bars should be; had shown him the way of a ship and taught him a respectful awe of the treacherous sea.

Jedediah had been his tutor in the art of making his way in the physical world; the rest of his education had been seen to by his father. George had been only two years old when the vicarage at Worthamstead, his father's parish three miles inland from Moorhouse, had burned to the ground. He had heard from friends of the family—his father never spoke of it—that Parson Nathaniel had watched quietly, like one in a dream, as the flames lapped with their long tongues from the windows of the square flint rectory; and that before they could stop him, he had calmly walked to the door, plunged into the inferno, and emerged five minutes later with the infant George kicking and wailing in his arms. When they had taken him by the arm to lead him away, the scorched cloth of his cassock crumbled under their hands; and when he turned his face to them, it was seen that the very flesh was roasted away, and his eyes with it.

In the fire Nathaniel had lost not only his sight but his wife, his eldest son, and his daughter. He had always been a strange and somewhat reclusive man; though his sermons had often been published and their fame had spread the length and breadth of the realm, he had steadfastly refused to accept the rich livings and preferments offered him. Instead, he had opted for a small flock and a simple life in the shadow of the huge Gothic church, built with the gold of devout wool merchants in the Middle Ages. In Parson Gurney's illness, memories of the cool shade of

the forest of pillars and the dappled traceries of light
from high windows on white stone floors twisted into
grotesque shapes and mocked him for a madman;
and when at last he recovered, he found himself drawn
more and more to the laudanum decanter, in whose
depths he found anew the sumptuous images that the
fire had stripped away.

But his dreams were peopled with demented
flames, from whose ashes rose, not the phoenix res-
urrected, but a gray, bent clergyman with a hideously
disfigured face and a small boy.

George remembered fondly the Greek, Latin,
and mathematics his father had taught him. In neither
the classics nor the mathematical arts could the old
man control his fantasies; utopian dreams would su-
persede dry historical realities; the possibilities of
squaring the circle were of far more interest than Py-
thagorean theorems and long divisions. But somehow,
during the years after Nathaniel abandoned the great
church with the burned out rectory at its side for a
small, dank, flint cottage overlooking the bleak salt
marshes of Moorhouse, George had acquired from him
a deep and catholic body of learning. It was not so much
a mass of knowledge as a quirky, unfocused interest in
everything about him, from the harsh and treacherous
shallow seas he explored with Jedediah to the most
abstruse speculations on the guiding principles of the
universe.

He had been thirteen years old when his father
died, his life guttering and fading like a candle flame.
On the day after the funeral, the lawyer had told him
where he stood; he had a tiny private income and
owned the Moorhouse cottage, but besides that pittance—less than a governess's wages—he was a pau-
per. It had taken Gurney ten minutes to decide what
to do. He had jumped on his pony and ridden pell-
mell the twelve miles to Great Hetchingham, home of
Sir Randolph Harbord-Coke. The baronet had been
one of Nathaniel's few friends, and he had met George
a few times; he knew him as a strange, wild lad,
clever all right but with a disturbing touch of the Jaco-

bin about him. Sir Randolph had always maintained
that what these free spirits needed was a stiff dose of
discipline, taken daily for five years; so when George
proposed to him that he use his influence to secure
him a post as midshipman aboard one of His Majesty's men-of-war in exchange for five years' use of his
minute income, he was delighted to recommend the
stripling to Jervy Hutchinson of His Majesty's ship of
the line, *Egregious*, seventy-four guns.

Gurney recollected himself under the curious eye
of the Norfolkman.

"I were sayin', you've got the cut of a navy man."

"So I have been told."

Something in his manner seemed to preclude further comment. There were deep-etched lines on the
young face, lines which said that here was a powerful
character which would not lightly reveal its secrets.
The seaman shrugged, touched his hat brim with a
callous forefinger, and rolled forward.

It had been a hard life in the 'tweendecks of the
Egregious. At first Gurney had rebelled violently
against the iron discipline, the constant living cheek
by jowl with a lot of callow landsmen, younger sons
of the gentry like himself for the most part, but with
no more seamanship than farm boys. His Jacobin reputation seemed to have gone before him, too. Frequent
applications of the bonsun's rattan to his posterior
failed to rid him of his unwillingness to suffer fools
gladly; while the quality of his seamanship raised eyebrows on the quarterdeck, his ready wit and often dis-
respectful tongue earned him many enemies among
the incompetent and the self-important.

It was not until after his first action, broadside to
broadside with the French three-decker *Gloire* off
La Coruña, that he had seen for himself the necessity
for a ship whose men worked, not as individuals, but
as a well-oiled machine of war. The noise and the
smoke, the crash of roundshot tearing through two-
inch oak planking, the titanic rattle of falling spars,
had left him curiously unmoved. He had watched as
his messmates trembled and wilted under their bap-

tism of fire; he had seen Ramsay, the third lieutenant, blown to a bloody pulp not six feet from where he stood at the signal halyards. Though the blood had pounded in his ears and his mouth had been dry as sandpaper, he had been conscious of a feeling of cool-ness, detachment even, which had allowed him to concentrate single-mindedly on his duties even as the foremast toppled slowly to leeward like a felled tree. In the midst of the fight he had become aware of Cap-tain Hutchinson's eye on him; afterwards, as the ship limped toward Portsmouth with a jury-rigged fore-mast, leaving only a few floating spars to mark the last resting place of the *Gloire*, the captain had called him in to one of his famous Saturday breakfasts. Gurney had been too busy eating—the midshipmen's mess had been supplementing their diet with rats for some time now—to give a good account of himself conver-sationally; but there had been something amounting almost to respect in the stout captain's expression as he commended George on his coolness under fire.

After that, life had become less hard to bear. The painful episodes bent over the breech of one of the windward 24-pounders had become less frequent, and the responsibility of his duties had increased to the point where he had been detailed to command the prize crew of a nondescript schooner which had been unwise enough to show the *Egregious* her topsails off Cádiz. He had made a good passage home, despite a sharp encounter with a Breton chasse-marée off the Isles of Scilly. A lucky (Gurney unwisely insisted) shot from the schooner's ridiculous long four-pounder popgun had carried away the Frenchman's topmast, and the schooner had limped into Falmouth ten days later with his prize in tow.

While the capture of the chasse-marée meant nothing significant in financial terms, the prestige it attracted was something else altogether; the fast, heavily armed French ships were playing merry hell with shipping on the south coast and in the western ocean, and frequently made mincemeat of vessels four to five times their size. Gurney found himself a hero in a

modest way, lionized by the press as one of the young
fire-eaters of Albion. Popular acclaim had done much
to blunt the edge of Captain Hutchinson's wrath, too.
While the captain had been justifiably incensed that
one of his hard-won prizes should have been put at
risk in such a quixotic venture, he found it difficult
to conceal his pride in a protégé who had so early
shown the Nelson touch. Others, notably Carruthers,
the *Egregious*'s dour and fanatically religious first lieutenant, did not trouble to temper their misgivings
with patriotic fervor. And Carruthers had friends in
high places.

It was on one of his forays ashore, in one of the
gaming clubs in Pall Mall, that he had met Mathias
Otway. He had been suspicious of the stout, ingratiating merchant from the start, but Otway had evinced
a flattering interest in the young acting lieutenant's
deeds and had presented him to his stepdaughter, the
Lady Arabella Mountolivet. Any reservations Gurney
might have had about his new patron had vanished at
his first meeting with Arabella. The two months he
had spent at Mendlebury House, Otway's pretentious
residence below Cranborne Chase in Dorset, had
passed in a twinkling; and when he left to rejoin
the *Egregious* in April, bound for the West Indies to
pacify the Caribbean, he was aware that there was a
space in his life that nobody but Arabella could fill.

The Caribbean had, at first, been disappointing.
Jervy Hutchinson had been forced to use the *Egregious* as a floating office building, anchored in the torrid
heat three miles off the disease-ridden city of Kingston. Gurney, now a lieutenant, had chafed under the
tedious routine of spit-and-polish, ceremonial, and
minor diplomacy. And still worse, while privateers and
pirates roved almost unchecked in the shallow channels where even frigates could not follow them, the
Egregious's men festered in the tropical heat without
even the thought of accumulating prize money to
console them. Gurney, half-mad with boredom, had
taken up a subscription from his shipmates and with
it had purchased an ancient sloop, a single one-pound

swivel gun mounted at her bow. After a stormy interview with Jervy, whose liver was showing signs of deterioration under the combined influences of inactivity and Jamaica rum, he had succeeded in persuading him to commission the sloop as H.M. cutter *Shrimp*. Gurney had packed his new command to the gunwales with men and supplies, and set off on an expedition which had resulted in his sending back to Kingston several prizes, and eventually returning himself in command of a sleek eight-gunned topsail schooner he had christened the *Vampire*. By this time his exploits had become something of a legend in the Gulf of Mexico, and Jervy came under some pressure to curb the activities of this young blood whose exploits bore more of the stamp of the privateer than of one of His Majesty's sloops of war. While the captain heartily disagreed with the correctness of this view, he had not been sent on this diplomatic mission for nothing; and as a compromise George had been promoted to full lieutenant and packed off home in the *Vampire* with dispatches from London, bearing strict instructions to look neither to port nor starboard but to head with all expedition for Portsmouth.

It had been a melancholy moment for Gurney when the *Vampire*'s anchor had plunged into the dirty waters of Portsmouth harbor. England was no longer at war; the huge naval machine which had assured her rule of the waves was being disassembled piece by piece, its officers languishing ashore on half-pay, bombarding a callous Admiralty with solicitations of work. Unless they had influence and connections; and both of these commodities, Gurney found, had become very difficult to come by in the hardheaded commercialism of peacetime.

Mathias Otway's attitude had undergone a subtle change, too. No longer could he bask effortlessly in Gurney's reflected glory; the young hero had turned suddenly into that least valuable of peacetime commodities, a half-pay lieutenant with plenty of nerve but no solid prospects. And his deepening attachment to Arabella also gave the merchant cause for concern.

It was no part of his plan that his beautiful step-daughter should marry some half-pay nobody; acutely conscious of his ignoble origins, Otway knew that he needed the connections that only Arabella's marriage to one of the great names of England could bring. He would provide the dowry, a sound investment by any standards; and God knew that there were few enough brides with Arabella's combination of brains, wealth, and beauty. In his more optimistic moments, Otway would gloat unrestrainedly over the prospect of being father-in-law—well, stepfather-in-law—to a duke. But Arabella seemed to have other plans. She was constantly in Gurney's company; they moved in the same circles since George had discovered that he could stay fed and financed by moving in society and playing the odd game of whist. Humiliating it was, to be sure; but how else could he see his Arabella?

Otway had been openly hostile when George had taken up Arabella's invitation to the November covert-shooting at Mendlebury, but enough of Gurney's reputation lingered on in the minds of others of his house party to bring him up short of dismissing the lieutenant from the house. And then he had been called away to Bristol after Christmas on pressing business—Gurney now knew what that business had been—and Gurney had discovered, in an attic where he was wont to dally with Arabella, the chest of bills of lading, letters, and manifests which revealed that his fortune was now founded not on legitimate trade but on the shipping of human cargoes from West Africa to the plantations of the Indies, a commerce punishable by transportation to Botany Bay since Wilberforce's Act of 1807.

That the act was even now honored nearly as much in the breach as in the observance made Otway's involvement no less reprehensible; Gurney had been shocked to the core by the abominations of the slavers in the Caribbean, and more than one bold black-birder had danced on air at *Vampire's* yardarm. He had seen in Otway's perfidy not only a route to Arabella's hand in marriage, but also the means to deal a body blow to the despicable traffic in which the merchant was involved. It was only the treachery of the keeper Watkins, whose conniving had landed him in his present pass, that had come between him and his goal. And now, on the quarterdeck of the *Lady Ellen*, beating to windward three hundred miles off the coast of Portugal, he gripped the rail and renewed his vow to come up with Otway if it was the last thing he did.

He was aware of a twinge of uncertainty, however. His vengeance was one thing. But what of Arabella, the goal beyond that feast of vengeance? Was it fair to expect her to wait for him? The *Lady Ellen*, as if in response to his doubts, stuck her round nose into a wave and stopped dead, then wallowed into the next trough. As fast as the thought had been born it died. Gurney smiled to himself, and the tenderness that always accompanied thoughts of her washed over him. She knew as well as he that the course he was following was the only one open to him; he only hoped that such a sentiment would stand the test of time. And a long time it would be, for ahead of him stretched the long road east. He could not take the Cape route— the danger of recognition was too great, and East India Company scuttlebutt might alert his quarry. But his consultations with his friend Cullompton of the Royal Society had convinced him that were he to cross the Mediterranean to Alexandria, he could trade his remaining gold to advantage, and that from there he could finance his passage to India and thence to Macao.

During the days that followed, as the *Lady Ellen* wallowed protestingly around Cape St. Vincent and towards the Pillars of Hercules, Gurney's day fell into an unvarying routine. He fretted at the slowness of the ship, the snaillike deliberation of the crew, and the constant headwinds; only by burying himself in his books could he make life supportable. He had resolved to learn the languages of the East, and had purchased an Arabic grammar at Hatchards. His fluency increased daily, aided by sporadic bouts of conversation with the villainous-looking Cornish second mate, who claimed to have acquired his knowledge of the tongue on merchantmen in the eastern Mediterranean. Gurney reckoned that simple trading would not have accounted for the Cornishman's vocabulary, which combined martial pursuits and lechery in equal parts; but he persisted, and by the time the lookout hailed the Rock of Gibraltar on the port bow, he could have passed muster in any rotgut rumshop from Macedonia to Tangier.

His face was once more taking on its mahogany tan, and the lines had faded from his cheeks. In the Mediterranean sunshine his leg, which often gave him trouble in the damp cold of more northerly latitudes, had begun to behave again, and his limp was now virtually imperceptible. His whole mood seemed to change as he watched the Rock of Gibraltar grow larger under the *Lady Ellen*'s stubby bowsprit; here, at the gateway to the South and East, the miseries and oppressions of the winter rolled off him like water from a duck's back. The warm aromatic breeze from the Spanish mainland coursed through his blood like wine; he was suddenly filled with an urge to laugh, to caper on the deck like a spring colt, to cock a mighty snook at those pompous milords, choked to the gills in their cravats and thick serge coats, posturing and pawing at each other in their fat, stuffy burrows in the side of the Rock. He looked guiltily around to see if anyone had noticed his momentary lapse. The crew were too preoccupied with their preparations for docking to pay any attention to their passenger, rum cove though he might be. Anyway, the novelty of his presence had worn off fast. Even Amos Sawyer, the man from Moorhouse, rarely exchanged a word with him since he had begun to associate with Trevose, the second mate. For Trevose, Gurney gathered, was not a popular man among his inferiors—not that he was physically violent; a merchant crew of this experience would never have stood for that. No, it was an essential *foreignness* in the man—the very factor in his character that had excited George's interest—which set him apart from the rest.

The *Lady Ellen* stayed four days in Gibraltar. Gurney found the heat and stink of his cabin unbearable, so he spent most of the time on deck, under an awning he had had rigged to one side of the wheel. Even here, the noise and filth were appalling—the hands were scrubbing the hold clean of its layers of coal dust prior to loading it with Spanish oranges—but he could not take the risk of an erstwhile naval colleague recognizing him ashore. He well knew the speed at which a rumor could travel; in an age where a letter might take four months to cross the Atlantic, an item of gossip could travel from Athens to London in mere days. So he closed his ears to the tumult, pulled a broad-brimmed hat over his eyes, and lost himself in the gargling complexities of the Arabic throat consonants.

A week later, with Naples only five days away if the brisk westerly continued to blow, George was sitting in the crow's nest talking to Trevose. Fifty feet below, the *Lady Ellen's* forefoot plowed stubbornly into the turquoise rollers; but up here, with the hum of the wind in the rigging and the creak of her spars— Gurney cast a nervous glance at the fishing on her topmast, which was working visibly as the crow's nest swayed fifteen feet to port, fifteen feet to starboard, like an upended pendulum—he felt a freedom from constraint, an exhilaration, which had nothing to do with the ungainly hull below. Trevose was watching him quizzically.

"You been to Naples before?"

Gurney shook his head, half his attention still suspended in the tilting of the horizon.

"Rum place, very. Cut your throat soon as look at ye, most of they buggers. If'n I may make so bold as to ask, what would be your intentions in they parts? Something in the mercantile line, mayhap?"

"Something like that. I propose to take ship for Alexandria, where I have business to conduct."

"Tricky, that. I wouldn't like to see you landin' up afoul of any of they sharks down there, pertickler if you're by way of carryin' anything in the way of valuables." The Cornishman refreshed himself from a black bottle. "So happens I met a cove hailed from Napoli way once, in Tripoli. Anyroad, I did him a bit of a favor—took apart some pimping lad as was after his hide—and he says to me, 'Trevose,' he says, 'if ever you're in need of advice or assistance down Naples way, ask for Mama Eugenia's, and mention my name.' And it strikes me, my young sir, that it would be no bad thing if I were to take you along to see Mama Eugenia and see what she can suggest."

Gurney grinned at him. "Thank you. I am deeply sensible of the service you do me. But first, may I ask what's in it for you?"

The Cornishman spread his hands deprecatingly. "I allus did say you was a quick one, Mr. Gurney. It's merely a matter of a small parcel that I'd like to get ashore at Naples. I'd do it myself, only there's a customs man there I've had some trouble with in the past."

"And what would be the contents of this parcel?"

"Oh, merely a few letters from friends of mine in Spain—Gibraltar, I should say."

"These letters would be of a political nature?"

"You could say that, sir."

"And you guarantee me a good passage to Alexandria if I take this packet ashore?"

" 'Pon my word, sir."

Gurney reflected. Political letters. The Kingdom of Naples was still in a ferment after the ejection of Bonaparte's younger brother and the installation of the Bourbon monarchy. Rumor had it that a popular uprising was imminent; he wouldn't be surprised if Trevose, with his obvious smuggling connections, were involved in some lay with ball and musket. Well, he held no brief for the arrogant Bourbons; as a democratic Englishman he could certainly stretch a point if it served his own ends.

"Very well. Your hand on it."

The two hundred gold sovereigns in the money belt under his shirt weighed Gurney down as he tramped up the steep hill towards the Via Tiberio. Five miles to the southeast, the crater of Vesuvius streamed a thin plume of smoke down the wind. Gurney called to the urchin carrying his ditty bag to slow down. Tall tenement buildings of gray tufa lined each side of the street, their balconies projecting confidentially towards each other. Above his head thirty conversations, each of them conducted with a gusto that would have done credit to your average bosun in a fresh northeaster, were in progress at the same time. Between the buildings, in the dark, narrow courts, long multicolored lines of washing hung like signal flags.

The street itself was piled high with mounds of refuse, and the air buzzed with large green flies. A mangy cur left off its rooting at the bottom of a heap which, by the smell, contained something very dead indeed, and snarled at Gurney. Grinning nervously— it was not that he didn't like dogs, he told himself without believing a word of it, but if this one bit him, mortification would set in for sure—he skirted the pile, keeping it between him and the dog, and looked up the hill for his ditty bag and its porter.

Negligence personified, the infant was sitting on his burden in the middle of a large and odorous puddle. Gurney gave him the back of a hand round his ear and tossed him a couple of soldi. From nowhere, a pack of ragged children pounced on the recipient of largess, and disappeared, a brawling, yelling, struggling knot, around a corner. Then, overlaying the noise of the women, children, donkeys, dogs, cats, and an ark of other beasts, came the clanging of the bells for vespers, a combined call to worship from one hundred and fifty belfries, towers, and steeples. Gurney wiped off his bag, slung it over his shoulder, and plunged into the dark mouth of an alley.

The wineshop was as Trevose had described it, a cavernous, dark room, cool after the heat of the evening. Along one side ran a rough counter, behind which great tuns rested on trestles. The rest of the room was occupied by a long table of unplaned chestnut set with crude chairs. At the far end sat three old men, who looked up curiously as Gurney entered, then returned to their discussions. He sat down and called for wine. He was finishing his third tankard—it was delicious, the bottle frosted with moisture from the cool cellars under the room where he sat—when Trevose drew up a chair, ordered a mug, and gulped down a liberal measure.

"Better. Much better. You have the packet?"

Gurney patted his breast pocket. "No trouble. They barely looked at me."

"Well, by God, they looked at me, all right. I had to stay on board till their backs were turned, then swim ashore." He spat into the sawdust on the floor. "If I'm not down with a quartan ague before the week's out, it'll be a miracle. And even so, I'm not sure I lost them. They've become devilish sharp since I was last here. Come along o' me."

Gurney planked a silver coin down on the table and hoisted his bag onto his shoulder. Trevose walked into the street, looking to left and right, then ran hastily back into the shadows of the wineshop. He caught the proprietor's eye and pressed a warning finger to his lips. The man jerked his head towards the back of the shop and continued to polish glasses as Trevose bundled Gurney through the door at the back of the taproom and out into a filthy back alley. As they started to run between the crumbling buildings, a clamor of voices broke out behind them. The word *Inglesi* featured prominently, interspersed with vehement denials—the wineshop owner was evidently holding true to his word. Gurney raised an eyebrow at Trevose, and they darted into the shadows of a tumbledown warehouse. Gurney caught a gleam from the long knife in the Cornishman's right hand.

Two uniformed men, each with drawn sword, wearing plumed kepis and highly-polished black knee boots, were approaching across a patch of waste ground. Gurney held his breath and pressed his shoulder against the wall behind him. As the two men passed—they were both smaller than Gurney; one of them wore a waxed mustache, and both sported oily

ringlets spilling from under their kepis—a rat scuffled
from a pile of garbage. The carabiniere with the mustache looked around, and gave a startled yelp as he
caught Gurney's eye.

Gurney forced a grin. *"Buona sera,"* he said, nudg-
ing Trevose, who was hiding his knife behind his back,
"marineri inglesi perditti. Dové il porto?"

The carabinieri were still suspicious.

"Carbonari." The one with the mustache pulled his
lips back from his teeth and drew his sword. Trevose
whipped his hand from behind his back and drove it
into the Italian's stomach. A look of enormous surprise
spread over the dying man's swarthy features, and he
folded up, clasping his belly. His colleague was
thumbing back the hammer on the pistol at his belt
when Gurney's boot smashed into his right kneecap.
As he bent forward, a hand like an oaken plank
crunched into the nape of his neck and he fell limply
to the filthy ground.

Trevose set off at a run, followed by Gurney. A
fresh outbreak of shouting at their backs told them
that the two bodies had been discovered, and as they
dived into the maze of alleyways across the waste
ground from the ruined warehouse, a pistol ball
whined over Gurney's head. Trevose led him through
twisting lanes and courts hung with washing where
beefy-armed matrons screamed at ragged children
from high windows, through a labyrinth of tunnel-
like alleys, and finally into a malodorous catacomb
which, Gurney guessed, had once been a sewer. The
sounds of pursuit faded, but Trevose kept up his un-
relenting pace. After a while, it became evident that
they were heading downhill—toward the harbor, Gurney thought, his chest aching and the wine in his
stomach slopping queasily.

Finally they emerged panting on a short, stony
beach, covered with refuse. Night had fallen, and the
stars were winking from a sky of blue velvet. The
waterfront buildings loomed like a black cliff behind
them; Trevose took his arm and tugged him impatiently towards a flight of steps. Gurney panted up the

slimy treads and came to a halt beside Trevose on a broad platform at the top. The Cornishman rapped a tattoo on the tall iron door; a small slit appeared, and a hoarse voice rasped a password. Whatever Trevose answered seemed to satisfy the watchman; a wicket creaked open, and the two Englishmen entered.

At the far end of a vaultlike chamber, dimly illuminated by a couple of hanging lanterns, was a huge, solid armchair surrounded by a litter of ledgers and papers, remnants of food, and empty wine bottles. In the chair sat—lay, rather—the fattest woman Gurney had ever seen. She was clothed, in the manner of elderly Italian women of a certain class, in a gown of black alpaca big enough to have made a fair-sized skysail for a seventy-four-gun ship of the line. Innumerable chins hung over the neckline of her garment; thin eyes, black as deadly nightshade berries, peeped out from behind puffs and creases of lard set above billowing jowls and an absurd button nose. Gurney was reflecting irreverently that she would have been a major asset to any traveling freak show he had ever seen when she opened her wet rosebud mouth and spoke. Her voice was clear and reedy as a little girl's. Its effect, coming from that gross pile of flesh, was grotesque in the extreme.

"Gooda evenink, my fren'sa." Trevose bowed, motioning to Gurney to do likewise. The Cornishman replied in Italian, and Gurney made his salutations in the same language.

"So. A little bird tells me you have had a little fracas with the carabinieri, no? Ah, *Inglese* with the yellow hair, I see you are surprised that Eugenia knows already." She indicated her gross body. "I have a big family—many sons; also daughters, cousins, grandchildren, and friends, such as yourself. And, to keep a poor old lady amused in the evening of her years, they . . . tell her things." The piggy eyes went hard and cold. "Now, you have some letters for me from our friends in Spain, I hear." The eyes stared unwinkingly as Gurney handed her the packet. The old woman read the papers it contained and threw them onto the pile at her side, chuckling.

"Good, very good. Now tell me what you require in exchange and I will see what can be done. But first, food and wine. Gonzalo!"

A child scuttled out of the shadows at the door, carrying a laden tray. As the small figure stepped into the circle of lamplight, Gurney caught his breath; this was no child, but a midget of about five-and-thirty. Donna Eugenia's silvery laugh tinkled around the grimy vaulting of the ceiling.

"Surprised, my brave young officer? At Donna Eugenia's the fit go work in the street; the halt and the lame serve as retainers in my castle. So eat, eat. I love to watch people eat." She made a face. "I myself peck like a bird."

Gurney watched fascinated as she posted four inches of salami and a half-pound of bread into her mouth and began to champ and snuffle like a sow at the trough. When she had finished chewing, her chins wobbled and her eyes seemed about to pop out; but a long gulp of wine from the bottle at her side seemed to compose her, and she turned again to Gurney. "Well, my fine young friend, you have done me a service, and one good turn deserves another. What can I do for you?"

"I should esteem it a great favor if you could show me a means of obtaining passage to Alexandria."

The donna seemed to lose herself in thought, twiddling her lower lip with a pudgy forefinger. "This is not easy, you know. It has been a bad year, with storms and guarda-costa accounting for many of my brave boys. But wait a minute. Cesare, my nephew, sails for Crete tomorrow morning at six. And from Crete, with the recommendation he will give you, you should have no difficulty in making Alexandria. Is fixed?"

Gurney thought fast. It had certainly been a rough year in the Mediterranean, and it should be no hard task to find passage from Crete to Egypt. And in his position he couldn't afford to pick and choose. Swallowing his apprehensions, he let his face relax into a broad smile and bowed deeply to the donna. "Six o'clock tomorrow with your nephew Cesare. Is fixed."

2

Cesare's face was as red as a turkey-cock's. He banged a hairy fist on the chart table. "No! And a thousand times, no! It is madness to do anything but run before such a wind as this. For twenty years now I am making this passage in my *Santa Maria*, and I know the dangers better than any man alive. With a southwest wind such as this a man does not trifle." He waved an arm toward the window of the dog kennel that served as the *Santa Maria*'s deckhouse. "Look for yourself!"

The window gave onto a threatening waste of water. The southwesterly breeze that had helped the ancient *Santa Maria* and her crew of eight down the west coast, past the isle of Capri, and through the Strait of Messina between the toe of Italy and the island of Sicily had, on the fifth day out, freshened steadily. Now the turquoise of the sea had changed to a dark blue-black, and white horses were beginning to bound on the wave crests. The waves themselves were steep and hollow; the *Santa Maria*'s deck was often buried in foam, and judging by the inky smudge of cloud approaching from the southwest, things would get worse before they got better.

At the moment, the *Santa Maria* was on a broad reach, one of her better points of sailing. The choice, as Gurney saw it, was either to take the risk of pointing her up toward the wind despite her dreadful performance close-hauled or—and this was Cesare's solution—to run before wind and sea and commend their souls to their Maker. This latter course was all very well, except that a day's sailing ahead lay the Cerigo channel between the northwestern tip of Crete and the long rocky fingers of the Peloponnesus. Though the gap was a hundred miles wide, it was studded with jagged reefs. No place to be running blind in a full gale. Were Gurney to have his way and head south, the *Santa Maria* would be crashing through a beam sea on her worst point of sailing; but at least she would stand a good chance of leaving Crete to port. What was certain was that she could not carry on much longer on her present course. The rollers were butting into her starboard quarter, and often she would be flung skyward, then slide, her sails flapping, into the trough. If the seas became any steeper—and the whine of the wind had risen in pitch during the last half hour—the *Santa Maria* would almost certainly broach-to, slew beam-on to the waves, and would in all likelihood roll over and founder. Gurney had all the deep-seaman's instinct to head for open water in a storm. The thought of running direct for so fearsome a shore as the Cerigo channel and, beyond it, the rocky fangs of the Cyclades, appalled him.

Cesare was sweating profusely. His face all of a sudden lost its color, and he sat down suddenly in the chair at the chart table, wringing his hands.

"Well?" Gurney's voice was insistent. "She's your ship, Signor Cesare. It's up to you what you do with her. But those are the facts as I see them, though I suspect I owe you an apology for having been so forward as to present them to you."

"No, no, please do not apologize." The Italian's eyes were imploring. "It's a comfort, a great comfort, to have your assistance in time of adversity, *per Jesu Maria e i santissimi angele*. But what shall I do? O my God, what shall I do?"

Gurney was extremely embarrassed. "But Signor Cesare, I repeat: this is your ship. And though I have had the presumption to advise you on the matter of our course, the final decision is yours alone."

The Italian's chest swelled with self-importance. "Very well. I, Capitano Cesare, *carbonaro* and naviga-

tor, shall take the con. We drive for the Cerigo gap.
Pah! It should be no hard matter. But perhaps the
Inglese signor would do me the honor of giving me the
benefit of his counsel from time to time?" He beamed,
secure in the knowledge that he had saved his face.

As they came back on deck, a sheet of spray blasted
over the poop and swept the length of the ship. Gurney barely noticed it, but it had a distinctly damp-
ening effect on Cesare's spirits. His face turned yellow
again, and his teeth began to chatter like castanets.
Gurney saw one of the crew make an offensive
gesture at his captain; two other men, loafing in the
waist, laughed behind their hands. Cesare turned
to Gurney. "S-suddenly I find myself indisposed. I
should be grateful if you could assume command until
such a time as I feel better in myself." And he slunk
below, to the open amusement of his crew.

Gurney rounded on them with a scowl, roaring like
a bull. "All right, you scum, the comedy's over. You
and you! Get forward, reef topsail, clew up main
course. You! Two reefs in the mizzen topsail, strike
spanker, and look sharp!"

However cowardly their captain might be, the crew
were none too bad—for an undisciplined rabble. It
seemed that Cesare was the only officer aboard. All
the other men did what they could when they felt
like it; there was no mate to drive them to their tasks,
no petty officer to chase laggard topmen up the mast
with a rope's end. But the *Santa Maria* herself was no
racing yacht; so sluggish was she, indeed, that Gurney
doubted whether smartening up her crew would have
any effect on her performance. She was somewhere
between a barge and a bathtub, her decks cluttered
with ramshackle wooden structures and piles of cargo. Her mainmast carried a huge, square main course
and an ancient grayish brown topsail fancifully
painted with a Virgin, a new moon, and at least a
platoon of stout pink *putti*. It was set far forward, with
the result that in a gale of wind abaft the beam her
blunt nose would dig violently into the seas as she met
them. Gurney noted with relief that as the men

gasketed the flapping and booming mainsail to the yard, her motion eased; she began to sail over the waves instead of crashing through them. But in this quarter sea she was still rolling alarmingly. He walked back to the wheel, balancing with difficulty against the corkscrew bucking of the deck.

"How does she feel?" he asked the man at the wheel.

The helmsman laughed mirthlessly.

"Listen, *Inglese*, this old tub goes to leeward faster than she goes forward on anything tighter than a beam reach. The only hope is to put her into a dead run, rip every scrap of canvas off her, and to hope to God and his saints she doesn't get pooped or hit a stone."

"Is there anyone aboard who knows the Cerigo gap and the islands beyond?"

"Only Giallo."

"Who?"

"Giallo Cesare. The captain."

Gurney grinned. Yellow Cesare. This was obviously not the first time that he had slid below when danger threatened. He started for the deckhouse. The helmsman called him back.

"He won't be any good to you now. Flat on his bunk blubbering his little eyes out, no doubt. If it goes according to form, he'll start praying next." The helmsman made an obscene gesture and tapped his forehead meaningfully with his forefinger. "Pity. Pox, you know?"

Gurney nodded, looked at the horizon. The sky to the southwest had darkened. A purple-black pall was racing towards them over the sea, drifts of rain hanging in dirty curtains over waters that even at this distance looked restless and turbulent. As the sun disappeared behind the cloud bank, twilight fell like a gray blanket. For a moment the wind seemed to falter; then it doubled in force, driving the *Santa Maria* up to her forecastle into the next wave. Gurney was bellowing orders as the ship staggered up again, water rushing in torrents from her scuppers. The main topsail split down the middle with a report like a cannon shot and flogged itself to tatters immediately; the ship careened wildly, sliding almost parallel to the breaking crests of the waves, her deck canted at an angle of forty degrees as the hands fought, fingers bleeding, with the iron-taut canvas of the mizzen topsail. Inch by inch they dragged it in and made it fast to the yard; and no sooner did their feet touch the deck than Gurney was driving them forward to the jib halyards, tailing onto the sheets, the veins starting from his temples with the effort, as the sails bellied to the deck. But the foot of the flying jib had jammed in its outhaul; the sail, spread under the *Santa Maria's* bow like a huge drogue, immediately dragged her stem deep in green water.

Gurney looked around him. The three men with him looked back expectantly. With a curse, he stepped onto the slippery, wildly bucking bowsprit and inched his way forward. As he wrestled with the two-inch Manila twisted in the block, he looked down. The *Santa Maria* hung suspended on the crest of a wave; then the water fell away hollowly beneath her, exposing her stem and six feet of weedy keel, and she plunged downwards into the trough. Gurney fell flat, wrapped his arms and legs around the spar like a monkey on a stick as the sea smashed into his back and he went down, down, the roar of water in his ears turning to a roaring laughter, Otway's laughter, the gross, leering face mocking him as he clung to the bowsprit, the pudgy hands—strong, incredibly strong —dragging relentlessly at his body; down, down, and the choking in his throat was Arabella, torn away from him, whipped by a great wind to the edge of a black abyss, and the wind was roaring in his ears and its voice was the voice of Otway again, and his limbs were plucked from their hold like straws, and he was lifted in the air and flung with unbelievable violence down again. His knees smashed agonizingly into a solid object, and he gasped, choking on bitter seawater; then the water receded and he found himself prone on the poop, coughing and sputtering, next to the open-mouthed helmsman.

He struggled to his feet, ignoring the helmsman's astonishment, and looked forward. There had been three men with him there; now there were only two, picking themselves up off the deck. He hobbled forward. Their eyes were glazed with shock, and they stood stupidly, gaping. Gurney shook one of them roughly by the shoulder. "Where's the other one?"

"I saw him go overboard with the wave that took you. But the sea threw you back, signor, while it kept him." Superstitious awe shone in the man's eyes.

Gurney suddenly realized he was trembling. He clenched his teeth against their chattering, turned on his heel, and limped aft. It was full dark now, and the rain was pouring down, cutting his face.

The helmsman showed his teeth. "It's not so easy, now. She begin to wallow like a buffalo."

And sure enough, there was a sluggishness about the ship's movements, a heaviness, which had not been there before. A dull rumbling, terminating in a solid thump, came from below. And again. Gurney cursed and ran for the hatchway, lighting a lantern as he went. The cargo had broken loose, and boxes, barrels, and balks of timber were crashing from one side of the deck to the other with every roll.

The lantern flung huge, grotesque shadows as it swung, and the moving carpet of boxes and crates slid from side to side, cracking and groaning like a glacier, smashing into the sides and each other. Gurney pressed himself against the great wooden cylinder of the mainmast as a huge hogshead rumbled past him and broke like an egg against the starboard side, spilling the olive oil it contained in a treacherous film over the soggy planking, where the careening crates spread it over the whole deck in a matter of seconds. On the port side, just on the waterline, Gurney guessed, some heavy object had splintered an area of planking some two feet square. As the *Santa Maria* rolled, a gout of water surged through the hole.

He ran up the companion ladder and stuck his head out of the scuttle.

"Four men, lanterns, and some tackles. Quickly. You! Set a storm jib."

The seaman waved and started forward. The storm jib should stop her swinging and broaching-to. If, that is, she weren't pooped . . .

Four hands clattered down the ladder, coils of heavy rope on their shoulders. Gurney concentrated on giving orders. It was fantastically dangerous business. In the leaping shadows thrown by the lanterns, it was almost impossible to see where he was putting his feet. And the footing was treacherous, glassy smooth with the spilt oil. Once he looked around to see a huge box of coarsely nailed slats bearing down on him in eerie silence. For a moment he froze, calmly assessing its course and speed; then, ever so carefully, trying not to rely on the friction of his soles on the deck, he waited until it was almost on him, fell towards it, grasped its sides with his hands, and somersaulted over the top as it cannoned into the side, making the whole ship shudder. He landed in a sprawling heap, picked himself up, and once more started to rope the wildly slewing boxes like steers, lashing them to the stout rings set in the keelson.

But the men were stumbling with fatigue. As Gurney bent to pass a bight of line around a heavy crate careening past him, he caught a whiff of alcohol on the breath of the man at his shoulder. The man's eyes were red, his breath came in gasps, and his movements were clumsy. A sudden jolt as the ship smacked into a yawning trough snatched the rope from Gurney's hand; he watched horrified as the crate slid, gathering momentum, towards the seaman, who was struggling towards him across the tilting deck. He shouted a warning, and the man looked up, horror dawning in his eyes, and made to leap out of the way. But his feet, covered in oil, slid from under him, and he crashed down onto the deck. Gurney distinctly heard the snap as his legs broke; he leaped across, secured the crate to the side, and dragged the screaming man to the companion hatch. He was unconscious as Gurney heaved him on deck and took him to the stern cabin.

Giallo was on his knees in the corner, a rosary in his hand, babbling Hail Marys. He had been sick several times. Gurney strode across to him, cracked him across the face with the back of his hand, and pointed at the unconscious figure in the doorway. Then, without waiting for his reaction, he went on deck.

The rain had almost stopped, though the wind roared unabated over the deck, the wet rigging shrieking like a pack of banshees. The moon shone fitfully through a scudding wrack of clouds; in its light he saw the log line, taut as a bowstring over the poop rail, shortening as a huge wave reared its white head over the quarterdeck. He roared at the helmsman; the wind whipped the words away as soon as he opened his mouth, and the glittering crest hung suspended thirty feet above his head. He dived for the mizzen shrouds as tons of water roared down onto the deck, buffeting his already weakened knee against the rail. The *Santa Maria* went down; then, when Gurney was sure she would never rise again, she seemed to shake herself and surged upward with such speed that the blood drained from his head. As he broke surface, surprised still to be alive, he saw the mainmast thrashing alongside, trailing in a raffle of gear, threatening at any moment to stave in the ship's already weakened planks. He looked around. There was no sign of the man at the wheel, which spun uselessly on its mountings; two men were already hacking at the mainmast's rigging. He grabbed an ax from one of them and severed the last of the shrouds. The spar floated free and disappeared into the raging waters to port.

It seemed that the wave which so nearly pooped the *Santa Maria* had done her a service. Relieved of the weight of the mainmast, the bows floated higher in the water. Looking briefly into the hold, Gurney saw that the sea was no longer gushing through the hole in the planking. He sent two men below with a sail and a tin patch, and set about preparations for riding the night out.

By the time the sky lightened in the east, he was numb with cold and exhaustion. The *Santa Maria* was drifting in the eye of the southwesterly wind; if his dead reckoning was to be relied on, they should by now have passed miles to the north of Cape Spatha, on the northwestern extremity of Crete, and between the twin islands of Cerigo and Cerigotto, at the southernmost tip of the Peloponnesus. His father had told him of Cerigo—Cythera, Aphrodite's island, whence she had traveled to the shores of Cyprus on her shell. Strange apparitions, maidens in flowing robes, Tritons, dolphins, drifted before his eyes. He shook his head to clear them, angrily concentrating on Otway's smugly grinning features. One of the hands appeared at his shoulder with a cup of coffee. He handed the wheel over and went to huddle under the lee of the deckhouse, sniffing the aromatic liquid and letting its heat warm his icy hands. The stiff tot of grappa in the cup sent a welcome warmth coursing through his limbs as he watched the first rays of the rising sun pick out the high mare's tails glowing pink against the fading indigo of the sky.

Two hours later the wind had dropped to a light breeze, and Gurney, invigorated by the growing heat of the sun, was supervising the lashing of a jury mainmast to the jagged stump of the one that had gone overboard in the night. A huge sea was still running, but the steep, hollow waves of the gale had given way to a long swell, which the *Santa Maria* rode easily under her lateen driver. The crew were in reasonable spirits, despite the loss of two of their comrades; but Gurney had caught dark mutterings against the cowardice of their captain—mutterings in what sounded like a Sicilian dialect, in which the words *vendetta* and *ommerta* ("vengeance" and "silence")—figured prominently.

A small Sicilian crewman in a stocking cap came aft toward where Gurney sat, walking lightly on the

balls of his feet. He had been in the hold earlier,
working neatly, efficiently, with a catlike grace which
belied his thickset figure. He smiled mysteriously at
Gurney—there was a strange expression of sorrow,
of inexorable purpose in his eye—and disappeared
into Cesare's cabin. Gurney shot to his feet as Cesare
wailed shrilly from within. Flinging open the door,
he saw the captain backed into a corner, the little
man six feet from him, staring into his eyes, his head
weaving from side to side like a snake with a rabbit.
Cesare was babbling in dialect, cowering away as
though he meant to sink through the very paneling
of the cabin. Gurney stood dumbfounded as the small
Sicilian waited for Cesare's tirade to die away into a
whimpering, crossed himself, and drew the blade of
a knife swiftly across the captain's throat. Cesare fell
on his face, kicking. A pool of blood spread across the
planking. The Sicilian spat at the recumbent form,
wiped his knife fastidiously on his coattail, and
strolled past Gurney out of the cabin.

Gurney, horrified, caught him by the shoulder. "For
God's sake, man! Why did you do that?"

The Sicilian met his eye with a level gaze. His pupils
were slightly dilated, cold as jet. "Through cowardice
he caused the death of one of my brothers and
smashed the legs of a second. His life is mine. It is our
way." And brushing Gurney's hand aside, he walked
slowly, head bowed, to the forecastle.

By noon Gurney had established a rough position.
It seemed that the storm had blown them farther than
he had expected—or more likely, that Cesare, whose
remains now rested on the seafloor some five leagues
astern, had miscalculated in his dead reckoning. Just
over the eastern horizon lay the Cyclades; the breeze
driving the *Santa Maria* southward at a snaillike two
knots should make them a landfall at Heraklion, on
the north coast of Crete, during the afternoon of the
next day. His eyelids were heavy as lead; the midday
sun, tempered by the cool wind, spread a pleasant
warmth through his body. He stretched out in the lee
scuppers and slept.

He was wakened by a hand on his shoulder. He got to his feet, his stiff muscles screaming in protest, and stumbled to the pump, ignoring the Sicilian plucking at his sleeve. The jet of water washed most of the sleep from the corners of his brain, and he straightened up, pushing the hair out of his eyes. The Sicilian was pointing to the east. Gurney strained his eyes in the direction of the man's pointing finger. At the limit of vision was a white sail. He went below and rummaged in Cesare's lockers for a telescope; eventually he found one, crusted with verdigris but still workable.

Steadying himself in the lee shrouds, he focused on the sail. Into the round frame swam a trim xebec, carrying a cloud of canvas. Even at this distance he could see a white plume of spray hissing from her forefoot, and as she came up into the wind, he counted ten gun ports picked out in yellow in the shining red of her weather side. He handed the telescope to the Sicilian.

"Well, what do you make of that?"

The Sicilian made no reply for a moment. He seemed to be looking for something. Then he grunted and handed the glass back, shaking his head. "We are done for, *Inglese*. This is the *Golden Horn*, the xebec of Kapraj Bey, whom they call the Black Crow of Izmir. These are his native seas, and I know only one man who came back to his fellows from the dungeons of the Crow. And he had no eyes and but a stump of a tongue."

A puff of smoke bloomed from her starboard bow, and a ball skipped lazily over the wavetops a pistol shot ahead of the *Santa Maria*'s blunt nose. The crew had fallen silent; all eyes were fixed on the sleek red ship as she set her course to intercept. A slight shiver of her royals told Gurney that she was as close to the wind as she could be; in his mind he plotted the converging courses of the two ships. In twenty minutes the *Golden Horn* would have the weather gauge of him; then all she would have to do was bear down on the *Santa Maria* and the battle would be

over before it was well started. Even if he turned
tail and fled, the xebec would catch him within the
hour. Unless . . .

He ran up the poop ladder and cupped his hands
around his mouth. "You all know who that is," he
roared. "We're dead men once the Crow gets his
talons into us. Me, I have a deep prejudice against
dying like a pig in a slaughterhouse." The crew were
nodding in agreement. "So which of you here would
rather go down fighting like men? At least we can
take some of those piratical scum with us." A ragged
cheer rose from the pitifully small knot of men in the
littered waist. "Good. Now listen closely."

As he explained his stratagem, the stiff face of the
Sicilian relaxed into a savage grin. Gurney detailed
four men to collect everything on the ship that could
be used as a weapon; then he took the wheel from
the helmsman and spun it hard over. The *Santa Maria*
turned towards the xebec and kept turning until the
lateen yard jibed across and she was returning the
way she had come, heeling slightly to starboard.
Gurney took three men with him into the hold. When
he prized the patch from the hole in the port side,
water splashed through; but the *Santa Maria*'s keel
kept the hole above the level of the sea. Yelling like a
madman, he cursed and kicked his two companions
into laying a stout iron-shod balk of timber, eighteen
inches in diameter and thirty feet long, flat on the
deck, directly below the hole. Then they lifted the
port end of the balk with a tackle rigged from a
beam in the deckhead and pushed ten feet of it outboard through the hole, lashing the other end snugly
against the *Santa Maria*'s stout keelson.

As Gurney returned on deck, the xebec was a couple of musket shots astern. He distinctly heard the
thunder of her sails as she went about, and despite
himself felt a pang of admiration. She was superbly
handled; her yards came round as one, and as her
sails filled on the port tack, she spilled wind from
her topsails so as not to overshoot the wallowing
Santa Maria. The gun ports on her starboard side

yawned open, and the snub muzzles of ten carronades
—twenty-eight-pounders, Gurney guessed—stared
sightlessly at him across two hundred yards of heaving
blue water. He made a sign with his hand behind his
back. The *Santa Maria*'s sails, unsheeted, spilled
their wind and flapped idly. She lost her way quickly.
Gurney felt the drag to port as the balk of timber
projecting from her side hit the water; then she came
onto an even keel and lay helpless, to all intents a
lamb to the slaughter.

A hail, in gutturally accented Italian, came across
from the xebec. "Not a movement, you dogs. I am
coming alongside. You are my prisoners."

Topsails backed, she drifted down on the *Santa
Maria*'s weather side. As the gap between them
closed, Gurney looked down. A wicked cutlass lay on
the deck at his feet, and the crew were crouched
under the gunwales. Each man had a weapon;
though firearms were pitifully low, Gurney guessed
that the knives that each of these men bore were at
least equal to pistols in the hands of others. For while
many of their lips moved in prayer, there was a raw
ferocity in their eyes which boded ill for a boarding
party. Gurney looked at the Turkish ship. Her decks
were thronged with men—at least sixty or seventy.
Ten to one. Impossible odds, but better to go down
fighting than to drown like a rat in an Aegean squall.
He felt a great calm spread over him; the red of the
Golden Horn's hull, the blue of sea and sky, seemed to
intensify as, foot by foot, the distance between them
narrowed. On the pirate's poop stood a tall figure in a
white turban, at his belt a great scimitar in whose
hilt splendid jewels glittered in the sun. Gurney
looked down at his own ragged shirt and breeches
and grinned. So this was to be the way of it; he, once
one of the foremost ornaments of His Majesty's Navy,
was to perish disgraced and banished at the hands of
a rabble of seedy Turks. But at least he would get his
blow in first.

The *Golden Horn* was twenty feet away; Gurney
held his breath as her lowering gunwale bore down

on him like a moving crimson wall. Then the *Santa Maria* seemed to leap under his feet, and the Turkish ship staggered as the great balk of timber projecting from the derelict's side drove deep into her hull below the waterline. Confused shouts came from the Turk's deck; then a whistle shrilled and the world dissolved in a roaring inferno of noise and smoke as the Turk loosed his full broadside at a range of no more than five feet. The *Santa Maria* sagged like a dying animal, her bowels smashed to flinders; and down from the deck of the *Golden Horn* leaped the boarders. As Gurney scooped up a cutlass from the deck, a club whizzed over his head, almost parting his hair; he ducked the next swing too, and slashed at his assailant's leg. The man went down, bright blood spurting from between his fingers, but Gurney had already turned away and was hacking at another club-wielding Turk, feinting with his blade until the man lost balance and exposed his side, coming in under his guard, and watching the eyes roll back as he slumped to the deck. Tugging his sword free, he leaped for the mizzen shrouds, yelling hoarsely as a pistol exploded in his face and a ball whizzed past, nicking his ear. The *Santa Maria* was low in the water and getting lower; the Turk's broadside had caved in her port side like an eggshell.

On the deck, the Sicilian shouted, and the crew gathered in a tight knot, back to back in the waist, their knives flashing as the Turks closed in for the kill. As Gurney watched, the Sicilian fell under the flailing hanger of a huge Negro, naked but for a loincloth; then the *Santa Maria* lurched and seemed to slide away under his feet. Gurney leaped for the quarterdeck rail of the *Golden Horn,* fingers scrabbling for a purchase, legs thrashing. He found a foothold on the deep strake which ran around the xebec's poop just below her rail, and hurled himself onto her deck.

A man rushed him, club upraised in both hands, exposing his naked brown chest. The point of Gurney's hanger caught him under the left armpit and came out between his shoulder and his ear. His club clattered to the deck and a look of astonishment came over his face. Then Gurney tugged his sword out of the wound, and the man's mouth opened. A vivid stream of blood spilled down his chest and he sprawled backwards.

From the corner of his eye Gurney caught sight of the *Santa Maria's* mizzen arching away behind him; then there was a great bubbling, and something ground and wrenched at the xebec's vitals. But Gurney's eyes were fixed on the man with the turban. The thin lips were twisted in a smile, and the black eyes were hard as chips of obsidian. He spoke, in grating Italian.

"So. Your pitiful tub has gone to the bottom of the sea. I think I only accelerated the inevitable by a year or two." He frowned, and the tip of his scimitar waved a delicate figure eight in the air. "But you, what is such a one as you, a Frank, doing on this grimy dung beetle of a ship? I see now why cowardly Italians found a sudden strength." He seemed to sigh, and took a sliding step forward. "I am displeased, very displeased, that so fruitless a seizing should have caused me so much trouble. You put a hole in my ship, you Frankish dog! And for this you shall not die easy. No, no." The eyes took on a faraway look. Gurney swallowed, scared for the first time. This man was mad. There was a coldness about him as if he were carved from stone. He took a firm grip on himself and breathed deeply. At the pommel of the scimitar, the jewels shot points of rainbow fire into the air. Below the white turban, the fierce eyes locked with his. Then he sprang, the blade of his cutlass arching in an axman's stroke at the turban. The scimitar moved in a blur, and a numbing shock crashed up Gurney's arm. The Crow seemed to look past him rather than at him, and nodded. Despite himself, Gurney half-glanced over his shoulder; the flat of the scimitar blade caught him on the left temple and he sank to his knees, head roaring and waves of blackness lapping at the corners of his vision.

The Turk stood watching him, face impassive, arms folded. Then he spoke. "You will learn, in the slave coffles of Achmet Bizound, that there are fates far worse than death. Even if you had the opportunity—and assuredly you never will—you would not lightly again cross the Crow. Sweet dream." And the flat of the blade rang again on Gurney's head. A gong started to sound, louder and louder, intolerably loud, and Gurney fell forward in the dark.

It was the flies that finally woke him, stalking through the gummy blood at his temple and buzzing around his mouth. He moved his head and groaned, pressing his face into the moldy straw that was his bed. Things were swimming and flickering before his eyes as he opened them cautiously. The left eye didn't seem to work; when he touched it gingerly with his finger—not knocked out, please God?—he found it was stuck together with clotted gore from what felt like a deep crater in his brow. With an enormous effort, he raised himself on his elbow and gulped water from the earthern bowl at his side. His stomach heaved, a wave of nausea threatened to overwhelm him, and he pitched forward on his face as the darkness rolled in again.

The second awakening was better. This time the sickness held off and his eye came into focus. He was able to drag himself across the floor, prop himself against the wall, and take stock of his situation. A cell it was, perhaps six feet by eight. In one corner was the pile of straw on which he had lain. Bright white daylight streamed in through the high window, casting a barred rectangle on the earthen floor. Through the window came the sound of many voices. Beyond the voices someone was screaming. The screaming spoke of pain without end; it was the sound a human makes when hope and thought have gone and what is left is only torment.

The screaming filled Gurney with despair. As his mind met and dealt with the pain in his head, pushing it into the background, the events of the previous day (Was it the previous day? Or was it last week? How long had he been unconscious?) came back to him. The Black Crow of Izmir. Slave coffles. But if it was a matter of a slave coffle, why was he in a cell by himself and not in the barracoons or on the auction block? He climbed to his feet and looked out of the window.

Outside a mob of people milled around a small square. Directly opposite him, a low, solid-looking structure crouched in the ground, gun ports covering the square and a battery on its roof threatening the sea, which lay blue and sparkling beyond the quay that formed the right-hand side of the square. To his left, a lofty cloister of columns and fretwork, surmounted by a dome and what Gurney, twisting his head inside the narrow embrasure of the window and cursing its agonizing throb, decided must be a minaret. The mosque.

In the middle of the square was a raised platform. The people went suddenly silent and craned towards it. Something red and shapeless was spread-eagled across a large wagon wheel, hung upright on the platform. The something screamed again out of a black hole in the red mask, and the huge Negro in a bloody butcher's apron spun the wheel again until the something's leg was close to him; then he began to pound at the knee joint, braced against the stout wood of the wheel's spoke, with the solid iron crowbar he held like a light walking stick in his right hand. The black seemed merely to tap at the joint, but the pounding soon took on a wet, crushed sound. The screaming rose to an animal bellow and died away as the head slumped forward on what had once been the chest. A bark of laughter from the crowd as the Negro flung a bucket of water at the ruined face on the wheel. Gurney stiffened. As the water sluiced the blood away, he recognized the Sicilian.

The door behind him crashed open, and his stomach turned to water. Two jailers, dressed in the filthy robes and stained turbans that, judging by the crowd in the square, were more or less a uniform in the village of Kapraj Bey, grasped him by the arms and rushed him out of the cell, his feet barely touching the ground. As they half-dragged him down the passage outside, with its long row of doors, the screaming in the square rose to a new peak of agony. Then it stopped short. Gurney found himself muttering a prayer.

Suddenly the ground was covered with lustrous tiles bearing intricate arabesque designs, and the walls receded on either side. At the far end of a kind of atrium, in which a little fountain ran a tinkling stream of water into a tiled pool of water lilies, on a pile of silk cushions set on rugs of marvelous richness, lay Kapraj Bey. He was not as Gurney remembered him, dressed for battle; now he wore a long dressing gown of richly brocaded silk, and his sky blue turban was crowned by a sheaf of peacock feathers. His slippery black eyes crawled over Gurney like snails, and he took a deep pull on the mouthpiece of an ornate narghile. The smell of hashish mixed with attar of roses filled the room.

"Welcome to my little home, Lieutenant Gurney."

His voice hissed and purred from among the cushions, raising the hairs on Gurney's neck. "I can see that you are surprised. It is because I know your name? Simple; that Sicilian pig told us everything he knew, even before my lovely Nkudu was properly started on him. Fool that he was, he did not realize that he could have had no information of interest to us; it is merely that from time to time we must put on a show for the populace, to keep them amused."

Gurney felt sick. The voice and the smell were nauseating. "What do you want with me? His Majesty's government has ways of dealing with vulgar pirates, you know; have a care."

Kapraj laughed, a silky laugh, and bubbled again at his narghile. "Oh, beautiful, beautiful. The English lieutenant threatens me with retribution. But may I remind you, English, that you're in no position to offer retribution. Nor will you ever be again. Tall young men such as yourself are in great demand in the interior, and I have some very interested buyers attending my next sale in two weeks. And speaking of retribution, there is the matter of some stove planks in my *Golden Horn*. I fear that I shall be asking payment of you for that. A rib for a rib, lieutenant."

"I promise you, whatever you call yourself, that you will answer for this. One day I shall see you dance on air at the yardarm, you slaving rat. You won't be the first petty thief I've strung up."

The room was suddenly very quiet except for the tinkling of the fountain into the pool, and even that homely sound now seemed invested with a sinister life of its own. "You are impudent, English. You try my patience sorely. We shall have to teach you a little lesson." A little spark of excitement twinkled deep in the wet black eyes. "Yes. A little lesson. Guards, take him to Nkudu. Tell him that I wish to count the lower ribs on the left side of this one's body. He will understand."

As the guards hustled him down the passageway and out into the glare and dust of the marketplace, Gurney's heart was cold lead. The crowd parted to let him through; at the end of the avenue of dusty clothes and impassive faces, the platform waited. His feet slipped on the bloody wooden steps, and he fell sprawling. Nkudu, the Negro, grasped his wrist in a huge soft hand and pulled him up onto the charnel boards. Blood and little splinters of white bone glistened on the wheel. His arms were manacled above his head, and the Negro's voice whispered in his ear. Gurney had a sudden urge to laugh. The man's voice was almost exactly like that of Monsieur Albert, the Frog crimper who cut his hair in London, caressing, insinuating.

"Ah, monsieur, how the serpent will enjoy to kiss your Frankish flesh." He traced a line below Gurney's left shoulder blade with his finger. "We shall start *here* and work downwards, I and the serpent, and monsieur's little white bones will peep out, just peep out because we do not want to spoil monsieur's value on the auction block, oh no, and only on the left side, for what we do must be close to monsieur's heart so he remembers, no?"

Gurney could smell the violet perfume of the Negro's breath. He turned his head and spat. As the saliva ran down his cheek, Nkudu smiled a wide smile, revealing teeth the size of dice, and ran his pink tongue over his thick lips. "Come, monsieur, let us begin."

Something that felt like a sledgehammer smashed Gurney in the ribs, and his knees gave out. A band of white-hot iron wrapped itself around the left-hand side of his chest, and his head crashed into the filthy spokes of the wheel. He bit his tongue to stop himself from screaming as the blood poured into his eye again from the wound on his temple and the fire spread down his rib cage like lava. A dull roar rose like steam from the crowd, but Gurney did not hear it, for his head was filled with pain and his lungs refused to function. When he tried to scream, he could not find the breath. In the red fog that filled his mind, a face grew that was Kapraj Bey's, grinning, the slimy eyes mocking, and then it filled out, developed hanging jowls and a sly smile. Otway opened his mouth and began to laugh, peals of triumphant laughter, and Gurney found his knees again, took a deep breath of agony, and wrenched at the gyves binding his wrists to the wheel. Then the face faded and left him washed over by a sea of torment that lapped at his body and sucked him down into nauseous silence.

3

The kite wheeled high in the brazen sky, balancing itself on the furnace-hot updrafts from the stony land beneath with tiny movements of its wing feathers. In all the rolling expanse of plain, brown with scorched

grass, stretching to the blue peaks of the Taurus
Mountains shuddering in the heat-haze to the east,
there was no movement. Unless you counted the
string of tiny figures, two on horseback and twenty-
odd on foot, in pairs, trailing a laborious plume of
brown dust up the long, dry valley toward the first
rank of the distant foothills. The kite cocked a wary
eye at the leader of the column, who wore a dirty
yellow turban and carried a gun; but it caught no
glimpse of telltale white eyes scanning the sky, so it
resumed its regular, patient quartering of the arid
grasslands.

They had been walking for five days now, and it
felt like five years. Gurney, a couple of pairs from the
front of the stumbling, cursing procession, eased his
shoulder under the weight of the yoke to which he
and his neighbor were chained, and strove to adjust
his stride to the smaller man's shuffle. His back and
the half-healed scars on his left side ached like hell,
and his yellow hair, gray with the dust of the trail,
lay plastered over his brow in thick, gritty strands. His
red eyes stared out of two holes in a mask of grime,
and his clothes hung in rags and tatters from his
body. He was limping badly; his feet were horribly
soft from the month at sea, and his shoes, never stout,
were developing thin patches in their soles which
boded ill for the future. Each step sent fiery needles
racing through his right ankle, where the musket
ball he had earned on the *Vampire* had left a mess of
scarred tendon and nerve. But already, the baking
misery of the first three days had passed. Gurney no
longer felt anger at the figure on the horse, brass-
bound musket slung across the inscrutable back and
long rawhide whip tapping negligently against the
right knee. In the slave coffles of Achmet Bizound,
resentment was a luxury that few could allow themselves and live, the mustachioed Turk had told them in
his vile lingua franca after the auction on the waterfront. Gurney had been incredulous, but now, as he
and his companions trudged mile after mile, hour after hour, toward the blue fangs of the distant moun-

tain range, he felt almost nothing. One foot slowly overtook the other, the dust rose, and the breath rasped dryly in the throat.

The horseman waved a languid hand at a horsefly crawling on his mount's shoulder, not so much to deter the fly as to demonstrate to the human cattle behind him that he, Achmet Bizound, had strength and to spare. He was not one to let foul dungflies from the middens of Shaitan creep and buzz where they would; he was a human being, with self-respect, paid servant in the retinue of the great Bey Suleiman Khimiz of Diyarbakir, itself no mean city. And he had impressed his importance on these miserable vermin, unbelievers most of them, in the market. They would not trifle with him—would probably think twice about trifling even with Ibrahim, squint-eyed son of a goat though he might be, bringing up the rear on his balky mule, since the black Nkudu had shown the Frank the color of his own bones by the harbor. He ran his tongue over his lips. Ah, but he had borne up well, that one. Not a murmur had he let out before he had swooned under the lash. That one bore watching.

Near the crest of a slight rise, he reined his steed, raised his hand, and shouted in Arabic. The file stopped dead, the slaves falling in their tracks, prostate on the gray stones, flies buzzing over them in a cloud. Gurney felt a dim irritation as the yoke caught him smartly in the neck and he was dragged to the ground on top of his companion, but he forgot it in a moment; all his attention was riveted on the boss-eyed Ibrahim, who had dived into a tumbledown hut at the side of the road and emerged with a bulging goatskin, from which he began to ration out two small brass drinking bowls of water to each of the slaves. He had started at the tail end of the line; even through his thirst, Gurney snarled as he watched him leer at the beautiful Greek girl in the last pair as she threw her head back to drink. She and her partner, a Macedonian maiden of some seventeen years, had been spared the heavy chains and dragging anklets worn by the men;

but even so, she looked exhausted, and dark circles
ringed her black eyes.

Ibrahim passed his tongue over his lips and leaned
forward, trying to get a look down the girl's bodice.
Then he darted a furtive glance around him, grinning
sheepishly. His grin widened as he caught Gurney's
eye, and he shouted something incomprehensible as
he made his way slowly along the line. The tinkle of
water being poured into the brass bowl was music to
George's ears; he watched greedily, avidly, as his yoke
partner's Adam's apple rose and fell in his scrawny
neck; his tongue was dry as sand, swollen in his
mouth. Ibrahim turned to him, showing him teeth the
color of rotten bananas and enveloping him in a blast
of sour breath. Gurney reached out a hand for the
bowl; the Turk snatched it away, grinning and letting
loose a stream of Arabic in which George distin-
guished the words *infidel . . . impure . . . hands*
and what sounded like a stream of imaginative insults.
George tentatively reached out once again, and the
Turk brought his riding quirt slashing across his fingers. He leaped back with a yelp of agony, only to be
brought up short by his chains and fall headlong in
the dust once again.

The Turk made drinking motions with his cupped
left hand, obviously delighted with the success of his
little joke, chiding in Arabic all the while, shouting
that Gurney, as an infidel, should no longer expect
to share a drinking bowl with the Prophet's chosen,
but should drink only out of his left hand, which, used
as it was for certain other unmentionable purposes,
would certainly not be offended by carrying water
to his impious lips. And so saying, he slopped water
in the general direction of George's left hand, chuckling as it ran between his fingers and soaked into the
dust.

George managed to lick about a teaspoonful from
his palm, then scrabbled in the dust between his feet,
panic-stricken. Ibrahim roared with laughter, scooped
up a handful of mud, and flung it in his face, shouting

at him to drink his fill. Gurney buried his head in his arms, expecting a haul of blows.

But it never came.

Ibrahim fell suddenly silent, and a rough hand shook Gurney's shoulder. He looked up. Towering above him, in black silhouette against the sun, stood Achmet, holding out a bowl of water. George grabbed it, his hands shaking, and poured it down his throat. Then he held out the bowl again, stammering his thanks. Achmet's lip curled. "I have no need of your thanks, Frankish dog. Think not that I give you drink from kindness of soul. No, I paid a fat price for you at the Crow's auction, and my neck stands surety for your safe arrival in Diyarbakir, five weeks hence. But I say again, expect not my sympathy; consider yourself a prize sheep in the flock of a provident shepherd who knows that the sheep go to the slaughterhouse, not at his discretion, but at his master's."

Often Gurney had told himself that death, any death, was preferable to bondage. He had even listened to Mr. Wilberforce's sermons and felt a powerful sense of righteous indignation at the wickedness of man's buying and selling his fellowmen like chattels. And when he had captured a blackbirder in the *Vampire*, he had been disgusted at the condition of the holds, where two hundred coast blacks lay chained in spaces five feet by seventeen inches. But never had he even considered that one day he might pass into slavery. And now with Achmet's words, the realization flooded over him. This was no accident of war, no brief period of hardship to be terminated by ransom or armistice; he, George Le Fanu Gurney, body, soul, and mind, was now and had been for the past five days the property of a greasy Turk, to be disposed of as and when he wished, for the rest of his natural life.

The Turk turned on his heel and strode back to his horse. George closed his eyes and listened to the blood pounding in his ears—now no longer *his* blood or *his* ears. Then he opened them again and looked

up and down the line. The foot travelers were a sorry
crew, by all accounts. Gurney thought back ruefully to
the time he had been ashore in Portsmouth, a ten-
der midshipman in charge of the press gang. Half his
companions here wouldn't have measured up even to
the low standards of a navy desperate for men. Apart
from himself, the women, and a couple of skilled
tradesmen who, the scuttlebutt in Kapraj's slave barracoons reported, had been seized from some unfortunate islet in the Cyclades, the coffle was a job lot of
Greeks, Macedonians, and Cypriots, good for nothing
but manual labor. They represented the last sweep-
ings of the crews of perhaps half a dozen fishing
boats and traders seized over the past twelve months
by the *Golden Horn;* the vile food and harsh treatment of the barracoons had left them little more than
dull-eyed skeletons. Achmet Bizound had scowled bitterly at the auction when he realized that in order to
secure the women, the tradesmen, and the Frank, he
would be forced to purchase the rest of the unprepos-
sessing rabble; but purchase them he had, and all
he could do now was pray to Allah that not too many
of them would die on him during the long march
ahead.

As George's eye caught that of the Greek girl, he
thought he caught a brief flash of sympathy in her
expression; but then her features were still as marble
again, and Ibrahim was watching her, moistening his
loose lips with his tongue. Gurney turned his face to
the horizon, screwing up his eyes against the glare,
counting the carrion birds soaring effortlessly in the
burning bowl of the sky. It seemed a long time before he dragged himself to his feet, bent his shoulders
to the yoke, and once more concentrated all his attention on putting one foot in front of the other.

During the next few days, the trail grew steeper
and the brownish scrublands gave way to lusher
vegetation, which in turn began to recede before
outcroppings of gray rock. The nights were cooler
now, and often in the daytime a chill wind would
creep down from the towering peaks of the mountains

through whose valleys they wound, turning the sweat cold on the slaves' skins. None of them were dressed for cold weather; most of them, including Gurney, had come dressed for the Mediterranean summer, and at nights they huddled round a pathetic fire—wood was scarce at these altitudes—shivering and cursing, each man pressing against his neighbor for warmth. Ibrahim sometimes aimed a kick or a blow at Gurney when he thought Achmet Bizound was not watching; Gurney grew to hate the man's squinting leer and his neighing laugh. Bizound seemed to have retreated further into his veil of inscrutability.

George's yokemate, in the intervals of bewailing his lot in a falsetto whine that grated on the nerves like a fork squeaking on a plate, his copper-colored face screwed up in a permanent rictus of self-pity, explained that in order to arrive at Diyarbakir (he had heard from a man in Macedonia who had a brother who had heard a story) they would have to cross five ranges not less precipitous than that on whose western slopes they were clinging like flies on a pitched roof. Each range was beset with an appalling variety of evil spirits—jinns, afreets, and apparitions of the most disgusting kind, including werewolves, of which Bizound was undoubtedly one. At the end of the mountain trails lay the gorge of the great river, the Tigris, an hour's walk wide and a day's walk deep, in whose depths the mighty waters sang constantly the hundredth name of God, and into which the unwary traveler would infallibly be lured were he not wearing the amulet of the Hand of Fatima, one of which the Macedonian happened to have spare about his person and which he would be pleased to sell to Giorgiou (the man had given up, exasperated, trying to pronounce Gurney's last name) for his eventide bread ration.

George declined absently. Despite his timorous nature, the Macedonian had displayed from the outset a commercial bent which was equaled only by his hunger for the hard bread and stringy goat meat that comprised their food. Early on in the journey George had succeeded in trading bread from two evening meals for the villainous sheepskin his companion wore around his shoulders; but now, as the temperatures dropped sharply when the sun dipped below the jagged horizon, the Macedonian was showing a tendency to burrow under the sheepskin as Gurney composed himself for the night. And the Macedonian carried a breed of flea which was the most virulent Gurney had encountered, even in the cabin of the slaver he had boarded off Havana.

He tried to compose himself for sleep, but despite his exhaustion sleep would not come. During the past weeks he had managed to avoid reflecting upon the position in which he found himself, but now the full horror of the situation marched relentlessly through his mind, the thoughts following each other with the same dull finality as the feet of the slaves shuffling towards their grim destination. Arabella would even now be sitting in some drawing room in Bath, sipping tea and discoursing politely with her aunts on some tediously suitable female topic, the fire that he loved in her banked against his return. But what guarantee was there that she could control that fire? Gurney knew full well that behind the demure face that she presented to the world was a keen mind and a capacity for hell-raising that demanded an outlet. It was in some measure that fire in her that had made him entertain the idea of chasing halfway across the world in search of his lost honor.

Voices from the past—first lieutenants, bosuns, Norfolk county gentry—reproved him for his rashness and assured each other smugly that the hothead Gurney would come to a bad end. He felt a familiar depression creeping over him. Those moments of absolute self-doubt that in his mind took the place of fear had always plagued him; Arabella was so good at cajoling him out of his black moods, stimulating him to forget himself in some outrageous exploit, but now, how much could he expect of her? He found himself wishing almost that she was like the other girls he had met in society, a creature so bound by a sense of propriety that she would either have thrown him over once and for all or waited, in a state approaching suspended animation, for his eventual return. He shifted restlessly under the sheepskin, trying to ease the ache in his left side. His depression settled deeper. As well to forget Arabella. How could he, here in the heart of Asia Minor, bound slave to a Levantine despot, pretend to himself that he was entitled to count on the affection of a woman he would never see again? A lump rose in his throat, and he drifted off into a miserable sleep.

As they descended the eastern slope of the first range, they were joined by a troupe of herdsmen—nomads, it seemed, riding horses, donkeys, and camels, their saddles padded with gorgeous, intricately worked rugs, their womenfolk creaking along behind them in wagons so ancient that Gurney could see no reason why their wheels should not fall off and the whole conveyance fall in splinters over a precipice.

Bizound had cursed as he saw their vanguard, seven figures silhouetted against the morning sun on a knife-edged ridge hundreds of feet above the track, rifles raised in an ambiguous gesture of greeting. But as they thundered down the slope toward him, plumes of dust flowing like wings from the hocks of their magnificent Arab horses, he had pasted an oily smile on his face and spread his hands in a gesture of pacific greeting. Since that time they had been traveling in convoy. It seemed that the nomads had sold off the major part of their flocks in western Anatolia and were now ushering the remainder of their sheep and goats through the rocky passes to their summer grazing grounds on the plateaus to the east.

The coffle's pace slowed to a snail's crawl—a welcome relief for the slaves, though Bizound fretted visibly and Ibrahim, jealous of the frankly appreciative glances the drovers cast in the Greek girl's direction, sulked at the rear of the file. There was little love lost between the herdsmen and Bizound, for they seemed scornful of one who made his living as a herder of men; but the arrangement was mutually advantageous. By traveling with Bizound, the herdsmen had put themselves under the protection of the bey's flag, which fluttered from Ibrahim's long lance; and by accepting the nomads as companions, Bizound was assured that he and his charges would remain unmolested by them. For though the hills were thick with bandits, there were none regarded as being so fiercely unpredictable as the nomadic drovers of Ughara.

It was a cold, crisp morning when Gurney awoke on the tenth day. They were camped in a bowl-shaped depression in a dry moorland; the air was thin and stung his nostrils as he huddled under his sheepskin for warmth, kicking the Macedonian in the ribs to clear himself a space. Sleep was out of the question, and he lay awake, teeth chattering, as the sun inched up over the mountains. The fires of the nomads had died to glowing embers; all was quiet but for the cry of a bird not unlike a curlew. The morning star paled as he lay, eyes fixed on the lightening sky. Soon the camp would be awake, the Macedonian coughing his morning cough, Bizound snarling at Ibrahim, and Ibrahim prodding at sluggards with his lance. Then the day would begin, the long dragging march from nowhere into nowhere.

He rolled over, bringing his knees up under his chin, groping for the rags he had stowed in the waistband of his breeches the previous evening, and began to wrap them around the heavy iron fetter on his foot. Many of the slaves had huge sores under their chains; Gurney, by dint of the sacrifice of much of his shirt and a proportion of his water ration, had succeeded in building up a ring of callus on his right ankle and on each collarbone, where the yoke rested. The Macedonian, who wolfed down his rations like a starving man, had not been so lucky. Even in the morning cold, the flies had begun to buzz, and as Gurney lay back, his task completed, his yokemate stirred restlessly as a huge bluebottle stalked across the half-healed scabs on his shoulders.

The walls of Bizound's tent bulged and flapped, and the Turk walked out into the light, adjusting his baggy pantaloons. He paused, rubbed the sleep from his eyes, stretched, and began his inspection of the drowsily stirring slaves. Gurney heard his sharp intake of breath and watched as he stooped over a huddled form on the ground. He lifted the wrist, held it for a moment; then he shrugged and let it fall. It dropped limply to the ground and was still, the fingers clawing spiderlike at the sky. Then he picked up a length of chain and tugged it.

Immediately there was chaos. As the men to whose yoke the chain was attached awoke and struggled up, they jerked the next pair painfully in the throat. They in their turn thrashed about, trying to get to their feet, pulling viciously at the next yoke down the line. Within seconds, pandemonium had broken loose, hoarse yells and cries of rage echoing down the valley to the peaks beyond. Two men began fighting, yoke partner against yoke partner, both of them sobbing hopelessly, raining feeble blows on each others' heads. Bizound's whip hand barely seemed to flicker, and one of the brawlers was writhing on the ground, black blood streaming from a long cut running from his right shoulder blade to his left kidney. Silence fell.

"From now on, you go unchained." The Turk poked with his foot at the corpse. "It seems that the cold was too much for our scrawny friend here. Too bad. But I got him at a knockdown price, so be it as Allah wills. But listen closely; I am magnanimous in my solicitude for your welfare, or rather for my master's whose chattels you are, but should any of you abuse my beneficence by attempting in any way to escape, I shall do him the honor of severing his left hand from his arm at the wrist. Ibrahim!"

The squint-eyed minion, bleary-eyed, breath stinking of last night's stale arrack, passed down the line with a mallet, striking off the ankle irons and levering the staples from the heavy wooden yokes. When he reached Gurney, he showed his broken teeth and struck extra hard with his mallet, bruising his ankle and jarring his knee. Gurney narrowed his eyes.

"There will be a reckoning between us, dog. Now

strike sure, else I will surely summon evil spirits to choke away your breath."

The Turk recoiled, awestruck at the cold rage in the yellow-haired Frank's voice, and passed on to the next in line. Five minutes later, the slaves stood rubbing their galls, stretching limbs long cramped by wood and iron. Gurney moved his shoulders and arms, reveling in the sensation, feeling for a moment as light as a feather. Then he caught the eye of Bizound.

"Aye, Frank, revel in your petty freedom," the slave master spat. "God knows that one grain of rice to a starving man is a full meal; but it does not hinder him from dying soon after, and may make his passing harder. Now take this thing"—he indicated the corpse at his feet—"and pile stones on it, that the kites reveal not our passing to brigands."

Gloom descended on Gurney like a pall as he stared down at the dead man's face. It was all very well to speak of reckonings, but what reckoning could there be between slave and master save the death of one or the other? And even then the master would take the slave with him. The only reckoning that awaited him was with death. For himself, he barely cared whether he lived or died; but then he thought of Arabella, and he felt a traitor's misery. Even if his bones were to feed the kites under this desolate sky, he would be free; but Arabella would be doomed to a life at Mathias Otway's whim; for Gurney had no illusions as to Otway's recuperative powers.

He dragged the pitifully light body to one side, his flesh cringing away from the drying sores on its wrists, scooped a shallow depression in the hard, stony ground, and laboriously piled stone after stone on the cadaver until he was satisfied it was safe from the carrion birds which already hovered overhead. By the time he had finished his task, the sun was well up in the sky, and his mouth was parched in the growing heat of the day. The nomads had struck their tents and were now a cloud of dust to the east;

Bizound was fretting to be gone, his whip tapping impatiently against his thigh, eyes screwed up anxiously as he scanned the gray hills to the left and right. Ibrahim had been at his favorite pursuit of watching the Greek girl. Her eyes met his fearlessly, as if daring him to come closer. Then Bizound gave the order to be off. There was a note of urgency in his voice that George had not heard before; he followed the direction of his gaze with smarting eyes, wiping away the sweat that poured down his forehead. On a distant ridge, about two miles to the west, he judged, something metallic caught the sun. Bizound spurred his horse around the gaggle of slaves like a New Forest herder around a flock of ponies, snarling at them to stir themselves. The two women were in a bad way, near to dropping from cold and exhaustion. George could almost see the thoughts passing through Bizound's mind.

"Ibrahim! Take the Greek up behind you, and I'll take the other woman." He pointed to the ridge. It was lined with flickering points of light, and as Gurney watched, a line of boulders resolved themselves into tiny figures, mounted on horses. "It's the bastard Kurds. Go for your life, and remember I paid ten times the worth of your miserable hide for that woman. Your head and your son's are surety for her."

Ibrahim paled and dug his heels into the mule's ribs, sweeping the girl up behind him. Then he settled down into the saddle and commenced to belabor his reluctant steed towards the distant dust cloud with the butt of his lance.

Gurney and his companions found themselves alone, the hoofbeats of their guards' mounts receding into the distance. "Run!" he shouted.

Some of his companions shook their heads. "Nothing can be worse than the Diyarbakir trail, let alone the bondage waiting at the far end," said a middle-aged Greek. "And who knows, perhaps the Kurds will be sympathetic to our cause."

"Well, I'm for after the nomads. Better the devil

you know than the devil you don't. Who's with me?"
And he turned and began to run, stumbling and slipping in the dust and pebbles, to the east.

Four men followed him, grunting with the unaccustomed effort. As they reached the brow of the
ridge, Gurney turned. Below him, like a historical
diorama in Madame Tussaud's Wax Museum, the
slaves who had remained behind stood in a tight
group, their leader, one of the Greek tradesmen, advancing toward a knot of fur-hatted horsemen whose
wings were already closing round him like the horns
of a crescent moon. The Greek's hands were outstretched in a gesture of surrender. Then the horns
closed, encircling the slaves. The Greek's mouth
opened in soundless expostulation. Then the short
spears rose and fell, and the slaves disappeared in
the melee of horsemen.

Gurney watched unmoved, conscious only of gratitude that he had made the right decision. Then he began to run again, keeping below the skyline, hoping
against hope that the Kurds had been out of their
line of sight when they had left the group. He motioned with his hand to his dazed companions and
crept towards an outcropping of lichen-crusted rock
fifty yards away. After he had ushered them into a
deep, shadowed crack, he backed in himself. A babble
of shouting and cheering came over the brow of the
ridge, and the Kurds—stocky men, with deep slant
eyes, white teeth, and coppery skins, on small wiry
ponies—burst into view, yelling and weaving their
mounts. Gurney cringed back into the darkness of the
crevice as one rider came straight for him, waving a
curved sword, leaning far down from the saddle. The
hooves thudded closer, the ground shaking under
their impact. Then the sword swept in a glittering arc,
and a tuft of grass not five feet from Gurney's head
exploded in ruins as the horse and rider hurtled into
the air, clearing the edge of Gurney's outcrop in one
bound. The horseman's companions cheered and
roared with laughter, and gradually the shouts and
guffaws grew fainter in the distance, until George

looked around and shook the shoulder of the man behind him.

Then he was up and running, the breath rasping in his throat, his chest full of red-hot nails, the blood pounding in his ears. His feet hurt, but he doggedly slammed one after the other into the sharp stones, rattling off a string of curses in time to his gasping breaths. At the brow of the next hill, he stopped in the lee of a gigantic boulder, hands on knees, trying to catch his breath in the shade.

Two hundred feet below and a quarter of a mile of steep, stony scrub to his left, the nomads had huddled in a circle, like sheep harried by wolves. The Kurds, obviously chary of taking on superior numbers, had paused too; both sides were making up for their lack of martial vigor with a stream of invective, but it looked as if there was a lengthy wait in store until one side or the other committed itself to an aggressive move. A breathing space, and none too soon.

The situation was bleak. Gurney took a long look at the drovers' perimeter. The swarthy herdsmen had all but disappeared behind their crouched camels and their wagons. He caught the glitter of sun on steel and saw Bizound's yellow turban bobbing rapidly through the throng. The tables were turned; now Bizound was the captive and Gurney was free to go where he would. He took a mental inventory of what he had about him. One shirt, tattered. One pair of breeches, similar. Two feet, bleeding. One head, still on shoulders by the grace of God. Not the ideal equipment for—he reckoned—a trek of at least a week to the nearest civilization likely to be friendly to a six-foot, fair-haired, blue-eyed infidel.

The nearest place of safety would be Syria, and that was too far away by half. No, it was time to become a slave again. He turned to his companions and switched into the lingua franca, forcing the words out with an effort. "You see that gully to the right of Bizound? It's our only hope."

A couple of heads nodded. The others looked blank. Gurney swore. "Translate, for God's sake!"

A subdued mutter of Macedonian didn't seem to make the prospective adventurers any happier about what they seemed to regard as certain death—Gurney wasn't too sure of their prospects himself—but the logic of the move eventually sank in, and they turned, traversing the spur up which they had just come, out of sight of the Kurds, heading to the right, where a thick blanket of thorny scrub lay over the ridge like a saddle. If they could reach the gully—the water-course that had formed the valley where Bizound and the drovers were ensconced, now dry after the spring spate—they could creep right into the heart of the beleaguered camp.

The scrub was overlaid with a carpet of flying insects. The thorns dug through Gurney's clothing as if it weren't there, and he clamped his teeth against the agony. He heard one man yelp as he plowed into the thicket, but then there was only a crashing as five heavy bodies trampled a path through the spiny bushes.

After fifteen minutes, the scrub began to thin out and the ground, which had been sloping into the valley at a steep angle, became flatter. Gurney motioned with his hand for his companions to stay where they were, and inched forward. Four hundred yards away, the Kurds still stood in a group, holding their horses. Their laughter floated down the wind to the thicket; one of them drew an arrow from his quiver and loosed it at the nomads' encampment, out of sight over a slight rise in the ground; a cheer signaled a hit. The bandits' attention seemed firmly riveted on their quarry. The smooth; gravelly slope down to the gully was completely bare of cover. About fifty yards. The short hairs on the nape of Gurney's neck prickled warningly. He took a deep breath, cast a final glance at the Kurds. All clear. He signaled to his companions to stay where they were, and ran, blasting out of the bushes like a hare from its form. His legs seemed made of wet leather, and suddenly he remembered a nightmare where he was running, running from a blazing house in a flat green meadow, and the flames were licking red in the grass, and no matter how he struggled, they were catching up with him, inexorably gaining ground ...

And then he was lying face down in the dusty bed of the gully, sobbing for breath. When he had recovered, he crept up to the lip of the gully and beckoned to the next man. The Kurds were still absorbed in their human target practice, and two more men dropped into the dried-up watercourse without incident. Now there was only one to come. Gurney beckoned him. Even at this distance, he could see the muscles on the man's face working. Then he rose to his feet, put his head down, and ran, arms going like pistons, toward Gurney's hiding place. He had taken about fifteen giant steps when he slipped and came crashing to the ground, raising a cloud of dust. Gurney held his breath. The man picked himself up and was blobbing clumsily toward the gully, eyes wide with terror, when the Kurd with the bow turned round, gave a shout of surprise, and with a single fluid movement nocked, drew, and loosed a shaft. The arrow caught the Macedonian in the neck. He somersaulted twice, staggered to his feet, then crashed face down on the very rim of the gully where Gurney and his companions lay hidden, his head lolling over the edge.

"Run!" hissed Gurney, starting off up the gully toward the nomads, bent double. As he approached the camp, he heard rapid hoofbeats thudding in the opposite direction. Then the hoofbeats stopped; as he rounded what he reckoned must be the last bend in the gully, a confused shouting broke out behind him. Then he tripped headlong over a scrawny brown sheep with a melancholy face, which bleated reproachfully and scurried out of the dip. He scrambled up, dodged a sweeping blow from a saber in the hand of a broken-nosed nomad, bellowed in English, and spun like a top, searching for the yellow turban of Achmet Bizound. A threatening group of drovers surrounded him, eyeing his strange garments and fair hair with suspicion; then, as the muttering was reaching an ugly pitch, the slave master pushed through the crowd. His black eyes took in the four men, and he snapped, "The others?"

Gurney shook his head, jerking a thumb beyond the perimeter of the defensive circle and running the edge of his hand across his throat. Bizound's face went gray, and his shoulders sagged. Far from making a profit on his expedition, he would take a considerable loss. And he would be fortunate to escape with his head. Still, such things were the will of Allah. He straightened up and yelled for Ibrahim, who swaggered over, casting glances pregnant with braggadocio toward the Greek girl, who was sitting cross-legged on a red and gold rug, her eyes fixed in a listless stare on the ground in front of her. The full weight of his captivity fell once again on George's shoulders, and he groaned aloud. The girl looked up at the sound of his voice, eyes wide, lips parted. When she saw him, she half-rose to her feet, then appeared to think better of it, and resumed her downcast attitude. But there was a new life in her face, tension in her body, and Gurney frowned, puzzled, as he was led away and told to sit on the ground and await further instructions.

As the day wore on, heated negotiations took place between Bizound and a white-bearded old civilian in a coffee-stained djellaba who appeared to be the leader of the nomads. It seemed that the slave master was trying to persuade the old man to deliver a ransom of sheep to the Kurds, who would then let them pass on their way unmolested. His arguments were given a point by the arrows which whizzed at unpredictable intervals into the camp, two of which spelled an end to the careers of swarthy herdsmen.

The camels crouched on the perimeter groaned and fidgeted as the sun rose to its zenith and began the long, slow descent toward the western horizon. At about four o'clock, Ibrahim distributed a bowl of water to each of the remaining slaves. So dispirited was he that he even forgot to prod Gurney in the ribs and taunt him as he passed by. Then the shadows lengthened, cooking fires were lit, and both camps, as if by tacit consent, settled down for the night. Gurney lay awake for a time, watching the stars wink in and out of a sky of black lacquer; then, despite his parched mouth and his stony bed, he went to sleep.

He was awakened by a firm pressure below his right ear. It was very cold; the white plumes of the sentry's breath, fifteen yards away, reddened in the glow of the dying fire. Silky hair brushed his cheek. He shook his head. Was it a dream?

A soft voice came from the darkness by his head, and warm breath tickled his ear.

"Be silent," the voice said in French. "It is I, Helena. Oh, but you were so brave today! When I saw you left behind, I felt my heart would break!" Gurney felt a profound sense of unreality, not unmixed with embarrassment. Then he pushed it aside. After all, these were hardly circumstances where formal introductions could be said to be *de rigueur*.

"Helena?" he whispered. "The Greek lady?"

"Yes. But quick! The pig Ibrahim"—Gurney saw her eyes flash angrily in the dim starlight—"has told me that when Bizound persuades the sheikh to make a bargain of sheep with the brigands, we shall be allowed to proceed. And the night after tomorrow night, we shall be at the caravansary of Ijmara, where Bizound meets his kinsmen. There will be feasting, and their guard will be down. There we will meet, you and I. Good night, my beloved." Soft lips touched his cheek, and she was gone.

Gurney lay awake for a few minutes, amazed. Beloved, eh! Well, she was as smart a piece of the right stuff as he'd seen in many a long day, though somewhat in need of a wash. He grinned, for the first time since he had left Naples. He was still smiling when he went to sleep. In his dreams he was racing Arabella across Cranborne Chase on horseback, and the wind on his face had the crisp tang of freedom.

The caravansary lay sprawled over the rounded crest of a small hill in the gently rolling plains of the eastern Taurus Mountains, its thick outer walls—for it had been a place of refuge in times past—shining solid and white in the light of the full moon. Close up, the impression of solidity could be seen to be false; roofs and stairways had collapsed, and lizards and small animals hunted in mounds of rubble printed with thick black shadows. The outer walls themselves, said by the wise to have been erected by no less a one than the great Iskander, were crumbling into ruin, mosses and dry creepers tugging them stone from stone. For what should the Sultan Mahmud care for this unprofitable outpost of his empire? What was there in this barren place, on a trade route from nowhere to nowhere, to draw his attention from the diversions and intrigue of the wondrous palace at the Golden Horn? The caravans no longer ran the route from Byzantium, by high Anatolia and the twin rivers Tigris and Euphrates, to Baghdad; the empire was shrinking like a fruit withered on the branch, its stone rotting at the kernel.

In one of the courts of the caravansary, a yard some sixty feet square, roofed like a cloister around the edge, a fire flung red reflections on the cracked stucco of the walls. Around the fire sat Achmet Bizound, his two cousins, and, at a discreet remove, Ibrahim. They had eaten and drunk well. Bizound had all but forgotten his catastrophic loss and was staring through lowered lids at the fire, humming a tune and taking the occasional deep puff at the mouthpiece of a narghile. Ibrahim had made an effort to obey his instructions to maintain ceaseless vigilance over the slaves, huddled under the shadows of the roof at the western end of the courtyard, but had indulged unwisely in the potent wine. Now he was torn between sleep and the necessity to maintain watchfulness, and had struck an at best uneasy compromise between the two.

Gurney, lying with his back to a pile of rubble, feet crossed and hands locked behind his head, watched

as his guardian swayed like an Indiaman in a short
sea. The gate to the yard lay in the eastern wall; he
could distinguish its every stone in the bright moonlight.

A stone rattled at his side. He turned, his eyes slow
to adjust to the dark after the brilliant moonlight of
the yard. White teeth shone in the fine planes of a
woman's face, and his pulse quickened as he recognized the Greek girl. He looked around. The other
slaves were dark bundles, sleeping the sleep of the
exhausted, stretched like corpses where they had
dropped after their evening meal. And the Turks in
the courtyard would be seeing other things than were
going on before their eyes, judging by the sweetish
smell of hashish that had been drifting across to him
for the past hour or two.

The girl's lips came close to his ear. "Lie down. Put
your head near mine." Gurney felt her warm breath
on his face. "Your name?"

"Giorgiou."

"I have been watching you these weeks; you are
not like the others. How is it that you are here?"

Gurney explained the circumstances of his capture.
Helena listened intently. When he had finished, she
snorted. "That still doesn't explain what a man like
you, an English milord—no, don't deny it—was doing
on one of the worst ships ever to sail out of Naples harbor. Still, no doubt you have your reasons. You have
been lucky at any rate." She laughed quietly. "I myself am here through bad luck, and bad luck only; but
you seem to have put your head into the noose, so
you have only yourself to blame if it tightens."

Gurney felt a little piqued. "Why do you say that?"

She laughed again. "Oh, I am sorry, Milord
Giorgiou. We are in no case to mock each other's
misfortunes, you and I. No, I myself was on the island
of Deimos, at the funeral of an ancient aunt I de-
tested, when yonder pig of a Turk came down like a
wolf on a herd of sheep, murdered my parents, and
swept me away."

The perfection of her French and her air of breeding

had given Gurney much food for thought during the past few days. "So where is your home, Helena?"

"Oh, I have many homes, and soon I shall have another, in the seraglio of this fat Turk." She laughed a brittle laugh, cut off by something like a sob. "You would not think that last year I was in the arms of your Lord Byron, gazing at the sun rising over the Piazza San Marco, would you? Or that my father sent me on the grand tour in a coach and four not three years ago? Ah, well, perhaps I have been too happy. But thank God I have found someone I can talk to. Put your arms around me, Giorgiou, and tell me what we shall do?"

Gurney did as he was told, tentatively at first, then with more enthusiasm as she molded her body to his, laying her cheek on his shoulder and whispering in his ear. He pulled the sheepskin over them, and they lay and talked while the fire in the courtyard died.

Bizound and his cousins staggered to their blanket-rolls, sped on their way by an overloud "good night" from Ibrahim, anxious to impress with his vigilance. They were soon snoring. Ibrahim, having examined his charges at long range, propped himself up on his lance in the middle of the courtyard. His head nodded for five minutes; then, with the air of one who has made a great and significant discovery, he went to the gate, lay across it so that it could not be opened without disturbing him, and composed himself for slumber.

The two watchers let their breath out at the same moment, and Helena clung to George. Somewhat to his surprise, he found himself clinging back. She moved her lips, and suddenly there was nothing between them. Gurney felt the heat rise as she pressed against him, the swell of her full breasts molding to his chest, her belly and thighs warm and welcoming. He ran his fingers down the little hollow of her spine, and she shivered, raising her mouth to his. Her eyes were deep and luminous in the dim moonlight, and they were open under the long dark lashes as their lips met. Then she moaned softly, accepting him, and the light spread through both their bodies, quiet and slow.

Some time later, Gurney woke up with a start, then smiled, feeling the warmth in the ground at his side. A slim hand waved from the women's quarters at the far end of the wall; then all was quiet, and he fell asleep once more.

He was reawakened by screams of pain. He turned his head in the general direction of the noise and saw Bizound beating Ibrahim viciously about the head and shoulders with the butt of his own lance. It looked as if the unwary sentinel were getting the cutting edge of what must have been a really titanic hangover. Gurney didn't feel sorry for either of them. There was a great well of laughter bubbling in the pit of his stomach, and even the gray drizzle which began to fall as they moved off could not dampen his spirits. The low hills were partially hidden by rolling banks of cloud, and often he could hardly see the man in front of him for the dense vapor. Once, as the procession wound around a hairpin bend, he caught Helena's eye; she lowered her lashes and looked demurely away, but there was a hint of laughter in the way she held her head that put a spring in George's step and sped the ground from under his feet.

Their lodgings that night were less commodious, huddled around a pile of rocks on a steep slope. Bizound, still scowling, forbade the lighting of fires. His cousin had left that morning, and from the constant glances he darted around him, Gurney gathered he was feeling somewhat naked. Still chewing his dinner of hard bread, George pulled his sheepskin over his shoulders against the clammy drifts of rain. The drops were larger now, and if it kept on like this, they'd all be drenched by morning. He thought wistfully of Helena's warm body.

Then she was at his side, pressing a hand to his mouth. "Quiet, I must be quick. I heard Ibrahim say earlier that we expect to be in Diyarbakir in six days, and that in the morning we take the Way of the Gorge. Is it tomorrow, then?"

A chill of real physical dread swept up George's spine. Hardly trusting himself to speak, he grunted. "Aye. If the weather's right."

"Good. Sleep well, dearest Giorgiou. And pray." She was gone in the darkness. Gurney suddenly realized that he had never heard her talk above a whisper. He closed his eyes and desperately began to pray. He was still trying, repeating the words of the Lord's Prayer, concentrating with all his might, but despite himself his mind scuttled off down side allies, retreating from his fear like rabbits from the heavy tread of the gamekeeper. At some point he went to sleep. When he awoke, he was chilled to the bone and stiff in every limb. There was a hard knot in his stomach, and he had to force himself to eat breakfast, telling himself that he would need all his strength and more besides if he was to get through the day. In the end, he compromised, shifting half his bread ration under the waistband of his trousers against future emergencies.

The rain was still coming down in long wet skeins as the party filed along the trail. The way was downhill now, the path hugging the right-hand side of a stream which trickled down the bottom of a broad valley. Below, the valley disappeared under a thick blanket of gray mist. The air was dead and still; movements and sounds fell mute, seemingly absorbed by the dense moisture. Gurney found it hard to breathe, had to force air into his lungs, fight off panic. Then, as they approached the point where the valley disappeared into the fog, Bizound raised his hand, and the column came to a halt.

"Behold!" cried the Turk. "In yonder valley lies the great gorge of the Tigris, the great river which in its humility bathes the feet of the cliffs of Diyarbakir, ere it plunges on, whither I neither know nor care. You are but four days from the palace of the Bey, which, unless he decides to sell you, will be your last place of existence. So look well at God's sky and the earth beneath your feet. This may be the last you see of it

for a long time." He motioned with his hand, and the
column moved slowly on down the slope.

As they moved off, Gurney elbowed his way cautiously to the front of the line, until he was walking a
couple of yards behind the swaying rump of Bizound's white horse. The party trudged into the mist.
Then the ground began to level out. The narrow path
on which they were walking swung to the left, and
after a quarter of a mile met a broad metaled high-
way, running straight as an arrow into the fog to
the eastward. From the dense mist to the right came a
droning roar as of mighty waters in a confined space.

As they stepped onto the metaled surface, Gurney
stooped as if to brush a biting insect from his foot and
picked up a twig of a spiny, gorselike plant which was
lying in the thoroughfare. Then he raised his left
hand and scratched his head. Behind him, Helena
sneezed violently three times.

Gurney looked at the impassive back in front of
him. The spines of the thorny plant in his right hand
dug into his palm, but he barely noticed the pain.
Then he leaned forward and jammed the twig into the
base of the tail of Bizound's mount.

The horse leaped vertically in the air and came
down kicking its hind legs at the spot where Gurney
had been a second ago. But he was away running to
the right, and the sharp hooves met empty air. Then
the horse took off at a bolting gallop, with Bizound
hanging on for dear life.

The file had come to a dead halt. As Gurney took to
his heels, Ibrahim sat on his mule with his mouth
open. Then, seeing his master disappearing into the
fog out of control, he squared his shoulders, couched
his lance, and dug his heels into the ribs of his mule.
As he left the line, Helena edged off the road to the
right. The mule's hooves thudded deafeningly in
George's ears: Ibrahim's face was twisted in rage, and
he waved his lance above his head. Gurney stood his
ground, hands loosely at his sides, feet planted apart,
until the Turk's blade was nearly at his chest; then he

twisted between the lance point and the body of the mule, reaching for Ibrahim's right wrist. His hands found their mark and locked. Ibrahim yelled once as he was plucked from the saddle; then he crashed to the ground and lay still.

George ran to Helena's side. "Quick. Back to the hills." She nodded wordlessly, and they began to skirt back towards the valley. The roaring of the river was loud in their ears, not a hundred yards away, Gurney guessed. For a moment, it was the only sound; then, faint at first, then louder, came a drumming of hooves and Bizound's voice, hoarse with rage, screaming Ibrahim's name. Gurney turned to Helena and jerked his head toward the hills. She tugged at his arm and set off across the stony ground. Then she seemed to falter, stumbled, and fell. He hurried to her side and held out his hand to help her up. She was deathly pale, and her breath came quickly as she pointed at the ground beside her with a trembling finger. Gurney looked down. There, lying coiled smugly on itself, lay a glistening black snake, its head raised threateningly, hissing.

"Did it bite you?"

She nodded, eyes big with terror. "What are we going to do? I don't want to die. Please, please, save me."

George looked ahead. Between him and the path stood Bizound, his face a mask of fury, arms folded threateningly. Behind him Ibrahim was shaking his head dazedly, staring at Gurney with malice in his eyes.

Bizound made the gesture of a courser setting his greyhound on a hare. Ibrahim drew a long curved knife and began to walk slowly towards the two fugitives. Gurney looked down. Helena's breathing was becoming stertorous, and her long black lashes were fluttering low over her eyes. Quick as a flash he stooped, grabbed the viper behind its head, and flung it at Ibrahim. Then he gathered Helena up in his arms, slung her unceremoniously across his shoulder, and began to trot toward the roaring gorge at his back. He heard

Ibrahim shout, and vaguely hoped that he had been bitten, but he wasn't hopeful. All he could do now was pray for a hiding place in the rim of the gorge.

A thousand-to-one chance. The mist swirled before him, and the roaring became suddenly twice as loud. The ground fell away at his feet to a jagged lip of rock that disappeared into the mist to the left and right; beyond the lip was a white nothingness which roared and bellowed like devils in torment. His breath rasped in his throat as he ran down the incline, muscles aching under Helena's weight. She was limp now, and her body was horribly awkward to carry.

There was no hiding place on the rim. The top of the cliff overhung whatever emptiness lay below; a fly could not have climbed it. Gurney let his shouldres drop, then turned as a stone rolled behind him. Ibrahim's face leered at him, distorted with malignant triumph. His voice was soft, almost caressing.

"So. We meet for the last time, dog of a Frank. You kept the woman from me. Now neither of us will have her. But at least I will keep my life." And he ran at Gurney, knife extended in front of him. George was too exhausted even to dodge. He took two steps back, and the Turk stopped, his eyes glittering. Then, with tiny, almost mincing steps, he walked forward, knife at Gurney's breastbone, forcing him and his burden toward the ghastly chasm behind him. Gurney looked to one side. Two more steps. A wet blast of air chilled the nape of his neck. He planted his feet firmly, bracing himself as Ibrahim came on, drawing his arm back for the final thrust. As the knife whipped up at his belly, he caught the blow on his crossed forearms; then he yanked Ibrahim past him, toward the gulf. The Turk screamed as he saw what must happen to him, and clutched at Helena's skirt, which was flapping in the wind. Then he was a scream fading into the mists below, and Gurney was teetering on the brink of the chasm, fighting for balance and losing. He was too far gone; as he and Helena pitched out into space, a freak wind cleared the mists below. The last thing he saw was the smooth, gray cliff

walls plunging down to a tiny ribbon of black water
touched with foam, a ribbon that grew wider and
wider until it smashed into his body, poured into his
nose and mouth, and sucked him, spinning and
whirling, down into its depths.

4

A light shone at the end of a long, dark tube. Not a
bright light, nor a particularly alluring one. But it
held out whole vistas of rich promise. Gurney knew,
somewhere in the roaring chaos of pain that filled his
being, that he had to squeeze down the tube and
reach the light or he was doomed. If only the elephants would stop bouncing on his back and chest,
forcing the air in and out of his tortured lungs, so he
could stop breathing and sink back into the bottom-
less black well yawning at the back of his mind. But
the light grew brighter, and as it brightened became
complex, formed shapes and patterns.

He coughed and forced his eyes open, closing them
immediately against the glaring sunlight reflected
from the hissing water on either side of him where
he lay. The surface his back lay on was undulant,
strangely pliant, as if it were alive. He tried to turn
his head, but found that he couldn't; the tearing ache
in his throat reached his lungs again, and he coughed
again, so feeble that the spasms left him too weak
to move.

Someone adjusted the woollen blanket that covered him, and forced a rough pottery bowl between
his teeth. Liquid, bland but with a sharp aromatic aftertaste, flowed soothingly down his throat. Then
blackness was over him again.

When he came to for the second time, he was looking into two eyes. He blinked, but when he looked

again, the eyes were still there. Amber they were, the pupils sharply outlined and surprisingly large in the brilliant sunlight. The eyes of a bird of prey. But there were lines at the corners which spoke of laughter, and the forehead, what could be seen of it between the thickets of the eyebrows and the shabby green silk turban, faded to the color of shallow stream water, showed only one resolute vertical line between the brows. The nose, however, reinforced the impression of the bird of prey. It jutted uncompromisingly from the forehead in a cruel hook, fine at the bridge, flaring only slightly to the delicately chiseled nostrils whose roots lay hidden in the dense growth of black beard, streaked with gray at the left-hand corner of the mouth, which covered almost all the rest of the face. The brows drew together; the man grunted in satisfaction and returned to the pestle and mortar between his feet, in which he was grinding a mass of something which smelled sharp and invigorating. Gurney got an elbow underneath his chest and hauled himself into a half-sitting position. Almost immediately he wished he had let well enough alone. The world spun around him, and he fought a wave of nausea.

"Sniff."

He sniffed. A blast of something powdery whistled up his nose, and for a moment he wanted badly to sneeze. But then a feeling of warmth and vigor spread to his fingers and toes. He stretched, feeling as if he had just awoken from a long and refreshing sleep, and looked around him.

The surface on which he sat seemed to be a sort of latticework of slender branches, supported by stronger members, covered with rush matting of great thickness and resilience. But most of its area was piled high with bales of goods—carpets in rolls, sacks of what could have been barley, great casks of wine, mounds of vegetable produce, and bales and bundles of other, less identifiable wares. On the section of the raft upstream of where Gurney lay, three donkeys lay in attitudes of abandon on the deck, long dark eyelashes lowered over their eyes. A contented cluck-

ing came from two coops of chickens, and a large
yellow dog rested its head between its paws by the
broad flat flagstone which, from the black patches
on its surface, must serve as the strange craft's cooking
range. The hammocklike sensation, he saw, was attri-
butable to the fact that his platform, some fifty feet
by thirty, was drifting at considerable speed between
the precipitous basalt cliffs of the river gorge.

And then it came back to him—the awful crash of
the water against his chest, then the feeling of sinking
into illimitable blackness, tumbled like a feather in a
whirlwind by the currents that had plucked Helena's
limp and unresisting form from his arms. He had
opened his mouth, and water had rushed in; then
there was nothing until the agony of coming back to
life.

The bearded man in the turban seemed to read his
mind. "Aye," he said, speaking in a precise, strangely
stilted Arabic which Gurney, who was now sufficiently
familiar with the language, dimly recognized as Persian in origin, "it is said that they who drown are
luckier than those who come back. But it seemed to
me that you and the woman were not bent on self-
ending. Even as I hooked you aboard, you struggled
like a landed fish, and you were breathing not at
all. There is much strength in you."

"But the woman—"

The man—he didn't look like a Persian, for all his
accent—gestured toward the bundle of blankets at his
side. "She was breathing badly from the viper's bite,
so she swallowed little water. I have given her that
which will ease the bite." He held up a bottle of thin,
slightly iridescent glass, half-full of a golden liquid in
which swam a tiny snake. "Pickled alive in olive oil.
I made a cut over her wound and poured in the oil;
its virtues fight the venom as the north poles of two
lodestones repel each other. She is ill, but she will
live."

Gurney was having difficulty in believing his eyes
and ears. To have fallen in with this amazing mounte-

bank was an outrageous stroke of luck. He bowed stiffly.

"I must make plain the enormous debt of gratitude which I and mademoiselle owe you for your help in our extremity. And," he continued, grinning, "I shall certainly make a sacrifice to Dame Fortune at the earliest opportunity. Permit me to introduce myself. I am George Le Fanu Gurney, and this is Mistress Helena, whose patronymic I unfortunately do not know, my unlucky fellow fugitive."

The bearded man remained grave, but his eyes twinkled. "It is indeed a great pleasure to have made your acquaintance. I am the Hajji Basreddin, whom men call the Eagle Owl. As to the matter of Dame Fortune, over the years and by dint of study I have become well acquainted with the lady, and have even had some measure of success in predicting her fickleness. Now, if you will excuse me." And Basreddin marched aft, pausing to scratch the ear of one of the donkeys, which browsed contentedly on a net of hay. He picked up a twenty-foot sweep from the deck, set it firmly in the trestle crutch at the stern— or rather, the side of the raft that happened to be facing upstream at that moment—and with a supple movement of the body sculled the huge floating structure into line for the descent of a set of rapids which spanned the riverbed half a mile downstream.

The banks of the river rose steeply for the next few miles, until the sky was a blue slit between the blackish gray walls of basalt. The raft floated in deep shadow, and a continuous plume of fine droplets rose from the surface of the smoothly rushing glides, cooling the air to the point where Gurney shivered and threw an extra sheepskin over Helena, who was still sleeping.

Basreddin was busy at his steering oar. The river, forced through a slender furrow carved in the basalt foundations of the plateau, hissed on its course with a power that belied the easy thunder of its swift passages. Where outcroppings of harder rock encroached on the already narrow gorge, the Tigris lived up to its name; it rose up and roared, showing fangs of spumy white which seemed fit to smash the ungainly raft to atoms. But Basreddin stayed calmly in control, infallibly picking his line through the worst of the chutes with a bend of the wrists at the oar and a slight inclination of the body.

Gurney was very tired and dozed fitfully, huddled against the damp chill in a soft, richly hued rug. The sky overhead became shot with fiery pinks and golds, then darkened; as the first stars winked into view against the indigo curtain of the advancing night, Basreddin swung the raft into an eddy which had dug out a deep bowl to the side of the main watercourse. He let it drift to the outside edge and pushed an enormous hedgehoglike contrivance of timber and boulders overboard with his foot. It sank immediately, dragging the rope which held it fast to the raft; and the platform, with its cargo of men, animals, and trade goods, lay anchored swaying in the still waters beneath a cliff which plunged, inky black in the darkness, from three hundred feet above vertically into the swirling pool at its base.

The bearded man unwound his turban, loosing a mane of black hair, stripped off his robe, and plunged into the river. He swam like an otter. Then he climbed back on board and disappeared behind a pile of merchandise, reemerging dressed in a long white djellaba with a dagger at his waist, the starlight striking darts of light from its jeweled pommel. He fell on his knees and prostrated himself to the east. Then he came to the section of the raft Gurney already thought of as the living quarters. He lit a fire on the flat stone, and from a hole in the matting nearby he pulled a string. Two fat catfish wriggled on the end. After he had gutted them, he salted them, slapped them with a pinch of some herb or other into a flat skillet, and settled the skillet on the fire. While the fish cooked, he broke out more hay for the donkeys, which moaned in gratitude, and threw a handful of some kind of grain into the chickens' wicker cages. He returned to the fire with two brown eggs, grinning with pleasure, and slapped flat cakes of dough on the hot stone beside the glowing ashes.

Gurney helped Helena eat. She was groggy, wandering a little in her mind, and her eyes looked through him, beyond him. When she had eaten half a barley cake and a little fish, she fell asleep again. Gurney wolfed down his portion in silence, his mind half on his rescuer. Or was it captor?

He could not but feel a strong sympathy with the man's delight in simple things; the way he could become part of his vessel, could find happiness in something as banal as an ordinary hen laying a commonplace egg. It went deeper than that, too. The precision of the man's movements, his skill with herbs—Gurney knew that the viper was more often deadly than not, and yet Helena looked to be well on the way to recovery under Basreddin's ministrations—was uncanny. It reminded George of the old woman Jedediah had taken him to see in her cottage by the bleak marsh at Stiffkey some ten years ago. She had a name for conjuring warts, righting wrongs by means more effective and lasting than fighting or countycourting. And Basreddin had that same look, the calm, fierce eyes with a spark of laughter lurking at the edge, the pupils that seemed deep wells of an elder wisdom. The bearded man's eyelids were lowered, and his fingers were tapping time to a soundless tune. Gurney cleared his throat and addressed him in Arabic as formal as he could muster, painfully aware of his lack of mastery of the niceties of the language.

"Sir. It is hard for a man to express his gratitude for so vast a service as you have done me. Mere words do not suffice. But for what it is worth, I must say that I am everlastingly in your debt for your kindness in a time of, ah, extreme difficulty." He cleared his throat again, reflecting that he would have to go on for some time in this vein. The Arabs expected it of a man, or so he had heard.

He racked his brain for appropriate phrases—the grammar he had studied in his cabin in the *Lady Ellen* had done nothing to prepare him for this—and prepared to start again. But Basreddin waved a dismissive hand. The fingers were surprisingly long and slender for a bargeman's.

"Enough, please, O Frank. It is the duty of the kelekyi to rescue live bodies from the river."

"Kelekyi?"

"I see you are new to our ways. We who pilot keleks, the great river-rafts"—he gestured at the piles of cargo—"are a guild with our roots in the Flood. Since time beyond remembering, men have plied this river in rafts such as the one on which we now lie, bringing the treasures of the rich mountain valleys to the dwellers in the ruins that once were cities and the reedy deltas of the plain. It was my forerunners in the guild who brought wine to the taverns of the twin cities of Sodom and Gomorrah. And before that even, we brought corn and wood to the ziggurats of Ashur, where the astronomer-kings gazed at the heavens as the fields about them became salt and went back to desert." A veil dropped behind his eyes. "And over the years, little by little, piece by piece, we learned the lore of the cities of the plain. We watched the floods of men surge and dwindle across the river flats, plying always our trade. The great river carries us as far as we need go, sometimes even to the gulf where the water is bitter and the sea sweats crystals of salt under the sun; then, at spate's end, we sell the lattice"—he thumped a timber with his fist—"load the skins on which we are floating—they are filled with air now—onto the donkeys, and we make the long drive up through the mountains to Anatolia, telling the tales we have learned on the drift down."

Gurney shook his head in wonderment. "Still, I find it hard to express my thanks to you. Is there anything—anything at all—I can do to assist you?"

White teeth showed in the beard. "Nay, nay, for you have given me a great new tale to tell. It is not every day two such choice fish as you come to my hook. Ah, how you whizzed out of the sky! Like a swooping osprey, no less. And you were wet inside as well as out when I got you with the boathook. A strange sight in this country of brown men, like a white frog. And the woman! A goddess, an angel, or a succubus from Iblis without doubt. Though I wouldn't have thought so with such a pair of drowned rats as you when I dragged you over the side yonder, you pale as death and she black with the viper's bite. Ah, no, you need do nothing to thank me. But wait. I have shared no time with a Frank before now, and I know not the workings of your mind. So now I ask you—why not share my journey to the reeds? For you have the eyes of a traveler, and if I did not mistake the one who looked over the cliff after you, and he who drowned before you, any bondage will be lighter than the one you have escaped."

It was almost too good to be true. And at the end of this river lay the Persian Gulf; of that Gurney was almost sure. And from there it was but a short step to India and a Company ship to the East. He smiled and extended his hand to the Turk. "Delighted, my dear fellow, nothing could give me greater pleasure. Your hand on it." He grasped the Turk's paw in his—the bones were small and birdlike, but there was a sinewy power in his grip—and shook it mightily. Basreddin looked a little pained, then threw his shoulder forward and returned the shake with a will.

Water chuckled and gurgled six inches below his ear. Dull gray moonlight shone on the densely patterned carpet spread overhead to catch the dew. Helena's breath came warm on his face. He started, rising like a cork from a limpid pool of half-sleep, and turned, his voice a rusty croak.

"What are you doing? You should be asleep."

"Pah! I have lain still for too long. My leg hurts like fury, but I had to talk with you. Are you for the gulf with this dervish?"

"This what?"

"Dervish. Did you not see the belt of his tunic—the octagonal buckle? The man is a Sufi, a wise one and a traveler. If you go with him, you run the risk of becoming like him. I heard your talk earlier, when you thought I was asleep."

A night bird screamed, and dark wings flapped at the cliff wall overhead. Gurney shivered a little at the desolation of the sound. "What do you mean, become such as him?"

"They have a way of seeing that is not as other men see. I warn you that you may never be the same again. Once I knew a man, a merchant, older than you, who took up with one of these in Macedonia. He wandered out into the wilds and was seen no more, until two years later a ragged beggar arrived at the village gate, sat down, and began to recite. When they of the village saw his face, they realized that it was he. But he had changed; years younger he looked, but for his eyes, which were old and wise with a frightening wisdom. He told a strange tale, in a high, cracked voice, about travels in fearful mountains, great hardships endured, and strange people met. Then he rose to his feet, went into the courtyard of his house—he had been a wealthy man—and laughed. He took flint and steel from his pocket, made fire, and threw burning paper into the hayloft. The flames soon spread from the stables to the house, and all his possessions caught fire. Most of the village had gathered to watch; it was a dry year and there was barely a spit of water in the wells, so watching was all they could do. When the roof fell and all was ashes, they looked around for the man, but he was nowhere to be found. On a nearby wall, however, someone had scrawled in charcoal—the schoolmaster swore it was the beggar's hand—'Let God kill him who himself does not know and yet presumes to show others the way to the doors of His Kingdom. Once I was a merchant; now God has made me ashes.' But the footsteps led away from the village until they disappeared in the bare rock of the mountains."

Each day the river was drawing the raft and its passengers closer to the Persian Gulf, the Indian

Ocean, and Otway. For some days now, Gurney had been trying to hold back from himself the knowledge that he stood a good chance of becoming far too involved with Helena. She had little of Arabella's wit and less of her keen intelligence, true; but in her there burned slow, exotic fires which seized his imagination, always the most vulnerable part of him. Was she too much of a distraction? Since their escape from the slave coffle, Gurney's purpose in his mission had returned with redoubled force; he had vowed that Otway would pay in full for his capture, beating, imprisonment, and enslavement; would expiate every last bitter drop of gall with gall of his own.

Helena, as was her way, seemed to sense his misgivings.

"Do not worry about me, Giorgiou. I know you have your quest, and that were I to come between you and it, I should be crushed."

Gurney looked her straight in the eye. "In all honesty, I sometimes do not know where my quest now lies—with you or with my quarry."

She tossed her head. "How can you concern yourself with me, a poor whore from an insignificant island, cast off like an old shoe by Byron, when there is a matter so important as your honor at stake?"

"Oh, my Helena, you are so dramatic. If you are a whore, you are certainly the most beautiful I have ever met. And the most talented." She blushed and looked away. "But how shall I do the right thing by you? As slaves, our love was something we stole from our owners; as free people, the matter is of considerably more consequence."

"You British are all the same. Even Byron, who fancied himself to be not as other men. Be reasonable. We agree well, you and I, and for the moment we can give each other much that is of mutual comfort. So let us love a little, not think of tomorrow, and see what occurs."

The sheer pragmatism of her attitude took Gurney's breath away, and he told her so.

"What? You, a cold English fish, tell me I am cal-culating and expedient?" Her eyes blazed. "Well, m'lord, what do you expect from a whore?"

"It was you who called yourself a whore, not I."

"Bah! You understand so little about women, do you not? It is your British education that makes pederasts of you all. Even Byron, mooning over a slip of a page. I a whore? By no means. Unless to control one's own destiny is to be a whore. In which case you are a greater whore than I could ever be."

"All right, I apologize."

"No, not enough. For days now you have been mis-erable, and do not think I don't know why. All I wish is that I find safe passage to Nauplia, and I think it will be hard to find. Do you understand?" She was having trouble controlling her voice, and beads of moisture were forming below her lashes. Gurney longed to hold her in his arms, but something in her face told him he must play the game to the hilt. "I understand," he said, and smiled. "Nothing could give me greater pleasure, my dear, than to assure your safe passage. But I hope we may at last have some little time together."

"Yes," she said, moving towards him. "At least we shall have that."

Then she was in his arms, crooning little words at him, taking his face in her hands and covering it with kisses. "Keep me warm, Giorgiou, for I am cold and our journey is very long." Gurney pulled the rug up to their shoulders and cast a glance at Basreddin's shelter of carpets fifteen feet away. It was dark and silent. Helena's body wriggled against him, and he parted her robe, feeling the heavy swing of her breasts in his hand. As they made love, he could still feel the tears flowing down her cheeks.

Afterward, as her breathing slowed and she drifted into sleep, Gurney lay staring downstream, at the water which connected him like a thread—the silver cord said by the Egyptians to join the sleep-er's soul with his body—to Arabella behind and Otway before. And he knew that this river and Helena and

Basreddin and the raft were the dream, and that
Arabella and Otway were the reality. Helena stirred
next to him and clutched at his body, and a chill
went through him. Was it now that Helena was the
truth, Otway and Arabella the dream? He conjured
up their images. When he thought of Otway, as usual
his pulse quickened and a thin, sharp knife of hatred
tickled his heart with steel; and as Arabella came up
before him, he felt he would break apart with yearn-
ing. He went to sleep running over their first meeting in his mind. He remembered every word.

In the chill devil wind that sighs down the Tigris
valley before dawn, Gurney shivered in his sleep and
flung his arms around Helena, drawing her to him.
Warmed by her body, he ceased to tremble and fell
again into a deep slumber.

Grease ran down Gurney's chin, and he probed
with his tongue for a bit of stringy mutton stuck between two teeth. Beside him sat Basreddin, gnawing
at a sheep's hock. On the other side was Helena,
dressed as a man in turban and djellaba, a curved
knife at her waist. The old trader, on the far side of the
fire, ran his eyes over the trio for the twentieth
time, screwing up his face against the red glow of
the smouldering dung in the center of the circle. Hajji
Basreddin, whom men called the Eagle Owl, he
knew from long ago—since he had first appeared on
the river, a stripling not yet in his teens. As usual, he
had picked up a couple of lost sheep on the way. The
one in the turban, the toothsome youth of the smooth
face, wouldn't last long. But he of the yellow beard—
he was a different barrel of tobacco entirely. Basreddin might have bitten himself off a Tartar there. The
Frank had the look of one accustomed to do and
think in his own way, without consulting others. Po-
liteness forbade the old man's asking how he came
to be here, but from his scars it was undoubtedly a
bloody tale and one worth the hearing should he
ever volunteer the information. But there was a closed
look in his eyes that made the trader feel that this

was not likely. The beardless boy had spoken, for the first time since the raft had come ashore near his night camp at sundown. He caught a few words, for every year his travels took him beyond the narrow straits of the Bosporus and into Macedonia, and beyond that, Greece, but he did not catch the import of what he had said.

Basreddin translated. "The child asks which way you are bound now, and where we are."

The trader folded his hands portentously over his stomach and prepared to lecture. For had he not traveled this way for forty years, since his early manhood, from the bottom of the great gorge to Greece, trading his wine for hashish in the uplands, then trading his hashish for wine again in the sunny hills by the Aegean? "Tell him, O Hajji, that my wandering feet will be bent toward the blue mountains, and beyond them to the turquoise waters of the sea of islands. Tell him further that we are at present between the teeth of Satan and the gullet of death, where few tread but the valiant and not-to-be-trifled-with descendant of the Prophet himself, Yuri Impatuk."

His little eyes sparkled with a sudden piggy glee as the boy turned to Basreddin for a translation. Surely beneath those robes he had seen the swell of a breast, and a goodly one to boot. This called for a little guile. He grinned and bowed as deeply as his seated position allowed.

Basreddin was watching him narrowly. "Truly impressive, O stout tower of commerce. The child professes himself both awestruck and flabbergasted."

The merchant's eyes were shifty now, and he spread his hands. "Is it the young one wishes to join me on my journey to the lands of Greece? For I detected his origins in his speech, and he is far from home for one so young and beardless." Oh, you beauty, he thought. Oh, you would warm my bed well on the long trail and fetch a fine price at the end of it. He licked his lips. "It would be a great privilege to me to be of assistance to one so close to the Hajji Basreddin. Assuredly, my place in heaven would be secure."

Gurney shifted abruptly where he sat. Helena looked, as usual, relaxed; but there was something in her face, that gave him pause. He did not trust this Impatuk, though, he reflected, he might be transferring his jealousy unjustly to the nearest convenient object. The merchant's eyes were shifty, and something seemed to be making him nervous; his fingers clicked incessantly at his string of amber worry beads.

Gurney caught Basreddin's eye, and the Sufi winked. His hands went to his waist, and a fold of his clothing, disturbed as if by accident, fell aside. The octagonal buckle of his belt shone brassy in the firelight, and the merchant drew a sharp breath. When the Sufi spoke, his voice was quiet but singularly penetrating, soothing but imperious. "You will forget that you have ever seen this child. Moreover, you will tell your jackal acquaintances, thieves and bandits to a man, that there is leprosy on my kelek and that they will approach it at their peril. Now, sleep."

Basreddin seemed to have grown hugely in stature. His eyes were strange and piercing below the heavy lids, and his voice seemed to shake the ground. Gurney was convinced that if anyone had spoken to him in that tone of voice, he would either have killed him or immediately done as he told him. He was still puzzling as he went to sleep.

In Gurney's dream he was sitting in a theater. On either side of him rows of steeply banked seats marched away, and in front of him the stage was brilliantly lit with lamps. He tried to get up and leave, but he found his body and his limbs refused to function. A figure ran onto the stage. It was Helena, her hair swinging as she came, dressed in a gown of muslin, damped after the old French fashion, which clung to her breasts and thighs. Her nipples showed dark through the diaphanous fabric, and she smiled at Gurney, beckoning.

Behind her on the stage the tall curtains of red velvet parted, and Yuri Impatuk, beringed hands washing each other with invisible soap, sidled out into the lights, eyes fixed on Helena and tongue running around his lips like a rat in a coil of rope. Gurney tried to yell a warning, but no sound came, and the tears squirted from his eyes as Impatuk seized Helena and cast her down on the stage, ripping the thin muslin from her body. She lay, strangely passive, as the obese merchant hitched up his robe and knelt between her thighs. Then he paused, looked up at Gurney, and waved; and his face was no longer the sallow one of Yuri Impatuk, but the falsely bonhomous gray and pink mask of Mathias Otway. Gurney found suddenly that he could move, and he ran across the awkward rows of seats in the orchestra pit, where the edge of the stage loomed over him like a cliff as he scrabbled at it, trying to climb it. A face, a woman's face, appeared over the lip, and Gurney assumed it was Helena's until he looked again and, against the lights of the stage, it made a blond aureole, and the voice screaming, "George! George!" was Arabella's, and he was shouting back and hammering desperately at the wooden cliff in front of him when he awoke, her screams ringing in his ears.

Helena was beside him, a sadness in her eyes. "You were dreaming badly, my Giorgiou. And who was in your dream?"

Gurney fought to dispel the repulsive images swirling in his mind. "You," he said. "And others. One other, in particular."

She sighed. "Aye. It would be she whose name you were calling as you woke. She is the lucky one. Still, *carpe diem*, as the snake said to the frog. Come here and I will drive away your evil dreams."

As the warm alchemy of her body worked in his mind, the dream faded. But somewhere, even as they joined beneath the glittering night sky, a voice—Arabella's voice—was calling, desperate, from the treacherous meshes of a net cast by Mathias Otway.

Two hundred yards ahead, the smooth waters of the river narrowed into a deep V, outlined in turbulent ripples. The point of the V lost itself in a white haze of water vapor; from beyond the misty curtain came a dull, angry roar. The raft began to swing about its center point, slewing clumsily across the current. One of the donkeys brayed suddenly and staggered to its feet. Basreddin stroked it soothingly on the head and whispered in its ear, and it grudgingly lay down again. Gurney, braced at the stern oar, pushed with his body against the handle of the sweep. The blade, normally responsive, trembled like a live thing. He began to sweat as the arrowhead of water came swiftly nearer. Basreddin had taken the bow oar, which projected like a movable bowsprit from the kelek's blunt prow, and was rowing, slowly, far too slowly, to put the ponderous craft back on course. If they hit the rocks sideways, they would go beam-on, the deck would tip, and men, animals, and merchandise would be flung into the boiling rapids.

Basreddin's shout was almost lost in the growing roar of the chute, but his fingers pointed unmistakably upstream. Gurney glanced over his shoulder, leaning hard on the sweep with his hip. Some three hundred yards astern, a low wall of water, its face flecked with dirty white, brown against the transparent metal of the pool, was rolling towards them. Then the deck jumped sharply under his feet, forcing him on one knee, and he fixed his mind on the rapids ahead, for the moment ignoring the bore behind. But his hands clenched hard on the smooth wood of the oar handle, and he whistled absently between his teeth as he heaved the stern of the raft around in the direction Basreddin had pointed her bow. They were racing diagonally between the stony banks, the current driving them through a deep, narrow channel, set on its downstream side with boulders, and upstream bordered by a sandbank. All around, water was smashing white into huge, jagged lumps of rock, blasting into the air, vaporizing from the surface of

the river. The spray was so thick that Basreddin was
a dim shadow forward. His dog whimpered, fur glued
to its body, tail between its legs, shivering miserably.
The tail of the raft fishtailed in an eddy, while the
bow, driven by the main force of the current, swung
uncontrollably. For a moment, it floated almost at
right angles to the swiftly flowing water; then the
downstream edge caught across two boulders and
stuck firm, and the water began to build up under its
bottom. The deck, pushed by tons of water, reared
up at a steep angle. Gurney, clinging to an oar, saw
Basreddin standing easily at his trestle, his face impassive, straining upstream. Gurney struggled up the
tilting deck and clung to the edge, driven by some
ludicrous memory of a bosun in a pinnace under sail
in a high wind ordering all hands to the weather rail.

Then the bore hit them, and the deck reared up at
an impossible angle, boxes and bales sliding down
into the foaming water. When Gurney thought they
must surely turn turtle, the raft lurched again. Clinging to the side, Gurney turned his head. The downstream edge was buried in a roaring welter of muddy
brown foam through which projected the gray rump
of a boulder. As he watched, it began to roll, levered
by the raft's vast bulk, and crashed on its side. The
raft collapsed back into the water, its inflated goat-
skins once more accepting the weight of the lattice.
The stern swung free, but the bow still held fast. Basreddin, keeping his feet with difficulty, knife in hand,
slashed at something below water level; then they
were away. Rocks flashed under Gurney's feet as they
whizzed into the tail of the rapids and ploughed
into the four-foot standing wave. Three more shocks,
each smaller than the last, and they were clear, running down another curving pool, a gray sandbank
rearing like a whale's back from the slack water on
the inside of the bend. Basreddin pointed, and the
two of them bent to their oars.

While Gurney tied up, he let his eyes rest on
Helena, pounding barley in a quern, the fine lines of

her back showing through her caftan, and he felt content. Then he cursed himself for a fool as he remembered why he was here, and once again Helena's image blurred and Arabella was there, pounding corn in the blazing sun. She turned and smiled at him, and suddenly she was Helena again. Gurney, testing himself as a man gingerly probes a sore tooth, found that he was pleased.

He plunged into the river to cool himself off, then crouched beside her. He had discarded most of his clothes and now wore only a loincloth and a turban to keep the fierce sun from the nape of his neck. His skin was a dark mahogany color, and his beard had grown. Had he been the kind to waste his time speculating on such matters, he would undoubtedly have wondered what George Le Fanu Gurney, lieutenant, would have thought of Giorgiou, now crouched before a breathtaking Levantine houri and a devious medicine man, scrawny knees at his ears, molding a piece of dough into a flat cake of bread on the banks of the Tigris, three weeks and God knew how many miles, rapids, and trade deals downstream from Diyarbakir, bound for the gulf.

"By God, but that was a bad one," he observed, planking his dough cake in a place on the hearthstone he raked clear of ashes. "I thought for a moment you were going to show a big loss this trip."

Basreddin shrugged. "Aye. It was a work of providence that the bore came when it did. But then it is the season of spates. I had hope to be past the cascades when it arrived; but I was . . . sidetracked." He smiled at Gurney. "Be that as it may, those are the last rapids before we reach the gorge of Al-Fathah, downstream some way. The spates will not disturb us now."

It was true; the banks of the river were flattening, and a shimmering heat haze blanketed the undulating plains as far as the eye could see. Gurney marveled a moment. Arabia Deserta by water! Strange sailing indeed!

The interior of the tent was thick with the smoke of hashish. Folds of grubby white woolen cloth threw the bedouin's face into shadow; only his eyes glittered, black as jet beneath straight brows. The coffee was syrupy sweet on Gurney's tongue as he sat entranced, listening half to Basreddin's chaffering with the patriarch and half to the sounds of the desert night outside the tent, the bleating of the penned flock of gloomy, flop-eared sheep, and the soft, intimate chatter of the womenfolk.

That morning, Basreddin had called a halt before noon. They had pulled into the bank beneath the shadow of a ruined city, a maze of bleached columns and slabs half-buried in drifting sand. The place seemed deathly old, a dry pebble rolled nearly to the bottom of a long, slow slope of decay. Even the river had lost much of its vigor; Gurney thought almost nostalgically of the swift runs and roaring rapids upstream. Here, swelled by the Great and Little Zabs, its source waters shrinking as the high mountains froze into late autumn, the Tigris rolled and swirled portentously enough, but its force was the slow, deliberate power of the aged and thoughtful rather than the zestful, reckless energy of youth.

Gurney had tried to talk to Helena, but she seemed distant and withdrawn. Perhaps it was the dead dryness of their haven that was weighing on her nerves. When he had asked her to come, she had refused, saying that she knew the desert bedouin and that she would be unwelcome unless disguised as a man. And anyway, she would like to be alone for once. Gurney could see her point; the kelek, for all its size, seemed to shrink day by day, until he was familiar with almost every box and bale, every thread of the latticework.

Basreddin, by contrast, had been almost loquacious as they loaded the donkeys with the last of the fruit (kept on ice in hay boxes since the green valleys of Lower Anatolia), sundry articles of gold and silver jewelry, pots of bright paint and perfumes, and a bottle of brandy.

"Today we make the journey to see an old acquaintance of mine, who is always in the wadi of the Tell el-Qarb at this time of the year, plucking up his courage to enter the suqs of Mosul in quest of new wives. Do not be deceived by his dirtiness and barbarism; he is rich and powerful and will show you a side of the world which in me is diluted by an excess of human feeling."

He grinned wolfishly. Over the weeks, Gurney had manufactured a pack of playing cards from thin slivers of bone he had discovered on the banks of the river. Basreddin had swiftly developed a fair addiction for whist, though outwardly he sneered at it as a game of pure chance, a pathetic apology for a man's game compared with his beloved chess.

But Gurney had observed in him a streak of barely controlled violence, an almost self-destructive urge to test the patience of Fate past the cracking point, which made him a born gambler. Today he was still smarting from a crushing defeat the previous evening. He seemed to regard Gurney as a kind of good luck piece, too. Though he professed amazement and disbelief at Gurney's tales of life in the West, of actions at sea between seventy-four-gun ships, of cities with populations in the millions, Gurney realized that for Basreddin he was a window on a whole new world of practical magic—the magic of iron, great machines and huge ships, engines that worked by steam power, and empires that stretched across oceans. For him, Basreddin was the Orient personified; the man was a master of hypnotism, conjuring, doctoring, and all the fakir's bag of tricks. He believed implicitly that the air about him was filled with spirits, good and evil, that the workings of destiny were already written on great tablets of jasper on the far side of the Veil; but he was not afraid to use any of his arts to stay fed and cheerful. For all his belief in the supernatural, he was certainly the most natural creature Gurney had ever met.

Basreddin waved a hand at the ruins that stretched away on either side. "Here there lived once the scholars

of the Old World, they who foretold the future from
the stars. Now only afreets and jinns wail through the
columns under the moon. My acquaintance dwells in
the wadi where once the king of this place had his
palace, all girt with canals and green gardens. He
knows that most men, particularly those with crimes
on their consciences, will not come here for fear of
the spirits. Therefore, he lives in peace."

And as the sun drilled into the windless gray sands
of the low hills and the donkeys grunted protestingly
at the end of their halters, Gurney relived for his benefit the lower gundeck of the *Egregious*, the pall of
smoke shot through with a double row of red flashes
as the powder exploded in the priming pans under
the gun captains' slow matches, the fearful noise of
seventy-four big guns hurling tons of iron into the
muzzle flashes of the enemy, the smash of ball into
side, the yelling of five hundred men. And on deck,
the continual whine and hum of musket balls, the
deeper roar of the carronades sweeping the enemy's
deck with grape, the rattle and crash of falling spars
and rigging. And over all, the trade winds, blowing
the rolling banks of blue smoke down to leeward in
the thick billows, and the sun, shining down on a
clear sea the color of emeralds and spilled blood the
color of rubies . . .

He awoke, as from a dream, when his donkey
roared and jagged at the bridle. The ruins were thick-
ly overgrown with spiny brush now, and his charge
was lame in its right forehoof. Basreddin lifted the hoof
and pulled out the thorn, clucking like a smith shoeing
a fractious horse. Then they went on.

"Not far now. Over the crest of yonder dune, where
the three columns stand, is the tent of our man. You
had me in another place then, Giorgiou; I hardly
knew where I was. It seems that you have much of
the fakir, the tale-teller about you. I begin to feel that
it is time for me also to see these huge ships and wide
waters, where men are so ingenious to destroy. Look
now! There is the palace of the king of the dead
city."

The camp was like many others Gurney had seen in the past weeks, a huddle of low, dusty, black goat-hair tents around which small children in dirty robes chased each other, yelling. Slightly apart, a straggling flock of flop-eared sheep grazed morosely at twigs of brush. The smoke from a fire, tended by the shapeless black bundles the desert Arabs made of their women, rose vertically in the still air. As they unloaded the packs from the donkeys and handed the animals over to a ragged, ancient herdsman for feeding and watering, Gurney smelt a strange odor of dung and oily cooking, overlaid with rich, musky perfume. A pair of luminous black eyes leveled a liquid gaze at him over a veil; long eyelashes fluttered alluringly. He ventured a commonplace. But the muffled figure ran off, a water pitcher balanced on her head, to the well, whose long lifting arm pointed to the sky at the far side of the encampment. He thought he heard a giggle, but he wasn't sure. Then Basreddin nudged him with an elbow, and he sighed, slung the heavy saddlebags over his shoulder, and bent to enter the largest of the tents.

Now Basreddin and the patriarch were talking fast, in low voices. The hashish he had smoked thrummed in Gurney's brain as he dragged his thoughts back to the scene before him. He shifted uneasily on his cushions, thinking nostalgically of the hard matting of the kelek's deck. The floor of the tent was covered in rich rugs, woven in patterns of arabesque which shifted and coiled in the dim light of the pierced copper lamp which hung from the ridgepole, striking a rich reddish glint from the chased silver coffeepot which sat on its tray at the patriarch's feet. Gurney's eye followed the coils of the decoration; he was getting lost, lost in a silver maze, going nowhere, but not caring. Then, floating in front of him, in the semblance of one of the stone saints from the church at Moorhouse, was the figure of Otway, lips peeled from his teeth in his unctuous Judas grin. And Gurney ran at him, but the silver roads twisted and curled away, and he was back from whence he came, staring glassily at the two swarthy figures locked in conversation at the other side of the tent.

Basreddin jerked his head in his direction. "Where lies your journey, O Frog?"

The words echoed in Gurney's ears as in a cathedral, and for a moment they seemed pure sound, without meaning. Then he pulled himself together. "My path lies from your gulf, through the snail seas, and eventually to one of the great ports of India. There I shall take ship for the seas of Cathay, where my adversary awaits me."

The patriarch raised an eyebrow. "Cathay is a far distance from here, Frank. You must bear a hard grudge to follow a man halfway across the world."

Gurney grunted. "It is a matter of a woman."

The patriarch shrugged and sighed. "By God, but you are young. Would that I had your vigor still, by the Prophet! But it seems to me, whose blood is cooling, that you could as well pick a ripe maid from the suqs of Mosul. And she would not carry you through barbarous places at her whim." Basreddin said something to him, speaking quickly. Too quickly for Gurney. The shadowed face darkened, and the swarthy hand, crusted with jewels, stroked the beard. "But the Eagle Owl tells me that it is a matter of the righting of a wrong by the sword. Well, that I understand; for women are plentiful in this world, but a man has only one honor. The Hajji tells me he would go with you. Honestly, I fear he is mad. For years I have told him he should settle, take some wives—my daughters had good dowries, and are not ill favored —and put his tents in the solitude of the dead city, next to mine. But he will always be searching for what is new, as if what he has already learned would not fill nine lifetimes of tale-telling."

Basreddin smiled. "Ah, you old fox, you know full well that in tale-telling you yourself would die ten thousand times, yet not come to the end of your inventions. Truly, you are the favorite son of the Father of Lies."

The old man ignored him. "My cousin, who lives

in a damp hole in the reeds in the place where the great river Shatt-al-Arab flows into the snail gulf, has a dhow, an old bucket he chanced to take from a man he had taken the trouble to kill. In the winter, when the breezes blow fresh, his people are wont to go in pursuit of shell. I shall give you a letter for him; mayhap he will be able to help you on your way."

The river seemed finally to have given up any pretense of direction. It was as if it knew it had almost completed its long journey to the sea and, now that its task was nearly done, could not be bothered to make the final effort. The kelek drifted idly, pushed towards the northern bank of the meander by the southerly wind. Gurney, nearly suffocated by the damp heat, swatted at a mosquito and prepared to fend off from the bank of soft mud looming to leeward. For days—weeks—now, he and Basreddin had been floating slowly through the vast, looping meanders of the northerly end of the Tigris delta. The rich pastures and arable lands lay far upstream, as did the teeming cities of Mosul and Baghdad. It was in one of the markets of Baghdad that Basreddin, to the accompaniment of much argument and sweet black coffee, had made his final deal; now they were on their way to fulfill their errand, the remnants of their cargo supplemented by a flock of sheep which lay stupid on the raft, munching hay. Kelek, sheep, and cargo were contracted to a small trading station downstream, where they would receive in exchange some store of gold and one of the black coracles that plied up and down this part of the river.

Gurney picked up a long pole at its balance point and held it poised at his shoulder like a javelin thrower. As the mudbank came up under the bow of the raft, he darted it into a patch of firm sand and leaned into it, pitting his weight and the resilence of the pole against the kelek's momentum. For a moment he hung poised, the pole bent like a bow, taking up the raft's movement; then, when he felt the movement of the mass of hide and timber shift direction, he leaned into the pole, straightening his knees. Ponderously, the kelek changed course, running parallel to the bank instead of directly for it; then the river began to curl in on itself in a long smooth oxbow, and the wind was heading them. At perhaps half a knot, the great raft drifted steadily toward the Persian Gulf.

Even in the blanket of wet heat that hung thick over the chocolate-colored water, Gurney could feel the nearness of the sea. It was not a conscious knowledge of its closeness, but something which crept up on him like a thief, setting his ears to ringing and sharpening his every sense. Helena and he, crouched in the shade of a carpet suspended on a frame of sticks, were trying to play whist. Beads of sweat kept running down his nose and plopping on the cards. Helena played well enough, though without Arabella's dash and precision. She was feeling the heat, too, as was the entire crew of the raft, human and animal. Finally, she threw her hand on the mat that formed their table.

"I concede. Damn this heat. Can't you move that carpet so we get a little breeze? No, don't. We'll only bake in the sun. Giorgiou?"

Gurney, who had been gazing absently at the queen of hearts, came to himself with a start. "Yes?"

"How long will it take us to get out of this . . . this *boring* land?"

"Lord knows. Not above another month, though."

"A month! I shall die of the tedium."

"Let us hope not."

The sea, the sea. Beaches, waves, azure deeps, and fast ships occupied the foreground of Gurney's thoughts, and Helena's words were thin, wind-whipped, barely audible, coming from a great distance.

"Giorgiou." Something in her voice brought Gurney back to the present. "We cannot continue in this way, you and I. You are becoming the prisoner of your dreams. Perhaps you have always been their prisoner. At night, when you call out in your sleep, it is not my name that is on your lips. Do you remember that I once said that were I to come between you and your quest, I should be crushed? Well, this quest, this dream of yours, this tedious descent into hell, is crushing me."

Gurney felt a dull ache in the pit of his stomach. "How so?"

"I am sorry, Giorgiou, but I have always been light-minded. I cannot cling to a phantom, a ghostly goal such as your revenge. All I wish is to be free at every moment. It is making me sad, Giorgiou."

"But, Helena, we are together now, you and I. Isn't that what matters?"

"In a way. But I know that when we escape from this limbo, you will once again become the British bulldog, intent on your quarry to the exclusion of all else. And in time you will come to resent me as a distraction from your quest."

Gurney was horrified. "Me? Resent you? How can you say this? You, who reminded me what it was to be alive, when I knew I was dead, in the slave gang of Achmet Bizound?" But gnawing at him was the knowledge that there might be truth in what she said.

"Yes, I brought you back to life. But as I brought you back, I awakened your demon once again; and now it will not leave you alone until you have fully accomplished what you set out to do. Enough, though. Come." She pulled her caftan over her head, stood a breathless moment on the edge of the raft, and dived. By the time Gurney followed her, she was in midstream, swimming strongly. He jumped in, the murky water closing over his head, and set out after her.

As he came up to her, she turned quickly and ducked him. He surfaced spluttering, grabbed her, and started back for the kelek, a low pile of baggage on the water, with Basreddin at the steering oar, gazing as always at his illimitable horizons. Her body was pliant and smooth in his arms, and for a moment he was overwhelmed by the beauty of her. Then she turned to him.

"Ah, my Giorgiou. This time you caught me, because I allowed you to. But I fear there will come a time when I shall leave you. And then you will never catch me."

On either side of the river, the reeds waved and clattered. As far as the eye could see, the slim spears of green, rooted in water and mud, rustled in great waves as the wind passed across them like cloud shadows. Gurney's shout sent a skein of ducks whirring from cover on the left bank.

"Land ho!"

Far ahead, a low hill, like the back of a lazy, mostly submerged sea monster, thrust up above the featureless plain of vegetation stretching to the horizon. A gray line—a wall of baked mud, Gurney guessed—ran around the summit, and two domes shimmered in the haze. Basreddin was at his side, shading his eyes with his hand. "Yes, that's it. So, if Allah wills it, we get rid of this floating midden and start for the snail gulf."

5

The diver, a lanky youth of about sixteen, breathed in and out rapidly and deeply several times, the air whistling in his throat. Like the rest of the crew of the *Jewel of Loveliness,* he was very thin, the bones of his elbows and knees sticking out in great lumps through the skin. After seven breaths, he grasped a heavy stone and dived into the sea, leaving hardly a splash. Gurney, watching over the side of the dhow, saw the figure plunge rapidly into the clear depths, trailing bubbles until it disappeared. The rope at his elbow played out for perhaps twenty fathoms, then stopped; the bubbles continued to rise, a few at a time, for a couple of minutes. Then the rope twitched twice, and he surfaced, this time twenty feet from the side of the dhow, and lay floating, gasping for breath. He paddled over to the dhow and dragged himself up the rope ladder trailing in the water at the lowest point of her sheer amidships.

Gurney hauled in the rope hand over hand. At its end was a net bag, and in the bag rested about a score of large oyster shells, crusted with corallike deposits. He passed the bag to an Arab who was squatting on the deck, a knife and a bucket of seawater at his side. The man inserted the blade of the knife into the hinge of each shell, and with a deft flick wrenched cartilage and shell apart and pulled out the meat, palpating it with his thumb. As he opened the fifth bivalve, he grunted with satisfaction and washed something off in his bucket of seawater, then held up his hand. Between his thumb and forefinger was a pearl about the size of a robin's egg. The crew of the *Jewel* cursed appreciatively but languidly; the diver lay panting on the deck, a trickle of blood seeping from his right ear.

For nearly two weeks now, Gurney, Basreddin, and Helena had been supercargo on the *Jewel of Loveliness* as she cruised—drifted, rather—down the Great Pearl Bank to the north of the Arabian coast of the Persian Gulf. Gurney had heard in London that the pirates of the region had been causing a nuisance of late, despite various punitive expeditions. But now, prostrate beneath the meager shade of the pearling boat's furled lateen sail, he wondered what good a punitive expedition would do. Far be it from him to accuse His Majesty's officers of falsifying dispatches; but on so treacherous a coast, with so vast a coastline to patrol, he had a strong suspicion that one British frigate more or less would make little difference to a determined corsair. And if there was one quality that defined the attitude of these gulf Arabs, be they corsairs or pearl divers, to the single-minded pursuit of wealth, it was determination. Even Basreddin, now squatting in meditation against the mizzenmast, had expressed surprise at the endurance of the crew of the *Jewel of Loveliness*. For not only did she stink abominably of rotting fish, but her five crewmen and her three divers were undoubtedly the illest-looking men Gurney had ever seen, even in the West Indies. When they had sailed from the mud village at the mouth of the Shaat-al-Arab, the maze of muddy creeks and flat, reedy islands where the Tigris and Euphrates rivers joined and flowed into—or rather merged imperceptibly with—the gulf, Gurney had been surprised at the relative youth of the crew. Not a man of them was more than thirty years old. But then Basreddin had told him the real reason. The boy panting on the deck would be finished as a diver in two years; and his heart, weakened by the rapid changes in pressure, would keep pumping his blood for another ten years at the most. The old were an expensive luxury in the land of the reeds. But on the other hand, the crew did not seem unduly worried by the prospect of short life. As long as they had the glory of the small, soft leather pouches of pearls they traded with the East India Company and a plentiful supply of good black hashish to smoke under the star-crusted sky every night, they were content. Allah, if He willed it, would keep the corsairs and the diver's madness far away. And if He did not will it so, who were they to question the divine judgment?

They had even agreed, with far less argument than either Gurney or Basreddin had expected, to commit themselves to a course which would traditionally bring down on their heads the worst possible luck: to allow a woman as supercargo. Helena had protested bitterly at being forced to wear the stuffy black garments, complete with veil, that were the everyday dress of the women of the gulf, but finally Gurney had persuaded her. Now she caught his eye from where she sat, at a discreet remove from her masters the menfolk, and projected even through the veil such a bolt of fury as should have withered him on the spot. He smiled at her, then abruptly stiffened his face as he became conscious of the diver's eyes on him.

As the light faded out and the first stars began to

twinkle in the deepening bowl of the sky, Gurney beckoned to Basreddin. "How much longer are we going to be here?"

"Their dialect is impure, and I myself find it hard to understand. But I have heard them speaking, and it seems that they intend to remain until the summer comes and the quas begins to blow."

"The qaus?"

"A summer wind which blows hard from the southeast."

"God, but we've got to be out of here by then. If we stay till the wind goes round to the east, we'll be bottled up until the winter comes around." Gurney ran his fingers through his hair.

"There is one thing . . ."

"Yes?"

Basreddin pursed his lips and spread his hands. "We have come down the coast as far as Hormuz, of which I have heard. It appears that in Hormuz there is a durbar, with much rejoicing and a profusion of distractions for the idle, at this time of year. In honor of a holy man whose tomb is nearby. Possibly I could persuade our fishing friends that they have spent too long at sea . . ."

Gurney leaned forward. "But how will you do this?"

Basreddin smiled slightly into his beard. "They are weak men, and avid for celebration at the expense of others. And curiously enough, I remember suddenly that my master Al-Hafiz once instructed me on this very day of this very month to make an offering of a tenth of all I had to my less fortunate brethren. In remembrance of my revered teacher, I must therefore make the gift. Also, I have the profits of my trading about me." He waved a deprecating hand.

Gurney had gone red beneath his tan. "No. I couldn't possibly ask you to give up your profits in my interest."

"In our interests, you mean. For I fully intend to accompany you to Cathay."

It took a moment for the implications of the words

to sink in. "To China?" True, he and Basreddin had come to know each other very well over the past months. And the man had saved his life, after all. But to accept his money—which is what, in effect, Gurney would be doing—would be to put himself under a different kind of obligation entirely. Never in his life had he put himself in the position of owing money to anyone, and he was damned if he was going to start now.

But Basreddin, as usual, was with him. "It would not be to place you under any obligation. Put aside your pride for the moment, and look with the eyes of right seeing. You are a happy man in that you have a goal. Myself, I have no goal but the perfection of my soul. But there is another part of me that wishes to experience the great sea, to travel where none of my kind have been before. And since you give me a purpose, I must do all I can in recompense." His eyes were boring into Gurney's, but in them was as much a pleading as a demanding. They were not as Gurney had seen them before, when he was trading, implacable and unforgiving. He pushed his scruples aside.

"Why not?" he said. "It will be a new experience for the both of us. I only hope you aren't seasick."

The lights of Hormuz glittered in the still water. Outside the harbor, a breeze was blowing from the northeast; but the anchorage, sheltered by a spur of high ground that projected two hundred feet into the gulf, was still as a millpond. The *Jewel of Loveliness* lay anchored two hundred yards offshore, with a kedge laid from her bow to the open water beyond the anchorage. At this time of year, the crew had assured Gurney, it was as well to count on the northeast breeze blowing for weeks on end.

He crouched in the stern sheets of the dhow, staring at the fires dancing in the water. Beside him, Helena, her veil flung back from her dark hair, was quiet too, absorbed in her own thoughts—a state in which she seemed to spend more and more time nowadays.

Gurney was dimly aware that something was changing between them, but the sea was in his blood now, and the scent of his quarry was rank in his nostrils. As for Helena, she spent her brooding times wondering at this young Englishman. When she had met him, it was as if each breath that he drew could have been his last; but with every league they had traveled down the river, he had changed before her eyes. In the slave coffle, the face had been rounded, innocent, surprised at the treatment meted out to its owner. A young face. On the kelek, though, the flesh had fallen away from the bones, and the eyes had become older and wiser, with a keen and questing stare, sometimes, that made even Helena shudder for his quarry when he caught up with that unfortunate, if treacherous, man. There was about him the look of a rangy hound that sniffs the air on a winter morning, then arrows away after the fox.

Judging by the number of fires and the music and hand-clapping which drifted to Gurney's ears from time to time, everyone was enjoying themselves a lot. He himself had declined the pressing invitations. He felt he should stay aboard in case anything went wrong. And besides, he could not bring himself to leave a ship unattended in a strange harbor. All his training rebelled against the idea, particularly since the *Jewel* was the only toothless pearling vessel in a harbor full of ships that looked much too fast for comfort. Anchored next to the *Jewel*, for instance, was a rakish felucca which entirely lacked the stoutness and solidity he would normally have expected of a fishing vessel. In fact, the only purpose Gurney could think of for her was as a fast, shallow-water, bombard-and-board ship.

For the thirtieth time in the past half hour, Gurney cast a wary eye around the harbor. All was quiet. His hackles rose as a scream, ending in a bubbling gurgle, came from the shore. But a burst of hoarse laughter cut it off short. Coast Arabs at their horseplay, no doubt. But the short hairs on his neck were still prickling a warning. Restless, he padded to the bow, then returned to his perch and resumed his vigil. Drowsiness crept over him; the lights on the water had turned into a slowly revolving fireworks display at Vauxhall when he suddenly felt Helena's hand on his arm.

"What's that?" she hissed, pointing. Was that a seal's head out there, at the periphery of his vision where the reflections shaded into blackness? He strained his eyes. Then he shook his head. "I'm not sure." Mind must be playing tricks. Too little food, too much sun.

He was lapsing into reverie again when the head reappeared. This time there was no mistaking it, though it broke surface only for a moment. The knife at his belt leaped into his hand, and he went flat on his stomach, motioned Helena to do likewise, and crept to the side. A minute passed. The hilt of the knife was growing damp in his hand, and his breathing was shallow. For there were no seals in the gulf, and even if there had been, they would not have come so close to the harbor. Of course, it could have been a log. But logs do not have white teeth that glint in the moonlight. Nor do they take a deep breath before they dive. In these parts, the Arabs learned to swim before they could walk; and they could swim underwater for five minutes. Gurney transferred the knife to his right hand and wiped his palm on his breechclout. Why should anyone be swimming, and swimming underwater, at this time of night? None of the pearlers would swim for pleasure, particularly in the garbage-strewn waters of the harbor, a veritable magnet for sharks; so it must be someone on business. And the only class of business anyone engaged in at this time of night was skulduggery pure and simple.

A rope creaked forward. The diver's ladder! They had left it hanging over the side when they had gone ashore, and Gurney had not thought to pull it up. He inched forward on his belly and waited, crouching behind the gunwale at the entry port. A hand—two hands—appeared over the rail. Then a head appeared, a blurred outline against the loom of the land. Gurney held his breath. As the man heaved himself up, Gurney grasped both wrists, pulling him off balance, planted his feet in his stomach, and fell backwards, hitting the deck with his shoulders. The intruder sailed over his head and thumped on his back between the masts. Gurney had picked himself up and was in midair even as the man landed, the breath driven out of his body with a noise like a punctured bladder; then Gurney was astride his prostrate body, a knee on each shoulder, knife point digging into his throat. Helena stood over them, with a stout wooden oar threateningly raised.

The man under him gasped for breath, but did not struggle. "Get off, you idiot," he said, "It is I, Basreddin. And keep quiet, for the love of your God."

"Thunder and hellfire, man," Gurney hissed, furious with relief. "What the hell do you mean by creeping back aboard like a bloody thief?"

"If anyone had seen me, we would both be dead. Those pirates on the shore—whom may Iblis fry!—have killed everyone of the crew of this vessel save you and me!"

"All of them? Eight men? Why, for heaven's sake?"

"Greed. The thin one—the diver—was foolish enough to boast of his riches. The idiot even showed them what I had given him. So naturally, our friends on shore assumed that each of the crew would be carrying a similar treasure. And that was that."

"How did you get away?"

Even in the darkness, Gurney could see Basreddin's eyes narrow. "That, my friend, is my business. Come, now. We must remove ourselves from this place and speedily."

"Right. Go forward and get the anchor. I'll make sail; then I'll come and help you with the kedge."

Helena watched Gurney as he hauled the rough grass halyards and the lateen yard inched up the mast. The muscles in his arms worked under the skin in the light from the shore. She wondered what had happened. Of one thing she was certain: that the Sufi Basreddin would not have gone into Hormuz for no reason. Therefore, it was quite obvious that he had knowingly goaded the drunken pearl diver into revealing his wealth to the piratical jackals who thronged the gulf ports. The rest would follow as night follows day. She shuddered, realizing once again the incomprehensible vastness and cruelty of Gurney's quest for his lost honor. As for Gurney, he was silent, angry with Basreddin for what he suspected had taken place. He had no wish, he told himself, to wade after Otway knee-deep in the blood of innocent bystanders, still less to smirch Arabella with its taint.

He grinned mirthlessly. Fair play. Well, that was all behind him since Otway had forcibly stripped him of his honor last February. All that mattered was to get to India, and to get there fast. He finished the halyard on its cleat with two half hitches and padded forward to where Basreddin was straining at the kedge line. The triangular sail flapped idly as the dhow inched out towards the headland. When she was directly above the grapnel, the breeze caught and she came up in irons, pointing to the northeast. Gurney ran aft and backed the sail, and her bow came round until the North Star twinkled above and behind his left shoulder as he stood at the tiller. The fires of Hormuz dwindled and died astern as the *Jewel of Loveliness* slipped into the dark night.

For the next five weeks, the wind blew steadily from the northeast. Only once did it seem that the *Jewel* had bitten off more than she could chew, and that was three days after her escape from Hormuz. While she was in harbor on the northern shore of the gulf to the east of Bandar Abbas to take on food and water, the qaus came whistling out of the south. The wind had bidden fair to pick up the dhow and smash her bodily into the line of dusty brown dunes between the harbor and the half-irrigated fields of the small settlement, but the anchor had held and a couple of days later, provisioned with water in plenty and a good stock of barley meal and dried goat's meat, they had put out to sea once again.

Gurney had profited by his time ashore. While Basreddin and Helena chaffered for supplies, he had engaged the head man of the village in conversation about fishing and the problems of navigation on that coast. They hit it off well, and eventually nothing would do but that Gurney should accompany the snaggletoothed old chieftain to his mud house, where, from a chest of oak bound with richly worked brass, he had pulled out the Admiralty charts of the coastline, vintage 1743. Not only did he stand by, beaming with pleasure, as Gurney traced the sections he thought important onto sheep's bladders, but he also presented him, with the air of a rajah bestowing the half of his kingdom on the successful suitor of his daughter, with an ancient, verdigris-crusted lump of brass which on closer inspection turned out to be a compass—probably considerably older even than the chart.

On their last night in the village, Basreddin had kept the entire population spellbound for an hour and a half with a narration of several of the less likely voyages of Sinbad. The subsequent rejoicings had gone on most of the night, and when they had nosed out of the anchorage at first light, the whole village had stood on the beach, shouting and firing long muskets into the air. Gurney had ducked and cursed, pushing Helena into the shelter of the deckhouse, as an overenthusiastic reveler, firing too low, sent a musket ball humming through the sail not three feet from his head. But Basreddin rebuked him for his ingratitude. Gunpowder was scarce in these parts, and its expenditure was a mark of great respect. Gurney spread his hands in exasperation and concentrated on trying to lay a course for Bombay, thirteen hundred miles to the southeast, with his crude navigational aids.

Often at night as he rode the tiny quarterdeck, the tiller a live thing against his hipbone, he thought of that thread that connected him with Otway ahead, Arabella behind. Under the slowly revolving constellations of the inky tropical sky, the phosphorescence

glittering at the dhow's counter, he could convince
himself that he was the dream and Arabella the
dreamer, his inventor. It was the fear that brought
him back; not a physical fear, of some emergency of
the moment, of pain or death, but a deep, rumbling
fear, a sense of his own impertinence in the face not
only of nature but also of the opinions of his fellows.
For he should have done the Right Thing—either
blown his brains out with a pistol or fled to Boulogne.
But instead here he was, flying in the face of nature
and the civilized world. And having initiated this
gesture—he sometimes wondered if, at its inception, a
gesture was all it had been—he had to go through with
it. Would rejoice in going through with it, naturally!
But the fear was fear of failure, that George Le Fanu
Gurney, the fire-eater, would be consumed by a fire
of his own lighting. For perhaps the first time in his
life, he felt utterly on his own. Previously, whether at
sea as a naval officer or on land in Norfolk or in the
drawing rooms and gaming halls of London, he had
always been a part of something that he knew. Now
it was as if his umbilical cord had been cut, and he
was drifting in a chaotic whirl in which he, Basreddin, and Helena were the only fixed points—dubiously
fixed, in the case of the last two.

Basreddin, for whom he had developed an enormous respect, remained largely mysterious; it was as
though his reference points were triangulated by
some process entirely alien to Gurney. But he thanked
God that the Sufi had turned up; after all, it was to
him that Gurney owed his life. Besides which he was
no mean fighter, and he certainly knew a thing or
two. Helena, too, remained a mystery. He had never
met any woman with her simple, direct approach to
life and its pleasures. Her body was like some marvelous instrument on which he and she together
made sweet music. There was an exotic fire to her
which elevated their lovemaking above a simple, animal need for solace. There were times when a mere
look from her could make the pulses hammer in his
throat, when for hours at a time they would tangle

and writhe in their sweat in the stinking cabin of the *Jewel of Loveliness*, then play like dolphins in the warm swells. But there were times, even in the extremity of passion, when Gurney would look at her face, flushed beneath its olive tan, the full lips parted, the thick lashes fluttering over her misted eyes, and feel the disturbing realization that she, too, was utterly alien to him. The language that each understood in the other was the language of the body. In a way, he reflected, she was like some irresistible drug, a means to transports of delight which left no residuum of guilt, no aftertaste. Gurney and she depended on each other as the human organism depends on food; but Gurney was beginning to wonder —as, to judge by her increasing periods of silence, was she—whether their special circumstances demanded special nourishment; whether they would feel a similar need for each other in different circumstances. Gurney could not decide whether she was beginning to cloy, as sweet things will, or whether his novelty for her was wearing off, leading her to cast her eyes elsewhere (had there, in the middle of the Indian Ocean, been anywhere else to cast them).

For all Gurney's passion for Helena, he was aware that the real link he had with sanity, the one thing on which he based his sanity in this mad wild-goose chase, was Arabella. He had meditated long on his vengeance on Otway. When he had embarked on the *Lady Ellen* at Rotherhithe, he decided, his thinking had been clouded by the kind of reflex which off Cuba had caused him in blind rage to drag himself up the quarterdeck ladder of Simon Le Maitre's privateer *Panique* and pistol its captain through the body, heedless that one foot was dragging behind him, smashed by a sharpshooter's musket ball from the *Panique*'s maintop. Since that time, the first flush of his anger had abated, and in the long days and nights of his voyaging it had cooled to a slow seething that he felt at times in the pit of his belly. What had become apparent to him was that his love for Arabella meant more to him than life itself. If, by revenging himself on Otway, he could win her back, then revenge himself on Otway he would. And it was not for his own sake alone that he was doing this. Arabella herself had cause to exact retribution from the man who had once intended—still did intend—to use her as a mere stepping-stone to his own sordid ends.

Gurney looked up at the moon, crescent in the sky. Under just such a moon he had ridden with Arabella at Mendlebury the day before his fateful conversation with the keeper, Zeb Watkins. The night had been clear, miraculously without frost, and he and Arabella were walking their horses down the back drive through the home coverts. Watkins, out late on who knew what errand, had touched his forelock to them as they passed through the gates into the home farm, and then they were out on Cranborne Chase, a great sweep of hill soaring before them, covered in tussocky winter grass. Arabella laughed and spurred her horse and was gone, a white blur speeding across the hillside in a thunder of hooves. Gurney shook his head and followed, bucketing in his saddle as his mount took the slope (Arabella always mocked his "typical sailor's seat") and breasted the brow of the ridge. Arabella was careening at insane speed into the deep splash of moon shadow that was the bottom of the valley. As he caught her, she turned, showing a flash of white teeth beneath her riding veil. Then they were galloping knee to knee along the old grass road that wound down the valley bottom, Arabella poised like a perched dove on the horns of her sidesaddle, towards an odd conical bump of hill crowned with a stone barn.

The air buffeted Gurney's face, and he felt his hat go, but he could not stop, caught up in the mad exhilaration of Arabella and the cool night air. She shouted to him, "Fifty guineas says I'm there before you!" Then she bent forward in the saddle, whispered in the gray mare's ear, and shot away from him like a bullet from a gun. When he came up to the barn, she was waiting, composed and demure, as if she were taking horse exercise in The Park; but there was nothing demure about the way she slid unassisted from her saddle and hitched her mare to the rail with a groom's knot, beckoning Gurney inside as she took off her hat and let her hair flow down in the moonlight.

The barn was full of winter feed, the sweet smell of the hay piled halfway to the roof, warm after the chill of the night. It was very dark, and Gurney stood still until he felt her hand on his arm. He spread his riding coat and they sat down. Her breath was warm against his cheek as she whispered, "Fifty guineas, my lieutenant. Or you can pay me another way." His lips sought hers, and they sank back into the springy hay. Her body was burning, lithe as a willow wand but soft and rounded under the serge of her riding habit. Gurney pushed her coat back and felt the swell of her breast under her silk blouse. She took his head in her hands and drew him down to her, moaning a little as she felt his weight. Then she pulled away.

"George, will you promise me one thing?"

"Whatever you will, my lady of the night."

"Be serious, damn you."

"Very well. What is it?"

"That if you are ever . . . like this . . . with another woman, you will never tell?"

He laughed. "Of course not; my lips will be forever sealed. Though how you could imagine that I could ever think of such a thing, God knows."

He drew her to him again. The flecks of moonlight shining through the broken tiles in the roof crept across the two bodies moving gently in the hay until the moon sank behind the hills.

Gurney sighed as he remembered that smooth darkness, shot with silver gleams and fanned by great opening petals of passion. Was she constant to him still? Even at this distance, he could not imagine otherwise, but the idea gnawed at his mind. If he could find temporary solace in Helena's arms, then

what would she be doing, she of the cool exterior
and the volcanic heart? But that did not bear thinking about. Gurney was committed now. He would
have her on no other terms than as a free man, honor
restored.

On the evening of the thirty-fifth day, Gurney,
straining his eyes over the bow as he had done for the
past week, saw a white speck drift over the horizon,
then vanish as the *Jewel* slid into a trough. He
climbed into the shrouds, his heart beating fast. If it
were only a European ship, they were nearly at journey's end. And none too soon; he, Basreddin, and
Helena had for the past ten days rationed themselves
to three pints of water each day, and the flour was
getting low as well as being mildewed by the constant sweating of the *Jewel's* hull. He found himself
talking to the ship, whispering encouragement as she
chopped her bow into each wave, riding her like a
horseman at a jump as she crested one roller and
slid down into the next. The strange ship was soon
hull-up on the horizon; screwing up his eyes, Gurney
could clearly see the three masts, each with its tier of
white sails, and from time to time a row of yellow
gun ports. He let his shoulders relax. She was heading,
according to his compass, more or less due east; that
should mean that she was in the final approaches to
the great port of Bombay.

The sun was low in the sky when the *Jewel of Loveliness* rounded under the towering stern of the Indiaman *John W. Higgins.* Two stories of gleaming glass
windows, glittering in the reddening rays of the sun,
looked blankly down at the *Jewel.* Gurney's hands
were suddenly trembling as he gripped the tiller. The
Jewel had been his world for five long weeks. The
sheer size of the Indiaman was one thing; but her
immaculate paintwork, the dully gleaming curlicues
of gold leaf that decorated the intricately massive
carving of her stern gallery, and the vast rudder,
whose ponderous movements bespoke mighty ma-

chinery in the bowels of the ship—these, to Gurney, who for months now had seen no engine more complicated than the shadoof, the simple weighted lever the Arabs used to scoop buckets of water from the river, were the awesome part. Suddenly he was back in civilization, and it was as if there were two men inside his skull, one a sophisticate, taking this profligate ingenuity for granted, and the other a pop-eyed primitive, amazed and openmouthed before a technology of which he had no understanding. He glanced at Basreddin. The Sufi should by rights have been far more shocked than him; but he was simply standing, staring from under lowered lids at the Indiaman.

A blue-coated, brass-buttoned man—by his reddish brown complexion, Gurney guessed he was one of the officers of the Indiaman—was leaning over the poop rail. The officer cupped his hands and shouted, "Hey, you! Nigger! Fruitee? Apple? Orange?"

It had been a hard trip. The fresh meat had run out only a few leagues this side of the Cape, and the passengers were restless and quarrelsome. Only two days out they were now, but the spoiled brats—particularly the ladies, blast them—couldn't wait. So he must needs bellow like a costermonger at every boat they passed, trying to satisfy their whims. As if those two black villains and their woman, practically naked, in a boat that was not only rotting visibly but that he could smell even from where he stood, would be carrying crates of fruit with them. The officer's temper, never far from the surface, boiled over at the three gaping, salt-crusted figures in the dhow. "All right, you black bastards, so you have no fruit. I know you haven't. You know you haven't. But our bloody passengers, bless their spoiled little hearts, have asked me to try. Just, *try, please, dear,* Lieutenant Alcott. Well, for two pins I'd put a roundshot straight through the bottom of your bloody little hooker."

The taller of the two men in the dhow bowed deeply, sheeted the mainsail, and veered away on the

Indiaman's quarter. A mocking voice rang across the water, singing a song popular some years earlier in the less salubrious haunts of Deptford:

> I would not join the navy, I was frightened for my arse;
> At the thought of cannon and musket shot, I turned as green as grass.
> I could not stay in England lest old Boney should invade,
> So I away to John Company to become a ladies' maid.
> Oh, I am a company officer, a perfect ladies' maid.

Then the dhow disappeared towards the eastern horizon, leaving Alcott crimson and openmouthed until the ladies came and patted him on the arm, assuring him that there, there, he was such a good kind man to have tried so hard to get them some fruit, and what nasty rude impudent savages they were. But the mortified Alcott still couldn't understand how an Arab fisherman in the approaches to Bombay could be singing vulgar songs in a perfect upper-class English accent.

As the swift tropic dusk turned to black night, the wind blew fresh from the west. Gurney and Helena sat beneath the rounded triangle of the sail, staring out over the smooth heave of the swell, now sharpening as the seabed swooped up towards the land. The moon was full now, and Helena's sun-darkened skin was almost black in its light, shining like satin. When she turned to him, she was smiling. Gurney felt a familiar heat rising in him as she laid her head on his shoulder.

"Giorgiou?"

"Yes?"

"When will we arrive in Bombay?"

"With luck, tomorrow."

She sighed, and a cloud passed over her face. "Tomorrow. That is soon, my Giorgiou. Very soon."

"Hmm." Gurney was perplexed, and was going to

ask what she meant. Of course tomorrow was soon.
But her lips sought his ear, and the exciting present
soon distracted him from thoughts of the morrow.

That night their lovemaking was more passionate
that it had been in weeks. Helena seemed to abandon
herself to the great tides of sensation that gripped
both of them, flung them at each other, and left them
drained and exhausted, only to return once again and
drive them to fresh heights. Gurney fell into a light
sleep with Helena twined about him like ivy, her
black hair spread across his chest and her breasts soft
against his side. She stayed awake for a little while,
watching the regular rise and fall of his chest, the
spikes of yellow hair plastered to the slick scar tissue
at his right temple, the square jaw firm and implacable even in sleep. Then she gently disentangled herself from him. Her eyes were dim with tears as she
kissed him, once, at the point where the flat ridges
of muscle at his stomach peaked at the point of his
rib cage. She lay back, pulled the blankets over her,
and whispered, "Good-bye, my Giorgiou." Soon she,
too, fell asleep.

When Gurney awoke four hours later, it was still
dark. He struck flint and steel and looked at the hour-
glass. Only a few grains of sand remained above the
narrow waist. His turn on watch. As he went on deck,
his brow was creased with thought. It was time to decide about Helena, Arabella, and the like. Although
it would never have occurred to him to question his
love for Arabella, there was no doubt that Helena
made a most agreeable traveling companion. Perhaps
she would continue with them to the East? Gurney
found himself wishing she would, and shook his head
angrily. Ridiculous. He had spent too much time with
heathen Muhammadans. Still, it would make life
easier if a man could have two wives. He grinned,
imagining Arabella and Helena pouring tea for the
local gentry in the drawing room at Mendlebury. Then
he dismissed the idea impatiently. Time enough for
whimsy and women when he was ashore in Bombay.

Basreddin, at the *Jewel's* tiller, was a patch of

blacker blackness against the stars. The moon had set some time previously, and the Sufi's voice was tired.

"Welcome. This has been a weary watch. I confess I shall be glad to see land again."

"Ah, you old bargee. Go and get some sleep, and we'll have you ashore in no time. Good night."

Basreddin went below, and Gurney balanced himself loosely at the tiller, following the swing of the compass card in the dim light of the improvised binnacle. Two hours later, first one light, then another, popped over the horizon until the invisible line where sky met sea blazed like a string of jewels, fading into the advancing dawn.

6

The dining room of Toby Waterford's house on Malabar Hill was a lofty chamber, the walls pilastered with white marble on a ground of sky blue. The furniture and pictures were in the new taste, that is to say about a year behind London; for Waterford was a man of some elegance, who appreciated the luxuries of life. Not for him the grubby penny-pinching of some of his fellow merchants; in his view, part of the mercantile skill out here was to maintain a certain style. For it was men like him, men living in the other elegant white houses on Malabar Hill, raised above the docks and stews of Bombay, that had made this the foremost trading city of western India. Indeed, it was said by many that Calcutta, since time immemorial the chief marketplace of the East, was beginning to become nervous of its western rival. Waterford pushed away his breakfast plate and sipped coffee from a thin bone china cup. The turbaned butler cleared the table and, according to ritual, placed a

copy of the *Morning Post*, folded twice, beside his
master's coffee cup. Waterford picked it up and began
to read, as he had every morning for the past five
years. That the newspaper was precisely one year out
of date, having arrived with a bundle of its fellows on
an Indiaman some four weeks ago, mattered not at
all to him. A creature of habit, he had always found
the digestive process was greatly eased by the post-
prandial perusal of a few soothing columns of close-
set black type.

The butler was at his shoulder again, clearing his
throat. Waterford frowned. "Well, what is it, man?"

"There is one without, sahib." A conflict of strong
emotions showed on the man's face. "He says he must
see you immediately."

Waterford's gastric juices gave a warning rumble.
"He must see me? Well, don't just stand there! Who
is it? What does he want?"

The butler looked deeply unhappy. "He says, sahib,
that he will tell you and you alone. He is a very violent man."

"Throw him out, then. Good God, what d'you think
you're doing?"

"But, sir, he is a sahib also. Or he is and is not a
sahib. If you take my meaning."

Waterford made a noise like a kettle coming suddenly to the boil and rose to his feet, flinging the
paper across the room. Ruined. Irretrievably ruined.
He didn't ask much. Only to be left in peace after
breakfast. But no, not only did sahibs-who-weren't-
sahibs come tracking up to his front door in droves,
but his servants didn't even have the simple sense to
throw them out. He sighed and went into the hall.

His visitor started to his feet, knocking over the
spindly chair on which he had been sitting. He apolo-
gized profusely and bent to pick it up, then straightened and bore down on the merchant. Waterford
kept a straight face with an effort. The man was about
twenty-five, he guessed, very tall and painfully thin,
with skin the color of tanned hide and pale, almost
colorless hair, cropped short over the square, clean-

shaven face. On the right temple was a scar, which was pulsing slightly as he lowered his head and brought his hand to forehead, lips, and heart in a salaam. Halfway through the gesture, he seemed to recollect himself and extended his right hand in greeting.

"Good day to you, sir, and my apologies for so early a call."

The voice was powerful but soft, and there was a strange accent to it, as if it were unused to shaping English words. Waterford returned the greeting, surveying his visitor with some puzzlement. The man stood up straight enough, and his eyes were level and confident. But his clothes were extraordinary, to say the least. The white duck trousers gave up the unequal struggle halfway down his shins, and his bottle-green coat had been made at least ten years ago for someone at least five stone heavier. On his feet he wore a disreputable pair of buffalo-hide sandals.

"I wonder if I could trespass on your good nature for ten minutes or so?"

Waterford had not become one of the richest men in Bombay by refusing to indulge his own curiosity, and he waved the young man into his bureau. They were silent until the butler brought more coffee. The young man put six spoonfuls of sugar into his cup, picked it up by the side opposite the handle, and slurped vigorously. Then, feeling his host's eyes on him, he colored.

"I am sorry, sir. I should certainly explain myself. But first I must apologize for my manners, which have been rather tainted by the time I have spent of late with the bedouin. I am George Le Fanu Gurney, late of His Majesty's Navy, and I was given your name a long time ago by Admiral Sir Jervis Hutchison, who had his pennant on the *Egregious,* on which I had the honor to be a lieutenant."

The merchant took a thoughtful sip of his coffee, to gain time. Though he read his newspapers late, he read them closely. And he remembered this man's

name. Something about a card scandal, if he wasn't
mistaken. Certainly didn't look like a cardsharp—too
clumsy, for a start. But you could never tell. He
looked levelly across his morocco-topped desk at Gurney, who was shifting in his seat, unnerved by the
merchant's silence.

"Good. I am always pleased to meet a friend of Jervy's." His eyes were several degrees cooler than his
voice. Not much hope here, thought Gurney, suddenly
miserable. He had permitted himself to dream a little
about his return to the world of the British Empire,
the world he knew, but now it seemed that he was
to be a stranger to his own as well as to the savage
and strange. An outcast.

Waterford watched his face fall, and came to the
conclusion that he had been right. The man was disgraced and guilty. He congratulated himself on his
perceptiveness.

"What can I do for you?"

Gurney was hesitant now. "I was wondering . . .
could you give me and my traveling companion some
advice on a passage from here to the China coast?
For it is there that we are bound, having but yesterday landed from Arabia."

"Arabia?" Waterford's voice was heavy with disbelief. Gurney leaned forward in his chair. The other
man's air of ill-suppressed impatience was beginning
to irritate him, and he took a couple of deep breaths
to quell his rising anger.

"Yes, sir, Arabia, whence I sailed in a misbegotten
pearling dhow, arriving yesterday. If you do not believe me, you may ask the quartermaster on the Indiaman *John W. Higgins;* he will have a recollection
of our meeting, I'll be bound."

Waterford pursed his lips and shrugged. "If you
say so. Now, as regards your passage east. There are
several ways. First, the Indiaman. It is none of my concern why you did not take passage on a Company
ship from England"—Gurney seemed to be about to
expostulate, but the merchant overrode him—"but I

assume there was good reason. Failing a Company ship, I suggest you sign on with a country trader on the Coromandel coast."

"Country trader?"

"Ah, I was forgetting. You are a stranger to these parts. The country traders buy from the Company and trade privately with the Far East. If you hurry from here to Madras—and it is no short distance—you may catch a late trader outward bound." He rose to his feet and bowed coldly. "And now, *Mister* Gurney, good day." His portrait by Zoffany stared arrogantly down at Gurney from the wall.

Dismissed. Gurney reddened. So his disgrace had spread as far as India. Had he been a leper, Waterford would have done everything in his power to speed him on his way east. But as it was, the man could not be expected to care whether he lived or died. He turned on his heel and brushed past the butler into the hall, knocking over another spindly chair. This time he did not stop to pick it up.

After the front door had slammed behind him, Waterford dabbed at his brow with a cream silk handkerchief. A most disturbing young man. It was far from surprising that England was too hot to hold him if that was how he usually comported himself. He sighed and walked through the open French windows and across the smooth green lawn to the rose garden, where the peacocks were preening and strutting in the brilliant light.

As Gurney descended the hill, leaving the tall white house behind him, the sea was an aching blue. A British merchantman was standing for home beneath a snowy pyramid of canvas, and he felt a momentary tug at his heart. Home, to Arabella. Then he turned and started back down the road to the teeming heart of the city.

The noise increased steadily. For the first time in his life, he knew what the Tower of Babel must have sounded like before it was laid low. Even London at its densest had never been like this. He plunged into

the thrashing, jostling crowds that jammed the alleyways and thoroughfares of the city, cursing and being
cursed, deafened by the noise, surrounded, cramped.
His disgust at Waterford receded before his curiosity.
After the long months of desert, river, and sea, the
seething streets of the great port were like a tonic.
Gurney usually hated crowds, but now he wallowed
in the throngs like a water buffalo in a flooded rice
paddy.

When he arrived at the temple steps where he had
left Basreddin and Helena, he could see no sign of
them. The temple formed one side of a square; in
front of it, three roads met. Gurney climbed the steps,
ignoring the beggars who plucked at his sleeve, until
he had a bird's-eye view of the crowd that surged
around the handful of scrubby palms in the middle of
the square. In one corner, away from the main thoroughfare, the crowd was thicker than anywhere else,
and in the middle of it he thought he caught a
glimpse of a green turban. He hurried across, using
his elbows relentlessly, and pushed to the front. Sure
enough, in the middle of a tiny circle cleared by a
couple of self-appointed marshals, Basreddin sat. Gurney gathered that he was just concluding the story of
two more of the voyages of Sinbad. Facing him and
translating the Arabic simultaneously into Tamil was
a dark-skinned boy of about ten. When the story
ended, Basreddin rose from the mat he had spread
on the ground. The square was emptying out.

Gurney looked around him. "Where's Helena?" he
asked.

Basreddin's face was an impenetrable mask. Gurney's heart began to thump in his chest. "Well? Where
is she?" His voice was higher than it should have been.

The Sufi wordlessly handed him a packet sealed
with red wax. Gurney tore it open and took out a
letter. A lock of black hair fell out, and he bent slowly
to pick it up. It lay like a question mark in the palm
of his hand, and for a moment he stared at it, certain of what it meant. Then he sat down in the dust
and began to read.

Giorgiou,

Do you remember that I said to you once that I was afraid that I should be crushed between you and your quest? I realized afterward that there was another possibility—that you and I would remain with each other for too long, that you would never return to the world you knew, and that you would hate me for keeping you from it. Do not try to deny it.

I have watched you now for a long time, and I have seen it in your eyes and heard it when you call out for your Arabella in your sleep.

Giorgiou, I owe you the greatest debt that any woman can owe any man: you saved my life and you gave me your love. But the burden of the debt is on my side only, and I cannot let you live to regret it. I have taken passage for Europe on a merchantman. By the time you read this, I shall be beyond your recall.

When I arrive in England, I shall send news of you to your Arabella. When you think of her, think sometimes of me.

Perhaps we shall meet again: until then, farewell. May your revenge be as sweet as our love.

Helena

The words swam before Gurney's eyes, and he let the letter slip to the ground. He should have known. Those silences, the barrier between them. Fool that he was not to have talked to her before now. Or had he wanted her to go? Was it true, what she said about being crushed? But, then, what had been his intentions? Only the night before, he had in his weakness postponed making a decision. And now it was too late.

A lump rose in his throat. He became aware that Basreddin's hand was on his shoulder. The Sufi's eyes met his. The face was impassive as ever behind the thick black beard, but the eyes were deep wells of pity and understanding. As they bored into Gurney's, it was as if Helena suddenly became smaller in his mind, and he became aware of his surroundings.

Then the eyes changed a little, and he found himself thinking of Otway. It was as if his heart had started to beat again. He rose to his feet and dusted himself off, filled with a sense of purpose. The pain was still there, but now it was a goal, driving him on. He looked eastward and vowed again that Otway would feel the weight of his vengeance, and soon.

Basreddin showed him an earthenware bowl full of copper coins. "We have not done badly," he said. "And were it not for this one who translates so nimbly, we would have fared ill indeed."

Gurney looked at the child. A singularly ill-favored infant, when you came down to it. His right arm was twisted and withered, and his whole body, naked but for a scrap of dirty red and yellow rag twisted around his loins, was covered with smallpox scars. But his eyes were bright with intelligence, and it seemed, from the way he followed Basreddin at a distance of about two feet, that having found a meal ticket, he was not lightly going to let it go. The brat spoke passable Arabic.

"What is your name?"

"Gupta."

"Where are your people?"

"I have no people. My mother was a widow. We were untouchables in a village. My mother got hungry, died with my brother. Men in the village throw stones, hit arm, hurt. Run like hell. Walk three, four months, come to Bombay. Like. Stay."

"Well, you'd better come with us. We're for Madras."

Gupta's face split open in a huge grin. "Very good, sahib." His eyes narrowed, with a shrewdness far beyond his years. "One thing. We eat often?"

Gurney laughed despite himself. "Twice a day. Come, we start now." And the three of them began to walk, out of the city, toward the mountains to the east.

That night he lay in a hut, thinking. In the patch of beaten earth that served as the village's meeting place, Basreddin and Gupta were regaling a fascinated crowd with their tales. Basreddin's nasal half-

chant and Gupta's piping translations, interspersed
with groans of wonder and shouts of laughter from
their audience, came to his ears, muffled by the crumbling mud walls. Gurney missed Helena's presence, but
the pain was dulled now, and his overriding emotion
was one of anger—anger at himself for having allowed himself to be distracted from his purpose. But
then, he told himself, he would never have found the
strength to escape from Achmet Bizound's slave coffle
had Helena not loved him back to sentience in the
mountains of Turkey. And she was safe, in good
hands. Basreddin had confessed to him that he had
helped her find a passage to England; Gurney had
been furious at first, but his fury had died under Basreddin's assurance that it had been at her own insistence; and it was better that Basreddin, with his
apparently infallible judgment of human nature, should
have chosen her a captain than that she would have
picked one at random. The sea passage home was
long, and a ship's company could turn ugly over a
single woman in the lonely months of voyaging. Particularly a woman as beautiful as Helena. Gurney's
hands clenched into fists as he thought of what might
have been. And she would give news of him to Arabella. She would be discreet, of that he was sure; but
that did not prevent him from feeling mean, treacherous. Lying in the mosquito-pinging dark, he made
Arabella a silent promise. He would look neither right
nor left until he had caught up with Otway and visited upon him his just deserts.

The mosquitoes were becoming impossible. He rose
and went outside, to the smudge fire in the meeting
square. The dervish and Gupta were seated side by
side, approaching the end of their epic, surrounded by
a rapt audience of some twoscore girls, the oldest of
whom must have been about thirteen. Their faces
were heavily painted, and their black hair, shining
with oil, fell in thick ringlets to their shoulders. Gupta,
looking up, caught Gurney's eye and rolled his eyes
and licked his lips suggestively.

When Basreddin got up, Gurney went over to him.

"What is this place? Those young ladies have a look of being, ah, no better than they should be."

"This is Chatoogly, a village of no note whatever, so Gupta tells me, except for the large number of its child whores. They are true barbarians, these honest Hindus"—this last as a spindly child of about ten summers undulated suggestively at him, throwing out her almost entirely flat chest and fluttering her eyelashes. "These are the brides of old men, who marry from vanity when they are on their deathbeds and the women are seven or eight years of age. When they die, the girls are left widowed, and they are consigned for the rest of their lives to the brothel."

"Good God." Gurney was appalled. "Barbarous indeed. Well, I'm for turning in. There's a long road ahead, and we should start betimes."

The next morning as they set out, nothing stirred in the village save a yellow cur, which barked at their heels as they marched up the dusty road toward the mountains. It was a wearisome journey, and for Gurney the days merged into each other in a long, pale, brownish, dust-clogged, poverty-stricken procession, trailing one after the other, each differing from the last only in the number of coins or the amount of millet in the begging bowl. The scenery and the poverty of the people were uniformly dreary, and his spirits flagged. His two companions found it more and more difficult to communicate with him; fever racked his bones, and he sometimes awoke in the chill of the night drenched in a sick sweat. His flesh wasted until he felt almost transparent; weak, stringy, blackened by the burning sun, he was sustained only by the knowledge that if he did not reach the Coromandel coast and Madras before the last of the traders left on the northeast monsoon, a year would be gone from his life in vain.

And there was a fire burning within him that had been fanned to flame by Helena's departure—the same fire that had driven him to set out from England in pursuit of his honor. But now, in his feverish thirst,

in the furnace heat of the sun and the bitter smoke of
the fires that swept down on the Deccan from the
hills, leaving barren earth and the skeletons of cattle,
his very life was at stake. It seemed to him as he
awoke each day to the misery of the weary journey
that it was only his goal—Arabella—that kept him
alive. Basreddin was eyeing him strangely these days,
and Gupta, who normally trudged along at the Sufi's
side, chattering gravely, his eyes darting about him in
his young-old face, seemed to have developed for him
a respect not inconsiderably colored with fear. As for
Gurney, in his fever dreams Otway mocked him,
beckoned him across the miles; and Gurney used the
dogged anger his dreams engendered as a furnace
uses fuel.

Then, when they had been on the road six weeks, a
curious thing happened. They had stopped for the
night at a small village of mud houses, and at nightfall, Basreddin, as was his wont, had unrolled his
mat on the baked and beaten earth of the square
and delivered his opening lines. Gurney was sitting
—squatting, rather—against the crumbling bricks of
a ruined house by the side of the square, awaiting his
cue to take the bowl around, when a voice hissed in
his ear. He turned, startled. Two luminous eyes were
staring at him. In the starlight, he saw the sticklike
figure of a sadhu with a mane of white hair leaning
against the wall at his side. The eyes, black and enormous, seemed to look right through him. But they
were kindly, not threatening, and he found himself
basking in the light that came pouring through them
as a lizard basks in the sun.

Suddenly he was filled with hope. He laughed as he
thought of the hatred that had filled him during the
past few weeks; now he saw that it was only guilt and
offended pride which had brought him so low. Lord,
they had money, they had lodging for the night, and
the end of the journey was in sight. Besides which,
it was a beautiful evening, the stars were shining like

diamonds, and the village girls were both alluring and allured. He got to his feet, suddenly very hungry. The holy man giggled and melted into the darkness.

Later, he told Basreddin of his visit, and the Sufi stared at him. "Giorgiou," he said, putting his hands together, "I have talked to the villagers long tonight while you slept in the shadows. There is no sadhu in this place. But one old man to whom I spoke remembers in his childhood just such a one as he of whom you speak. Even at that time, the sadhu was burdened with years beyond counting; and even then, he was an inspirer of heroes. Truly, it seems that you have been visited by a ghost."

The next day they met a caravan from the coast, a creaking procession of bullock carts mounded with cheap and gaudy Birmingham cotton. From them they learned that the last of the country traders was reported to have left Calcutta and to be heading down to Madras to take on cargo for the Far East run. If the teller of tales and his companions wished to take ship, they should be sure to arrive within the next ten days. This would not be difficult, for even with the bullock carts it had taken only seven days.

On the evening of the fifth day, the sky ahead was a dirty yellow in the evening light. Gurney inquired of a peasant as to the reason. "It is the dust from the hooves of the million cows of Madras," the man replied.

The citizens of the great city of Madras liked to think they were hard to impress; but the three travelers under the chappati seller's awning attracted more than a few curious glances. The one with the face like an owl, chatting amiably with the untouchable child, had a strange air of foreignness; but the one with the blue eyes and fair beard, whose face bore the lines of great pain even when you discounted the scar at his right temple, had the mien of an Englishman. True, his limbs were emaciated and his ribs stuck out from under his brown skin like the ribs of a basket, but there was about him of scrawny strength, a sense of coiled threat, which put the more impressionable in mind of Rama in one of the more warlike of his aspects.

Gurney pointed down the slight slope toward the blue line of the horizon. Basreddin nodded, took Gupta by the arm, and they set off for the docks, the dervish continuing his animated discouse, illustrating it with many pointings and waves of the hand, and Gurney forging a way through the dense mass of small, dark Tamils who clogged the streets, accumulating like wreckwood in the eddies and flowing in all directions in the center of the thoroughfare. But he noticed none of them. His eyes were fixed on the straight blue edge of sea at the end of the road.

7

Ingo Baulch, captain of the *White Rajah*, had only five minutes ago roused himself from a deep, open-mouthed slumber, and as a result was looking at the world with a somewhat jaundiced eye. He sat on the edge of his cot and bellowed for Fong, his Chinese servant, pouring himself a shaky tumbler of brandy. The half bottle he had drunk at noon was sitting uneasily on his stomach, and from time to time he belched corrosively; but after he had choked down a couple of good swallows, he felt better.

Fong, who had been listening at the door, judged the moment auspicious and entered, carrying his master's voluminous breeches. As he aided the obese Baulch in cramming his huge buttocks into their duck coverings, he grinned and hissed in his teeth. "Three men, seamen, boss, come see, on deck."

Baulch nodded and belched, screwing his podgy

face up in a grimace of disgust. Then he knocked back
a final gulp of brandy, settled his round black hat
(once, in earlier and less alcoholic days, he had been
the pastor of the Unity Tabernacle, in Limehouse)
on his head, and stumped up the wormy steps that
led from the stern cabin of his ship to the waist.

On deck, Gurney, Basreddin, and Gupta were
crouching on their haunches in the shade of the port
bulwark. The sun had not yet settled behind the towers and hovels of the great city, and the wind had
dropped; even here in the outer harbor, the air
was stiflingly hot. Baulch looked the trio over with an
eye that refused to focus properly. Ordinary enough
men, he thought. Something funny about the tall feller, but he looked sound enough. And sound crews
had become less and less easy to find over the past
few trips. He smiled, unctuously. Gurney raised his
eyebrows a fraction at the fat jowls twitched back
from the moist lips.

"Well, well, well. Well," Baulch chuckled fatly, en-
gulfing the three of them in his oily condescension,
"do any of you speakee English?"

Gurney nodded curtly. The hair rose at the nape of
his neck; this man was too much like Otway for comfort.

"Good, good, good. Then you can interpret for your
friends. Hmm? Hm? Hm? We run a happy ship." A
sweeping gesture of his pudgy arm took in the rattan
shelter at the break of the high forecastle, under
which four or five lascars lay, eyes glazed, round a
lighted lamp. "Though we can't afford to pay what
the Indiamen pay." The piggy eyes were suddenly
flinty and suspicious. "One rupee the quarter, and
think yourselves lucky. Yes? Yes. Yes." Gurney
nodded again.

Baulch made a sign, and Fong darted back into the
aftercabin, returning with a large leather-bound book,
an inkwell, and a pen. Baulch began to write in a
shaky hand. Gurney could just read what he set
down. He headed a new page of the ledger, "Three

Heathen Hindoos Shem, Ham, Japheth. Signed on this day July 10th, anno 1820, five annas weekly, all sound."

Gurney frowned despite himself. "But it's only June yet," he blurted out.

Baulch drew himself up to his full five feet four inches, his brows drawn low over his red eyes. "And what is that to you?" A hand darted out; Gurney felt his ear gripped firmly between two moist fingers. Baulch pulled his head down until they were nose to nose. The sour brandy on his breath blasted warmly into Gurney's face. "Who taught you to talk back to your betters? And, for that matter, to read? I am watching you, and I hope for your sake that you are as good a seaman as you are a forecastle lawyer. If you don't like the contract, you can get yourself off the ship."

Gurney sprang back, quivering with rage. Basreddin caught his elbow with a warning hand. George calmed himself, relaxing as he had learned to do in the past four months, assuming the whine of the aggrieved beggar. "I'm sorry, sir, truly I am. 'Course, not for a moment was I suggesting that . . ."

Baulch puffed up like a turkey-cock and waved a dismissive hand. "Consider the incident closed. But don't do it again. Now. Your marks." Gupta signed with a shaky cross, Basreddin with a flourishing scrawl of Persian script, and Gurney, in a deliberately crabbed flourish, with "J. Keats." Baulch looked down briefly, said, "Capital, capital, capital," turned on his heel, and disappeared down the companionway to his day cabin, leaving Fong behind on deck with his three new hands.

The Chinaman, having assured himself that his master was safely out of sight, spat juicily at the closed cabin door, jerked a thumb forward, and said, patronizingly, "Pigman drinkum now all night, number one rum. You going there quick quick. Maybe two day, maybe three, we sail Macao, chop, chop. Next year, we get Macao. Then I go overside. But you stay here on ship, because you dumb animals. Now go."

And Gurney, seething, turned meekly on his heel and shuffled toward the men at the forecastle, followed by Basreddin and Gupta.

If this were not the last ship heading out of Madras for the China seas for months, and his discreet inquiries at the quayside had confirmed that this was indeed the case, the captain and his henchman would have been lying unconscious on the deck, and the three travelers would have been long gone. Gurney sighed, clambered up the forecastle ladder onto the foredeck, and ran a professional eye over the ship that would, by the grace of God, be his home for the next few months.

It was apparent that whoever had built her had taken considerable pride in his work. But it was equally apparent that his profession had not been that of shipwright. While every beam end, plank, and spar that could bear ornament was carved to within an inch of its life in the ponderous baroque style of a hundred years ago, the lines of the ship resembled nothing so much as a landsman's idea of a Spanish galleon.

Her three masts were innocent of topgallants. Gurney guessed that under such a press of canvas she would wallow like a pig in labor, but he doubted that the bilious Baulch would ever have summoned up the courage or commercial enthusiasm to put it to the test. And the spars that remained, made, like the rest of the ship, from dark brown, stringy teak timbers, were cracked and many times fished. All in all, however, given light breezes from abaft the beam over the whole of her voyage, the *White Rajah*, in his opinion, stood a reasonable chance of reaching her port of destination. Though a reasonable chance, as Ivo Dauncey had often pointed out to him over a hand of whist in the gaming rooms at Vernon's, might be no better than fifty-fifty. Gurney had always ignored such precise calculation of odds, preferring to trust to an indefinable something he referred to (to himself, naturally;

he would not have dreamed of mentioning it to anyone else) as his luck. It had carried him unscathed—
well, almost unscathed—from the West Indies, through
the gaming hells of London and disgrace across
the Mediterranean through Turkey, Arabia, and India
to Madras; and there was no reason he could see that
it should desert him now. Not that he wasn't superstitious; he held as talismans his devotion to Arabella
and his burning hatred for the conniving Mathias Otway, and it seemed that any action performed in furtherance of these widely separated, yet closely linked,
attachments could not but have a successful outcome.
At times he felt like a new King Arthur, protected
like the king by a talisman of invulnerability which
would turn away the bullets and blows of his enemies provided his cause was just; and at others he
cursed himself for a drawing room romantic, a fowler
after wild geese, for deliberately putting his neck in
jeopardy for no other reasons than will-o'-the-wisps
of love and vengeance. But it was scarcely practical
to reflect on such philosophical matters at this moment in time.

He turned to Basreddin. The Sufi had been very silent of late, reserved and withdrawn, leaving the plan-
ning of their everyday life to George and limiting
himself entirely to the role of traveling fakir. Almost
as if he believed in those conjuring tricks, thought
George, while admitting inwardly that he did too, and
with some justification.

Three days later, the *White Rajah* dragged herself
out of the harbor under dirty topsails. The sun was
only just above the water; a sickly breeze blew off the
shore, filling the sails with the stench of the city. A
fine, gritty dust was in the wind. It got into Gurney's
eyes and ears and crunched between his teeth as he
finished his morning rice.

Baulch, in his cabin, was setting a course, for the
thirteenth time in his life, for the Sunda Strait between Java and Sumatra. His Negro mate, Jamshid,
stood at his shoulder, puzzling over the stained chart

on the table, pretending to take an intelligent interest.
Jamshid's profound stupidity was equaled only by his
enormous strength. He had spent the dawn hours
clubbing and flogging the crew into some semblance
of activity, and had now come, as was his custom at
the beginning of the *White Rajah*'s trading voyages,
to bask once again in the warmth of his master's ap-
proval.

Baulch, who had been refreshing himself without
benefit of sleep since six o'clock the previous evening,
was in full flood. All the rhetoric of his days at the
tabernacle returned to him; he saw his trade as a
new mission to the heathen Chinese, himself as a new
Carey, for salvation bound. "Oh Jamshid, my black
brother," he pontificated, "though your skin, as the
sublime Blake himself points out, is black, I know
your heart is white. And as we stand together, on the
brink of a new voyage to parts unknown in quest of
the salvation of the yellow heathen"—Baulch, in his
own way, was a great romantic—"it is fitting that
we lift up our voices in prayer to our maker." Jamshid,
a devout Muslim, but an even more devout toady, fell
shamelessly to his knees. Baulch, in deference to his
grossness and intoxication, rose to his feet, bowed his
head, and planted his beringed hands on the chart
table. "O Lord," he extemporized, "give us fair winds
and calm sea on this, our great journey to enlighten
the dwellers in darkness. And may each penny spent
give of its increase a hundredfold, and the black pox
take the swine of an agent who sent us off last of all
this year, with a load of brummagem cotton and
moldy opium. And grant us," he said, recollecting himself, "the ability to live together, white and black, master with man, as brothers in the sight of the Lord.
Amen. Now get up on deck, Jamshid, and larrup the
hide of any of those bastards that isn't earning his
daily bread."

Jamshid rose to his feet, grinning. That was an in-
struction he understood. As he closed the door behind
him, Baulch was pouring himself another glass of
brandy, his lips moving in silent prayer, bestowing

large and emotional blessings on the city of Madras
as it receded into the heat haze beyond the broad
windowpanes of the stern gallery. A pink lizard ran
across the ceiling, and he greeted it with a solemn bow.
It was an old friend of his.

After the initial flurry of activity as they left the
harbor, the *White Rajah*'s crew had settled back into
something approaching their customary state of apa-
thy. The rattan awning had been rerigged, the long
pipes were out, and the musty fumes of opium spread
through the forecastle quarters where Gurney lay on a
rush sleeping mat, hands locked behind his head, eyes
closed in thought. Two days ago, the forecastle had
been slimy with filth and crawling with vermin. It
had taken some persuasive talk and some equally telling blows to get it scrubbed out with salt water and
to get the lousy matting replaced and a new piece of
horn to glaze the only porthole. Even after its spring
cleaning, it stank; but for the moment, the sun not yet
being well up in the sky, it was the coolest place on
the ship.

Basreddin and Gupta were crouched forward by the
bulkhead that separated the sleeping cabin from the
sail locker. The dervish was in the process of teaching
the boy chess; already his precocious pupil had
snatched two games away from him, and Basreddin
was even now knitting his dark brows until they
seemed to merge with his great beard as he tried to
avoid a humiliating draw. Gupta laughed as his teacher, exasperated, swept the pieces into their pouch
and pushed the board away. Basreddin swatted at
him with the back of his hand, but the child ducked
and ran for the deck, hotly pursued by Basreddin.

Gurney climbed laboriously to his feet and walked
out into the sunlit waist of the ship. There was a still-
ness on deck, a frozen quality, even to the normally
motionless opium smokers. All eyes were on the break
of the poop, where Jamship, his black skin glistening in
the sun, leaned nonchalantly, paring the calluses on
his palms with a long knife. But his attention was not

on his task; his gaze was fixed on Gupta, who was standing awkwardly, as if checked in mid-stride, by the starboard gunwale. Jamshid sheathed his knife and slowly extended a finger towards Gupta.

"You. If you have strength and to spare, go you up the shrouds there and tell me what you see."

Gupta looked up the steep ladder of rope to the platform where the topmast sprouted from the main, and gulped.

"Well?" The mate's voice was taunting. "An untouchable need fear no disgrace in cowardice. I had forgotten."

Gupta walked to the shrouds and began to climb, his withered arm hanging uselss. Gurney could see his knees shaking as he swung out over the lee side, and began to pray, very quietly, to himself.

As the child reached the maintop, Jamshid raised his head. "What do you see?"

"Nothing."

"What do you mean, nothing? No sea? No sky? No land? Take a better look; perhaps the mast obstructs your view. Higher!"

Gupta began to climb again, his step more confident. Gurney breathed a sigh of relief. The small coffee-colored figure arrived at the topsail yard, stopped, shaded his eyes with his left hand, and swept the horizon theatrically. Jamshid scowled. It was no part of his plan to be made fun of by the little devil. Then a smile of satisfaction spread across his face, and he bellowed, "To the yardarm!"

Gupta hesitated, looking at the narrow spar that extended twenty feet out on either side of his perch. Then he grinned. Not so different from the rope trick, really. And much more interesting. He'd show the Owl that he was big enough for more than magic tricks. Then maybe they'd give him a knife like the one the black man had. Yes, a knife like that would be a great satisfaction. Below his feet the main topsail billowed, a huge belly of grayish white canvas. The deck looked absurdly small. His stomach lurched as he imagined the fall through eighty feet of emptiness to the unyielding timber of the deck. But he pushed the thoughts to the back of his mind and placed one foot on the yard. The best way would be to emulate the monkeys he had seen on their trip through the jungles of the interior—to run so fast that he would have no time to lose his balance. He raised his arms to balance himself and ran.

As he started, Gurney held his breath. Even the opium smokers were absorbed in his plight; one, more enterprising than the rest, was offering six to five against the boy's making it and finding no takers. Gurney remembered topmen running the yards on the *Egregious;* but they had been men of two years' experience, fit and strong, not malnourished children, cripples to boot, seeing the ocean for the first time.

A gust of wind, not much more than a puff really, pushed the ship over to leeward. The boy on the yard was nearly at the end now, but he faltered and windmilled his arms, trying to regain his balance. As the gust passed and the *White Rajah* righted herself, Gupta seemed to give up the idea of regaining the yard and launched himself in a desperate dive for the starboard brace, the long tackle running aft from the end of the spar. Gurney found himself shouting, roaring at the child to hang on, and started for the shrouds, bounding up the mast to the crosstrees and fighting his way to the topmast shrouds to the yard.

Gupta was twenty feet away, clinging desperately to the brace with his good hand, his face gray with fear, whimpering. George called across to him. "Don't worry. Hold on! I'm nearly there."

Then, not trusting himself to run the yard, he found the footrope with his feet, bent over the spar, and sidestepped quickly toward the starboard end. Gupta's cries were growing more desperate. Gurney was leaning toward him, when the child opened his eyes and seemed to see him for the first time. He grasped his wrist firmly and swung him onto his back; then, shouting at him to hold on tight, he grasped the brace and began to swing hand over hand toward the deck. His muscles cracked and yelled with pain, but he kept going until he could bear no more. Then he loosened his grip and slid, palms burning, to the rail. Gupta jumped down from his back and slunk away forward.

The men in the waist were studiously unconcerned. But Jamshid was glowering, fists clenched at his side, livid at being deprived of his fun. Gurney absently mopped the blood from his hands on his loincloth and stood on the poop, looking down at him. Jamshid beckoned to him, snarling. "Come down here where you belong, you blue-eyed scum. Nobody told you to stick your nose in, did they?" Gurney looked around him. Basreddin caught his eye, but George shook his head, deliberately ignoring the mate. "Come the festering hell down here, you pig!" Jamshid was almost beside himself. George grinned at him engagingly but made no movement.

As the Negro started up the steep companionway toward him, Gurney's right leg tingled in anticipation. When the head came to foot level, the tense muscles of his lower back, thigh, and calf blasted his instep into the jaw with the force of a cannonball. The black head snapped back with a sound like a carriage wheel on thick gravel, and the body slid down the ladder and lay limp, curiously boneless-looking, on the deck. Basreddin bent over him and lifted one eyelid with his thumb.

"Dead."

Gurney climbed slowly down the ladder, limping slightly. As Basreddin bandaged his hands in the forecastle, he said nothing.

Gupta was already asleep in the corner.

Baulch was laboring in the grip of strong emotion. In his own mind, he was again in the pulpit of the tabernacle, thundering damnation for the many and salvation for the few to a huge flock on a Sunday evening. As his rhetoric reached its climax, he clutched the poop rail convulsively, and flecks of spittle showered the crew assembled in the waist. Gurney feared that the captain would fall under an apoplexy at any moment. His sagging jowls were a fiery red, his hands were swollen and purple. His eyes, bloodshot with lack of sleep and excess of brandy, bulged from their sockets as he ranted hellfire over Jamshid's body, sewn up with a stone of bricks in an envelope of matting by the boarding port. He drew his sermon to a close on a virulent threat and said the grace with a ponderous amen. His voice sounded alone. The crew, some through linguistic difficulties, others through religious differences, and Gurney because he was thinking about something else, were silent. Baulch exploded. "I said amen, bugger you all! And when I say amen, you bloody well say it with me and like it. Hear? Hear? Hear? Now, handsomely. Amen. And tip him overboard." Apparently satisfied with the apathetic mumble that passed for a full-throated unison roar aboard the *White Rajah*, he went below as the waters were closing over his mate's body.

Five minutes later, Fong took Gurney by the arm and tugged him toward the captain's cabin. Baulch was sitting in an overstuffed chair of red velvet behind a table on which stood the inevitable broad-bottomed decanter of brandy and a thick glass tumbler, half full, much smeared and fingerprinted. When Gurney entered the cabin, Baulch looked at him owlishly and belched. "So you're the black bugger who murdered poor Jamshid, eh? Eh? Eh? I should certainly hang you at the yardarm—probably shall, sooner or later." He took a deep draft of brandy, fixed his eyes vacantly on a spot on the deckhead, and fell silent. After a couple of minutes he seemed to recollect himself, and glared at Gurney. "Hmph. Well. Well. Well. Seems you're the only seaman on this ship now. Poor Jamshid. Gone to meet his Maker, poor bugger. And unsaved." His voice died away.

Gurney watched him narrowly. Delirium tremens, for sure. The man was a wreck. Jamshid, bullying swine that he was, must have run the ship virtually single-handed. Baulch came to himself again and leaned forward over the table, hissing, "And what do

you want? What the hell are you doing in my cabin?" Then he seemed to collapse on himself. "Poor
Jamshid. Better make that blue-eyed bugger mate.
Only seaman on ship." He fell back in his chair and
drained his tumbler. The red eyelids fell over the
boiled eyes, and he lost interest in the proceedings.
Gurney bent over the chart spread on the table, mem-
orized course and position—not that they meant anything—rose, and left the cabin. As far as he knew, he
was the only blue-eyed man on the *White Rajah*.

Gurney wiped the seawater from his face with one
of Baulch's towels and cast a wary eye over the
White Rajah's sails. She was wallowing along, bucketing in the long swell, under topsails and driver, the
warm southwesterly breeze blowing over her starboard beam as she plowed through the rollers toward
the Sunda Strait, the narrow gateway between Java
and Sumatra. The main topsail was not drawing well;
it flapped every time the *White Rajah* yawed in a
trough. George pointed and yelled, "Braces, there!"
A bleary-eyed lascar, part of the watch on deck, began the long negotiations necessary to get a group of
men together to tail onto the line; it was not until
ten minutes later that five men hauled on the brace,
which one fit man could ordinarily have handled with
relative ease, and with a great show of panting and
struggling brought the yard into trim.

Three hours later, the wind died. The waves were
smooth and oily, and the *White Rajah* slopped this
way and that, her spars clanking and crashing, trans-
fixed by the sun like a moth on a pin. In the still air
the heat was awful, and the smells of the ship—astern,
the saloonlike atmosphere of Baulch's cabin, com-
pounded of bad brandy and the cheap scent with
which he doused himself to hide the brandy; and
forward, the stink of opium and sweat from the crew's
quarters, mixed with the all-pervading reek of the
heads—sat on the decks like a thick fog.

Gurney had moved his predecessor's possessions
out of the deckhouse amidships, which was the mate's

perquisite, and because it was large and spacious, had asked Basreddin to share it with him. Gupta lodged forward with the crew. The air in the cabin was almost unbreathable. The punkah on the ceiling, pulled by a Malay who had been caught thieving from a forecastle companion, merely paddled the volumes of baking air from one place to another; the cooling effect was minimal. The charts that had been in Baulch's cabin were now stowed in the locker below the table at which Gurney was sitting, frowning; the captain, finding that the blue-eyed savage was more than capable of running the ship by himself, had retreated into a limbo of brandy and hellfire from which he showed no signs of emerging. Gurney took Baulch's sextant from its case and strolled aft for the noon sight.

Basreddin was at the wheel, deep in conversation with Gupta, balancing easily on the viciously corkscrewing poop. As Gurney finished his sight, he saluted ironically. "Greetings, O captain. Can your magic give us a wind? He who sits below is cheerless this day and begins to stink and sing."

Gurney smiled and shook his head. "I'll see what I can do. Has he been acting the fool again?"

Gupta pointed at the deck between his feet. "Since eleven o'clock he has been singing missionary tunes, banging on his floor like a sick donkey. If you go to his cabin, be sure he does not bite you. If you go mad, too, we all all lost."

The door to the captain's cabin was locked. As Gurney turned to go, the steward Fong shuffled to his side, simpering and bowing, a key in his hand. "Capting much trouble in head, come up mast to fight devil. Fong lock door so capting no go." He smirked. "Capting drunk, so maybe capting lose." He unlocked the door, waving Gurney in.

The mess in the cabin was worse than last time, and he raised an eyebrow at the Chinaman. The small man spread his hands in a disconsolate gesture. "Lars time I come to make shipshape, he throw glass at my head and call me reptile. So I no go in more except bring him more liquor."

Gurney nodded and stepped over the threshold. Baulch was sitting on a chair facing the bare teak bulwark on the starboard side, a rapt grin on his shivering red face, his fingers performing complicated virtuoso scales and trills in the air in front of his bulging stomach. Gurney stood to attention—after all, the man was the captain—and said, "Morning, sir. Just come to check the glass." Then he walked to the fore bulkhead and inspected the barometer. He looked at yesterday's reading scrawled on the slate beside the instrument. The mercury stood a full two inches lower. He glanced covertly at Baulch, who favored him with an affronted glare and played a doom-laden run of minor chords resolving into a crashing major on his invisible organ. As Gurney hurried out the door, the captain was pulling out tiers of invisible stops before launching into the last movement of his private Dies Irae.

On deck, the opium smokers lay in their usual places, the blue smoke from their pipe bowls curling vertically into the still, thick air. Gurney had organized the fifteen men into two watches, according to seagoing procedure, but it seemed to have changed nothing. The watch below spent all day on deck, and the night watches spent most of their tricks snoring in the scuppers. The usual custom of the country traders was to take off sail at night, leaving only one man to guard against storm, wreck, and collision. But Gurney had taken it upon himself, in view of the musty cotton goods and opium rotting in the hold —to say nothing of his personal mission—to dispense with tradition in the interests of speed.

He glanced apprehensively to the southwest. Sure enough, the horizon had lost its knifelike definition. Sky and sea—it was difficult to make out where the one stopped and the other started—had deepened to a dirty black, and in the far west a huge mountain range of anvil-topped thunderheads towered into the blue. Gurney leaped shouting into the knot of smokers. He picked up a rope's end from the dirty splintered deck, and flailed it about him to left and right. The men cowered out of his way, but to no avail; he drove them, yelling and cringing, into the shrouds and flogged them onto the yards to take in sail. Ten minutes later, the *White Rajah* was stripped down to bare poles, but for a pocket-handkerchief storm jib, and was rolling like a dead dog under the sun, which was now circled with a ring of dirty haze. Gurney's ears were singing, and he saw Basreddin's Adam's apple bob as he swallowed to clear his hearing.

The storm smashed into the *White Rajah*'s stern like an earthquake. The storm jib disintegrated before their eyes, the figurehead plunged deep into a wave, and the stern slewed parallel to the swells. The ship heeled over on her beam ends. Gurney and Basreddin clung to the wheel as the deck leaned steeply away, until they were hanging, their feet unable to grip. Gupta slithered past, wailing; Gurney grasped his wrist and hung on, but it was slippery, and he felt his hold weaken. Then the boy was wrenched away down the steepening slope to leeward and disappeared into the raging foam of white water where the poop rail should have been. Numb with horror, Gurney saw the longboat, torn from its davits on the starboard side, arc ponderously over the waist, smash to flinders on the mainmast, and plummet into the sea to port. Then something cracked with a sound like all the trees in the world falling, and the *White Rajah* staggered, reeled, plowed around head to wind, and came upright, water spewing from her decks, jouncing and battering in the huge, steep head sea.

Gurney dashed stinging salt water from his eyes and automatically began his inventory of the ship. Miraculously, the foremast had gone as she lay on her beam ends. It lay wallowing in the vicious sea at her bow, acting as a sea anchor, held fast by a tangle of cordage. His knees went weak as he realized how mi-

raculous their escape had been. If the mast hadn't
gone, if a freak cross-sea hadn't battered the ship
onto a more or less even keel as she lay broached-to,
the cargo would have come crashing through the deck
and they would at that moment have been sinking
through the black water towards the oozy bottom
of the Bay of Bengal. Like Gupta. He bowed his
head, and a lump rose in his throat.

He tore himself away from his thoughts and ran
his eye over the ship again. The rain was roaring
down so thick that he could see no further than ten
feet in any direction.

"Take the helm," he bellowed in Basreddin's ear.
The Sufi nodded, his beard blowing out in front of
his face in a black cloud. Gurney started forward.
Damage was surprisingly slight. One longboat was
gone, and the other was stove in, though not entirely
beyond repair. The foremast was a ragged stump rising twenty feet above the deck, and the foredeck was
a treacherous mesh of rope. The crew were huddled
in the forecastle ankle-deep in filthy water, and
Gurney had to beat them out on deck, drive one
party to chop away the foremast before it smashed
the side in, and another to sound the well and man
the pumps. By nightfall, the *White Rajah* was bucketing northeastward before the gale, driving through
the Andaman Islands under bare poles.

"Sumatra," said Gurney. The *White Rajah* lay be-
calmed beneath a blue bowl of sky, the long swell
rocking her sleepily. To the southwest, a long, low
streak of land topped with woolly white clouds lay
across the horizon.

Basreddin looked blank. "But Sumatra should be to
the east, Giorgiou. Can it be that that filthy storm
took us so far northward?"

Gurney shrugged. "Seems so. The wind must have
gone round to the south, which would have blown us
to hell and gone." He pointed to the chart he held
unrolled with a hand and a knee. "Look. We will
have passed south of the Nicobars, and that will be

the north coast of the mainland. What a bit of luck, eh?"

Basreddin did not look convinced. "I have heard those in the forecastle—though you and I know they are ignorant scum—tell tales of this way. The Strait of Malacca. Tales of shallow seas, rocks like a dragon's teeth, eaters of the flesh of men, sudden storms. Sometimes I rue the day I sculled from the sweet waters of my beloved Tigris."

"Sweet waters be damned. Never have I seen mud so thick flow so fast as in that sewer." Basreddin's face darkened, and Gurney cursed himself for overstepping the mark. "No, Bas, you're right. Many's the time I've longed for the raft of late. But don't worry! Soon we see far Cathay, the seas of the South and East, the spice islands and burning mountains!" Basreddin seemed mollified. He showed his teeth, and his eyes glittered beneath his bushy brows.

"Burning mountains I shall believe when I see them. Some bald old fool once told me in the northlands that he had seen Elbrus ablaze. Undoubtedly the man was mad."

"Aye, well, you may be in for a shock, Bas. Come nightfall I shall expect you to recant and apologize in full. Now, why don't you take yourself to a pipe of opium? You will find it soothing, I suspect."

The Sufi frowned, turned on his heel, and disappeared into the cabin.

The *White Rajah* had driven five days and nights before the storm, and then the wind had dropped as soon as it had risen. The crew were mostly asleep, sprawled like dogs on the damp mats in the forecastle. It had been touch and go, with the mighty winds blasting at the ship's high poop, driving her blunt nose deep into the troughs of the rollers. Gurney and Basreddin had found themselves clinging to the wheel together, desperately spinning the spokes against the hull's unwieldy slew as she tried to broach for the hundredth time under the toppling peak of a wind-steepened swell.

Last night, as the wind and the day died together,

Baulch had appeared on deck for the first time since Jamshid's funeral, his face gray. Gurney, his head spinning with fatigue, was almost pleased to see him. The trader had been almost cringingly grateful—had chased him off to his bunk to get some sleep, protesting in a voice only slightly slurred that he was resuming command. George had been too tired to quarrel. But now, as he washed the last of a hard biscuit from his mouth with a swig of creosote-thick black coffee brought him by Fong, who had at last, it seemed, decided that he was officer material, he felt ready for anything. Granted, he was stiff and bruised, and the skin of his hands, hardly healed after his long slide down the main topsail brace with Gupta, again throbbed like fire. But his head was clear as ice, and the fresh morning air filled his lungs.

So this was Sumatra, of which he had been told by the extraordinary Mr. Raffles, to whom Arabella, ever the ardent botanist, had introduced him at a reception after the opening of Parliament in 1817. A gentle man with kindly but distant eyes, he had waxed lyrical about Java, the mysterious island he dreamed of securing for the crown. Gurney had been fired with enthusiasm by the quiet, curiously forceful diplomat in the black and white, almost clerical dress; he had looked forward to reading the final draft of his great history of Java when it appeared; but Otway and ruin had come between him and that enlightening experience. He shook his head. His facial muscles had tensed into a tight grin, and his fingers drummed nervously on the rail.

As the morning wore on, a light breeze sent cat's-paws across the oily heave, and the *White Rajah's* sails filled slugglishly. The water at her stern coiled and eddied, and the helmsman felt the wheel bite satisfactorily as he paid off to stop the wind spilling from the puff of the main topsail. That day and the next they ran east southeast, into the five-hundred-mile funnel of water that extends southeasterly between Malaya and Sumatra from the Andaman Sea.

On the third night the land lay closer on either side,

and the winds had become fluky and fitful. The
steady monsoon breeze, corrupted and led astray by
the encroaching coastlines, deserted them, and the
crew sweated as Basreddin drove them continuously
to the braces to haul yards around to take advantage
of the slightest puff of breeze. Gurney thought often
of Gupta, who had wished to ride the elephants of
Java and see the man-apes of its jungles. But he
thought more often of the shoals and reefs for which
these straits were notorious. Moreover, the seas here
were largely uncharted.

The land, by his calculations, should be about four
leagues away to starboard, if land it could be
called. The coastline chart was marked as indetermi-
nate—a mass of rivers, sandbanks, and swamp. The
leadsman, invisible in the blackness forward, called
out the changing depths.

Then his voice stopped, cut off in mid-cry with a
strangled squawk. Basreddin moved fluidly into a
fighting crouch on deck at Gurney's side, his knife
gleaming dully in a glint of starlight. Gurney flung
his straw hat aside, because its paleness was conspicu-
ous—indeed, that was part of the reason he wore it.
His only other clothing was a dark ocher loincloth.
The air, heavy with the chlorine smell of the luke-
warm water that gurgled under the *White Rajah*'s
counter, was thick in his throat, wet and hot. He
strained his ears into the silence; runnels of sweat
coursed down his face, and the blood pounded in his
ears.

Then, above the rattle and creak of the *White Rajah*'s progress, he felt two distinct thumps, as of ship's
boats coming alongside. He sprang for the rail. A
swarm of small black shapes, indistinct in the thick
darkness, were swarming up the side, silent but for
the whisper of callous feet on the planking. He
shouted a warning, and they were on him, a flood of
tiny men. Gurney had only his clasp knife, but he
crouched back to back with Basreddin and together
they wove a ring of steel which for a moment drove
the invaders back.

Then there was a shout from above, and he looked up to the crossjack yard. A tiny shape grew rapidly until it resolved itself into a black savage swinging at the end of a rope and wielding a club like a croquet mallet. Gurney leaped in the air, dodged the mallet, and slashed at the rope, which parted. The savage, to judge by the thin scream which trailed into nothingness over the side, became a late snack for the sharks. Gurney found this immensely funny and was laughing as he turned again to the mob surrounding him; but there was a cracked edge of hysteria in his voice.

Basreddin was fighting, whirling, hooking his blade through two of the dark figures. One of them went down without a murmur, but the other yelled and fell back over the cliff of the *White Rajah*'s side into the sea. Then Gurney saw a pair of eyes flash white. He drove his foot into his assailant's stomach and whirled to free himself of the clawing hands at his knife wrist. Then clubs rang agonizingly on his head and shoulders, and, a titan overcome by monkeys, he crashed headlong on the deck.

8

The yellow splash of light from the portholes in the forecastle companion hatch had moved three feet up the fore bulkhead when Gurney felt the heave of the deck lessen. The *White Rajah* had been reaching to the fitful southwesterly wind for three hours. From the motion of the ship he guessed that they must be coming into the lee of a headland.

Basreddin, a bundle of rags at his side, cocked an eyebrow as Gurney crept across the cabin, picking his way through the bundles that littered the deck. Through the yellowed horn of the single porthole in the larboard side he saw a long, low strip of dark green. Mangrove. He had come across them before in the West Indies. A difficult, swampy coast, perfect country for corsairs. The shore would be honeycombed with creeks and estuaries, inaccessible except from the sea. And the seaward approaches would be very difficult. Reefs, shoals, tiderips—it was not for nothing that the early circumnavigators had named this part of the East Indies the Impassable Isles.

"This may be somewhat difficult. I have heard of these coast Dyaks before. Their custom is to strip their quarry of what is obviously valuable and sell their crews to the inland rajahs. And when there is a lack of fresh meat ashore, they have been known to supplement their short rations with human flesh."

And those who ended up in the pirates' stomachs would be very lucky ones, he reflected. Quite apart from malaria, yellow fever, and other even less agreeable diseases, the Sumatran rajahs were not renowned for their charity to their human chattels. Better a swift knife in the throat than six months of living hell and a fly-blown grave on the village dunghill.

Basreddin cast a sour glance at the crew, huddled apathetically on the splintered planks at the after end of the forecastle. Most of them were glazed with opium. They were only too well aware of what lay in store. No help could be expected from that quarter. Baulch was silent, crouching in a corner, twisting the rings on his pudgy fingers in abject terror.

"We will gain nothing by force. Discretion, as you told me once before when I wished to spit at that fat drunkard"—he jerked his head towards Baulch—"must be the better part of valor. We must disappear." Gurney's eyes raced down the littered forecastle. The door of the sail locker in the forward bulkhead hung open. A mass of canvas had spilled onto the deck when the Dyaks had rummaged through its contents. But the *White Rajah*'s spare sails had been rotten, a mass of mildew and rust spots. They wouldn't look there again. He tugged at Basreddin's sleeve and pointed. The Sufi nodded.

"One moment. I must speak with the Fat One, or he will squeal like a pig."

He went aft and whispered in Baulch's ear. The trader's bloodshot eyes rolled, and streams of sweat poured down his jowls. But after a while, his hands stopped trembling and fell relaxed in his lap. Basreddin made a rapid gesture in front of his face and slid back to Gurney's side.

"He will remember nothing—not even that we exist. Come."

The anchor cable roared out close to Gurney's head. The slatting of the unsheeted sails came muffled by the layers of canvas he had pulled over their bodies. He held his breath as the forecastle door crashed open, and the lascars wailed in terror as they were flogged into the waist of the ship. Baulch's fruity voice, raised in protest, was cut off by the abrupt crack of a rattan cane. Hoarse shouts urged the *White Rajah's* crew into the waiting boats, and a yard creaked outboard to swing the bundles of booty after them. Gurney let his body go limp as the thump of tholepins receded into silence. The sweat poured off his face as the minutes ticked by.

The ship was uncannily quiet. Long months at sea had accustomed him to the creak of wood under stress, the rattle of cordage against spars, and the crash of water against her sides. The absence of noise was unnatural. The *White Rajah*, though by any normal standard a vile old tub, had been a living thing with a personality and a language all her own. Now, in what would undoubtedly be her last anchorage, she was a dead hulk. The click of the latch on the forecastle door seemed to echo like a cannon shot. Bare feet padded on the deck a yard away. Someone was going through the bundles on the deck. Gurney groped for his knife. The footsteps came closer. Gurney inched his canvas covering aside and pressed a warning on Basreddin's forehead.

Peering through a fold of sailcloth, Gurney saw a brown Dyak dressed in a dirty sarong rummaging through a ditty bag. With an exclamation of disgust the Dyak flung the bundle into a corner and took a long swig out of a black bottle. As the pirate turned his attention to another bundle, Gurney rose smoothly to his feet, knife reversed in his right hand. The Dyak half-turned at the rustle of canvas. His eyes widened, and he was going for the long, wavy kris at his belt when the pommel of Gurney's knife slammed into his temple. He flopped to the deck with a grunt. Gurney studied him with fascination. He was about five feet tall, thin to the point of emaciation. The skull showed clearly through the flesh of his face, and the dark lips snarled back from blackened teeth filed to points. His body was crisscrossed with knife scars.

"Don't finish him yet! He's going to be useful." Basreddin grunted disapprovingly. "We're going to need a pilot to get out of here. I only hope that he was a lone wolf. Truss him up."

There was no sign of life as they crept astern, bent double under cover of the bulwarks. Basreddin was dragging their captive by the hair. The door of the companionway to the aftercabin was closed. As Gurney raised the latch stealthily, Basreddin covered him.

On the bottom step of the companionway sat another chocolate-colored native, staring out of the windows of the great stern gallery. In his right hand he held a kris. He was humming softly to himself, his matted hair swinging as he rolled his head from side to side. As Gurney watched, he staggered to the corner and was violently sick. Basreddin brushed past, leaped on him like a puma, and chopped him to the deck with the edge of his hand. As he tied him up, Gurney caught the stink of raw brandy. He lifted the panel over Baulch's wine locker. It was empty.

"This will smooth our path. The only liquor these heathens get is palm wine, and precious little of that. They'll all be howling drunk by nightfall."

The *White Rajah* lay at anchor in the tidal mouth of a river. The tide, two hours into the flood, surged

past her weedy sides, holding her bowsprit pointed
firmly to seaward. Gurney guessed she was anchored
only by the bow; that would mean deep water under
her keel. He walked over the rich carpet to the windows. A long musket shot to starboard was a landing
stage and a kampong of sun-browned palmetto huts,
built out on stilts over the black water. On either side of
the village and on the far bank of the estuary, dense
thickets of mangrove probed the ooze with their
gnarled roots. The sun, low in the west, struck a blaze
of color from the jungle; the branches of the trees
were matted with creepers and orchids, and rainbow
flights of chattering birds flitted in and out of the
dense foliage. Gurney's eyes traveled down from the
luxuriant treetops to the waterside. The wind had
died, and the water was glassy as it eddied through
the roots. A large reptile plopped under the surface, leaving only a spreading ring of ripples to
mark its passing.

Gurney shuddered, then got a grip on himself.
Damn it all, a man could afford to shiver with gothic terror in the drawing rooms of Bath, but here and
now there were more urgent things to attend to.

The *White Rajah* was not the only ship in the
anchorage. To port lay a country wallah of similar antique type. Four or five small cutters, petty Dutch
coastal traders probably, were anchored close to the
landing. And a hundred yards astern lay a lean, low,
two-masted schooner. As she swayed to an eddy of the
tide, Gurney saw that her masts were finely raked
and her hull had the lines of a thoroughbred. One
of the old breed, built in Baltimore for a privateering
man, he guessed. This would bear further examina-
tion.

Basreddin called him forward and pointed through
the half-open door of the cabin. The longboat lay
moored to a tiny quay on a bare islet surrounded
just above high-water mark by a palisade of sharp-
ened bamboos. The islet lay in the middle of the
seaward channel. Gurney's practiced eye told him
that the slight right-hand bend of the estuary would

have built up a shoal to starboard. He filed the information away in his mind for future reference. The captain and crew of the *White Rajah* stood in a disconsolate group on the small landing. A villainous-looking Dyak with blue tattoos on his forehead was searching them one by one. Any articles of value were tossed into a sack held by his companion.

As Gurney watched, it was Baulch's turn to be searched. The fat trader's face bore a vague, puzzled look, as if he'd forgotten something important. Gurney focused his glass carefully. The tattooed savage grabbed Baulch by the shoulder and yanked him to his knees. He struggled to his feet again, shouting with rage, purple wattles quivering, shaking his fist at his tormentor. The Dyak pressed the point of his kris into Baulch's neck where it bulged over the stained collar and repeated the order. Baulch emitted a squeal of rage and terror and made as if to turn on the man with the sack. The kris moved a fraction of an inch. Baulch gave a bubbling scream and fell to his knees, blood squirting rhythmically from a neat hole below his left ear. As his head fell forward, the kris flashed down in a blur of polished metal. The head, blood gushing from the severed arteries, rolled away from the twitching body. The tattooed guard went through the corpse's clothing methodically, grunting with satisfaction as he found the watch and silver hip flask. He had some difficulty with the diamond on Baulch's swollen finger. After a short struggle, he put the hand between his teeth and bit down into the first knuckle. He spat the ring into the bag; the finger stayed obscenely in his mouth. He chewed it absently, as an African chews sugarcane.

Gurney lurched back, bile rising in his throat. He half-fell down the companionway and sat head between knees, white as a sheet. Basreddin, toying with his beads with noncommittal fingers, raised his eyes heavenwards. "Like a swine he lived, like a swine he died. So be it." Gurney blinked, trying to rid himself of the picture of that finger wagging in the corner of the Dyak's mouth.

He began to run over the situation in his mind. Obviously, they would have to escape by sea. A fit man couldn't hack his way through that snake-infested, poisonous jungle; and he and Basreddin had been living on salt junk and rice for too long. The answer had to be a cutting-out expedition. Basreddin and he could handle the *White Rajah* in a pinch, though God knew it wouldn't be easy. But if they could get a crew together, they could take that schooner astern. She was a neat little ship, she wouldn't draw more than twelve feet, and she'd go like an arrow. They could use one of the Dyak captives, now gagged and bound in the empty lazaret, as a pilot. The tide would be turning at about one in the morning, and dawn would break at five; given the land breeze and the last of the ebb, they should be out and away before the Dyaks had time to blink. He trained his glass on the schooner again. She looked handy enough. Her two fore-and-aft mainsails lay furled along their booms. The square topsails on the foremast, clewed up into clumsy folds on their yards, were beginning to bang and slat in the sea breeze. Twelve men should be complement enough for the moment. And if she was as good as she looked, by God but she'd be a valuable prize! And Gurney's by right of salvage.

He turned to Basreddin. "You're going on a recruiting drive. In half an hour it'll be pitch dark. Could you swim to that island against the tide, do you think? We'll need a crew for that schooner."

"Nothing is impossible. But I am glad that the Fat One—peace be on his hog's soul—has lost the contents of his wine locker."

The capture of the *White Rajah* and the valuable slaves in the prison compound would be an occasion for rejoicing. By three hours after sunset the whole village would be reeling drunk, sentries included. It shouldn't be difficult to move around unnoticed. Gurney glanced out of the window.

The longboat, with three argumentative and probably half-drunken Dyaks aboard, was making an erratic course through the twilight to the village. The two savages left to guard the stockade shouted after them, each holding up a black bottle. The men in the boat laughed and waved back as they tied up among the other small craft at the landing stage and disappeared among the huts.

"Think you can take one of those boats from the landing? You'll have to muffle the tholepins with a bit of rag, or you'll make enough noise to wake the dead."

"When my fire burns, it burns without smoke. Have I not told you, O my friend, of my escape from the Afghan caravansary after my walk to Nuristan? There I left the souls of seven Pathans burning in the pits of Shaitan. There are ways in which a man may move more silently than the ghost of a shadow, and of these I have some small knowledge."

It was pitch dark when Basreddin, his body oiled and wearing only a loincloth, crept spiderlike down the ornate molding on the *White Rajah's* aftercastle. He slid noiselessly into the water and disappeared into the blackness, a long curved knife clamped between his teeth.

On shore the feasting had started. A huge fire on the stamped earth behind the huts cast their high rooftrees into sharp relief against the lowering eaves of the forest. The reflected flames danced in the water to a dull throbbing of drums. A single voice wailed a monotonous chant, punctuated by many-throated roars of applause. The smell of wood smoke and roasted meat drifted into Gurney's nostrils as he fretted on the red velvet of Baulch's overstuffed chair, slapping irritably at the cloud of mosquitoes buzzing around his head. The savory smell might well be coming from the late owner of the cabin. Gurney looked at his watch. Then he took off his clothes and packed them into a tight bundle. Lashing the bundle to a cork life belt, he climbed into the water on the larboard side and let the tide carry him down toward the schooner.

The Dyak with the tattooed forehead sat with his back to the bamboo of the prison stockade, looking at the lights of the village. He took a long swallow from his bottle and cursed the foreign dogs for making their vile noise. The prisoners had been restless ever since he had taken the head of the one like a pig. A powerful feeling of self-importance took over as the brandy hit him. It was a noble and worthy thing, he felt, to guard the human merchandise on which his fellow tribesmen depended for their livelihood. Although those mud-eating wretches who had arrived today would hardly fetch more than five rupees a head. Still, there were consolations. His betel-stained teeth showed in an anticipatory grin as he thought of the one like a pig crackling on the spit over the fire pit before the long hut. His woman would save him a succulent piece of lower back for tomorrow. He slapped at a mosquito on his left shoulder and peered fuzzily at the puncture mark.

Basreddin, prone in the water ten feet to his right, laid his thumb along the inside of the wickedly curved knife in the classic fighter's grip. For a split second every muscle in his body relaxed as he sighted on a spot an inch below the Dyak's left shoulder blade; then he rose from the water. The Dyak half-turned; then a forearm like a steel bar clamped across his windpipe, and the razor-sharp blade sheared through the wall of his chest cavity and punctured his heart. Blood poured into his lungs. When Basreddin let him go, he slumped sideways, a red trickle seeping from the corner of his mouth. Basreddin stripped him of his sarong and kris and tipped him carefully into the turbid water.

Five minutes later, the second sentry came around the stockade, humming in unison with the chants drifting over from the village. He chuckled with delight when he saw the sarong-clad figure face down in the mud, snoring heavily, an empty bottle overturned beside him. He had never liked Fadrak, and when the chief heard about this, there would be a

cutting. He drew his foot back to kick the recumbent
figure. He would enjoy the cutting.

His mouth fell open as the drunk opened a pair
of wicked amber eyes and sprang to his feet. Basreddin hit him under the jaw with the heel of his hand
before he could shout; his teeth crunched together,
and as his head snapped back, the Sufi's knife drove
up below the breastbone and sliced his aorta. He
sprawled on his back, eyes staring sightlessly at the
stars.

Basreddin lifted the bar from the compound gate
and slipped inside. A small fire guttered at the far
end. In its light, he saw rows of half-naked bodies
stretched out on a carpet of foul-smelling filth. The
fetid air was alive with mosquitoes, and there was a
continuous babble of men delirious with fever. By the
side of the fire was a shelter of rotting palmetto.
Basreddin pulled the gate shut behind him. As he
crossed the enclosure, men shrank away from him,
raising their arms as if to ward off blows.

In the shelter, the six men playing cards in the
feeble firelight huddled closer as he entered. They
had a different look from the rest; their backs were
straighter, and they spoke with quiet control. In English. One of them, a vast hulk of a man with an
empty socket where his left eye should have been,
spat into the fire.

"And what is it now, you black bastard?" he growled.

Basreddin smiled. "I am here at the orders of Captain George Le Fanu Gurney, late of His Majesty's
Navy, on a recruiting mission."

The big man's jaw dropped. Then a slow grin
spread over his battered features. The cardplayers
had forgotten their game. Basreddin squatted on his
heels, and they gathered around him eagerly.

"Are you all from the same ship?"

"Aye. Schooner *Duiker* lyin' there in the anchorage.
I'm the mate. Name of McIver."

"How many more of you?"

"Five. There was eighteen of us when those black

dogs brought us in, but eleven men and the skipper went under with the heat and fever."

"Are there others here that you trust?"

"Aye, half a dozen good lads besides us."

"Then assemble them as silently as the drifting eagle of your homeland; be sure that there is one who understands the ways of artillery. I shall return with a boat. Listen for the cry of a northern gull at the gate."

Basreddin slid into the tepid murk like an otter. He swam in a state of light trance, ignoring the dying flames from the village fires. When he was fifty yards from the bamboo piling of the landing stage, he rolled onto his back, letting the tide carry him, regulating his breathing so that only his nose and the lower part of his face showed above water. As he came level with the end of the jetty, he dived deep, breaking surface in the middle of a group of boats. Most of these must have come from the Dyaks' other quarries; Basreddin inspected them rapidly and chose a light seven-oar gig. Then he clambered along the pilings to the shore, where he crept under the raised veranda of the hut nearest the jetty. Two minutes later he was asleep.

His eyes snapped open an hour later. Unsteady footsteps were thudding on the matting above his head; a woman giggled and a bead curtain swished shut. The festivities were coming to an end. The chanting had stopped, and apart from occasional bursts of slurred yelling, the village was silent. Basreddin crawled out of his hiding place. Great swathes of cloud covered the stars, and as he made his way back along the pilings, the first drops of rain dimpled the smooth water. By the time he reached the boats, it was falling in torrents. As he dropped off the last pile and handed himself toward the gig, he muttered a prayer of thanks. The village had disappeared behind a curtain of water; no hostile eyes would see him now. He pushed the gig into the tide, set his oar, and sculled with a smooth figure-eight movement of the wrists toward the island.

The rain had stopped, and the stars were breaking
through the clouds as Gurney finished his inspection
of the schooner. He was well pleased with what he
had found. She was a neat little ship, about two hundred tons, probably fast in a light breeze and sturdy
in a blow. And she had teeth. Ten twelve-pound
carronades were snugged to their ports below, and a
long, sixteen-pound stern chaser crouched on either
side of the cuddy aft. An ideal armament for a small,
fast ship. She could swoop in, deliver a formidable
weight of metal, and stand off in the twinkling of an
eye. Gurney, sitting in the aftercabin in inky darkness, wondered what she had done since leaving the
Baltimore yards. He guessed that it had been more
than pleasure cruising. He would be a sorry seaman
if he couldn't get a ship like this away from a rabble
of savages. If Basreddin's mission was successful. Gurney had a sudden picture of himself as a landlocked
Flying Dutchman, compelled to wait for all eternity
for a cutting-out crew that would never arrive in this
world or the next.

To distract himself, he hunted out a dark lantern
and made a cautious inspection of the magazine and
the stores. The musket racks were empty, and the
stock of loose powder was low. But the powder bags
and shot for the carronades and the sixteen-pounders
were untouched. Gurney looked at his watch and
doused the lantern. Two hours till dawn. Time Basreddin was back. He climbed on deck through the
hatch between the two great masts. The village was
dark, quiet except for the occasional barking of a dog.
The air was cool, freshened by the rain; the stink of
rotting vegetation had been washed away. A faint red
glow came from the prison island. Against the chir-
ruping of tree frogs and the constant chattering from
the fringes of the jungle, the plaintive screech of the
herring gull sounded strange and incongruous.

Gurney's mind snapped back to the choppy gray
seas and cold east winds of the Norfolk winter. He
was absorbed in his memories as Basreddin, shivering

in the cool air, led a procession of vaguely distin-
guishable forms up through the midships entry port
on the larboard side. He beckoned them below,
made sure that the hatch cover was secure and the
gun ports were sealed tight, and relit the lantern.
Its flickering light cast grotesque shadows on the
planking above their heads as Gurney looked around
at the haggard faces. Basreddin, wrapped in a blanket, radiated a feeling of suppressed excitement.

"Who here has sailed in this ship?"

Five men stepped forward. McIver, the one-eyed
bosun, tugged his forelock.

"What happened to your captain?"

"Dead of the black vomit, sir."

"Are you all healthy?"

"Nothing that real food won't cure, sir."

"Very well. Now then. I am going to take this ship
out of here in one piece. I claim the captaincy of
this vessel by right of salvage. Objections?"

No one spoke.

"Good. Where's the gunner?"

Another figure stepped forward. "Me, sir. Used to
be a navy man, sir. Frigates."

"Name? Ship?"

"O'Shea, sir." The man seemed to check himself and
stared miserably at his feet.

"Not, by any chance, the *Hermione?*"

O'Shea nodded dumbly. In 1799 the crew of the
frigate *Hermione* had revolted, butchered their officers, and handed their ship over to the enemy. The
mutineers had been hunted down systematically ever
since, and most of them had met their ends dancing
on air at the execution dock.

"Well, O'Shea, I should think that we're all what
you might call outlaws here. If you lay a good gun,
I'll not lay a noose on you." The seaman's weather-
beaten face relaxed. "And now for the rest of you.
We leave at dawn, and we'll be in a hurry. I'll knife
the first man who speaks above a whisper or shows
himself above the gunwales. McIver, show these men

the ship, and quietly. Basreddin, I'd be obliged if you could fetch me our . . . pilots." The Sufi grinned and slipped away.

A faint glimmer of light was showing in the eastern sky when McIver returned. "She's no bad, sir. I've taken the ties off; we'll be up and away when you wish."

The schooner, anchored by the bow, was now held by the ebb tide, her nose pointed firmly inland. McIver would have to anchor her by the stern and cut the forward cable; that way, she would swing toward the harbor entrance. And the land breeze, the convection current set up by the interaction of the warm sea and the night-cooled land, should do the rest. If it blew.

But there was no time for doubt now. They would cross those bridges when they came to them. He called O'Shea.

"How many guns can you fire with six men? You'd have thirty minutes to prepare yourself."

"Sure I could load, lay, and fire the whole starboard battery meself with two men for the powder and shot in ten minutes."

"Good. You'll kindly do just that. And load up the stern chasers as well; we may have unwelcome visitors. When she swings, I want you to put five shot into the landward end of that jetty. Then stand by the chasers."

Gurney paced up and down in an agony of impatience as the dawn rose pink in the sky. Basreddin had returned from the *White Rajah* with his human cargo; the Dayaks lay squirming on the deck in the schooner's Spartan aftercabin. The village was waking up; thin plumes of smoke rose vertically in the still air, and women's voices chattered across the glassy water. There was not a breath of wind. Soon the savages would realize what was going on aboard the schooner; then it would be the end. Gurney resolved to die fighting rather than face the prison stockade.

Then Basreddin, dressed in brilliant patchwork robes and an emerald-green turban, stalked out of

the aftercabin, spread his prayer mat on the deck,
and prostrated himself toward Mecca. Then he rose,
drew himself up to his full height, and began to
chant in a high, piercing voice an invocation to the
wind afreets.

Gurney goggled and rounded on him, cursing.
"You damned idiot heathen, you'll be the death of us
all. McIver! We'll have to try drifting her out on the
tide. Up sails!"

A cloud of white canvas inched up the schooner's
masts, flapping idly in the motionless air.

"Bower anchor!"

The schooner, head anchor warp chopped with
one ax blow, drifted down the tide. Gurney looked
desperately around him as the stern anchor caught
and held. The water was still glassy, though inland
the treetops seemed to be moving; but that could be
a trick of the light . . .

Two sarong-clad figures rushed onto the jetty ges-
ticulating wildly. They were joined by others. A puff
of smoke and a bang was followed by the whizz of a
musket ball.

"O'Shea! Fire as you bear! Afterguns first!"

The schooner's deck juddered at the roar of the carronades. The first ball took the group of Dyaks clean
in the middle, knocking them about like skittles; then
the jetty disintegrated into a mass of flying splinters.
But somehow, a boatload of Dyaks was even now
paddling out toward the schooner, which lay at an
angle to the tide, knocked off true by the concussion
of her broadside. The savage in the bows was loading
a swivel gun. Gurney looked inland again. A cat's-
paw of wind ruffled the surface of the water between
the mangrove clumps.

"Stern anchor! Cast off!"

Now the schooner was free, drifting across the tide
to the open sea. Or the mudbank, if the wind didn't
reach her. Gurney found himself cursing, teeth
clenched as he spun the brass-bound wheel, the rudder wagging ineffectually in the water.

The first ray of sun struck the main topmast.

Gurney glanced behind him to starboard. The boat
with the swivel was a hundred yards away now; he
could see the sweat shining on the bodies of the
paddlers. And on the starboard bow the mudbank
of the prison island, exposed by the ebb, loomed ter-
rifyingly close. The hair on the back of his head lifted.
Suddenly, the flapping white masses of canvas
cracked taut, and the wheel spun through his fingers
with a new purposefulness. He pushed the spokes
hard-a-larboard. The schooner, like a horse stepping
onto soft grass from an icy road, came together under
his hands. McIver ran shouting along her flush deck,
trimming the long-unused jibs and bracing in the two
square topsails. The deck surged beneath Gurney's
feet as the hull bit the water and white bubbles began to cream in her wake. O'Shea came on deck,
grinning delightedly. Gurney pointed out the Dyak
craft, now three hundred yards astern and losing
ground rapidly. The Irishman nodded and peered
along the barrel of the long, sixteen-pound chaser.
He made some adjustments, stepped back, and pulled
the lanyard just as the Dyaks swivel gun banged
and a fist-sized chunk of wood flew out of the raised
cockpit coaming by Gurney's left hand.

The sixteen-pounder bucked and roared, and the
Dyaks' bow dissolved into a froth of blood and
splinters. Gurney stuck his head down the companionway and bellowed for Basreddin. The Sufi climbed
on deck, dragging after him a glassy-eyed Dyak.

"This barbarian dog will pilot us. I have made certain ... suggestions to him, so he will not deceive us.
I find that his tongue has many points of similarity
with that of a certain magus I once met on the waterfront at Ibadan, and his will is weak. Incidentally,
it is well that my intercession with the wind afreets
was successful."

Gurney shook his head in disbelief, but said nothing. One day this fakir would fake once too often,
and then they'd all be in fiddler's green.

Basreddin grinned at him. "As your Book says, O
unbelieving dog, 'O ye of little faith!' Trust me! But

now listen to the wisdom of this ill-smelling navigator."

Two hours later, Gurney handed the helm over to Dutch Pieter, the blond, scar-faced coxswain Basreddin had brought from the prison island.

"Take her ten points to windward and keep her there. Basreddin! We'll keep those savages till we put in for water. Then we'll dump them in a boat, and they can take their chance. Now I'm going to take a look at this ship. She has too many teeth for a simple trader, and privateers are out of style, more's the pity."

The cargo space under the smoke-reeking gun deck was jammed with tin-bound mango wood chests, each bearing the stamp of a heart quartered. The John Company stamp. Gurney smashed his bare heel into the nearest chest. It was packed with spherical objects about the size of twenty-pound shot. One of them had fractured, and out of the cracks oozed a black, treacly substance. A musky, perfumed stench filled the hold.

Basreddin tugged thoughtfully at his black beard. "Allah has been bountiful. Truly it is said that he who sits under a tree long enough, though he may not frequently eat peaches, will certainly have a sufficiency of firewood."

A slow smile spread over Gurney's face. "We're rich. There must be at least seventy chests here. Seventy chests of the finest Patna opium."

9

The newly painted letters on the schooner's bow gleamed with spray as she knifed her cutwater deep into the swells. George Le Fanu Gurney, captain of the free ship *Vandal*, late the *Duiker*, of no par-

ticular allegiance, grinned wolfishly as he stood braced
against a windward backstay, gazing beneath the long
mainsail boom at the western horizon. Far beyond
that horizon was the muddy coast of Cochin China;
and ahead lay the protruding belly of the Chinese
mainland. Crawling on that belly was a louse he
meant to crack.

Ten days before, the *Vandal* had sailed from Singapore after a lengthy careening. It had taken Gurney
and his men nearly a week to scrape the barnacles
and yard-long weed from her copper; but she had
three knots more speed as a result. Then there had
been water to take on and the obligatory visit to the
commander of the fort. But Farquhar, the commander, had been a kindly man and had expressed
more than a little envious admiration for Gurney's
exploits. He had put all his facilities, such as they
were, at the *Vandal*'s disposal, and given him a letter
of introduction to one Hamish Gordon, a merchant
last heard of trading from Hong Kong, a bay ninety
miles to the southeast of Canton.

Gurney had worked his new crew, scoured from
among the malcontents and ne'er-do-wells of tiny
Singapore harbor, like a Tartar. The *Vandal*'s complement now numbered some sixty men—small
enough by navy standards, but trained to a hair.
The ship's rigging was tuned like a racing yacht's,
her deck shone, and her guns gleamed with grease.
On her two masts she carried three foresails, two huge
fore-and-aft sails, and three topsails. Now, driven by
the northeast monsoon blowing steady over her starboard bow, she was beating to the northward like a
greyhound. Despite her press of canvas she rode the
long, trudging rollers like a cork, curtsying her way
through a sea where most ships would have been
taking green water over the bowsprit.

Gurney had slept little during the past weeks.
Even when the running of his ship was not requiring
his full attention and he lay in his narrow bunk with
the creak of the rudder pintles in his ear, Otway's

face would rise before him wearing that terrible unctuous smile.

He felt a touch on his arm and turned. Basreddin was watching him, his eyes troubled.

"You are stretched very fine, O companion of my travels. The lust for vengeance may be its own undoing. I felt your anger as I toyed with a novel end game."

The Sufi had kept very close of late, spending much of the day with his chessboard and emerging from his cabin only in the night watches. Gurney, on the infrequent occasions he gave the matter any consideration, reckoned that the wide gray waters on every side were at the root of his silence. To a man whose principal experience of seafaring had been floating down a river on a quarter-acre of raft, the *Vandal* must seem like a cockleshell in a whirlpool.

"As I followed the moves of your baraka—your spirit—I found the red bishop threatening the white queen. I know it is in your nature to move impetuously after your goals; but I fear that when you break your enemy's tree, he may use it as a cudgel against you. Remember that the most circuitous route may prove the swiftest in the end."

Gurney nodded and turned away. McIver was coming aft, balancing his bulk springily against the solid heave of the deck.

"We'll have the main topsails in. And call the men aft."

"Aye, aye, sir." The one-eyed Scot filled his lungs and loosed a brass-throated roar. Two hands sprang to the halyards, and the huge triangle of canvas collapsed into the fork of the gaff. Jago Pendethick, once a navy topman, sprang for the ratlines and brailed home the billowing sail. The *Vandal* fell off the wind, her motion easing into a long, slow corkscrew as the helmsman ran the spokes through his fingers.

Gurney climbed onto the rail and ran his eyes over the expectant faces below him. "As you have doubt-

less realized by now, I am not one of your nabob
yachtsmen, and this is no pleasure cruise. But it is a
fair deal more rewarding than feeding the sharks in
that stinking Dayak mud puddle or rotting your guts
with Singapore brimstone, so I'll thank you to give me
your full attention. We're sailing in a ship with a
changed name, which some of you may think bodes
ill. I remind you that the duiker is a kind of deer—
fast enough, but a timorous beast at the best of times.
Well, the *Duiker* has been eaten by the *Vandal*.
For the benefit of the nonclassicists among you, thirteen hundred years ago a band of gentlemen of the
Vandal persuasion went through the whole of Europe
like an ax through a maggoty cheese. In one lifetime,
they were masters of the world. And while the com-
petition has become stiffer since those times, every
man jack of you will have money enough to be master of his own destiny if he comes along with me. I'll
not overstep the bounds of human decency if my
parties deal fair with me; but by the gods I'll slit the
belly of any fat goat who tries to come between me
and my deserts. So if I ask you to follow me into hell
and tweak the devil's tail, I'll expect you to be close
at my back. And if any man of you feels he'd be on
the laggard lay, he can take himself off this ship, and
now's the time to start swimming. That's all."

He jumped from the rail and went below, slamming his cabin door on the babble of voices that
broke out behind him. Basreddin entered and seated
himself on a locker. After the steward had brought
coffee and left, Gurney raised his eyebrows.

"Well?"

"They are for you. I watched them all. You handled
them well."

Gurney grunted and leaned back in his chair, lock-
ing his hands behind his head and stretching his
weary muscles. Outside the porthole, small pudding-
shaped clouds hung in the evening sky. The sun was
dropping toward the horizon, blazing an incandescent
road across the darkening sea. He knew he could

sleep now. Basreddin finished his coffee and rose to leave. Gurney only just made it to the bunk before unconsciousness rolled over him in a dark wave.

Some fifteen ships lay at anchor in Hong Kong bay. Some, like the *Vandal*, which swung at her mooring in the outer harbor, bore the marks of the long passage from the Sunda Strait and beyond; others, by their cluttered top-hamper and the absence of any but the most rudimentary sailing gear, had obviously been at the same mooring for years. Gurney steadied himself as the longboat drove through the gentle swell, easing his neck against the unaccustomed roughness of his collar. He smiled at the irony of it: here in a harbor surrounded by the mountains known as Kowloon—the Nine Dragons— and fortified villages of mud inhabited by the most mysterious race in the world, he had donned a stiff collar and neckcloth for the first time in months. He sighed and mopped at his brow with his handkerchief.

The *Maid of Perth*'s mooring would be her last. Originally a bark of some thousand tons, she now lay anchored by weed-crusted cables, dismasted, her upperworks extended haphazardly into a bewildering labyrinth of wooden structures. As the longboat passed under her stern, Gurney saw that the gallery had been extended and built higher. Jasmine and climbing roses twined over the balustrades and her tall French windows were curtained with bottle-green velvet. On her port side, a huge derrick was lowering a net bulging with boxes and sacks into a lighter manned by lascar seamen. The longboat came alongside an ornate companionway, and a dapper Chinese in a black frock coat and varnished top boots led Gurney up the steps to a dark red door with a highly polished lion's-head knocker and a plate which announced this to be the Far Eastern office of Hamish Gordon, merchant. The Chinese ushered Gurney along a corridor hung with framed share certificates into a paneled cabin, took his hat, and asked him his business. Gurney handed him Farquhar's letter, and he bowed himself out.

Gurney looked around him in disbelief. The cabin had been turned into a countinghouse. Along one wall were ranged six sloping-topped desks, and facing them, as a schoolmaster faces his pupils, was a single, larger one. All were unoccupied. He noticed that while the stools ranged abreast had plain wooden seats, the seventh was covered in leather and comfortably padded. Below the skylight a punkah paddled the air languidly, worked by some unseen mechanism. The room—he could not for the life of him think of it as a ship's cabin—had a musty smell of dehydrated ink and moldered quills, overlaid with a tang of spice and a whiff of salt. The door opened, and the Chinese appeared, beckoning. "Mr. Gordon will see you now."

Suddenly full of trepidation, Gurney walked along another narrow passage, this time hung with meticulously executed botanical drawings, into what had once been the stern cabin of the *Maid of Perth*. A small, heavyset figure advanced across the rich Bukhara rug, hand outstretched in greeting.

"How d'ye do, Captain Gurney. Have a seat, have a seat. I'm Hamish Gordon."

The voice was Scottish. Lowland Scottish, at a guess. Gordon sat down behind a Louis XV escritoire covered in papers and specimen vases, motioned Gurney into a chair, and thrust his hands into the pockets of an old-fashioned lapped coat liberally dusted with snuff.

"Well, we'll not beat around the bush. I've read Farquhar's letter about ye; he seems very taken with ye, and he's a man of sound principle and judgment. Now. Would ye be so good as to tell me the purpose of an errand that brings ye to the courts of commerce when right-thinking folk are sleeping or following the noble pursuit of horticulture?" His heavy eyebrows sank in a quizzical frown. Gurney was reminded of a small, humorous animal peering out of a hedge.

"I have seventy-five cases of Patná opium that I must sell."

The eyebrows shot upwards; the eyes lost their humor. "That ye must sell, eh? And how, if I may make so bold as to ask, did ye come by it? Ye're very young to be carrying that kind of cargo in your pocket."

Gurney leaned forward in his chair, his face flushing. "I don't think my age has anything to do with the matter in hand."

"My apologies, my apologies. But be that as it may, I must hear how you came by it."

Gordon listened intently while Gurney told his story. Toward the end he rummaged in his pockets, produced a yellow handkerchief and a large horn snuffbox with a cairngorm lid, and inhaled a copious pinch of snuff up each nostril. He dusted his long chin and upper lip, sneezed violently, and resumed his attitude of rapt attention.

Gurney gave him only the bare bones of the story, omitting all mention of Otway and dealing only sketchily with his naval career. When he had finished, Gordon sat back in his chair and proffered his snuffbox.

"Well, well. Quite a tale. Ye'll have a peat?"

Gurney declined, and Gordon sat in deep thought for some time. At last he looked up, his eyes shrewd.

"Ye've reasons for not wishing to go to Canton, then, to the Factory? Aye, well. If ye don't want to discuss them, I suppose that's your business. I could take the mud off your hands, though. I'll tell you frankly it's no' the price you'd get if you took it up the river yourself. Ye'll know that there's only one place you can dispose of it—at the Factory at Canton. It seems that His Serene Pomposity the Emperor will have no foreigners on his land; but such is the greed of the man that he authorized a European compound in Canton. There's no' enough room there to swing a cat, though. Myself, I prefer to sit well out of it. Canton's only ninety miles to the northwest of here, and I reckon this place has possibilities. In fact, I'm negotiating for a plot of land over that way"—he pointed to the Kowloon peninsula—"with the local mandarin. All very secret, ye ken, and a bit time-consuming. And things are a little sticky just now."

Gurney drummed his fingers impatiently on the arm of his chair. "Why's that?"

"Och, it seems that the John Company have got it in their heads to make a big killing with the opium. As a result the price at the Factory has fallen from two thousand dollars to fifteen hundred; a lot more mud's going in illegally, and the emperor's getting a wee bit savage. They say it's because most of his army are overfond of the pipe, and it interferes with their maneuvers. But I reckon what he's really worried about is the drain on his silver. Before some bright lad had the idea of selling the Chinks opium, they didn't need anything the West could produce. So when we wanted their tea, we had to pay cash on the nail, and it disappeared into nice big jars in their nice big treasure houses. Now they pay us for the opium—in silver dollars, because for your Chinese silver is the color of money, not gold—and we pay them for their tea with those same dollars. And I don't have to tell you whose side bears the larger profit margin, with the Company controlling the Patna opium crop. But be that as it may, how does a thousand dollars a chest sound as a price for your cargo? I'd offer you more, only there's some funny business going on at the moment, which means I may have to keep it in my warehouse for some time."

Gurney fought to control his emotions. Seventy-five thousand dollars! Sixteen thousand dollars apiece for Basreddin and himself, and the rest the crew. So much for navy prize money! He fingered his chin thoughtfully. "That seems a reasonable enough offer, Mr. Gordon."

"Good. Well, that's settled—subject to inspection of cargo, mind. Ye'll join me in a dram? No hurry, no hurry. Wong!"

The Chinese factotum hurried into the room with

ā silver tray bearing a square decanter, a jug of water, and two heavy lead-glass goblets.

"Slainte!"

Gurney raised his glass and drank. After a year of crude native firewaters, the straight malt slid over his tongue like ambrosia. The Scot chuckled. "Ah, but it's good to see a man who likes his dram. I have the water shipped from Deeside at the spring melt, and the whiskey's my brother's distilling."

After half an hour of talk, Gordon led Gurney on a tour of the hulk. The aftercastle, with its counting-house, Gordon's quarters, and a glass-topped conservatory filled with plants from all over the world, fascinated Gurney. And the rest of the ship, a labyrinthine complex of storerooms, warehousing, and chandlery, gave him cause to marvel at his host's apparently limitless scope of interest. In his well-stocked library were books in five languages, protected against the salt air by sliding fronts of plate glass; and in his warehouses were pins and muskets, pharmaceutical goods and chiming clocks, marine supplies and hair ribbons. By the time Wong bowed himself up to them and told them that the Vandal's dayboat had returned, Gurney felt as if he'd known the other man all his life.

"You'll dine on my ship?"

"Thank ye kindly. I'll take the opportunity of inspecting your cargo before the light goes, if I may?"

They threaded their way through the moorings out toward the Vandal's anchorage. The harbor was busy in the late afternoon; sampans rocked by, and the occasional junk, its rail lined with inquisitive yellow faces, veered to take a closer look as the longboat, eight oars dipping as one, carved a straight track toward the Vandal's sharply raked masts.

Gurney cast a covert look at Gordon as McIver and his sidemen piped them alongside navy-style. The Scot was nodding approvingly to himself, obviously impressed by the easy discipline of the men at the rail, the freshly pipe-clayed sail covers, and the gleaming brass strakes. Scruffy, bearded, and bare-

foot these ruffians might be; but they exuded a
confidence as sound as any you'd find on a navy ship.
At the entry port, Basreddin bowed deeply. Gurney
signaled McIver to dismiss and called the Sufi over.
Under his arm he held a thin sheet of ivory covered
in neat Arabic script. Gurney introduced him.

"Mr. Basreddin has prepared the cargo manifest.
Shall we check the goods first? We'll dine in about
an hour."

Four hands lifted the hatch from the hold, and Gordon climbed down, followed by Gurney and Basreddin. The merchant examined the chests. "The stamp's
all right, at any rate. Pass me your chisel." With a
practiced wrench, he levered the top off one of the
cases—not the one nearest him, Gurney noticed. No
booby, this Hamish Gordon. He pulled out a ball of
dried poppy leaves, gashed it with his chisel, sniffed
at the black, treacly juice, and nodded.

They climbed out of the hold and into the broad
stern-cabin. The slight breeze blowing through the
open portholes was a welcome relief after the dense
muskiness of the hold. Gordon lit a candle, scooped
out a blob of opium with the point of his knife, and
watched intently as it bubbled, smoked, and burned
away to hard, black ash. The saloon filled with pungent blue smoke.

"Good. There's no cow-flop in this lot. Ye'd be surprised at the makeweights that some of the brethren
try to pass off as the number one mud. Only last
week there was a whisper going around that some enterprising gentleman had tried to sell Mr. Otway a
load of molasses." Gordon smiled with pleasure. "They
pulled him out of Macao harbor three days later. He's
a bad man to tangle with, that Otway."

Gurney's hands clenched on the arms of his chair.
But as he started forward, Basreddin's warning look
drilled into him, and with a mind-cracking effort of
self-control he sank back into his seat, the cabin spinning around his head.

"A man may come to an evil end through over-
caution as well as rashness; the raftman and the foot

traveler both avoid the ford when the river is in spate."

"True, true." Gordon, surprised, was looking at Gurney with narrowed eyes. The younger man had gone white as a sheet, and the scar on his temple throbbed. "Aye, he's a bad lot, this Otway," he resumed thoughtfully. "He's made many enemies in the three ports. A greedy man. It's been a long hard job reaching terms with the mandarins, and it's the likes of Otway who will finish by ruining the trade for everyone, wi' their smuggling and their politicking. But you seem to recognize the name?"

Gurney's face was set in a grim mask. "I have . . . crossed this man's path before now, in England. He was ever one to deal crooked and make enemies."

"And by the way you speak, I'd be ready to guess that you fit the latter category like a nut its shell. Well, far be it from me to cross you. The man's a plague and a blight."

"You say he's a smuggler? What need, if there's a free trade at Canton?"

"Well may you ask. And ye must understand that what I've heard is only rumor. But it's rumor well founded on solid information. You know from your voyage on the *White Rajah* that your Company controls all sales of Patna opium, selling to the country traders who deal with the Factory at Canton. But Malwa opium—grown in Rajputana—isn't under Company control. So when this Otway had to leave England in a hurry—by the looks of things, you know more about that than I—what did he do but buy the whole Malwa crop for the year, about four thousand chests in all. I hear that he had to mortgage all his ships and most of his other assets to raise the cash. But then he found that the country traders in India and at Canton, fearful of losing Company goodwill, wouldn't touch the stuff. So Otway had to hire American skippers who didn't give a fig for the Company, and arrange alternative means of distribution on the Chinese mainland. Anyway, he's a cunning man. And the Chinese are a weird lot—worship their grandpas

and their emperor, but would do either of them down
for a brass farthing. Corrupt as bedamn and ambi-
tious as tinkers' wenches, the lot of them. But the
Cohong, the group of merchants who deal with the
Factory at Canton, are pretty much under the imperial thumb. So Otway found this half-Jesuit Chink who
knew of a mandarin who runs a fortress-village called
Haipo, to the west of Macao. The mandarin's called
Han Sat Fen, and he's an ill-reputed devil if ever
there was one. They say that he's trying to break the
Cohong monopoly so he can make himself the richest
single man in China; and in an empire like this one,
where human life is no' so dear as in ours, money—
silver dollars—and political power are boon companions. So Otway is providing this savage with the
means to start a popular rising—at a price. If he
comes out of it with his head, I'd guess he'd multiply
his original investment by about twenty. But it's
a dangerous game he's playing, not only for him
but for all of us trying to turn an honest penny in
these heathen parts."

"But how's he putting the stuff ashore? It's a hellish
tricky coast over that way, and I can't see a deep-sea
merchantman agreeing to go anywhere near it."

"He's got himself a wee deep-sea harbor on an island called Klimhoa about twenty miles off Haipo.
They say that Han had the seaward approaches and
the mainland passage charted, and presumably he
passed his information on to Otway. But Otway keeps
very close. I suspect that his Americans pick up charts
of the approaches in Manila and that Han collects
from Klimhoa in one of his fifty-oar galleys—centi-
pedes, they call them."

Gurney and Basreddin exchanged looks.

"Would you excuse us for a moment? Please help
yourself to a glass of brandy." When they returned
to the cabin ten minutes later, Gordon was gazing at
his glass with some distaste. Gurney laughed. "I'm
afraid it's not as good as your malt. Singapore brimstone, in fact. Well now, Mr. Basreddin and I have a
proposition we'd like to put to you. I'm sure it will

be to our mutual advantage, but before I begin I must enjoin you to the strictest secrecy. May I have your word as a gentleman?"

Gordon decided that he liked this young man. God knows he was sick of the petty meanness, the pomposity, and the pretentions of the likes of Otway. The East had a way of corrupting mind and body; he'd watched too many fresh young bucks turn cynical and devious under its insidious spell. There was directness about Gurney, and behind the engaging exterior he sensed a core of steel. And the black man, for all his weird ways, seemed straight enough. "Aye, ye have my word."

As the light faded and ships' lanterns began to glow yellow in the black water, Gurney began to talk. The wakes of passing sampans lapped against the *Vandal*'s waterline, rocking the cabin lamps gently on their gimbals. The level of liquid in the brandy bottle sank slowly. Gordon listened intently, eyebrows dancing with a will of their own on his broad forehead. Basreddin stroked his beard thoughtfully while Gurney's voice, quiet but insistent, droned on.

When he had finished, he looked inquiringly at Gordon. The Scot clapped his hands to his thighs, threw his head back, and roared with laughter. "Remarkable! And completely illegal! But by God I like it! I'm your man. Gi'e me your hand on it."

Gurney got up and fetched pen, paper, and ink from a locker. He wrote two laborious paragraphs on each sheet—it was a good three months since he'd last put pen to paper—signed his name at the bottom of each page, and passed them over to Gordon, who signed, put one in his pocket, and gave the other back to Gurney.

Duplessis, the cook, had used his pidgin to good effect in the shore village of Ka Sai Chin. After a dinner of burgoo followed by local fish and two brace of ducks roasted in the Pekingese manner, Gurney and his two companions felt relaxed and expansive. As the brandy circulated and conversation became general, Gordon waxed lyrical about the beauties of the Kowloon peninsula and his botanical finds there.

"But I was under the impression that Europeans couldn't land, except to trade," said Gurney.

"Ah, but there's trading and trading." Gordon smiled. "These poor sailormen sitting out here all year must have their diversions; the local mandarin, though not a man I'd trust very far as a general rule, turns a conveniently blind eye to the occasional leg-stretching excursions. And there's a full-fledged grog-shop for those desirous of exercising their elbows, though I wouldn't recommend it to a man not tired of life. And there's old Joe Apoo's bathhouse too."

Gurney had had just enough to drink to take this as a challenge. "Very well. Steward! Get the gig along-side. We're going to see Mr. Apoo and get clean."

The little half-caste girl's eyes sparkled knowingly, and Gurney patted her bottom as he went out the door. She wiggled and said, "Prease to come back soon, makee more number one good time."

Gurney had half a mind to go right back into the little room with the low bamboo bed and the smell of joss sticks. La-liu was really most talented, and it was so long since he had set eyes on a woman except in his dreams that he had almost forgotten. La-liu had reminded him, and forcibly; her tiny body was de-lightful, and she had provided ample evidence of the legendary Oriental skill in the amatory arts.

He turned and went down the corridor, pressing some coins into the hand of the old Chinaman whose eyes, slitted under his pillbox hat, glittered with min-gled cunning and avarice. Gurney hiccuped slightly. Old Joe's gin was a loathsome brew, but it certainly put an edge on the evening.

The Chinaman parted the bead curtain, shook hands with himself vigorously, bowed, and let Basreddin and Gurney out of the house. As the old man closed the street door behind them, a hunched figure stum-bled drunkenly out of the shadows, tripped on a lump of refuse, and sprawled full-length in the road. A bottle rolled into the gutter, and the man began to sniffle. Gurney bent down and yanked him to his feet.

The drunk began to mumble in English. "Oh, thank you, kind sir. It'sha hard world full of Chinkies and ruffians for a poor rat catcher like me wotsh far from 'ome by the crool wickedness of a villain of a squire." His breath reeked of rotgut rum. He swayed and would have fallen if Gurney had not caught him by the scruff of the neck.

Gurney turned to Basreddin, his eyes chips of blue ice. "Well, well, well. May I introduce you? Mr. Basreddin—Mr. Otway's friend Zeb Watkins, through whose good offices we find ourselves here today."

The drunk's teeth began to chatter.

"Get a grip on yourself, you sot. You're coming with us. And when you've dried out, we've got a lot to talk about, you and I."

10

The hands of the brass chronometer screwed to the bulkhead of the aftercabin pointed to half past twelve. Gurney massaged his temples with his hands, for his head was throbbing dully. It had been six o'clock by the time they had lugged Zeb aboard, and then there had been work to do.

Basreddin stuck his bearded face around the cabin door. "I have brought you a gift from the Gordon." He tossed a bundle of clothes on the deck.

Gurney had foresworn yesterday's fripperies in favor of his usual ragged linen shirt and canvas breeches; but the time was fast approaching when he'd have need of decent clothing.

"Did he give you the bills of lading?"

Basreddin produced a packet from the folds of his robe. Gurney tore it open, inspected the contents, and

grinned. "Thanks. We'll discuss this later. In the mean-
time, let's go and take a look at Mr. Watkins. He
should have dried out by now."

The air of the sail locker where Zeb had spent a
troubled night was thick with the stench of vomit.
Gurney picked the cringing Dorsetman up by the
scruff of his neck and dragged him through the hatchway onto the foredeck, where he collapsed in a heap.
"Pieter! Get me a bucket of water." The coxswain
brought a brimming pail. "Sling it over his head." Zeb
spluttered and choked as the salty stream sloshed
over him, gluing his grimy gray locks to his forehead.
Bloodshot yellow eyes stared with ratlike ferocity
at his tormentors. Gurney prodded him gingerly. "On
your feet!"

Shaking his head bemusedly, Watkins struggled
upright. He was a small man, sallow of complexion,
clad in rags which had once, apparently, belonged
to a well-to-do merchant but which were now tied
together with string and crusted with filth. Gurney
didn't like to think what had become of the original
owner. The shifty eyes widened in recognition. Watkins shrank back, holding his head in his hands.

Gurney raised a quizzical eyebrow. "So you remember me, do you, scum? It's a long time since we
were rabbiting together on Badbury Rings. I'm surprised that you haven't looked me up since. But then,
I was forgetting. You could hardly consort with fugitives such as myself, bound servant as you were to
the Very Honorable Mathias Otway, merchant and
gentleman." The bantering expression was still on
Gurney's face, but his eyes were hard. "I think you'd
better tell me how you come to be here and in such
a state as this. Pieter, get him a pannikin of rum;
he'll need it."

Zeb was trembling like a man with the ague. He
was unconscious of anything but a crippling terror.
This scarred and stained brigand, brown and hard
as a mahogany log, was the pink-cheeked snotnose
of two year ago? Searching back in his fuddled mind,
Watkins decided that he'd be lucky if he got out of

this alive. The pannikin rattled against his teeth as he drank. He all but gagged as the fiery spirit coursed into his queasy guts. Gurney waited for the dose to take effect. The man's body appeared to fill out, and a bright patch of color appeared on each cheekbone. The rheumy eyes grew crafty.

"Well, master, it started after you left Mendlebury after that disagreement you had with Mr. Otway. It so happens that I'd come into a little money about then, what with Mr. Otway leaving and all, and I thought, well, I might as well take meself to Dorchester fair. I had a few drinks at the fair and got talking to this Gypsyish sort of lass, and she took me back to her wagon. Then damn if I don't come round the next day in a lugger in the Channel five miles off the Needles. When I ask where I am, the bastard of a skipper gives me a crack on the head and tells me I'll find out soon enough. So I says, 'Look here, when Mr. Otway finds out about this, he'll have the runners on you in no time flat!'

"He sorto' laughs, 'Oho, my beauty, so your precious Otway's going to save you from the wicked press-gang, is he? Well now, you might be interested to know that it was Otway's agent at Lymington as gave me a guinea to deliver you—where you'll find out soon enough.' That night they took me on a merchantman heading downchannel, and they told me that Mr. Otway had signed me on as supercargo for the China run. Then they put me to work."

He shuddered at the recollection. "I wun't go up them masts, not to save my life. So that hog of a third mate, he finds out my profession ashore. 'Rabbit catcher, eh?' he says. 'Well then, you can try your hand at the rats. We've got a cargo of cotton stuff and loose biscuit, and they're running wild below.' So I spent the next six months lookin' for rats in the bilges, sleepin' in a corner of the hold. And when they landed me here, I got one of they Chinee letter writers to send word to Mr. Otway, being as how I'd heard he were at Macao. But he never answered. And I couldn't get a berth on a merchantman on account of my not being a seaman trained, and the neuralgy. I were near on my last legs when you came along. An' very glad I am to see you, too, sir." He eyed Gurney, working his hands fawningly.

Gurney smiled at him sweetly. "A moving tale. But I think you've left a few things out. Before Mr. Otway left England, did you not assist him in the— let me see, how would he have put it?—'deflation of a coxcomb'?'" Watkins seemed to shrink in his clothes. His face turned the color of putty. "Thirty pieces of silver to spend at Dorchester fair, eh, Watkins?" Zeb's teeth were chattering again. He shook his head desperately, clutching the rail as if the ship were pitching violently.

"Pieter, tie this man to the main topsail halyard and show him the view. You'll find that a sudden flow of blood to the head refreshes the memory wonderfully. And if by any chance the recollective powers aren't improved in the next twenty seconds, I'll tell this Dutchman here to let go the halyard. It'll foul the decks, but I'm prepared to let that happen this once."

A violent shove knocked Watkins sprawling, and a noose pulled tight around his ankles. He yelled with terror as he was hauled to the main truck a hundred feet above the deck, where he swung dizzily, head downward. He was almost too terrified to speak; gobbling noises came from his throat, and he clutched desperately at the smooth, unsympathetic main topmast.

"Oh, no, we can't have that." Gurney smiled grimly. "Drop him ten feet, Pieter." The Dutchman let go a short bight of rope. Watkins fell like a stone and was brought up short with a sickening jerk, screaming with horror. "No, no, I'll do anything, just let me down for the love of God." Gurney nodded, and Pieter and the mate, controlling his laughter, lowered away until Watkins lay in a whimpering heap on the deck.

"I don't believe in flogging. But any more trouble out of you and I'm prepared to make an exception.

You'll sling your hammock with the rest of the men, if they'll have you. Now get out of my sight."

"Port your helm!"

The man at the wheel spun the brass-bound spokes deftly. Gurney peered into the darkness as the *Vandal's* bowsprit swung into line with the *Maid of Perth*, a patch of blacker darkness in the gloom. The longboat with its crew was lost in the darkness forward; only the slight creak of rowlocks and the taut towrope betrayed its presence. Basreddin, at the tiller of the longboat, saw the side of the hulk rear beside him like a cliff.

"Easy all. Ship oars." They were drifting slowly forward now. Basreddin knew that the slight stern breeze would keep enough way on the *Vandal* for her to come alongside.

Gurney watched as the rail glided by eight feet above his head. A rope came snaking down, and O'Shea leaped to make it fast to a bollard on the *Vandal's* quarter. Other hands lowered thick hempen mats over the starboard side. The schooner gradually lost way. As she came to a dead stop, bow and stern lines were made fast, and four men padded into the waist to remove the hatch covers of the main hold.

There was soft hail from the hulk. "*Vandal?* Stand by." The derrick creaked out overhead. From it a heavy tackle dropped slowly into the hatch. A minute later four mango wood opium chests swung upward in the gloom. As load after load of opium swung away into the night, Gurney bit his nails and fretted. Once, when a lashing parted and a chest crashed onto the deck, he almost shouted with rage and shock. He couldn't fail now. Not after eighteen months of stinking pork and cold rice, blazing sun and icy cold.

He was lucky to have found Gordon. Gurney's opium was being transferred here instead of at Canton. Eyebrows would certainly be raised if Gurney

were to sail for Canton in an empty ship. What
would be the point? Tongues would wag, and it
would be only a matter of time before news of his
presence reached Otway. And then the fat would
really be in the fire. So Gordon and Gurney had
drawn up a private agreement to transfer the mud
under cover of darkness. And there was another transfer to make which was best undertaken out of sight
of prying eyes.

A double blast on a bosun's pipe announced that
the last chest had left the hold. Gurney held up a
warning hand to O'Shea, who was standing at the
stern line. "Bide your time. I've a little present for
you. Here it comes now."

Out of the murk a huge tarpaulin-wrapped bundle
was descending. O'Shea grinned as he recognized the
long, graceful barrel and chunky carriage of a great
gun. "Sixty-four-pounder, sir? She's going to take
some stowing. One bounce out of her and we'll have
a hole in the side you could sail a trawler through."

"Very well then. Get forward and see to it. We'll
have her in the hold for the moment." O'Shea scuttled
below to direct the placing of the new cargo.

A rope ladder rattled down the side of the merchantman, closely followed by Gordon, who landed
on the *Vandal*'s deck with a thump.

"Och, but I'm getting too old for this sort of thing."

"You're lucky to be alive at all, the way you were
behaving last night."

"Ah well, nothing ventured, nothing gained. Though
that's no' a very profitable philosophy for a respect-
able merchant such as myself. Here, I've brought the
bills of sale and five thousand dollars on account. Oh,
aye, and here's a drop of comfort for the long eve-
nings." He pressed a large black bottle into Gurney's
hand. "Highland dew. Slainte." Then he disappeared
up the ladder into the night.

Gurney passed the word to cast off. The longboat
took the strain, and the *Vandal* drew gradually ahead
of the *Maid of Perth*. When she was well clear, Gur-

ney gave the signal to bring her head to wind and
hoist the longboat into its davits. Ten minutes later
the moon, bursting from behind the distant rain
clouds of the Chinese mainland, revealed the *Vandal*
creaming to seaward under a white cloud of canvas.

Two weeks later, the *Vandal* lay in the anchorage
at Pin Mau, one of the countless uninhabited islands
that stud the seas to the west of Macao. Beneath her
keel was six fathoms of clear blue water. Two ramshackle Chinese fishing boats, matting sails furled,
were moored astern. Their owners, whose terror at
their capture a week ago had been somewhat mollified by a lavish gift of dollars, squatted on the strip
of silver beach that connected the two tree-clad islets.
They watched in mystification as the foreign devils
aboard the sleek black schooner hammered, sawed,
and scrubbed in the blazing noonday heat. The *Vandal's* sides shone with a new coat of black paint. Her
rails and strakes were gleaming with varnish, her gun
ports were picked out with bright yellow, and under
her bowsprit was a new figurehead. Basreddin had
occupied himself on the passage from Hong Kong in
carving it from a block of mahogany; it represented
the head of a Tartar warrior. From each corner of
the grimacing mouth trickled a scarlet thread of
blood, and on the brow of the pointed helmet was
emblazoned the Sufi octagon.
O'Shea, the gunner, was supervising the finishing of
a new gun port to larboard of the bowsprit. He had
talked long with the captain; now the *Vandal* was
to become the most fearsome engine of death and de-
struction in the South China Sea. Her ten carronades
could hurl a blizzard of iron at an adversary at either
broadside: her long sixteen-pounders could effective-
ly discourage enemies astern; and the sixty-four-
pounder, firing steel shell fused and packed with
gunpowder, would give her the forward firepower
of an entire battery. Volnikov, the giant Russian carpenter, had strengthened the deck forward, and now

the three tons of bronze and oak crouched threateningly in its tackles, muzzle staring over the bow, ready
to vomit a whirlwind at any challenger.

Astern, Basreddin and Mather, another of his re-
cruits, were donning blue canvas smocks and three-
quarter-length trousers. Mather was an experienced
small-boat man. He had wound up in Singapore as a
result of a disagreement with the skipper of the Cali-
fornia sealer in which he had sailed Canton-bound
from the Aleutians. The sealing captain had failed to
realize the foolishness of tangling with his best skinner
until Mather's blade had ripped his belly from groin
to solar plexus; and then it had been too late.
Mather had leaped overboard into an open boat and
had somehow navigated himself the two thousand-
odd miles to Singapore by way of Manila. He had
taken some time for even Basreddin to subdue; but
on a dry ship, he had proved true as the steel of
the flaying knife that was his constant companion.

Basreddin nodded a farewell to Gurney, who was
seated on the low cabin hatchway. He and Mather
climbed into one of the fishing boats. Mather was
carrying a sack, which wriggled and squawked. Two
hands holystoning the deck smirked as the incongruous pair—Basreddin had refused to take off his turban
—set the sail and bobbed out into the open sea.
Gurney called one of them over.

"Belay that for the moment. I want you to get up
to the main truck and watch that fishing boat. If you
see any movement, tell me immediately." The man
swarmed up the shrouds, shinned up the topmast,
and took up a precarious perch on the broad wooden
button at the top. Zeb Watkins, picking oakum in
the waist, watched him and shuddered.

As Pin Mau shrank astern, Basreddin shaded his
eyes and looked eastward. The three peaks of another island were beginning to show above the horizon; soon, from the tops of the swell it stood up
clear against the surrounding sea. He looked around.
Pin Mau was still visible, though it sank from view
in the troughs of the waves. He grunted to Mather.

"There. Klimhoa. Down sail." The matting collapsed on the boom, and the American lashed it down with lengths of grass rope. Basreddin opened his sack. Two cormorants fell squealing into the bottom boards. "Now we fish."

Mather looked on with puzzlement as the Sufi fastened a brass ring around the neck of one of the birds and motioned to him to do the same. To the ring was attached a long silk cord, whose free end he tied to the thwart. He then picked up the flapping bird and tossed it overboard. It sat in the water for a moment, eyeing him peevishly. Then it started to preen its black, oily plumage. When it had finished its toilette, it began to swim in a spiral. Suddenly it dived. Twenty feet of line ran out before it surfaced, beak pointed skyward. Mather shook his head.

Basreddin looked at him with an air of self-satisfied wisdom. "You will observe, O Frankish dog, that this bird has not eaten all day. Thus when it sees a fish, it will dive in pursuit. If the fish is small, it is swallowed. If it is large, the ring prevents it passing into the belly of our feathered ally, and it lodges in the throat. Would that I could attach a ring to the gullets of you unbelieving swillers of ardent spirits. Here, take the line." Basreddin then extracted a spyglass from its leather case and fixed it on the distant loom of Klimhoa.

When they returned to Pin Mau two and a half hours after sunset, there was a fair-sized basket of fish on the bottom boards. The next morning at dawn they set off again; but it was not until four o'clock on the afternoon of the fourth day of watching that Basreddin closed the glass with a snap and ordered Mather to hoist sail. On the horizon to the south of Klimhoa was rising a pocket-handkerchief-sized smudge of white canvas. Three hours later, the sampan was two miles upwind of a bluff-bowed merchant vessel of about three hundred tons burden. The last rays of the setting sun were lighting up her topsails as Basreddin tilted his conical straw hat forward over his eyes and unshipped the long sculling oar.

"When we come alongside this vessel, you stay in the boat and protect her against harm. You have your weapon?" Mather ran his thumb along the wicked edge of his knife and smiled. "But wait. Do not use it unless you must. Rather, feign the idiocy of the humble Cathayan. Myself, I have some small business to transact with the Frank who commands this vessel."

The captain of the bark *George G. Smeeton* was in a rage. For a day and a night he'd been following the chart Otway had given him; it was a damn tricky business keeping to the channel in this shallow waste of tiderips and knife-edge reefs, and he'd hoped to be safe in harbor by nightfall. Now he'd just have to anchor. Provided that the hook didn't drag and the bloody Chink pirates didn't make mincemeat out of him, he should be all right, but he wouldn't be really happy in his mind until he was safe under Otway's guns in Klimhoa anchorage.

He stumped into the day cabin and poured himself half a tumbler of whiskey, cursing the fever that shook his fleshless body and rattled his teeth against the rim of the glass. Two more years out east and he'd be dead. It was only the burden of his gambling debts that kept him here at all. And he didn't trust that slimy bastard Otway further than he could throw him. But he couldn't afford not to trust him; his mud bounty was five percent better than anyone else's. And five percent of $170,000 was a lot of money. He stared at the twilit hulk of Klimhoa through the large windows of the cabin and aimed a string of tobacco juice at the spittoon.

A slight movement behind him spun him around. By the cabin door stood a stooped figure in blue pyjamas, straw hat in hand, emanating a penetrating smell of fish.

"And what in the devil's name do you want, you heathen Chinese beggar? Who told you to come down here? Get out chop-chop or I'll slit your ears." He advanced threateningly on the slight figure.

The voice which checked him was unexpectedly soft and firm, with a trace of accent he couldn't identify. "It is simply that I and my brother, humble fishermen of this coast, have come to see whether we can provide you with some of the fruits of our labors." Basreddin straightened up and advanced a couple of steps. "But I see that you are not a well man. May I suggest that you rest? Rest . . ."

The captain's head swam. He sat down precipitately in a chair, waves of drowsiness sweeping over him. Through a great lassitude he seemed to hear the smooth voice trickling with the silvery insistence of a mountain waterfall. Everything was happy, peaceful. Of course he would give this wise and placid peasant what he wanted. He had but to ask. And then his poor, fever-racked body could sleep, rocked in the arms of the great mother sea . . .

By the time Basreddin finished copying bearings and soundings from the sheet in front of him, the light was fading fast. When the mesmerized trader awoke from his trance, he would remember nothing. He tucked the paper in the waistband of his trousers and strode to the door. Reassuming the waddle of a Chinese peasant, he scuttled across to the entry port, picked up the empty basket from the deck, simpered and bobbed his head at the uncaring seamen, and dropped into the sampan. The night breeze freshened in the sail as they nosed off toward the western horizon.

11

The galley and the heavy spritsail barge lay sprung together, lurching and corkscrewing in the short swell. In the helmsman's kennel on the barge, the horn lantern swung sickeningly to the ungainly wal-

lowing of the vessel. Otway, counting the paper-
wrapped rolls of silver dollars from the lacquer chest
between him and the Chinese, had never felt more
uncomfortable in his life. Even the steadily mount-
ing pile of coin in the sack at his side was no con-
solation; he knew he was going to be sick, and soon.

The Chinese, not a man given to humorous reflection as a general rule, was finding it hard to keep his
face still. The greedy barbarian opposite him, rivulets
of sweat running down the creases of a jowly face
rapidly greening with seasickness, was a contempti-
ble figure. The foreign mud that the lord's men were
at the moment transferring from the lighter to their
fast, fifty-oared centipede, would reap rewards on a
scale larger than this Otway could dream. Twenty
more such cargoes, and Han Sat Fen would be in a
position to challenge the emperor himself. And he,
Liam Fong, would be at his master's right hand, with
power of life or death a finger wave away. Like his
master, Liam Fong was a man of boundless ambition.

As the counting ended, he rose to his feet and
bowed courteously, bracing himself against the teetering of the deck. Otway, grunting, made as if to rise,
failed, and waved a dismissive hand. Liam's eyes
narrowed as he turned away and scaled the rope
ladder to the poop of the galley.

The rendezvous had been set for a point some five
miles to the south of Klimhoa, at the center of a
maze of reefs and channels. The wind blew fresh off
the mainland fifteen miles to the north. Despite the
three-quarter moon, which blazed from a star-
studded velvet sky, Liam Fong felt secure. No imperial vessel would risk the appalling loss of face
involved in a shipwreck in these waters; and besides,
did not his master and the barbarian Otway have
the only charts of the perilous return passage to
Haipo? He sniffed the wind. It would be a hard pull
home loaded with fifty chests of mud, but, in the
words of his revered ancestor, the road to power is
strewn with boulders. And boulders roll easiest across
the bodies of men.

Otway did not see the galley pull away into the darkness. He was hanging over the side of the bucketing barge, vomiting his heart out.

Gurney folded up the chart and drew the shutter over the dark lantern. Shrugging his shoulders deep into his coat, he took a deep breath and went on deck. The *Vandal* lay hove-to, borne up into the wind by the ebb tide. It would have to be within the next ten minutes, if tonight was to be the night. The channel in which his ship lay was the only route, as far as he knew, between Klimhoa and Han's fortress-village. And with full warehouses at Klimhoa, Otway would waste no time in making his trade. He looked around him, thrusting his hands deep into his pockets against the chill of the breeze.

The *Vandal* was completely blacked out. Her white sails were wetted to a shadowy gray, and earlier that day McIver had supervised the coating of her snowy deck planking with a thick layer of black mud. The only light came from an occasional speck of phosphorescence as a wave broke against her windward bulkwarks. Against the loom of the nearby islands, she was simply a lighter area of shadow.

Basreddin, the hood of his djellaba pulled low over his forehead, was scanning the heaving waters astern. Then he stiffened and tugged at Gurney's sleeve, pointing. Gurney strained his eyes and caught a spark of phosphorescence—about three cables downwind, he estimated. The dim luminescence resolved itself into a line of white foam. He felt his heart pounding; the blood sang in his ears, momentarily blotting out the muffled creaking of spars and cordage. The mate was at his side.

"McIver, bring her round. Starboard tack."

The mate slid away; the hands took the strain and heaved on the fore topsail braces. As the yards came round and the sails filled, the *Vandal* began to turn. Her great fore and main booms inched out over the port gunwale as the sails caught the wind and the deck tilted under Gurney's feet as he took the helm.

O'Shea, a dark shape in the bows, waved a hand. McIver, watching the sheeting of the topsails, saw the stars wheel overhead; and the *Vandal* surged towards the distant line of oar splashes like a killer whale after a wounded cachalot. She was approaching the centipede from dead ahead. O'Shea took up the final pressure on the linstock of the sixty-four-pounder. The oar splashes, foreshortened, were now two blotches of white flanking a dark bulk. Gurney waited until he could hear the thud of the oars and the grunt of the rowers before he gave the signal.

There was a blinding flash and the *Vandal* seemed to stagger in her tracks as the huge projectile, more than half a hundredweight of fused black powder, blasted from the sixty-four-pounder's enormous barrel and smashed through the high forecastle of the centipede, burying itself deep in the cargo before it exploded with a volcanic roar.

Gurney's ears were still ringing from the concussion when McIver began shouting new orders. The galley had stopped and was now being blown across the tide by the wind. The *Vandal* turned hard astarboard, and as she turned, O'Shea's crews gave her the full weight of the port broadside.

Liam Fong had been blown off the poop by the first explosion. As the shrieking rowers struggled to get free from their benches, the world erupted into a blizzard of flying metal and jagged wood splinters. What was left of the deck was covered with groaning, screaming men and things that had once been men. Pungent black smoke billowed from the hold, and flames cast an infernal light on the twisted faces of the dying. But, Liam noticed with shock, the only sound came from the sinking hulk of centipede. Was that a shadow flitting past outside the orbit of the flames? He dismissed it as a fancy caused by demons. Most agonizing was the fact that while the barbarian Otway had the silver, he, Liam, trusted lieutenant of the Lord Han Sat Fen, soon to be divine, had none of the mud. And with such shame a man could not live. As Liam drove the knife into his stomach, the

sea hissed in through the wounds in the centipede's
side.

*Letter to the Exalted Barbarian Eye Ot Weh
from his Self-Effacing and Unworthy Partner in
Mutually Advantageous Commerce, Sat Fen of
the Obscure House of Han.*

It has come to the attention of your unworthy
partner in trade that one of the vilest of his
servants, the oarsman Ping of the unseemly
House of Wan, was brought under the roof of
this Eye by a poor woman who had found him
on the shore of the island of Pisman in a state
of extreme physical and mental distress. This insignificant and unpleasant-looking oarsman told
the following tale before he appropriately ex-
pired, happily leaving no sons to mourn him.

"A demon of remarkable size and extraordinary ferocity appeared out of the wind and
planted a thunderbolt of exemplary but devas-
tating violence in the hull of our ship, which then
took fire, burning many of those whose rightly
laborious task it was to ply the oars. The demon
then roared angrily, causing a sudden rain of
wood, iron, and fire, which had the effect of de-
priving of life those unworthy toilers who had
escaped the first onslaught. This one saw with his
own admittedly defective eyes the henchman
Liam take his life in a noble and fitting manner;
then the bark sank beneath the waves, taking with
it his humbler companions. Providence cast before this one a large balk of timber, which
supported his short-lived carcass through a bewildering and tedious succession of tide races to
the inhospitable shore."

At this point the loathsome Ping became in-
capable of further speech, possibly due to the
fact that his ignoble head was struck from his
shoulders by his inquisitor.

It is of course a joy to me that one so fortunate
as yourself should have received the silver, while

an ill-principled and incorrectly observant villager such as myself should have lost both coin and mud. And the news that we will pay only half the normal amount of silver for the next consignment of mud and the one after that will undoubtedly impress you by its fairness. If not, your humble partner would remind you that the Isle of Klimhoa is part of the dominion of the Divine One, and were a chart of its approaches to reach the Imperial Constabulary, your well-conceived mercantile activities could be terminated rather abruptly. Let us hope that our next exchange, which will be consummated seven days from now at the same place under the ceaseless vigilance of a greatly increased force of arms, will have a happier outcome.

As the interpreter finished reading, Otway grabbed him by the scruff of the neck and flung him across the room. The little Eurasian scuttled out of the shack and down the makeshift quay, where the coolies were loading chests of opium from a shabby American merchantman into a spritsail barge. Drawing a long pipe from his sleeve, he squatted, tweezed a small blob of raw opium into the flame of a little oil lamp, and settled down to smoke.

Otway sat at the high stool behind the rough deal desk and gnawed his nails. It was impossible. It had to be a trick. No man alive could find his way through those channels without a chart, and he was sure that only Han and his trusted captains had copies. If Han Sat Fen was trying to back him into a corner, he'd chosen the right time. The four principal cargoes, brought with almost the last of his dwindling capital, were due into Klimhoa in ten days. He had one hundred and twenty chests of mud in the warehouse now; even at half price, he'd make something on the next load. And if he could renegotiate by the time the big consignment arrived, he should come out on the right side. If not . . .

Otway shivered.

So many cases on the open market at Canton would push the price right through the floor. He'd have to start again from scratch—if, that is, Jardine, the Scot who held the mortgages on his last remaining assets, didn't foreclose. It had been so much easier in the blackbirding days, before that young whelp Gurney had come sniffing round Arabella and upset the apple cart. You could talk man to man with those slavers, scum through they were; but these yellow devils were full of more tricks than an organ-grinder's monkey. There was only one thing for it. If he wanted to come out with the shirt still on his back, he'd have to go along with Han and take his medicine like a man. Otway reached for the brandy bottle, poured himself a tumblerful, and began to write.

The lookout on the galley strained his eyes into the murk ahead. Here, in the narrowest channel in the Klimhoa passage, was where danger would most likely lie. With the flood, the tide raced through a forty-yard gap like a mountain torrent; even now, with the tide on the turn, the calm water moiled and eddied with a sullen turbulence. The only sounds were the collective gasp of a hundred oarsmen as they dragged the oars into their chests, the chunk of rowlocks, and the hiss of the centipede's hull through the water. Han was taking no chances on this expedition. Thirty men, armed with swords and pikes, were clustered in the waist; each of the rowers had a club and a knife. Mounted high at poop and forecastle were six bronze cannon, richly chased with grotesque beasts and dragons, gunners at the ready, slow matches glowing in their tubs. Empty, the galley was a fleet enough vessel. Now, her only cargo fifty thousand silver dollars, payment for one hundred chests of opium, she sped through the windless night like a seal.

McIver flung the last of the buoys over the stern of the longboat, took the dark lantern from its locker, and flashed it twice to starboard.

A hundred yards away, at the other side of the

channel, a light shone briefly in reply. Between the *Vandal's* two longboats, on the surface of the water, lay a tangle of netting, buoyed with seine-net corks. The *Vandal*, all sails furled, not a glimmer of light showing, lay anchored at bow and stern where the channel widened to seaward.

The inside bow oarsman of the galley never knew what hit him. As he chopped his blade into the water for a new stroke, the oar seemed to take on a life of its own; it leaped out of the rowlock and smashed into his chest, crushing his ribs as it flung him and his mate over the side. Screams and yells drifted across the water to Gurney, and the dark bulk of the galley faltered and stopped. He nodded to the stroke oarsman of the longboat; the man's teeth showed in his blackened face as he bent to his oar.

The deck of the galley was in chaos. Oarsmen tugged at their blades to free them from the invisible encumbrances in the water; those who succeeded and tried to start rowing again became entangled, while the officers ran up and down the central catwalk screaming orders and striking out with the butts of their pikes.

Gurney cupped his hand to his ear and turned toward the *Vandal*. He heard the clacking of the capstan and saw her swing gradually to cover the centipede. A light flashed twice at the waist. "Down!" he roared. The longboat's crew flung themselves on their faces in the bottom boards as the *Vandal's* broadside erupted, blasting a sleet of grapeshot over their heads to sweep the decks of the Chinese. "Give way: 'ware nets!" The longboat leaped forward in the water, then coasted the last twenty yards to the drifting galley.

"Board!"

As Gurney heaved himself over the side, cutlass at the ready, he felt the wind of a bullet on his cheek. The decks of the galley were a charnel house. A figure rose up in front of him; he slashed at its head with his sword, and it fell away. Two more, one wield-

ing a spiked club and the other shortening his grip
on a pike, closed in. He pistoled the pikeman, feinted
at the other's head with his cutlass, and slipped in a
pool of blood. The fall knocked the breath out of
him, and he rolled to one side as the club whizzed
down, dealing him a glancing blow on the temple. As
if in slow motion, he saw the man's face twist into a
grin as he raised his arm for the coup de grace;
then the grin spouted blood, and Basreddin stepped
from behind him, fastidiously wiping his knife blade.

Gurney scrambled to his feet and looked around
him, dashing blood from his eyes. The forward part
of the galley was half-hidden in smoke. Basreddin
gestured with his thumb. "We cleared up forward.
The sting remains in the tail."

On the poop, the Chinese were fighting a desperate
rearguard action. At the head of the ladder a half-
naked giant was laying about him with a long sword;
as Gurney watched, McIver, backed by a knot of
boarders, rushed at him, parried his thrust, lost his
footing on the ladder, and fell. Gurney shook his
head to clear the red mists which threatened to overwhelm him.

"*Vandal!* To me!"

Smoke-blackened and bloodied, his men rallied in
the after part of the waist and hacked their way
to the poop ladder. Mather the sealer, bleeding from
a long slash below his shoulder blade, hefted his
skinning knife by the tip. The giant at the head of
the poop steps was aiming another slash at McIver
when Mather threw. The keen blade caught him in
the throat and he fell spread-eagled, clawing at the
hilt as the life bubbled out of him.

McIver, Basreddin and Gurney at his back, was
up the ladder like lightning. About a dozen Chinese
were clustered around a cannon, levering it around
to cover the waist of the ship. As they came over
the poop rail, Gurney saw the gunner press the slow
match to the firing hole. He knocked Basreddin
flat and dived for the deck as the world dissolved
into flame. Ears ringing and nostrils filled with the

stink of burned hair, he went for the gun crew like
a berserker, hacking, stabbing, gouging; then there
was a giant concussion at the nape of his neck, and
he sank into a deep well of droning silence.

*Letter from the Provincial Eye Han Sat Fen to
Barbarian Ot Weh in which Heaven asserts its
Just and Righteous Wrath.*

Be informed that the undignified and treacherous acts of such foreign dogs as yourself will
no longer receive the benisons of divine tolera-
tion, as in the past. Vengeance will come like
the thunderbolt from Heaven. Tremble, O moth
about to be shriveled by the Sun!

Otway's jaw dropped. The room swam before
his eyes. What could this mean? Two days ago he
had spent the night in the stinking wheelhouse of
the barge, wallowing in the swell at the rendezvous
point, waiting for a galley and fifty thousand dollars
that never arrived; and now this letter. And in three
days the whole of the 1820 Malwa opium crop would
be sitting in Klimhoa harbor. He had to make his
peace, and make it fast. But what in the name of
the devil was going on in that yellow savage's mind?

He called his interpreter. The man was obviously
terrified. "I want you to visit Han Sat Fen personally
and find out what's going on." Rather him than me,
he thought; I'll at least get out with a whole skin.

"But, Mr. Otway, that letter carries the superscrip-
tion of absolute condemnation."

"Poppycock to your absolute condemnation. Just you
get yourself over to the mainland and arrange a rendezvous with Han." The man cringed. Otway's face
had gone a dangerous purple, and he took a threatening step forward. "Now get yourself off the island!
Nielsen!"

His Danish sailing master climbed to his feet from
the bamboo chair where he had been sitting in the
afternoon sun.

"Make sure this rat gets to Haipo by tomorrow morning."

By God, but he'd pull the fat out of the fire yet. There was too much at stake for some trumpery Chinese swell to interfere at this stage of the game.

Night was falling as the sampan carrying the interpreter set off for the mainland.

By noon the next day, four large merchantmen were unloading in Klimhoa's horseshoe-shaped harbor. They had arrived on the morning tide, aided by a brisk westerly breeze blowing out of a clear sky. Barges and lighters plied constantly between the quay and the ships as Otway and his captains sat around the mahogany table in the aftercabin of the largest of them, the *Pride of Miskatonic*. The captains were expansive, jovial even. After they had unloaded and taken on gravel ballast, they would sail up to Canton and take on the green tea that their fellow Americans enjoyed so much. And this run would put enough silver in their strong rooms to found a tidy little fortune or two. The brandy bottle had circulated freely when a boy came into the cabin and whispered in Otway's ear.

Otway smiled a fat smile of satisfaction. "Send him in. Gentlemen," he said, "this is the moment we've been waiting for. Our messenger from Mr. Han Sat Fen, the other party in this deal."

The cabin door burst open. Nielsen, his face crusted with dried blood, lurched across the table and fell, scattering bottles and glasses. His bare back was crisscrossed with welts; around his neck hung a blood-stained bag. His lips moved, but at first no sound came. Otway bent his ear close. The Dane mumbled incoherently; then his eyes snapped wide open and he screamed, "They sawed him in half in the marketplace! I saw them! Like a log of wood! O my Christ!"

Otway clamped a hand over his mouth. The captains had jumped to their feet; one of them bent and opened the bag around the unconscious man's neck. Out of it rolled the severed head of the interpreter.

Morrison of the *Pride of Miskatonic* was the first

to speak. "Can you please vouchsafe us an explanation for this, Otway?"

But Otway was staring through the stern windows, across the green headland with its white strip of beach, toward the horizon. Like pale yellow butterflies on a field of cornflowers, the matting sails of a squadron of junks were bearing down on Klimhoa. And with the wind blowing directly into the harbor mouth, that could mean only one thing.

The man with the bandaged head in the dress of a Chinese fisherman pulled a telescope from the bottom of the boat and put it to his eye. Between him and the peaks of Klimhoa, the Imperial Regional War Fleet was sailing in full line of battle. Gurney passed the glass to Basreddin.

"Gordon was telling me that the Chinese naval philosophy is based on a book called *The Essentials of Fire Raft Attack*. Written in 1412 A.D. about a battle fought sixteen hundred years earlier. Rum bunch, if you ask me."

"In this instance it seems that the teachings of their ancestors have guided them well. Look, Giorgiou."

Gurney watched as the Chinese fleet hove-to about a cannon shot off the wide mouth of Klimhoa harbor. He saw a puff of smoke blossom from the deck of the leader; then the sea burst into flame, a long dancing wall bearing down on the four towering merchantmen and their smaller satellites. He watched in shocked fascination as a flicker of flame ran up the rigging of the largest of the ships. Within an instant it was blazing like a torch, and tiny black figures were leaping into the sea below. Then the other ships caught fire, blooming first with flame, then with a thick, oily black smoke which rolled eastward down the wind, blotting the island from view. He shut the glass. When Basreddin began to pull homeward against the stiffening breeze, Gurney mechanically bent his back to his oar.

He hardly saw the black pall over Klimhoa or the blazing torches that had until moments ago been proud merchantmen. He was back in the Dovecote Inn, with Arabella's perfume in his nostrils, the firelight casting red reflections on the ceiling. All that time ago, in another world, he had told Arabella that he would not rest until he had ruined Otway and made him acknowledge his treachery. Well, the first part of his bargain was filled; now he had only to accomplish the second and he would be free—free for Arabella, if she was still true to him. He put the doubts from his mind and rowed on, back to the harbor where the *Vandal* lay ready for sea.

12

The brass plate on the door of the stone building read, "Consulate General of His Portuguese Majesty." Gurney, uneasy in high collar and cravat, bright coat of blue broadcloth with brass buttons, nankeens and Hessians, rapped smartly.

A hoarse, booming voice rolled from inside. "Who the devil is it?"

"George Gurney, of the *Vandal*."

Slow, heavy footsteps crunched across the floor within, and the door opened. "Well, don't just stand there; come in. Ah. Excuse me." The short, stout man waved a hand at an extinguisher-hatted Chinese sculling a sampan on the smooth waters of the river which flowed past the bottom of the stone stairs from the counting house veranda. The Chinaman waved back and signaled with upraised fingers toward the island on the other side of the Pearl River.

"Sorry, lad," said the Portuguese consul, in the accents of Newcastle upon Tyne, "my night out. Off to Hainan island yonder for a turn this evenin'. Man's liver takes a bad beatin' without a bit of walkin' exercise. Dam' Chinks." He scowled, darkly. "Three times a month we get over there for a promenade. Other times, cooped up between the city walls and the Pearl River. No kind of life. Been here since 1811. Leaving soon. Sit down, sit down." Gurney, bemused by these rather one-sided conversational overtures, allowed himself to be piloted to a deep leather chair and opened his mouth to speak. But the consul resumed. "Good God, haven't introduced self. Shockin'. Davidson's the name, Bill Davidson, consul of His Majesty, er, never can remember the feller's name, king of Portugal. God knows how or why, but it's been good enough for the Chink and the Portuguese these ten years, and it's no' bad for me." His rheumy eye, black and hard for all its bleariness and veining, bored into Gurney. "And you are Gurney, eh? Can't say I understand what I've heard of ye—oh, aye, your name's been round the town—but I suspicion you've come here to sell me some gewgaw or other, eh? Aye, it always happens so. Those hoity-toity factors won't deal with the fast boys like yourself, and you all end up with Old Bill at the consulate. Well, if what I hear is true, it'll be a pleasure to deal with ye."

Gurney forced his way into the old man's monologue. "What do you hear?"

"Aye, well, not exactly what I hear, but it has come to my notice that one Mathias Otway has been running around town like a mad thing, and my old friend Hamish Gordon implied that maybe you and your lads would have a hand in that."

Gurney started forward in his chair. "Gordon told you—"

"Steady, lad. Calm yourself. Hamie's an old friend of mine, and I know well he's not tradin' in the mud unless it comes cheap and accidental. So when he gives me the agency on yon load you sold him, naturally I have to inquire as to where it comes from. Mud packed under the Company's seal's dangerous stuff to have in your hands without a good reason."

"And about Mathias Otway?"

"Well, it could be a bad slander, but he's been behaving very strange syne he came back down the coast. And I did hear a whisper, from an American who had maybe spent too long in old Joe Apoo's grogshop back in Hog Lane, that he'd had a commercial misfortune among the islands. Quite ferocious, was the American feller. Claimed he'd lost his ship. You wouldn't know anything about that, I suppose? But that's not a fair question. Your business?"

"I have silver that I would exchange for gold. Dollars, I hear, are at something of a premium now that the emperor purposes to ban the tea fleet, so I shall be looking for an advantageous price."

The Portuguese consul's brow grew lowering, and he quivered a little. "Aye, and it's yon damned unscrupulous East India Company playing God again for the benefit of we heathen. Why can they no' leave well enough alone? They had a nice thing going when they were growing the mud and turning the blind eye to its import, but they're greedy. No sooner do they see honest independents like myself turning the odd dollar with a chest or two than they want all the proceeds. So what do they expect? In the city there"—he jerked a thumb behind him, toward the towering walls of Canton—"there are a million people. And maybe fifty thousand of them are opium addicts. It's the same all over China, they say. Army officers, civil officials, professors, the best and the sharpest, dreaming their lives away for the profit of the Company. So no wonder the emperor gets itchy in his dragon books, or whatever he wears on his holy feet. We're ruining the country and we must take our medicine. And there's a bright side. The cargoes of tea that get back to England first this year are going to fetch a hell of a lot of money, even if the leaf's not too good. Someone's going to make a fortune." He shook his head. "Still, it's a chancy thing, all right. A game for a desperate man or a young man. Otway, now there's a man who's desperate enough." The small, shrewd eyes looked levelly at Gurney. "Can ye spare a day tomorrow? There's a thing I'd like to show you, downriver. Young Man."

Gurney felt he was being dismissed, so he rose and

bowed to the curiously impressive figure in the over-stuffed chair. "Certainly. Tonight I lodge at Canton, but tomorrow I return to my ship at Whampoa. I presume it is in the deep water anchorage that your errand lies?" The northerner nodded. "Good. Then perhaps after we have made our tour, you will join us for dinner on the *Vandal*? Though the ship is small, we have acquired a tolerable cellar."

Davidson bowed gravely once more and ushered Gurney to the door. Then he went to his desk, called for fresh pens, and began to write. He was still writing and chuckling in turns when the time came for his promenade, but he waved his companions impatiently away, and they set off without him. Old Bill was obviously onto something good, and wild horses wouldn't drag him off the scent of money.

Bright and early the next morning, Gurney reported to the jetty of the consulate. Davidson was waiting for him, sprawled in the cushions at the stern of a six-oared barge, ornately carved with mythical beasts, the white crusted with red lacquer and gold leaf. Gurney had slept indifferently, and his head ached. The cigar the consul was smoking smelled vile, and he began to feel somewhat bilious. But the cushions were soft enough, and the varied traffic on the Pearl River soon diverted his attention from his ills. The dirty green-gray waters were thick with boats of all shapes and sizes, from the dirty little cockleshells sculled by ragged, emaciated Chinese in conical hats to the great gong-booming barges of the mandarins, huge eyes painted at their bows, driven by forty well-fed paddlers, their muscles gleaming with oil.

Gurney became aware that the consul was lecturing him, somewhat in the manner of a tour guide. It was a relief to lie back in the cushions and let the stream of talk flow over him as his headache receded. The traffic thinned out as they went downstream, and soon the dull landscape of paddies and walled villages, each with its spirit pond, stretched to the green mountains on either side.

The day had started cloudy, but the sun was break-

ing through the clouds as they came in sight of a
jumble of buildings, boats, and mastless hulks, over
which towered a tall, nine-roofed pagoda, its eaves
brilliant green. Beyond the pagoda rose a forest of
masts and spars. Gurney strained his eyes for the
Vandal's, but could not be sure of her in the thicket.

Davidson pointed. "Ye see there, in the center of the
channel." The masts seemed to get taller in the general direction he indicated, and Gurney nodded. "Tea
ships. Two of them, come up fast on the off chance
the emperor makes the ban. I know a man who could
fill 'em both, though I don't know if he will or not.
Ye'll see what I mean when we come closer."

Twenty minutes later, they were lying head to the
current in the channel, the oarsmen holding water.
Davidson waved a hand. "Well, there they are. On
your right the Indiaman Nabob, ten years a fast run-
ner. On your left, the bark Swallow, out from Liverpool on her maiden voyage; never carried anything
but ballast and a bale or two of brummagem linen."

Gurney ran his eyes over the Nabob. Nothing much
to get excited about, he thought, as his eyes wandered
towards the Vandal, whose steeply raked masts were
visible upstream. The Nabob had the lines of your
run-of-the-mill East Indiaman, a little sleeker and
finer perhaps, but not so as you'd notice. Fast of her
kind, for sure: indeed, were she to rid herself of the
pernicious habit of striking topsails at night, she
would be the fastest thing on the sea over a nonstop
run from here to the West India dock.

But the bark was an entirely different kettle of fish.
Beside the Nabob, she looked like a racehorse beside
a hunter. The hollow sharpness of her bow, her long,
low freeboard, and her scooped-away, slender stern
gave her the same lines as the Vandal's. But she was
half again as long, with a prodigious volume of her
below the waterline. Either she would go like a rocket
or—Gurney looked up at her three towering masts
and her enormous bowsprit—a puff of wind would
blow her right out of the water. Be that as it might,
she was a true Thoroughbred of a ship, and one

ideally suited to the carrying of a light cargo like tea
in chests. But Davidson was shaking his head.

"Aye, she's a pretty enough thing now, and fast as
all get out, they say. But God, I'd hate to see her in a
blow. They say that she turned her captain's hair
white on the cruise out. What d'ye say?"

Gurney reflected. "I can see why she'd be a fickle
one. But she came through the side of a couple of
typhoons out there if she came in this week, so it
can't have been an easy cruise. Myself, I'd like the
handling of her before I delivered judgment. But that's
all very interesting. Thank you, Mr. Davidson. And
now, may I offer you the hospitality of my ship?"

His mind worked furiously as they were pulled to
the Vandal's entry port. Davidson looked at him out of
the corner of his eye. Then he leaned back in his seat,
rubbing his hands. It looked as though he had a deal.

Davidson had finished a fourth glass of brandy and
was leaning back in his chair in the Vandal's stern
cabin, his waistcoat unbuttoned. It had been a long
dinner, and the sun was dipping over the mountain
peaks to the west. Gurney's face was a little flushed,
and his hair hung in yellow spikes over his forehead.
He felt slightly breathless, but he wasn't sure whether
that was the result of the heat or of the information
Davidson had brought with him.

Unlike Gordon, whom he had found congenial company as much because of his strange botanizing
quirks as because of any pecuniary or strategic advantage that might arise from his advice, Davidson
seemed to live only for the political and financial in-
trigues and scandals that ripped through the Canton
Factory like squalls through the doldrums. Gurney
leaned forward and pushed the decanter back to Davidson, who poured himself a generous slug and settled back again.

"So you want a passage home, do you? Seems to me
you couldn't do better than to get a berth on the
Swallow yonder. I won't say I'd go—I'm too old to be
riding racehorses; but if she can get through the forties

with all her masts, she'll be home safe while the *Nabob*'s still puffing up the Azores. And you could do worse than take a share in her cargo. With the way the Hoppo's acting up—he's the number one Chink, ye know—the lads are saying up in the Factory that we're going to be damn lucky to get any tea out this year at all. It's those bloody swabs trying to bring the mud price down to edge out the private traders."

The only apparent effect the drink had on Davidson was to knock the diplomatic mask aside a fraction, so that the august body he had previously called John Company had been relegated to "those bloody swabs." Likewise, Otway, about whom Gurney had been pumping him discreetly, had become "that preaching hound."

Gurney nodded. "So the *Swallow* will have her cargo soon?"

"Aye, and the *Nabob* too. Ye'll probably see the barges loading now. Listen." And sure enough, across the water came a regular pounding thud. "That'll be old Gippo Hawke at it again. He's the *Swallow*'s master. Never stops, that man. Drives his men all day and night. The *Swallow*'ll be a tight ship if he has anything to do with it. D'you know what they're doing over there?"

Gurney shook his head, and the northerner snorted. "I can see you haven't been in the merchant service for long, seaman though you must be to have come this far." The brows drew together. "But that's your business. What's happening down in the *Nabob* is that they're laying sacks of saltpeter out over the dunnage, maybe bundles of bamboo or some such, and then they're wetting with saltpeter and they're bashing it flat. They'll roll it with a hogshead of water, then they'll cram and jam the tea chests in on the top of that, nigh on twenty thousand of the little beauties."

Gurney was interested. "How could a man set about getting himself a part of the cargo on the *Swallow*?"

"Nothing to it. Come to that, I'll handle that for you, and get you the passage too. Oh, aye, that gives me great pleasure. I'll take ye over in the morning and introduce you to Gippo. Ye'll have much to discuss, as one or two of the things he's done are very much of the warlike persuasion." He winked broadly. "Now give the brandy a fair wind, and we'll drink to a speedy and safe passage. God's blood, but I'll even put some money on myself. Strictly as a wager, ye'll understand."

"A wager?"

"Aye. When all the shares are sold out, the lads sometimes get together and make book on the ships homeward bound. Harmless fun, ye know. Except when the wagers are of a size where they'd buy out crews, ships, and men five times over. This year, there's little tea, so I'd guess big money will be out, either for the cargo or the race. But don't you fret; old Bill'll get you in on the ground floor with Gippo. The man owes me a favor." And he laid his finger alongside his bulbous nose, winked again, and concentrated fiercely on lighting his cigar.

The day turned out hot, and the air from the sea was thick and humid. Mathias Otway was mopping his crimson face with a soaking handkerchief as he puffed out of the countinghouse squeezed under the towering walls of Canton. It was worse than he had expected. The men he called his "bankers"—though he now saw them in a clearer light, the damned shylocks—had not accepted his regrets at the loss of their capital with a good grace. Indeed, it seemed that only two possibilities remained. One was to return to England, hope to realize enough to pay off his debts by the sale of his remaining assets, and in all probability finish by rotting with the other insolvent debtors in the Fleet prison. The other was to go into voluntary exile with what remained, to sit on some island, ruler of a petty kingdom of natives, till fever got him or his henchmen turned on him.

For Otway, the admiration of those he liked to consider his peers was the stuff of life, so neither prospect pleased him. He puffed stertorously against the tapes of his gray, clerical sort of waistcoat, eyeing with disgust the human refuse flopping and snoring alcoholically in the gutters of Hog Lane.

Just inside the doorway of Ben Bobstay's House of Salubrious Refreshment, Zebedee Watkins poured a couple of glasses of rotgut gin down his grubby shirtfront and lurched into the narrow, filthy street. Though the man was clearly three sheets to the wind, he looked oddly healthy. His face was covered with greasy dirt, true; but it was no longer the blackish gray of the hopeless derelict, and his eyes were clear, if still shifty. Someone with a keen sense of smell would have found it curious that while his clothes reeked of alcohol, his breath smelled of nothing stronger than onions.

Otway stopped to let the drunk reel past, looking down his nose with the air of offended piety which was second nature to him. His heart missed a beat as the drunk paused, seemed to recognize him, and extended both hands. Watkins! Otway had always been terrified by the prospect of physical violence, and for a moment he thought the derelict was going to attack him. But a rotten-toothed grin wavered in the stubble of his chin, and Otway found himself greeted as an old friend—as a long-lost brother. Watkins poured out a highly colored account of his tribulations to date, omitting, curiously enough, any reference to Gurney, the *Vandal,* or the opium trade. From inside the doorway at Joe Apoo's, just down the street, Basreddin watched with narrowed eyes. Then he smiled to himself as he heard Otway's fruity tones.

"My poor dear fellow! A fearful tale, tch, tch. But let it be a lesson to you. The demon rum thinks nothing of dragging such as yourself through the mire of indignity." He glanced at Watkins, who was gaping idiotically. Strange. The man had been quite sharp once, sly, even. Well, thank heavens nobody had told him at whose instigation he'd been pressed. Still, the thing now was to get away, to go and see some men who could perhaps help him out of his difficulty. But Watkins had him by the sleeve, was whispering hoarsely in his ear. He tried to shrug him off, fumbling for his purse to drive him away with a silver dollar. Then his fingers froze. He looked quickly from left to right, grasped him by the elbow, and hustled him into an eating house across the street.

Basreddin smiled again as the black-clad merchant and his ragged charge disappeared through the beaded curtain. Then he headed for the waterfront, where the *Vandal*'s longboat was waiting for him with six stout oarsmen. As they pulled downriver from the pier, they passed a string of huge, bulbous barges, shaped like half melons, piled high with orderly stacks of tea chests, dragged by galleys filled with straining rowers. A white man stood by the helmsman, dressed in dirty canvas breeches, a glazed round hat, and a blue guernsey with white lettering arcing across the chest. Straining his eyes, Basreddin read, "*Swallow*. Liverpool."

Most of the merchants who lived in the cramped quarters of the countinghouses and storerooms of the Factory tended to a certain stoutness. Exercise was hard to come by, and though the impassive Chinese butchers who sold pork and beef were undoubtedly puzzled by the bristly barbarians' appetite for great greasy chunks of roast meat, their produce was cheap and good. Edward Morningside, however, was an exception to the general rule. He was a lanky man, cadaverous of feature, with sour, dyspeptic breath and a stoop to his shoulders, much given to incongruously bright clothing. If you had asked him for a description of himself, he would probably have told you that he dressed well and tended to a fine and contemplative melancholy. In fact, he looked gaudy and sulked often. And he was not a good man of business. It was laziness that had made him allow himself to be bullied to this ghastly place, and it was laziness that kept his business running at a slight, though unremarkable, loss, while almost every other merchant within a thousand miles counted himself a failure if he did not double his investment every year. And it was laziness of mind that had made him, in what he had thought was a real coup, pay five times the right price for the cargo of the *Nabob*.

The *Swallow* rode at anchor in the back of his mind, her sharp lines and forest of spars a perpetual reproach. He prayed, when he could be bothered, that she would lose a spar on the way home: for of one thing he was sure, with the conviction of the persistent failure. Short of heavenly intervention, nothing would get the *Nabob* home first in a fair race. He sighed, his watery blue eyes fixed absently on one of the gold dragons, each a foot long, which snaked across his scarlet waistcoat. Life was really very sad at the moment.

Soon he would have to write another of those letters to his father-in-law: "My lord: the exigencies of my expanding interests make it imperative that I recapitalize, and due to misunderstandings in the trade community here my normal avenues of credit are closed to me. I beg you therefore to consider further reinvestment in my enterprises." And the old buffer would make a hell of a fuss and wonder aloud yet again why his damn fool daughter had married not only into trade but into a merchant house which couldn't keep its books balanced, let alone show a profit. He sighed again and pulled his watch from his pocket. Ten o'clock. Time for his opium pill. The tenth that day.

As he was washing the bitter bolus down with a glass of water, there was a commotion in the outer office, and the door banged open. Before him stood a large, portly man in clerical black, with a gray waistcoat and a purple face down which the sweat coursed freely. Morningside noted with a light shudder of distaste that the man's collar was losing its starch. He looked as if he would be dissolved away by noon. Morningside smiled affably at the stout man, whose face was vaguely familiar, and waved him into an upright chair. His feet began to glow as the opium crept through his veins to the back of his neck, then enveloped his brain in a golden tide. Little sparks of multicolored light began to dance in the furniture and across his visitor.

The stout man spoke. "Otway. My name's Otway. Mathias Otway. Edward Morningside." It was not a question. Little tremors of desperation flickered in Otway's eyes. "I'll come straight to the point, no beating about the bush. You own the cargo of the *Nabob*, don't you?" Again, it was not a question. "I. Want. That. Cargo. Name your price."

Morningside rocked a little in his chair. Even through the opium, this was a shocking suggestion. Still, business, he told himself weakly, was business. Best start the negotiations somewhere. Be reluctant. "Well," he said hesitantly, "it's good tea, on a good ship, in a good year, what with the ban. So"—his dull eyes narrowed—"I should be asking a premium price. If I were selling."

Veins bulged over Otway's collar, and he started forward in his chair. His eyes rolled wildly, and he spoke in a sort of inarticulate roar. With an effort that turned his face nearly black, he got himself under control. "I—will—offer—you—precisely *three times* what you paid for this cargo. And I know exactly how much that was. The ship sails soon. I want an answer. NOW!"

The last word was a bark. Morningside jumped, then sat quivering, the cozy fog of opium pushed aside by the enormity of the suggestion.

"Three times? I shall have to think this over—"

"NOW!"

"Really, sir. Ah . . . what are your terms?"

"One-third cash. The other two-thirds a note, payable on arrival in England."

"And what if the *Nabob* loses the race? You may, if you will forgive my saying so, sustain a severe reverse."

"And what the hell business is that of yours? You're back in pocket, hard cash, with the one-third; and you know my bankers. I know you're in Queer Street at the moment. If it makes any difference to you"—

he bent over the desk toward Morningside and hissed between his teeth—"*I know the* Nabob *will win that race*. But only if I own her cargo."

A huge pile of silver dollars reared up before Morningside's inner eye, chinking seductively. He slumped back in his chair. After all, a bird in the hand . . . He stood up abruptly, reeling a little. "Done," he said. "Fu!" A Chinese factotum trotted into the room, inscrutable yet, Morningside felt, scornful. He would show him.

"Draw up a bill of sale for the *Nabob*'s cargo. This gentleman will go over the terms with you."

The day was hot, but Otway was shivering slightly as he stumped back toward the river. He touched the bill of sale in his breast pocket. The one-third of the purchase price of the tea in the *Nabob*'s hold represented his entire cash recourses. And when the note for the balance fell due, it would swallow up double the value of his remaining assets in land and stocks. He curled his lips to relax the taut muscles of his face. If the *Nabob* didn't get home first, and first by a clear day, he would land in the debtors' jail. And he had no illusions about the feelings of his erstwhile friends in London. True, he had been tolerated in the salons of the *ton*. But even the cardsharp de Fauvenargues had condescended to him. He was an interloper, a parvenu, and he knew it. No, unless he could restore his fortunes with one coup, he was doomed. Be that as it might, this was not the first time he had walked the knife edge. And with the advantages he expected from the cooperation of Zebedee Watkins, the odds were very definitely stacked in his favor.

Nonetheless, as the eight-oared boat took him through the hurrying evening traffic on the river, his stomach growled nervously. A string of tubby barges struggled upriver, and he shifted on the seat, trying to find a more comfortable position. That meant that the *Nabob* and the *Swallow* had finished taking on cargo. They would be leaving Whampoa on the morning tide tomorrow. He snarled at the helmsman of the gig. "Move, you yellow bugger. D'ye think I've got all night?"

The man shrugged and spat juicily over the side without shifting his grip on the tiller. Otway bent forward and shifted his weight again. His pelvic bones were already getting sore on the hard thwart. As the lights of Canton dimmed slowly astern, he wriggled impatiently. The gig pulled steadily downriver.

While Zebedee Watkins had seen more desirable resting places than the narrow bunk he had been allotted in the forward deckhouse of the *Swallow,* he reckoned, all in all, that he wasn't doing too badly. Indeed, there was a certain luxury in his surroundings, though, he thought, thrusting out his jaw in pride, anything would look luxurious after his gloryhole in the *Vandal.* He clasped his hands behind his head and whistled between his teeth, trying to turn a knothole in the boards of the top berth into the alluring bottom of a Parsi girl he had seen in Macao, and failing.

A smell of frying onions drifted to his nostrils and he went on deck, hobbling slightly. His muscles were still stiff from his three days at the sheerlegs, swaying up the nets of tea chests for stowage by Chinese coolies under the eagle eye of Fairweather, the third mate, in the *Swallow's* holds. But even during the stowage of the cargo he had found time to befriend the cook. He licked his chops. Ever since he could remember, he had been a little better fed and a little less hard driven than his fellows and even his betters; and all this because, wherever he had been, be it an English country house or a Chinese grogshop, he had made up to the cook. As his hands reached for the polished brass knob of the galley door, someone caught his shoulder with fingers like a vice. Watkins cringed, started to give an explanation, then dried up as he recognized his captor. God, but that stringy brown varmint did give him the shivers, with his turban. He twisted like a hooked eel, but the fingers stayed firm.

Basreddin bent down and hissed in his ear. "Your master would have speech with you, O scourge of the four-legged. So bid your stomach be silent a moment and come with me." And he marched the now unresisting Watkins astern, along the *Swallow*'s long flush deck to the after companionway.

As the two men entered, Gurney was sitting alone at the mahogany table beneath the skylight, his blond hair shadowing his eyes, bent over a ledger. Before him on the table was an inkwell, and in his left hand was a quill pen. He looked up at Basreddin and Watkins, blotted the page, and rose to replace the ledger on a shelf at the port side of the saloon. Then he turned, hands clasped behind his back, and walked slowly across to Watkins. He stood facing him for a moment, looking into his eyes. Zebedee quailed and bowed his head, shuffling from foot to foot.

"Watkins."

"Aye, sir."

"Do you wish to get home safe?"

"Aye, sir."

"Do you wish to rot in jail when we land?"

"No, sir."

"Then have a care, Watkins. I have my eye on you. Remember, I am your master now, not Mr. Otway. I am relying on you to turn a deaf ear to his suggestion. Now get away with you."

Watkins scuttled forward; the galley door closed behind him, but he was soon back on deck. His appetite, it seemed, had disappeared.

Gurney plumped down on a locker and crossed his feet. "Well, Bas, I don't think that runt will give us any trouble. What's your opinion in the matter?"

"One such as him will always keep a whole skin on the journey rather than lend it at interest by the wayside."

"Hmm. I don't know about that." The man was getting more obscure every day. Obviously feeling his oats. But then all these months stewing on the China coast weren't doing anyone any good.

"Keep your eye on him, whatever happens. Don't

let him out of your sight if you can help it." Basreddin
sighed and spread his hands. "All right, Bas, I know,
I know. Through the pits of Shaitan would you go
before your eye deviated a weevil's foot from his nox-
ious visage. Yes?"

The Sufi grinned. "Yes, that was more or less what
I was going to say. Old man."

"Good. Did you see McIver this afternoon?"

"He sent his compliments and said he'd be sailing
at six o'clock in the morning."

"Lucky devil. What I wouldn't give to be on the
Vandal now."

"He who owns the cheetah must often hunt on the
back of an elephant."

Gurney grunted. "Cheetahs, elephants, be that as
it may. If I have to make polite noises at any more
poxy East India merchants, I swear I'll turn into a
dancing monkey." He kicked moodily at the paneling.

Basreddin's eyelids drooped. "Have no care for the
far future. Tomorrow brings troubles of which a man
knows nothing; and behold, if a man know the day
of his death, how then shall he live content?"

"Write that down and send it to Otway. He's going
to have greater need of philosophical counsel than I."
And Gurney muffled his face and strode on deck to
stare at the *Nabob,* two hundred yards across the
dark waters. Her riding lights struck yellow fires from
his pupils, and for a moment he looked like a hunter
tense in his machan as he hears the roar of the tiger
in the bush nearby. In one of the staterooms, Otway
would be draping his flabby bulk in a nightshirt and
preparing for bed. Check, you bastard, thought Gurney.

13

The fiddler standing on the *Swallow*'s capstan played a long major triad and scraped into a droning, rhythmic chantey. Slowly at first, then faster, the bare feet of the men at the capstan bars, forty pairs, including the cook, yes, even Watkins, slapped and scraped on the deck. The windlass clacked until the *Swallow*'s bow lay vertically above her anchor. Then Gippo Hawke, a huge, square man in a blue reefer and a cap with a peak that almost covered his small green eyes, bellowed from his place at the wheel. "Fore and main topsails! Driver, halyards, there!"

Two great canvas sails fell with a rattle on their clew lines, flapped once, and filled to starboard in the fitful breeze blowing from the north.

"Capstan!"

The bower anchor inched up from its lair in the ooze of the Pearl River and hung under the bow. As Gurney watched, the rice-thatched huts and wooden jetties of the anchorage began to slip slowly astern. The *Nabob*, a little slower, had waited for the tide to turn before weighing anchor; but as the *Swallow* passed between the twin pagodas to seaward, Gurney saw white canvas blossom from main and foremasts, and as she went hull down behind a low island, the masts started to move. They were no slouches, the *Nabob* crew. Gurney knew a good crew when he saw one, and those people were some of the best he'd seen, outside a navy.

Then the wind died, and until sunset the two ships slowly trailed each other past the tree-girt mountainous shores, finicking their sails to catch the puffs that sometimes rolled down the valleys, but mostly drift-

ing, now pointed downstream, now at right angles to
the current.

Gurney stayed below until the porthole in his state-
room was nearly dark. He came on deck as the river
went into deep shadow. The *Swallow* was running
with the wind on her quarter, and the shore was
slipping past very quickly now. Gippo gave the wheel
to the pilot, a small, wizened Chinese in a quilted
canvas jacket. His white teeth flashed in the dark
face. "Not bad, eh?" He disliked and mistrusted the
shore and shore folk, and showed it. But now, with the
sea near at hand and the breeze freshening his face,
he was unrecognizable as the surly martinet who
had driven hands to make sail in the morning. He
pointed astern. "Look at yon tub of nails. Plowing
through the river like a bloody farm boy."

Gurney looked up at the great driver, a taut wall of
canvas soaring to the gaffpeak lantern high over the
starboard rail. The *Swallow* was straining like a hound
at the leash, her wake bubbling and muttering under
the overhang of her counter.

"We'll not be long for the Bogue," said Hawke, ges-
turing over his shoulder at the *Nabob*. "We'll see the
last of her for a while too; this one sails three feet to
her two in a light air." And he stumped into the waist
to confer with his first mate.

George stretched and yawned, breathing deeply.
Though the night air was tainted—the Chinese, he
heard, being a parsimonious folk little given to waste,
fertilized their fields with human ordure—it tasted
clean and fresh after the soupy, humid muck at
the Factory.

It was clear to the eye as well as the lungs. He
leveled his glass at the *Nabob*'s poop, which had just
come into view around a bend, and caught a
glimpse of her captain, impassive in the half-light
from the binnacle. Beside him, lips working, great
bags under his eyes, his whole face twitching, Otway
stared at a chart as if he could force the ship by sheer
power of will out of these fitful breezes into the solid
monsoon winds.

Gurney smiled without humor and closed the glass. The man looked old—twenty years older than Gurney remembered him. Beaten. For a moment Gurney felt an emotion that approached pity. But then he thought of Arabella, doomed to spend an eternity in exile should she marry a man dishonored, and he knew that only two alternatives lay ahead. To give way to pity would be to lose forever the chance of vindicating himself in the eyes of the world—perhaps also to lose Arabella, for who could blame her were she to have second thoughts about throwing her brilliant future away on a proven cheat? Or he could allow his stratagem to run its course and crush Otway utterly before the very eyes of the rich and powerful circle into which he had aspired to clamber over his stepdaughter's life and Gurney's honor. He ran his hands through his hair and stared to seaward, reviewing the possibilities.

Otway could not but be aware of the chance he was taking; but experienced whist player that he was, he would undoubtedly realize—had realized before, as Gurney remembered to his cost—that evens were good odds, and would count on the owners of the *Swallow* to be of like mind. A flip of the coin. What could be fairer than that? Win a fortune or spend the rest of your life in a debtor's jail. A sporting proposition, one to warm the blood of a gambler. If you were a gambler. Which Otway, however he might flutter the cards in the drawing rooms of London, was not. The only way he would let so much ride on an even chance would be if he were convinced not only that the coin had two heads, but that it was being tossed by someone in his pay. Like Watkins.

Gurney suddenly felt extraordinarily pleased with himself and laughed, genuinely amused this time. Otway, the cardsharp, the mighty nabob, over a barrel! Caught with the best bait in the world—his own vanity.

For Zebedee Watkins, now snoring, full of illicit biscuit, in the forward cabin, was for the second time in his life the hinge of great events. Otway was laboring, it seemed, under the impression that his sod-den—well, odoriferous, anyway—ex-employee was in a position to perform certain acts of sabotage to the *Swallow*'s upper rigging which might—would cer-tainly—mean the *Swallow*'s incapacitation in the dan-gerous seas off the Cape. While the *Nabob* might, in passing, fly a sympathetic signal—if, that is, she ever came in sight—it was unlikely—implausible in the ex-treme, in fact—that she would pause in her home-ward dash.

But only Gurney knew that Watkins was far from being the *Swallow*'s star topman, as Otway believed. Indeed, he had had to pay Gippo Hawke a fair sum even to get him to have the man aboard. And it seemed to him unlikely that the rat catcher, even were he to succumb to the doubtful allure of his for-mer employer, would be able to do much to cripple the *Swallow* in his new role of supernumerary cabin boy. And just in case, the *Vandal*, under McIver's command, would be shadowing the *Nabob* home. Mc-Iver had instructions to use his discretion. Gurney smiled. McIver, bless his Scottish heart, could be re-lied upon to be discreet.

Gurney waved a hand at the *Nabob*. Nobody waved back, and he went below, chuckling. The Nel-son eye. "A man disgraced," said the unwritten rules of honor, "does not exist. He is invisible." And oh, thought Gurney, how that swine was going to wish he had worn spectacles.

When he awoke, the *Swallow* lay hove to on a sheet of misty water bordered to left and right by rugged dark cliffs streaked with green. At their base, smooth bastions of stonework pocked with gun ports stared at the ship like a row of empty eyes. Gurney pulled on a pair of trousers and a shirt and ran up the companionway, wiping the sleep out of his eyes with the back of one hand and buttoning his coat with the other.

Gippo Hawke couldn't have been to his bunk, but he looked as fresh as if he had slept a full eight hours. He was directing a string of pidgin at a Chinese who handed him a piece of paper, which he signed and returned. The Chinaman bowed, shook hands with himself vigorously under the long sleeves of his robe, and climbed nimbly over the *Swallow*'s low freeboard into the high-pooped barge alongside.

Hawke bellowed his orders, the yards came round, and the Bogue forts, guardians of the mouth of the Pearl River with their few score of antique cannon and lazy coolies, slid astern. The four four-pounders on the *Swallow*'s starboard side banged, then banged again; the answering salute came rolling over the water, each report a little behind the puff of smoke from its gun. Gippo was already shouting at his men to reload with ball, close ports, and secure all. From now until London, the *Swallow* would show her teeth only in anger.

To the eastward the sun was rising out of a gray bank of misty cloud; it was already hot on Gurney's face. Within half an hour the Bogue was sinking behind them as the estuary widened into Canton bay. Gurney swept the horizon with his glass. There, sure enough, were the *Vandal*'s topsails, hovering just out of sight of land. He redirected his gaze at the Bogue, hazy in the morning mists. As he watched, the *Nabob* struggled into view, backed her topsails, and lowered a boat.

Hawke looked back and laughed. "She'll be needing her anchor for sure. Yon Chinese pipsqueak gets very tired after he's done a couple of trips of a morning, and tends to refresh himself until about noon. Well, no hearts are breaking here, I guess. And now, a bit of breakfast with you, Mr. Gurney?"

"By all means."

As they went below, the breeze struck firm in the *Swallow*'s skysails. She heeled and bounded forward, southwest into the broad Bay of Canton, headed for the Sunda Strait, the Cape of Good Hope, and home.

14

It was bloody difficult to tie a cravat. Gurney had forgotten how difficult in the three months, three weeks, and two days since the *Swallow* had slipped over the horizon from China. He braced his back against the pillar of his bunk and planted his feet firmly against the bucketing of the short gray sea. Though it was mid-August, the weather was blustery and lowering; as he had come below, flurries of rain were blasting across the muddy waters of the Thames estuary. But through a hole in the mist he could see the white houses of Gravesend to port, serene above the great untidy sprawl of the navy dockyards, now a mere shadow of their wartime selves, and Gurney, who had long ago told himself that he could expect nothing from England, felt a sharp pang.

He made a grimace at the looking glass. He was still tanned to a dark mahogany brown, although the weather had started to give out two weeks ago. The scar on his right temple shone pale against his face, and his eyes looked back out of the glass mockingly. But their mockery was tinged with worry. Since his triumph over Otway, he should, he assured himself, have felt happy as a lark. But revenge in itself was not enough. He had been away two and a half years, and he had no illusions about the changes that had taken place in him during that time. And if he had changed, what then would have happened to Arabella? Would she still be attracted to a new, hardbitten, cynical Gurney? And, more to the point, would she have waited? Aye, two and a half years was one hell of a time. The full weight of the risk he was taking pressed heavily on his shoulders for a moment; then he ran his fingers through his spiky fair hair, settled his shoulders in his coat, and returned to the deck.

Basreddin, muffled in a long brown cloak like a Franciscan friar's, was leaning against the port rail, watching the gulls fighting over a bucketful of galley scraps Watkins had just flung overboard. The Sufi gestured at Watkins. "He has been good, our friend, has he not? Though I feared for a moment, off the Cape of Good Hope, that he might delay us by dying of the seasickness."

"Aye, that he has. And I'll wager he's pleased to be seeing these shores again. Eh, Watkins?"

"Yes sir, that I am. Never thought I would, to tell ye the truth, sir. Thankin' ye kindly, sir." Watkins tried desperately to keep his eyes from sliding away from Gurney's level gaze.

"Blast you for a flanneling swine, Watkins. Get away forward, there, and back to Cookie, or we'll have you up to the maintruck again in no time flat." Watkins paled and scuttled forward, the bucket clanking as he ran.

The banks of the Thames were narrowing steadily. Houses and wharves began to cover the water's edge. Basreddin was muttering to himself in an undertone and started when Gurney gripped his arm.

"My dear friend," said George, "never have I seen you so discomposed."

"Never have I seen such engines. Truly the Tigris is long and the great seas are broad, but here are marvels utterly beyond the understanding of man. Even Bombay, compared to this, is as a candle beside the sun." He shook his head, half-wondering, half-appalled.

For his part, Gurney felt no particular sense of awe. He was more disturbed by the tainted thrill of homecoming and his apprehensions about Arabella. The docks, as far as he could see, were only docks, and rather dirty ones; certainly they were extensive, but then so was London. More to the point was the fact that he was still in disgrace as far as the world knew; he had not seen the *Vandal* since the cape, when she had come within hailing distance to tell him that the *Nabob* was a good seven days astern and, barring accidents, right out of the running.

The *Swallow*, a swan among coots, was now foaming through a thickening crowd of wherries, barges, luggers, smacks, and miscellaneous cargo vessels of every shape, size, and description. Gippo Hawke was bellowing almost constantly, and canvas was disappearing from the lofty yards like snow from a sunlit mountain. Heads turned toward her, and here and there a cheer went up. Gurney's pulse quickened.

"They'd not be cheering like that if the *Nabob* were home first."

Hawke frowned, trying to hide the elation that was making his eyes sparkle. "Aye, there's many a slip 'twixt cup and lip. I shan't be content until we're alongside a solid dock and the tea's in the warehouse, without a sight or a smell of the *Nabob*."

"You're right, of course. But I can't help thinking . . . Perhaps you'd like a little wager on it?"

Hawke's face cracked into a broad smile, and he gave Gurney a roundhouse clout between the shoulder blades. "A wager, forsooth! You young whippersnapper! Not content with most of the tea in China, you're trying to relieve a poor old seaman of his hard-won gold! Away with ye!" Beaming all over his face, he stumped off, bellowing at the hands on the yards.

The fore topsail shrank to pocket-handkerchief size, and the ship pitched gently as she slowed and her wake caught her up. Gradually, very gradually, wind and tide under her counter, she inched upriver, past great yards of timber with grubby Baltic schooners moored at their docks, past depots where barges, their tan spritsails black with dust, unloaded coal onto enormous piles. And gradually the vast open yards gave way to tall buildings, cliffs of masonry with cranes at their upper doors, and long, low, stone warehouses.

The rain had stopped, and as they drew abreast of the West India dock a flood of sunlight fell on the spars of the ships moored in the basin. Gurney swept the hulls with an anxious eye, searching for the *Nabob*, which would look positively slender among her matronly sisters. There was no sign. Suddenly the day was hot and bright, and he took out a handkerchief to dab away the sweat that broke out on his temples. Boats darted out for the *Swallow*'s mooring lines. Slowly, steadily, the blue water between her side and the quay narrowed. Then her fenders bumped once, very softly, and she was still.

Gurney closed his eyes for a moment, then opened them to a roaring. He looked up to the edge of the quay, five feet above his head. The lip of masonry was lined with jubilant faces, openmouthed, cheering hoarsely. Home. Safe. Then he remembered who he was, turned and grasped Basreddin by the arm, and hustled him below. It was not yet time. He was still an exile. But it would be soon. Very soon. He took pen and paper, then struck his head around the cabin door and shouted for Watkins. As he wrote, the man pattered down the companionway. From the way his feet shuffled and slid on the deck, Gurney deduced that he wasn't sorry to be home.

"Take this to Romeo Copley at the Three Tuns in Whitechapel. And Watkins. In case you should have thoughts of deserting, there is a reward for this errand. Fifty guineas. You will receive that sum on your return here, with a reply from Mr. Copley. Now take yourself off and stay out of the alehouses!"

Gurney was trying with little success to concentrate on the game of chess he was losing to Basreddin when the door burst open and Watkins rushed in, panting, hotly pursued by the diminutive Copley. George leaped to his feet, spilling the chess pieces across the cabin, and violently shook his hand. The little man looked pleased.

"I can see you haven't got no weaker, Mr. G. Gawd, I thought I'd lost my flipper." He leaned closer and whispered hoarsely in Gurney's ear. "Oo's the dusky gentleman, then?"

Wrinkling his nose against the powerful aroma of gin on the actor's breath, Gurney introduced him to Basreddin. "You two should get along famously, being the most gifted mountebanks I have ever in all my days stumbled over. But first, a little business." Romeo rubbed his hands and sniffed meaningfully, his long red nose quivering with anticipation. "Does your brother still run that lugger out of Maidstone?"

"Yes sir, Lieutenant, certainly."

"Good. Take him this letter and tell him to wait at midnight every night from now until the full moon on that bearing. Someone will come and pick it up. I'll see he's none the poorer for it."

Romeo's eyes bulged at the weight of the purse Gurney tossed him. "Tare and 'ouns, Mr. Gurney, where did you come by that? I don't know what the world's coming to, even without your turning up black as my hat—beggin' your pardon, Mr. Basreddin—and covered in gold. Where you been?"

"China, Romeo. Where the streets are paved with gold. And where fat merchants like our mutual friend Mathias Otway may slip on a dog's turd and end up face down in the gutter. Now, on your way." And he made as if to snatch the purse from the Cockney, laughing as the small man whipped it out of his way and sprang nimbly for the door.

The *Vandal's* decks were darkened; the only light came from the binnacle and from the red and green lamps to port and starboard and the white lantern at her gaffpeak. The breeze blew cool, but not cold, from the southwest, and a long swell was running. According to McIver's calculations, they were about thirty miles south of the Needles. Ten miles to windward, the *Nabob's* topsails were invisible in the darkness. But he knew they were there; he had taken station on her at dusk, and according to Mr. Gurney's orders, was following her from in front. Mr. Gurney was undoubtedly up to his tricks again. McIver chuckled as he spun the wheel to spill a little wind from

the *Vandal*'s fore topsail. Well, all he could say was
God help the victim, whoever he might be.

A week previously, the *Vandal*, flying upchannel
under every rag of canvas she possessed, had made
rendezvous with Romeo Copley's brother's lugger off
the North Foreland. That same night she had gone
about and returned the way she had come, despite
the mutterings of some of her crew, who were returning home for the first time in ten years; and two days
later she had dropped anchor in a cove near the
cliffs of the Golden Cap, where Mr. Gurney, the darky
Basreddin, and a veiled woman had come aboard,
leaving their horses in the care of a groom ashore.
And since then it had been quite like old times. Mc-
Iver, though he would never have admitted it, had
become heartily sick of creeping up the Atlantic just
over the horizon from the *Nabob*, and now that the
Vandal was under full sail again, he felt a new
man.

He chuckled again. Mr. Gurney had been barely
recognizable as he had handed the lady aboard.
Doubtless he was trying to make an impression. At any
rate, his breeches were white as snow, his dark cloth
coat fit him like a glove, and his collar came close
to his ears. Not that he had anything to worry about.
Her Ladyship seemed very pleased to see him. Mc-
Iver was blowed if he knew. He'd seen Mr. Gurney
cool as a cucumber in some tight spots. Once Volnikov, the carpenter, had got at the rum and come
at him with a chisel. But was he worried? Not Mr.
Gurney. He'd given him one of those looks, grabbed
him by the wrist, and laid him a clout along the jaw
as had put him in his bunk for a week. And now Her
Ladyship had him like a dog on a string. McIver waggled his head and tut-tutted a bit. Then the hatchway
behind him slid open, and his captain's head appeared over the coaming. He looked round, bade
McIver a good evening, then spoke to someone inside.

"Would you care for a turn on deck, m'dear? The
starlight is most effective, and we must not miss the

final minutes of the chase." His voice sounded strangely stiff. McIver waggled his head again.

He came on deck, handing Arabella up after him, and they walked, arms linked, to the after rail. They were quiet for a moment; the cabin had been stuffy, and the cool air was fresh and clean. Almost dead astern, a gibbous moon hung over the water, looking as though it could plunge hissing into the sea at any moment. Arabella's hand was soft in the crook of his elbow, and without realizing it, he put his arm around her unresisting waist. It felt like the natural thing to do. But frankly, George told himself, speech was out of the question. Specks of phosphorescence glimmered in the wake, and the Milky Way arched overhead in a great bow. Whatever the trials and tribulations of the past few years, Gurney knew they had been worthwhile.

Arabella seemed to catch his mood. She always did. "Oh, George," she sighed, leaning on him a little, "how beautiful it is! And to think that out there Mathias Otway is sailing along!"

Gurney cleared his throat, which was suddenly hoarse. "Never you mind about him; I've a couple of gentlemen aboard who will take good care of him in a few hours. Now then, I don't want you to take cold as soon as I've found you again. Come below and maybe Bas will give you a game of chess. Ye've beaten me often enough in all conscience."

She smiled at him, and in the moonlight her eyes were shining. Gurney felt, as usual when he was near her, that his hands were several sizes too big and that his shoes were larger than his feet. She was so . . . fragile. Aye, that was the word. Fragile. Then he recollected that she not only rode a horse like a lancer but could also outsharp him at whist any time she liked, and he felt better.

"No," she said, "I'm quite warm, thank you. Let us stay out here a little longer and watch the moon set."

Gurney demurred for the sake of form, then again put his arm around her. "I could really believe I had never been gone, but for this ship," he said.

Arabella smiled again. "As far as I was concerned, you never were. I thought of you constantly and prayed for you until my knees were sore. And when I read in the newspaper that the *Swallow* was coming upchannel with the first of the year, I *knew*. I just knew. And when Romeo brought your letter, I nearly fainted." She giggled. "I fear we shall have to visit my poor aunts in Bath. When I escaped, she was having one of her tea parties, a gaggle of old hens discussing what they call literature and I call gossip. In my haste, I knocked the teapot all over Lady Gwendover and stole my cousin's phaeton to get to you." She sighed. Gurney held her tighter.

"Are you quite well?"

"Of course I am, you fool. Happiness always makes me puff like a grampus."

They laughed, then stood silent.

"Arabella?"

"Yes?"

"Will you . . . ?" Gurney gulped. The *Vandal*'s stern slid smoothly down a wave.

"Yes. Of course." The stern came up again. Gurney, for the first time in years, was taken by surprise by the motion and had to clutch at the rail.

Basreddin, coming on deck, turned hastily forward and engaged McIver in loud conversation about the weather, apparently oblivious of the fact that the glass was high and that he had had an identical conversation with the mate earlier in the evening. At length Gurney disengaged himself and escorted Arabella to the wheel. He bowed ridiculously formally to Basreddin, and coughed. "Bas, may I have the honor of presenting to you my future wife?" A simper spread itself across his face.

Basreddin beamed. "Many felicitations to you, o falling frog." His English was weirdly accented, but grew in scope daily. "And may I express the wish that all your other wives may be as fair and shapely as she at your side, and that her loins be filled with sons, in the name of Allah, the Merciful and Bounteous." He stopped. Gurney had Arabella by the arm; she was frowning, and he appeared to be explaining something in her ear and trying to suppress his mirth at the same time.

Basreddin looked helplessly at McIver, who was making strange rumbling noises at the wheel. "What did I say?" he asked. A ringing slap sounded by the companionway to the stern cabin, and Gurney emerged, shaking his head and rubbing his ear.

"All right, that's enough of that." he growled. "Women. And bloody Arabs. Now, let's get down to business and take that Indiaman. I don't know how your fellow countrymen do it, Bas. Better three hornets' nests and no water for miles than a slighted woman." He barged McIver off the wheel and roared a string of orders, spinning the spokes through his fingers as he shouted. The *Vandal* came round almost in her own length, leaving a deep U of phosphorescent wake as her booms crashed over on their tracks and her forefoot bit into the rollers. Gurney grabbed a ship's boy by the ear.

"Right, you, Hawkins. Get up the mast, and as soon as ever you see a light, let me know. Watch out on the port bow; that's where it should be." The child squeaked an "aye, aye, sir" and sprang for the weather shrouds.

The ship's motion was sharper now that she was sailing into the swell. Under her press of canvas, the bow at times buried itself, bowsprit and all, in the black waves, and from time to time a sheet of spray whizzed across the deck, soaking the men at the sheets and braces as they fought for each puff of wind. The *Vandal* throbbed under Gurney's fingers as he guided her, a jockey on a huge racehorse, through the gleaming rollers under the stars. The compass card before him had stayed rock steady on the bold black W for about thirty minutes when the lookout's voice floated down to him, reedy and thin over the rustling roar of the wake and the creak of the rigging.

"Light Hooo! Port teeen!"

Gurney held his course until the light was dead

abeam, perhaps four or five miles away. He called
Basreddin and McIver and pointed. "Well, McIver?"

The Scot nodded.

"Yes, sir, that'll be her right enough. She aye had
her mainmast away back."

"Good. We'll go round under her stern just to make
sure, though. O'Shea! Gun crew ready?"

"Aye, sir."

"I hope we don't require their services. Deuced embarrassing, that could be."

"Aye, sir." The understatement of the year. If the
Vandal fired on a Company ship in the middle of the
English Channel, her entire crew would be eligible
for the hangman's noose, no arguments to the contrary accepted. Sometimes McIver seriously doubted
his captain's sanity.

"I don't like it, sir."

"No, no, nor do I, nor do I." Gurney had clearly
forgotten what he was supposed not to be liking.

"Basreddin! Are our two bloodhounds ready?"

"Yes, Giorgiou, snuffing for blood, each one of
them."

"Very well."

Basreddin had escorted two thickset individuals,
dressed in black breeches and coats, their calves
straining at white cotton stockings, from the forecastle. Even in the dark, they had an unmistakable air of
determination.

Gurney laughed. "The secret weapon. Good, very
good." Someone opened a hatch aft, and a stream of
light poured on deck. "Douse that light, God damn
and blast you, whoever you are! Oh. Sorry, my sweet,
but would you . . . ?"

The light disappeared abruptly as Arabella
slammed the hatch.

Soon, the Indiaman was fully in view, a tower of
lights, glimmering and wavering yellow over the water. Gurney took the *Vandal* up to within fifty yards
of her and held his position alongside, spilling wind
from his mainsail to keep his speed down. She looked

right. Then he put his helm hard up and rocketed under her stern. As she passed the two tiers of plate glass, only forty feet away, he saw her name board, its gold leaf a little worn after the long pull round the Cape, but plain as day in the light of her stern lantern. He nodded to McIver, who cupped his hands around his mouth and hailed, "Ahoooy! *Naaabob!*"

A thin reply came across the water, much torn and weakened by the wind. "What ship is that?"

McIver cleared his throat and caught Gurney's eye, then returned the hail. "Mail packet *Rapid*. Letters for Captain Evans."

"Very good. I am coming about."

The lights at the *Nabob*'s mastheads came into line, then spaced out again as she hauled her wind and lay wallowing in the troughs. Gurney nodded to McIver, then sprang for the longboat as it was lowered handsomely from the davits to leeward. As they rowed over the short stretch of water between the two ships, he heard the sound of teeth chattering. One of the "bloodhounds" was looking very sick indeed. Well, not long to go now, thought Gurney. The Indiaman's side reared up at them like the belly of a sea monster, a fringe of weed showing in the lamplight on her copper.

Then they were alongside, and Gurney leaped for the shrouds as the longboat came to the top of a wave, paused, clinging like a fly as it sank away from him, and then hauled himself onto the broad deck. Behind him the two bloodhounds struggled clumsily on board to the grins of the Indiaman's sailors.

Gurney strode aft to the steps at the break of the poop, beckoning them to follow. A short, florid man in a cocked hat and a blue coat with a good deal of gold braid at wrists and shoulders stood at the head of the steps.

"Captain Evans?"

"At your service. What the devil do you mean by coming alongside at this time of night, letters or no letters? I find it hard to understand that any communications should be so important that I must heave to in the middle of the bloody Channel to receive them when tomorrow will see me fair to Dover."

"I fear that there is some misunderstanding. I bring no letters for you. My mate may have overstepped the bounds of truth somewhat in his hail, but we felt that you would be more inclined to stop were we to address you in that manner."

"What? No mail?" Captain Evans was spluttering like a damp firework. "Then who in damnation are you, you young whippersnapper? This is piracy, blast you, piracy!"

"No. Piracy it is not. Call it rather the liberty which any owner may take with his own property."

Evans stood open mouthed a moment, and Gurney and his two henchmen rapidly scaled the steps and brushed past him.

"His own property? What the bloody hell do you mean? Coming aboard my ship on the high seas and telling me it is your property? Confound you, sir, but we shall soon see whose property this is!"

"Excuse me, but I think you should see this." Gurney unbuttoned his coat and pulled out a paper, which he handed to Evans. Evans screwed up his eyes, then snorted in exasperation.

"I can't read this here."

"Then I suggest that we go below, and you can peruse it at your leisure." Evans complied grudgingly, and they trooped into his cabin. He plumped himself down behind his desk, propped a pair of reading glasses on his blunt nose, and read. When he looked up, his mouth was set into a tight line.

"So. Bought the cargo, have you? Even before we've landed." He shook his head. "Quicker every year. God knows what the world's coming to." His eyebrows came over his eyes. "But what I want to know is what right have you to come on my ship, cargo or no cargo?"

Gurney waved a nonchalant hand at the bloodhounds. "I and my associates here have come to discuss business with one of your passengers. Perhaps we could send the steward for him? Mathias Otway is his name."

Evans boiled over again; but the young man held him with a gesture. "A moment, I beg of you. May I crave your patience while I say what I must to Mr. Otway? Then you shall judge the case on its own merits." There was something in his eye that gave Evans pause. He shrugged.

"Have it as you will." He rang a bell for the steward. Gurney sat down in a deep chair, and the two bloodhounds took up positions one on either side of the door.

Footsteps sounded outside, and Gurney gripped the arms of his chair hard for a moment, then relaxed. Otway entered. He must have been asleep, for his hair was disarranged and his face was puffy, still creased from the pillow. When he saw Gurney, his mouth hung open; then the skin of his jowls turned the color of ashes and began to sag.

Gurney crossed his legs and beat a tattoo with his fingers on the arm of his chair. For a moment the two men faced each other below the lantern swinging to the roll of the ship on its gimbals. Gurney felt very calm, more curious than vindictive. When he had last seen the merchant's face in the light from the *Nabob*'s binnacle downstream from Whampoa on the Pearl River, it had been full-fleshed, bloated. Now, despite its puffiness, it was haggard. The man seemed to have aged thirty years in three months. The flesh had fallen away from under the cheekbones and at the temples, and the neck was a mass of loose wattle. Inarticulate gurgling noises rattled in his throat.

"Good evening, Otway," Gurney said, joining his fingers. "I must apologize for having dragged you from your bunk, but I had to get to you before the mail packet brought the news tomorrow. Otherwise you might have remembered an urgent appointment on the wrong side of the Channel."

Otway looked as if he had been hit by a thunderbolt. He stood stunned, in the middle of the cabin.

"These are the facts of the matter, which you would have learned from the packet tomorrow. Firstly, the *Swallow* arrived some twelve days ago, and I am happy to say secured an excellent price for her tea. But I fear it rather spoiled the market for you. Quite apart from any wagers you may have outstanding. Secondly, your friend Zebedee Watkins has been in our confidence these six months and more, so I have to inform you that he was not enthusiastic to damage the ship on which his masters were sailing. A materialist, Watkins, and a deeply practical fellow, whatever you may say about his morals. But then you could not have known that I was at the back of your . . . misfortunes in the China coast, could you? I should have been skulking in Boulogne, brooding, or getting killed in a duel by your friend de Fauvenargues.

"My apologies. I am wandering. Thirdly, I spoke to your agent in London straightway after I had bid for the cargo of the *Nabob*. He readily accepted what I offered him for it, not only because it was a fair and honest price—far less, I may say, than the one you paid—but because after what I had told him, he felt in need of hard cash to regularize your position there. Which, I believe, leaves you with a note outstanding to Mr. Morningside's London agent, which you are not in a position to meet when it falls due on the day of sale of the cargo under your feet. Not so fast."

Otway had half-turned to the cabin door, but it was now blocked by the bloodhounds, who were leaning against it with folded arms, a look of grave but kindly concern on their faces.

"Good. Stay where you are, as there are a couple of other points I should raise. Where was I? Ah, yes. Fourthly, I have the honor of announcing my betrothal to the Lady Arabella Mountolivet, your ward, and I must say that I do not grieve at having to forgo the pleasure of asking your permission. For I believe that your guardianship lapses if you go to prison for debt. Which brings me to my fifth point. These gentlemen here"—he waved at the bloodhounds, who took up position at each of Otway's elbows—"are my bailiffs. Mr. Toomey, Mr. Briggs—Mr. Otway. Mr. Otway—Mr. Toomey, Mr. Briggs. Forgive the sketchiness of the introductions. Captain Evans," he bowed deeply to the small Company man, who sat astonished behind his table, "I must apologize for burdening you with two extra mouths to feed for a couple of days. I trust this may cover their passage." A chamois purse thudded onto the table.

He then walked very close to Otway, whose head was hanging on his chest, and put a finger under his chin. The head rolled up, the eyes shocked and glassy. "Oh, and one last thing, Otway. I have here a paper that sets out in full your liaison with de Fauvenargues and your conspiring with him for my disgrace. I would like to make a bargain with you. I for my part will remain silent about that part of your activities on the China coast which was actively contrary to the interests of the merchant community, provided that you will sign this paper as being a true and faithful record of the events of February 1819. Agreed?"

Otway nodded. Gurney took him by the arm and led him to Evans's desk. The flesh of his biceps was flabby under his coat, and he emanated a sour smell of defeat. Otway signed the paper, and Evans witnessed it. Then Gurney spun on his heel and walked out of the door. As he was leaving, he half-turned.

"I will not say farewell, for I confess that I do not care how you fare. But I will make a last agreement with you, though I realize bargains mean little to such as yourself. If I promise never willingly to cross your path again, will you do the same for me?" Otway mumbled an incoherent obscenity. Gurney's eyes were cold as he turned. "Sweet stay in the Fleet, at any rate. Gentlemen, good evening." The door slammed behind him.

When Evans returned to the quarterdeck five minutes later, the *Vandal's* masthead light was bearing away to the northeast. By the time he had cursed and yelled his ship under way again, she had disappeared into the gloom.

A Special Preview
of the exciting opening
pages of the second
SEA DEVIL adventure.

GURNEY'S REWARD

by Sam Llewellyn

1

High in the West Tower of Sea Dalling church, Charlie Jarvis was cleaning the light. Whistling between his teeth, he scrubbed at the greasy film of soot on the caloptric reflector, burnishing the polished tin with his frayed cuff. Then he trimmed the wick with his knife, struck flint and steel, lit the flame until it burned to his satisfaction, extinguished it, and crossed the stone-flagged floor to the north window.

Below his vantage point, the delicate Gothic pilasters and traceries swept vertically down to the rough grass and neat stones of the graveyard. Beyond the vicarage, with its paddock and copse, the cottages of Sea Dalling sprawled down the gentle hill to the Cut and Captain Gurney's shipyard, set behind the sea wall. And beyond the sea wall, the grey-green marshes sprawled out, shot with tidal creeks, towards the slate of the February sea, threatening under a dark bowl of sky.

Charlie shook his head. She were fair to blow again tonight, by the looks of it. How they nor'easterlies did mess up that reflector. Still, Sea Dalling Tower was the brightest light on the North Norfolk coast these days, and the fishing lads had Captain Gurney to thank for that. Used to be there was nowt but a little fire of coals up here; the bones of the smacks and wherries out on the sandbars off the Point had their own story to tell about that. He were none too bad a boy, that Captain, even if his idea of a boat looked like something you'd whittle a stick with. Charlie shook his head again. If he'd had the light in afore brother Tom put his smack on the Hood in a gale, Tom might still be here. He sighed, and turned his gaze inland, down the long straight mile of the Sheringham road.

A horseman was driving his mount towards the village. Even from where Charlie stood he could see the gouts of mud on the rider's black cloak and the lather of sweat at his horse's withers. Rush, rush, rush, thought Charlie, fingering his cutty pipe. Bloody impatient. He turned, clumping in his heavy boots across the floor to the low door which gave onto the one hundred and five steps down to the west end of the church. As he let himself out of the door in the nave, he looked quickly round, then genuflected to the altar and slipped into the churchyard. Bit of a bloody Dissenter, that parson. And a hell of a tongue. Catch a man at his proper devotions and hold him up as an example to the parish come Sunday, more'n likely.

He was under the slate roof of the lych gate when the church clock boomed the first stroke of noon, and his step quickened. As he started to walk towards the village, he heard hoof beats and a voice halted him.

"Hey! You!"

He turned. The rider was approaching at a trot. Charlie was not sure he liked being addressed in this way, but he was an accommodating man, and the rider, from his boots and his flat-crowned hat of muddy beaver, was obviously Quality. He removed his pipe from his mouth.

"Aye, Sir?"

The voice was imperious. "Where will I find Captain George Gurney, my man? Come, don't stand there with your mouth open, speak!"

Charlie, scenting largesse, swallowed his pride. "Mostly this time of day he'll be down the yard there. Down Staithe Street."

"Good. Look here, take my horse, would you? I'm cursed sore and I'll walk. Put her in a stable—there is an inn here, I suppose? Of course. And take this."

Before he knew what was happening, Charlie found himself with a shilling in his right hand and the reins of the horse in his left, watching the stranger's back receding down the hill towards the Cut.

The stranger was in an extremely poor humour. As he stumped down the rutted and potholed track that was Sea Dalling's main thoroughfare, he cursed roundly at the abominable Norfolk roads, the burnt beef and sour ale that had been his breakfast some six hours earlier at the Bell in Norwich, and that potbellied under-secretary at the Horse Guards who had seen fit to uproot him from London in mid-winter and send him on this zany's errand.

He rounded the corner of the netshed at the bottom of Staithe Street, and found himself on a broad, sloping hard, covered with small craft. To his right, inside the sea wall which blocked his view of the open sea, the hard was fenced off. Inside the fence, the ribs of a large ship in the early stages of building sprang from their spine of timber, and beyond, two low, black hulls, one of them showing signs of near-completion, lay in the slips. In and on the ships swarmed more men than the stranger would have thought possible in a village the size of Sea Dalling.

He passed through the gate, walking stiffly, and picked his way through the casks and the piles of timber towards a weather-beaten shack which leaned wearily against the sea wall. A stout man of some forty years looked up at him from a table covered in rolls of paper, and fixed him with his single eye.

The stranger cleared his throat. "Captain Gurney?"

"Nay, lad, the name's McIver. The Captain's out wi' the caulking gang on the *Vampire*." The beetling brows lowered. "But may I ask your business?"

"My errand is with Captain Gurney and with him alone."

McIver shrugged. "Aye, well have it your own way. Though there's nae much that's the Captain's business he doesn't share with us. Come, I'll take you to him."

The Scotsman set a cracking pace over the slips, and by the time he came to a halt under the knife-edged bow of the furthest of the hulls, the stranger's mood had, if anything, deteriorated. McIver cupped his hands round his mouth and bellowed "Captain! Company! Could be a bailiff, could not be. Very persistent."

The knock of the caulking hammers stopped, and Captain Gurney dropped down the side of the schooner as if the eighteen feet were four, and looked the stranger up and down. His manner, the stranger felt, was insolent in the extreme.

He was a tall man of about twenty-five, strongly built, with a spiky mop of fair hair much clotted with pitch from the caulking. The eyes he turned on the stranger were pale blue and faintly quizzical.

"Good day to you, Sir." The eyes flicked up and down once. To the stranger's mind came the conviction that he was being weighed on an extremely sensitive scale. "I have not the pleasure of your acquaintance, I believe."

"Perhaps the letters that I bring will remedy that."

"Perhaps. Come with me, if you would be so good." The young man turned to McIver. "Get the lads back to it, and make sure that they pound those seams well. Keep 'em warm."

McIver grinned and nodded, and swarmed up the frowning bulwark with an agility surprising in one of his solid construction. Captain Gurney and the stranger set off across the yard.

"Letters, you say," observed Gurney. "They must bring urgent news indeed, judging by the state of your clothes. You rode from Holt?"

"From Norwich."

Gurney looked at his visitor with a new respect. "Norwich, eh? Twenty miles if it's an inch. Good travelling. Come in here out of the wind." He pushed open the door of the shed, swept rolls of paper from the desk and the two crude beechwood chairs, and sat down, waving a hand at the other. "A glass of cognac against the weather, perhaps? You must be chilled to the bone." He poured. "Your health. Throw a billet on the fire, would you? And now, perhaps you will tell me what brings you out in the east wind in this most inclement weather. Cuts like a knife, that wind."

The stranger handed over a packet, thinking as he did so that this somewhat work-stained gentleman obviously was not as sensitive to the rigours of the climate as he pretended. His top-boots of brown calf had seen better days, and seemed rather more ventilated than their maker had originally intended. The tar-stained trousers tucked into the boots were little better than canvas, and as for the shirt—well, perhaps a ruffled silk shirt without collar or cravat was customary morning wear in North Norfolk in February, but in London it would be thought rather chilly than otherwise. As Gurney cracked the large red seal and perused the contents of the packet, the scar that ran across his right temple from eyebrow to hairline pulsed and a red flush spread from his collar—or where his collar would have been had he been wearing one—to cover his face. He sprang to his feet.

"So you are Morpurgo? It seems that I owe you an apology. My dear Mr. Morpurgo, how can I ask your forgiveness? Jervy Hutchinson must be my dearest friend and patron. How is the old windbag? And what is this that he says you must tell me?" The stranger was shivering now, his muscles stiffening. As he opened his mouth to speak, his teeth clacked like castanets. "But it can surely wait. Come, before you take an ague. Mrs. Cox at the Dun Cow will have dumplings a-boiling, and they will warm you."

Morpurgo liked to think that he was a man who would rather harbour a grudge than otherwise, but he found himself disarmed by the Captain's confusion. So he gracefully allowed himself to be steered up Staithe Street, through a herd of cows milling aimlessly by a milking shed, into the snug of the Dun Cow, where he was confronted with a quart tankard of very dark ale and a heaped plate of dumplings with the flavour of ambrosia and the consistency of stiff glue.

The Captain left him to struggle with this repast and dived into the taproom, whence soon came raucous shouts of mirth and a clattering of stout boots. As he was swallowing the last of the ale, his host returned.

"Finished? Good. We'll away to the Hall now. That old thief, Charlie Jarvis, has just learned that he'll get no second shilling for walking your mare to the stables. Ready?"

Gurney set off inland at a cracking pace, turning to the right on the rutted coast road. "I must apologise for the state of the roads. We've been here only a couple of years, and they say it takes a time to make the acquaintance of the magistrates." He grinned ruefully. "I fear the magistrates are none too taken with me and mine. The yard, you know. They seem to have some notion that I'm in trade. Well, damn them, if I'm in trade, so is old Jervy. How is the old boy, anyway?"

Morpurgo pursed his lips and looked tactful. "The Admiral is in passably good health and spirits, Captain, though somewhat troubled by the gout."

"Somewhat troubled, eh? I'll wager that isn't the half of it. I remember once when we were off Kingston in 1812 I rolled a two-pound shot against his foot." He shuddered at the memory. "Double watches for a week. He's a tartar, that one."

"Indeed." Morpurgo reflected that had he not stumbled against the Admiral's stool three days ago he would in all probability be comfortably ensconced in St. James' at this very moment instead of tramping the rural wilds with this cheerful ruffian. "Yes, he is indeed a hard taskmaster. He seems to think highly of you, however."

"Aye, well, that's his hardship. You wouldn't think it from the uproar he made when I suggested he commission two new schooners from my yard here! Deuced Yankee privateer's hookers, he called them. But he'll learn. He'll learn."

Morpurgo hid a saturnine smile in the collar of his cloak. It was as the Admiral had said. A fireater, this one, and well primed for what the Navy had in mind for him. But that would keep.

The two men had for some time been walking along a lane, open on the one side to rolling plough dotted with stands of oak, beech and elm, and bordered on the other by a high flint wall. As they rounded a curve in the wall, a tall wrought-iron gate guarded by a lodge came into view, and Gurney opened the wicket to let his visitor pass. An elderly man digging over the patch of garden behind the lodge doffed his hat, and Gurney waved to him cheerfully.

"Afternoon, Arthur." He turned to his guest. "Welcome to Sea Dalling High House, Mr. Morpurgo. I trust that we shall be able to make your tiresome journey worthwhile."

Three hundred yards later, the beechwoods that arched over the drive gave way to an open expanse of parkland, set here and there with oaks, leafless under the grey sky. Directly ahead of the walkers, a pile of grey masonry lay across a slight rise in the ground. Morpurgo blinked. Much of the house was entirely ruined. The central mass—Morpurgo, who knew his architecture, having been on the Grand Tour not ten years ago, immediately thought of it as the bailey— was festonned with ivy. The west wing appeared still to have a roof, though it sagged badly at the ridge, and on closer inspection proved even to be glazed as to its windows; but the east wing was little more than a pile of rubble, its windows gaping sockets, the tall tower at its easternmost tip a truncated tube of masonry, like a maimed fang. Extraordinary. Morpurgo stole a glance at his host, striding at his side whistling, hands in pockets.

"A . . . unusual residence, Captain Gurney."

"Unusual? Oh, you mean the east wing. I suppose you're right. Still, it's home. And there's Arabella."

A horsewoman was approaching, her habit flowing out behind the snow-white rump of her mount as she thundered across the green grass of the park towards them.

She reined in, slid from the saddle with a lithe grace, and flung herself into Gurney's arms. Morpurgo turned hastily away and became improbably interested in her horse. By the time he had fully apprised himself of the fact that it was an Arab, about fifteen hands, and really a stunning lady's steed, and was feeling guilty about the lack of apples in his pockets, his host and the lady had disentangled themselves. Morpurgo tore his gaze away from the horse's reproachful velvet eye and found himself face to face with one of the most beautiful women he had ever seen. He was dimly conscious of Gurney's voice, a long way away.

"Mr. Morpurgo, may I present my wife? The Lady Arabella, Mr. Morpurgo. Friend of Jervy Hutchinson's Come all the way from London to see us. Charlie's got his horse."

The Lady Arabella smiled, and Morpurgo rocked a little on his heels. He was by no means a man for the petticoats, he liked to think, but those eyes! Great pools of violet where a man could drown and die happy. That mouth! A red bow framing teeth of white jade, set in a face with skin like thick creams and bones chiselled by angelic sculptors . . . He realised that his own mouth was hanging open, and shut it with a click, bending hastily to kiss the proffered hand.

"How delightful that you should have come to see us. I fear you may find us a little barbarous after London, but you must tell me all that is going on there. I so seldom pass time there since George pressed me into service at Dalling." But the dazzling smile she turned on her husband said that she would never consent to be anywhere else. Morpurgo was surprised to find himself overwhelmed with jealousy. "Well, Mr. Morpurgo, I shall see you later. I must away and see to the baby pheasants. Perhaps I could show you them?"

Gurney had Morpurgo by the arm. "No, my dear, we'll go up to the house. Poor fellow's half dead."

"Very well." Gurney assisted her into the saddle and she cantered towards the lodge, her golden hair streaming out beneath her little hat.

By this time Morpurgo was near exhaustion, and he almost had to trot to keep up with Gurney. Like a man in a dream he allowed himself to be ushered through the oaken door of the bailey into a great stone-flagged hall where a log fire blazed in a gigantic hearth and two greyhounds leaped at his face, licking enthusiastically at his nose and mouth. He dimly remembered being shown a surprisingly comfortable bedroom where a tub of hot water stood steaming before a roaring fire, washing the mud of the road away, and sitting in a tall wing chair attempting to review the papers whose contents he must use later. Then he slept.

Round the long mahogany table in the Great Hall at Sea Dalling High House a buzz of conversation mingled with the candlelight, and died in echoes in the darkness that lay in the corners and vaults of the high ceiling. There were six people at dinner. Gurney, at the head of the table, was engaged in animated conversation with his right-hand neighbour, a stringy lady of about thirty-five, clad in an extremely unsuitable gown of white silk, who was explaining with many gestures what sounded like the plot of a novel. Gurney was enjoying himself. Euthymia Henry's novels were a byword at Dalling, as their complexity of plot was equalled only by their ferocity of language; she spent most of her waking hours attempting to find a bookseller who would publish them for her, but the letters of rejection she received were invariably so shocked that Gurney could never see why she did not give up the battle. But as Euthymia's genteel voice continued to rattle in his right ear, he hardly heard her anguished account of her latest reverse at the hands of Mr. Murray. He was watching the other end of the table.

Arabella was looking happy, though Mr. Morpurgo was proving rather difficult. A very stiff one, that. God knew how Jervy stood that long face glooming at him over the morning mail. Truth to tell, that probably had a lot to do with his presence here. But at Arabella's other elbow sat the inimitable Sir Patrick Fitzcozens. Paddy claimed to have broken every bone in his body at least once, mostly due to sudden and violent partings of company with a long succession of horses, and on each fracture hung a lengthy and amusing tale. Even Morpurgo appeared to be taking an interest, damn him. He should be making himself pleasant to Isabel, George's reforming Quaker cousin, sitting at his left, sipping water from her wine glass.

"Don't you think so, George?"

He turned to Euthymia with a start. Cursed absent-minded, he was getting these days. Old age. Second childhood at twenty-six. "Ah, yes, indeed, Euthymia. Do you not agree, Cousin Isabel?"

Cousin Isabel tucked her chin firmly into her square white cambic collar and pursed her lips. "No, George, I do not, and I am surprised at you for asking. If Euthymia wishes her heroine to be violated by a pack of Spanish brigands, that is her business. For myself, I wish no part of it."

Gurney sighed mentally. The fading Euthymia, with her Byronic visions of odalisque-hood, and the blooming Isabel, who, however hard she tried to hide her beauty behind the plainest of Quaker clothes, was magnetically attractive to the opposite sex. And they always ended at each other's throats.

Euthymia drew herself up. "I merely mean, my dear Isabel, that we women, like a free people, must be *mastered* if we are to bloom to the full. Poor weak creatures that we are without the gentlemen."

"Oh, poor, Euthymia! Really, I declare that I think you are touched in the head to babble so. If a farm-wife can work with her husband in the fields—yes, if Arabella can ride and look after the house while George is in the yard, whence then comes this cult of enslavement and idleness that you propose?"

"Enslavement and idleness never! Call it rather the means to enjoy to the full the arts and letters of our civilisation! The leisure to divert ourselves with the fruits of men's minds. To build Temples to Beauty and worship there!"

Isabel looked grave. "Precious little beauty have I seen in the Fleet and the Marshalsea, Euthymia. While you and your like are drinking tea and reading silly novels in your Temples of Beauty at Bath, the world ignores you and life goes on, raw and dark."

Euthymia, surprisingly, smiled. "Raw and dark! Oh, Isabel, in your prison visiting and your praying there is a great poetess struggling for expression! What a loss you are to the Palaces of Culture!"

"Heavens, woman, enough of your silly vapourings." Isabel's cheeks were colouring, and her pleasantly-rounded breasts heaved beneath her drab dress. Gurney was beginning to feel a little desperate. It looked as though he would have a full-scale battle on his hands if he did not act, and act quickly; but he was by no means at his best when it came to stepping between such redoubtable females as these.

He looked imploringly down the table and caught Arabella's eye. It was sparkling with mischief. Gurney saw her signal unobtrusively to the footman, and then she broke the silence. "Perhaps, Euthymia and Isabel, we should leave the gentlemen to their port?"

And may God have mercy on their souls, thought Gurney, as the ladies left for the drawing room. Still, Arabella could keep those two apart without difficulty. As the door closed behind them and the footman drew the cloth, the three men pulled their chairs together. Gurney extinguished all the candelabra but one and passed the port.

Fitzcozens was visibly shaken by his vision of Isabel.

"By cracky, George, she's a game one. I'm not sure I don't mean to have her."

"She's too much of a handful for you, Paddy. And besides, she'd never have a smashed-up pagan like you."

"We'll see." Paddy, presumably to steady his nerves, tossed off his glass and leaned back in his chair. "We'll see. Meanwhile, give the decanter a fair wind, sharpish now." He drank again. "That's better. Ye know, I might join the ladies. You two will want to be talkin' about London, no doubt. Cursed boring place. Rotten Row, forsooth! Call that riding?" And so saying, he got to his feet and limped from the hall.

Gurney turned to Morpurgo. "Well, now, Mr. Morpurgo. I doubt very much that old Jervy sent you here for the sake of your health, bracing through the air may be."

Morpurgo touched his hands one to the other, steepling his fingers. The candlelight threw his hollow cheeks into dark shadow as he cast his head forward and cleared his throat, looking down at the table in front of him.

"You should know, Captain Gurney, that we at the Admiralty have been following your progress with some interest since your return from the East and your ah, *resignation* from His Majesty's Navy."

"But not with enough interest to commission the ships that I build."

Morpurgo spread his hands. "Unfortunately, this is beyond my sphere of influence and competence." Pompous ass, thought Gurney, sipping his port. "My field is rather more political, and it is for this reason that Admiral Hutchinson asked me to visit you here."

"I heard a whisper that Jervy was tied up with a lot of devilish dark stuff. Didn't sound like him, but with you lawyer sailors it's always damned hard to tell."

Morpurgo's face was blank, uncommunicative. "Really? How idle gossip does travel, to be sure. Be that as it may, the Admiral sent me to ask a favour of you on behalf of His Majesty's Government."

Gurney slumped back in his chair, eyelids half-lowered. Morpurgo thought he might be drowsing, but when the pale blue eyes opened again they were keen and bright. "All right, enough beating about the bush. What does he want?"

His visitor made a gesture expressive of distaste at his bluntness. "Very well. You are aware of the current situation in Greece and the Aegean?"

"Only that the Greeks are struggling to cast off the shackles of Turkish rule, and seem to be making quite a good job of it. Isn't Byron here?"

"He is. But this does not bear on my errand. As to the Greeks making a good job of freeing themselves from subjection to the Turk, they are doing quite the reverse. The story you see in *The Times* is that promulgated by certain gentlemen in whose, ah, pecuniary interest it is that the news from Greece should be encouraging to those with money to invest in the cause of Liberty."

"Gurney's eyes were wide open now. "You interest me strangely," he said. "Proceed."

"Yes. The facts of the Greek situation are as follows. The government, which at present is in possession of neither funds nor power, is in the hands of Prince Alexander Mavrocordato, as you probably know. What you probably do not know is that the noble Greek Klephts—brigands—whom Byron finds so romantic are a greedy rabble, perpetually at odds and just as ready to fight among themselves as with the Turkish oppressor. You may also remember—my sources imply that you are by no means an innocent on the Stock Exchange—that a loan has just been opened in support of the Greeks. Frankly, given the nature of the gentlemen who are promoting this loan, I should consider it a most unwise investment; but that is neither here nor there. What concerns us at the Admiralty is the almost limitless possibilities for further dissension in the Greek ranks that this huge sum of money opens. It will be a veritable Apple of Paris to the factions, and might result in a fatal division at a most inopportune moment."

Gurney was perplexed. "Why should this moment be more inopportune than any other? They seem to have rubbed along all right for the past couple of years."

Morpurgo drummed his fingers impatiently on the table. "My dear Captain, please do not be so naïve. Do you seriously imagine that a European country could be in a state of complete topsy-turvydom without some Great Power or other seeking to benefit from the situation at the expense of its neighbours? And in Greece, everyone wants a finger in the pie, if only to keep Russia out. You will probably be aware that Russia is hanging a mighty weight of troops at Turkey's northern borders. Well, it has come to our attention that Mehemet Ali of Egypt may be heading for a landing on the Peloponnese with a large Fleet; and this Fleet is led by men who fought under Old Boney himself." He leaned forward in his chair, his face earnest. "Captain Gurney, the situation in this troubled land may shortly become desperate."

"Come, come, Morpurgo, enough of this 'troubled land' stuff," Gurney shook his head. "You don't really expect me to believe that you've come all this way just to give me a lesson in politics? Where do I fit into all this?"

"I am coming to that. A few days ago, one of our agents returned from Greece with disquieting news. Certain papers of critical importance, whose contents I cannot at the moment divulge, even in the strictest confidence, disappeared. We know how and where, and our agent was confident that they could be retrieved, but their retrieval is a mission which demands rather special skills as well as the complete trustworthiness of whoever carries it out. I believe that you are acquainted with the problems of sailing such waters as the Aegean, Captain Gurney, and that your ship the Vandal is ideally suited for the task. Furthermore, it has been suggested to me that you speak the necessary languages. To this I would add that you would have the satisfaction of aiding the new Hellas, a project which must be close to your heart, for I know of your love of the arts and sciences."

Gurney laughed, shortly, "Quite a change of tune.

Squabbling brigands in one breath, and the new Hellas in the next. Well, Mr. Morpurgo, I fear your errand has been in vain. My commitments here are heavy. I must deliver the two schooners you saw to Aberdeen by May. What is to stop you sending a frigate of His Majesty's Navy to collect these documents, and have done with it?"

"What stops us is the need for discretion."

"Very well then, why can't your agent pick them up and deliver them to the Navy in the Ionian Islands? They belong to the Crown, do they not?"

A curious smugness spread over Morpurgo's face. He looked like a card-sharp who has just succeeded in manoeuvring the ace out of his sleeve and into his hand. "We cannot send our agent because he is not a free man at this moment. In fact, he is the captive of the Mainiot Klephts in the Peloponnese, and is, I hear, in daily peril of his life. It seems that only the fact that he knows that in the same place as these documents there is a considerable quantity of treasure keeps him alive." He looked sharply at Gurney, who was finishing his glass and appeared to be on the point of rising. "I should have thought the prospect of a treasure would be rather appealing than otherwise to one in your position, Captain. It is an expensive business, running a shipyard and managing an estate of this size."

Gurney decided that he definitely did not like this smooth and insinuating individual, but there was certainly something in what he said. Those two ships on the slip were financed by a series of heavy loans, secured by the estate and the yard itself. The one thing he could not afford to do was go off on one of Jervy Hutchinson's wild goose chases. Not only was there the delivery of the two Aberdeen ships; he needed a constant stream of orders to keep his credit good, and even working full out it would take him two years to get out of debt. "No," he said. "My commitments here will not permit me even to consider going."

Morpurgo sighed. "Dear me," he said mildly. "This is a great disappointment. I shall be forced then, to tell certain people in London that you are no longer taking your responsibilities seriously."

"My responsibilities? Let me remind you that I am no longer a naval officer, at your beck and call."

Morpurgo smiled his irritating smile. "I was not referring to your, ah, *patriotic* responsibilities, Captain. No, it was your *financial* responsibilities I was meaning. Those loans which, I believe, finance your shipyard at present. If you persist in your refusal to perform this service, I regret that I shall be forced to apply pressure to your bankers; pressure which will give them no choice but to foreclose."

There was a silence. Gurney stared at Morpurgo in astonishment. "Did I hear you correctly?" His voice was cold and dangerous. "You threaten an English gentleman in his own home? You, an assistant to Jervy Hutchinson? Good God, man, Jervy would never hear of such a thing."

"Yes." Morpurgo's smile was smooth and hard. "Admiral Hutchinson is indeed a gentleman of sentimental and outdated ideas. But he is now more concerned with matters of policy than of execution. I put it to you that you are faced with a simple alternative. Either you undertake this mission and thereby earn not only a considerable treasure but the goodwill of His Majesty's Government; or you fall into financial ruin. And your debts, if they are foreclosed, are now sufficient to put you and your wife into the Fleet."

Gurney's hands clenched convulsively on the arms of his chair. "Am I to believe that you are sitting there, having eaten my dinner, telling me that you will put the people of my village in the poorhouse and my wife in jail if I do not do your dirty work? I have killed men for less, Morpurgo. For much less."

"But you will not kill me. Be reasonable, Mr. Gurney. Oh, and another thing. This spy you are to rescue is well-known to you. A Mohammedan fellow, who goes under the name of the Haji Basreddin."

"Basreddin?"

"One and the same."

Gurney leaned back in his chair. "Mr. Morpurgo, you have, I perceive, been playing with me. The mere mention of Basreddin's name would have sufficed. I do not share your opinion that friendship is secondary to consideration of property and finance."

"How rare, how very rare." Sarcastic. "Well, then, you can pretend to yourself that it is friendship alone that animates you." The eyes narrowed. "But bear in mind that if you fail, your money and your lands are forfeit. There are still those in the Admiralty who would love to see you fail."

"I shall not fail."

"Let us hope not, for your sake and that of your dependents. Now, a toast to a successful enterprise?"

Gurney stood up.

"I think you have drunk enough of my wine, Mr. Morpurgo." He picked up a handbell from the table at his side and rang. The butler appeared. "Mr. Morpurgo is leaving us now," said Gurney. "Please have his horse brought round to the door and his bags packed."

"Very well, Mr. Gurney." The butler withdrew.

"We sail," said Gurney, "in three days, on the morning tide. Tell that to your masters, you dog. Now, get out of my house. And if you speak so much as a word to a living soul, I will kill you." And taking Morpurgo by the elbow, he led him to the front door and put him outside into the cold Saturday rain.

Gurney sets sail on the Vandal for the Isles of Greece to rescue an old friend. However Gurney's plans go awry and he finds he must choose between fabulous riches and an almost certain death.

Read the complete Bantam Book.
Available July 1st wherever paperbacks are sold.